A Ranger's Homecoming

Karlene Tura Clark

Karlene Clark

Copyright © 2011 Karlene Tura Clark

Cover art by Kami Jo Baxter

All rights reserved.

ISBN: 146361120X
ISBN-13:978-1463611200

DEDICATION

There was a group of people behind the "voices" of each of the characters within this book, giving me the "what if" and "how about..." every time I got stuck. Thank you to Jesse Black, Alex Nguyen, Jonathan Jääskeläinen, Mike Surber, Tarek Hariri, and my wonderful husband Terry.

Your ideas made me laugh, made me cry, and made this story.

Karlene Clark

ACKNOWLEDGEMENTS

Thank you to those who were willing to read the rough drafts, push me to keep going and kept coming back to ask "more?" when I found myself facing a blank page.

Thank you to Travis Gaddie and Holly Wheeler for being my inspiration, both in your speech and mannerisms.

For my various gaming groups that constantly supplied me with silly comments or deep truths. I kept notes and I used some of the things you said!

Dad, thanks for supporting me and knowing I could do it.

Karlene Clark

PROLOGUE

A long abandoned home was such a sad thing to see. It was sadder for the young woman to know that someone lived within the empty walls. Oh, there were things, but nothing really personal. It was more a mausoleum to times long past. It broke her heart to see the empty walls, the empty drawers... but the place was far from empty. A beautiful library, if more than a little dusty, was just down the hall from what had been a little girl's room. The room held the presence of happier memories, but no sign of life. No toys, no pictures, not even pretty curtains anymore.

It was as if the owner wished to hide what had been; as if he wanted to forget his past, but couldn't assuage the guilt he lived with yet today. She respected the space, much as she did the large chairs in the front entry. Four almost-thrones, all covered in dust, but still holding an important place in the owner's mind.

Well, nothing for it. The man that owned the home was often away in the wilds, preserving nature and protecting it from those that would destroy it. She had promised to look after the place in the owner's absence. And she would. That person deserved to come home to something more than dust and old memories.

She wouldn't eliminate the memories. Oh, no; never that! Memories made the owner who he had become, someone she wanted to be closer to.

He was far from the rumors of being a shadow guardian, yet he did shy away from most people. "And now," an old story-teller on the island often ended tales she knew were about Amil, "they say early in the morning, you can see faintly two figures – one a woman, and one a little girl, happily skipping down the old road, fading with the mist as the sun gets higher and higher. And if you ever go to the cliffs near here, late at night, you can see a dark figure staring out to the sea, his cloak whipping about in the wind... waiting... watching..."

She listened; listened to the "children's" stories about the ghosts and the mystery person. Then she went to work. She wasn't the wife or one of the daughters he had lost so long ago, but beauty and energy could heal so much. The chi must be balanced for the home to heal. She planted flowers outside the door, dusted the place from top to bottom, found the things in storage, returning lamps and vases to tables, ordering curtains for all the rooms... then placed a small alter in the room that had belonged to a little girl so long ago. "Rest well," her petite form bowed to the altar, "I'll protect him now."

Chapter One
Just One Kiss

Just a few weeks earlier, Annelise Erickson had made some decisions. She had finally realized that she had fallen in love with a man that didn't seem to understand that... or was too stubborn to consider it. No matter. She wanted to show him how much he mattered to her. And that had started with her cleaning his place.

It had been obvious on first sight that he was used to mostly being alone or only having other men and his wild animal friends tramping through it. But there had been so much potential. She had found things packed away and wanted time to start making it look like a place he would actually want to be in again.

Spotting her old friend Duval in his red leathers and plate mail next to the man she loved, she noted that once again Amil stood as he always did: the tip of his long bow resting on his boot and his dark hood pulled low over his face. He claimed no vanity, but she knew the scar across his face bothered him.

"Hey Squirt," Duval greeted Annelise, the bubbly little monk in a white gi, as she approached the group. Her brown hair bounced in time to the spring in her step.

"Good evening, Anne." Amil smiled to her.

Such a difference in the two men. Duval she'd known since she was little, he was just a little older than her, and, since she'd always been petite, he'd always called her Squirt. He was a proud vidu mage, slightly vain in needing to even have fancy filigree on his armor.

Amil was another matter. As dark skinned as Duval was, Amil was that light. Dark leathers with a minimum of metal, he was an old elven ranger that had suffered too much. And yet Annie found herself intrigued by him. He was just a little taller than her own five foot frame, but he carried such an air of authority to him, even hidden beneath his cloak's hood as he usually was. "Hi, Amil." She greeted him first before giving Duval a playful annoyed look, wrinkling her nose at him. "Do you *have* to call me that?"

The slender vidu pretended to think about it for a minute as Amil said "No, he doesn't." Amil wasn't sure what it was that made him feel protective towards her. He had first thought it was thinking she was like one of his daughters, but she was way too happy and effervescent to be like them. She was totally unlike his deceased wife, so it wasn't that either. He frowned beneath a hunter green hood that was pulled low over his face.

Amil refigured his thinking when he saw the smile on the young dark elf's face and the way Anne took it all as a joke.

Annie stuck her tongue out at Duval, saying quite happily, "I don't like you."

"I'd say it's his way of showing affection towards you," Amil quietly offered.

She reconsidered. "You think so?"

"No," Duval rolled his eyes, oozing sarcasm in his words. "I actually can't stand you."

"You're such a liar, you ... you...." she grinned, taking in his dark complexion and his white hair, so like frosting to her mind, "cupcake."

"Anne..." he tried to sound like he was offering a warning, but it didn't quite come off that way while he smiled. She knew it, too, laughing in delight. "Why don't you just get over here and plant your butt between Amil and me?"

She gave them both a cheeky grin, standing so close her toes touched Duval's where he sat on the bench. "Gentlemen should always stand up for a lady."

Amil was already standing, leaning on his bow like a staff. At the same time, Duval pulled Anne down to sit beside him. "Might help if a lady was present."

"Noooo!" She patted the bench, looking beseechingly up at Amil.

"You could just stand next to him. I'm pretty sure Amil doesn't bite."

"Why?" She playfully nudged Duval. "Have you checked?"

"Nah, Dante told me so."

She snickered. "He'd know."

"Yeah, he said Vil checked up on it for him."

Annie felt a moment of unwarranted jealousy, narrowing her eyes as she glanced at Amil. "Vil kissed you?"

The old ranger looked completely lost on their conversation. "Ah... what?"

Duval nodded sagely, even as his words were teasing. "Yup,

right over there by the food merchant."

Ignoring that, she addressed Amil. "Dante kissed Vil. But so did Duval, which is kinda disgusting, but then if Dante told Duval that Vil said she kissed you...." She paused for a breath.

Realizing she was spilling information that not everyone sitting around needed to hear, her friend cut her off. "Wait... hold on there... what?"

"That's what you just said, isn't it?"

"Right," he nodded to her.

"So... what?"

"Exactly." Duval grinned as she blinked dumbly at him.

She crossed her arms, giving him her best wet-cat expression. "Don't be dumb, Du."

"Meditate on that, Squirt." Knowing how much it bugged her, he ruffled her hair. "Besides," Duval whispered, "you've got a boy-toy right there you should be spending time with, instead of sitting next to the crotchety vidu."

With wide eyes, her jaw dropped. "Duval!"

Amil coughed to keep from laughing while Duval merrily gave in to his. "Go on... go get him."

Annie sighed, turning to Amil. "Sorry Duval's a pain in the butt."

"It's not a problem." Amil was in fact thoroughly enjoying the interplay between the old friends, even if he didn't know the people Anne was mentioning. The girl was pure sunshine and joy to him. Nothing ever seemed to get her down.

"Someone," Duval said in his best high-handed tone, "has to make up for Miss Cute here."

"I am *not* Miss Cute."

"Ms. Cute? Mrs. Cute?" Duval continued to rib her. "Her Highness, the Royal Cutie Pie?"

"Don't you have a girl for Dante to steal away or something?"

The fun faded as Duval gave her a frosty look. "Dante can't have 'Lex. You know that as much as I do."

She did know. Duval was desperately in love; the kind that was the "I'll die for you and will always come" variety. They had been through hell and back, only getting stronger for it. She wanted that someday, too. "Oooh. I hit a nerve," she teased, grinning playfully at him.

"And you know it, too, you little munchkin." He returned the teasing, letting her know he understood her intent. She laughed as he had hoped. "Don't you and Amil have trees to hug?"

She happily responded by sticking her tongue out at him. "I'm just the *mascot*."

Again, Amil smirked beneath his hood. She had started following along on his patrols of the forests, often times just as quiet as any of his rangers. They had all taken a liking to her, and at her teasing insistence, she had been made an honorary member... the mascot, as she had happily had embroidered on the back of one of her outfits.

"Okay," Duval shrugged, "Go find some honorary trees to hug."

Annie smiled brightly at Amil, talking to Duval. "He's the tree hugger."

Duval saw the way Annelise was looking at Amil. He also saw the way Amil was carefully guarding himself. All the same, he couldn't help a small smile at her obvious interest in him. "Should I leave the two of you in peace?"

"No," Anne barely let Duval finish talking.

"That was quick."

She smiled sweetly at Duval. "I want you to get to know him."

"But I already know him. That's Amil."

She had started falling in love with him at some point, and wanted validation from someone who knew her that it was okay... or to tell her she was out of her mind for feeling this way. "Yeah, but you don't *know* Amil."

"Do I want to?" Duval's lips quivered in mirth.

Silent until now, Amil cleared his throat. "I don't want him to ... *know* me. I'm not really into males."

Anne laughed, backing closer to Amil. "But since you're supposed to be in charge of me while I'm away from home, Duval," she stood possessively, but her eyes sparkled in fun. She knew her dad worried and didn't put it past him to send a friend as a protector. But best to let Duval know she knew it was why he and his wife had come to Lareah. "Don't you need to report back to my dad or something?"

"Why would I..." Duval paused, slightly incensed. "Where

on earth did you come up with such an outlandish idea?" He had in fact been asked to keep an eye on her as she settled in with creating a new dojo. "...Vith," he swore, knowing the game was up. "Right, right," Duval waved a hand to make them stop. "Okay, so I'm 'in charge' of you. Shouldn't you be... I dunno, trying to sneak off to kiss or something?"

"Not everyone has to go in a closet for a kiss, Duval."

"You do it in public?" Duval grinned, giving her an exaggerated wink.

She blushed, eyes going wide. "Not 'it'!"

"Now that I *know* your father would have some troubles with," he laughed. "Amil, if you're kissing this girl in public, I'm going to have to give you a very public thrashing."

Anne backed further up against Amil. "Oh, no you don't!" Her posture again was defensive, belying her teasing words.

"Her dad would want it that way." Duval nodded to Amil, for all appearances as if he were serious. Too bad his tone of teasing gave him away. "Ease up, Squirt," he placated when he saw her ire rising. "I'm joking."

There was something about her that could flip from so contemplative to this cute small dog mannerism of jumping and almost barking in protectiveness at those she felt threatened something she cared about. "I don't think anyone is needing to hurt anyone here." Amil gently pulled at a lock of her hair.

Duval noted how the elf's quiet words relaxed her. "As long as he doesn't hurt you, I'm okay with the two of you being an 'item'." He pointed a finger at Amil. "But if you do," he warned, "you won't be able to find a deep enough hole to hide in."

Amil smirked as Annie leaned ever so slightly against him and whispered, "I'll help you."

"That's not helping, Annie." Duval rolled his eyes.

"Ehmm, yes of course. Big brother role."

"Not related. Just keeping an eye on her."

"But you are kind of a brotherish person," Annie teased.

"Yeah, yeah. Don't remind me." Duval tried to sound irritated.

Annie leaned against Amil and grinned. "I just did."

"Hmm... such bickering," Amil commented, poking her in the back which only elicited a giggle from her.

"Giving her a hard time, Amil. I have since she was old

enough to give it back. Which was... what, about two years ago?" He grinned broadly.

She stuck her tongue out. "No. Since I got teeth." She playfully snapped at him.

"Alright," Duval leaned back on the bench, crossing his ankles out in front of himself. "So how am I supposed to get to know your boyfriend better?"

"Ask him stuff."

"Amil, Stuff?" He made it sound like the most important question he could come up with.

Amil responded by reaching into his pocket and pulling out a small amount of lint and a few copper coins, which he tossed to Duval. "Stuff." He nodded once, sagely.

"No!" Annie wanted to be irritated with them, but knew they were acting obtuse on purpose. "Like... if he's my boyfriend." They had been on "dates" per her playful agreement with him: she would happily clean his home; in exchange, he would take her out at least once a month for a meal. It had led to several kisses over the months, but nothing had ever been formally said between them about what was slowly developing. She smiled up at Amil, waiting, not realizing she was holding her breath.

"Okay. Are you her boyfriend? Her siblings had to go through this. Did you go through the official channels for it? Fill out the three forms?"

"Aye," Amil played along. "I filled the dash eighty-eight form along with the ninety-two eleven."

"What about eleven eleven B?"

Anne looked between them, trying to decide how badly they were mocking her.

"Ah... well," Amil smiled at Duval over Anne's head. "I was told the new form was the questionnaire at the end of the test."

"Yup, that's right."

"...questionnaire?" Annie tried to interrupt.

Duval ignored her. "And you passed the test last week, so I guess you should be able to officially date her now. Make sure all dates occur in appropriately lighted and chaperoned areas."

Annie blinked. "Wait... chaperoned????" Now she was indignant!

"I've got that part covered," Amil cut in before she could

start in on her friend again.

"Right. He's got a wolf and a panther." Duval nodded towards the two creatures contentedly lounging behind Amil.

"Oh them!" Annie happily exclaimed. "I like them."

"Both of whom," Duval went on, "are under orders to lick feet if it looks like the situation is going to go into designate three dash five B."

Anne gave him a blank look. "Huh?"

"Commonly known as 'second base' or 'Rook taking Knight'." The corners of Duval's mouth twitched up into another smile.

Annie put her hands on her hips. "Is that like Dante's game of 'Knight takes Queen'?"

"Ah, no. Not exactly. His is more like... umm... Bishop takes Queen. To bed."

Annelise smirked. "That's the one that creates pawns?" She pointed back at Amil. "He had pawns... I mean, kids... before."

"He doesn't need any," Amil answered about himself. He didn't even want to consider the possibility of losing another child, especially a daughter. But this situation, here and now, giving Anne a bad time, was another matter.

More laughter came from Annie as she looked to Amil again. "You don't want more someday?"

He didn't want to disappoint her, but he couldn't see himself risking his heart like that again. Instead, he smiled and offered a faint nod. "I suppose at some point."

"That works." She rewarded him with one of her room-brightening smiles. "So where did your fuzzies go? Hunting?" She had seen the wolf and panther stretch just a short time ago before padding out of the city.

"My Fuzzies?"

"Mmhm!" she answered cheerily as Duval snickered behind his hand, faking a cough.

"Oh. Hm." He smirked at her terminology. He had always just called them by their names. "Probably being lazy and asleep."

She looked between them. "What? They *are* fuzzy. And cute. Like Amil is!" she declared merrily.

"I'm... fuzzy and cute..." It was a description he couldn't remember anyone ever using on him.

"Apparently," Duval offered with a laugh.

"Odd... I don't feel fuzzy and cute."

"Nooo!" she laughed. "Just cute!"

"Oh hey," Duval remembered, "you and Amil should go check out the new tavern. Just opened up a few nights back."

"We'll save it for when he comes back." She glanced back at Amil, a little worry showing in her eyes.

"Comes back?"

"Mmhm," she nodded to Duval. "He has to go on a major secret mission to his homeland to do something he can't talk about."

"Aye. I have to go back home. They have asked for my return."

"Huh. Be careful, whatever it is."

"Of course," he said with a slight nod.

"But it's not to get married." She smiled. "I asked."

Giving the breath of a laugh, Duval shook his head. "I'm sure you did."

"Promise you'll be safe?" She turned and threw herself into Amil's arms. She didn't want him to go. He had told her stories about past wars in his homelands, and how things had remained settled now for a very long time. Now he was called home again to help those long unused to fighting. She worried for his safety. "I'll miss you."

"Of course," he repeated, wrapping his arms around her in return. "I'll miss you as well, Anne."

"And," Duval promised, "I'll keep an eye on her until you get back, Amil."

He hadn't considered that Anne – strong, independent Anne – would need someone to look out for her. But then, she was impetuous. His heart constricted, despite his mental protestations. Now he would worry about her. "You better." He hoped this friend of Anne's would understand the need he had to know she would be protected.

In return, Duval offered the slightest nod. "Don't make me have to come looking for you." Without saying it, without needing to scare Anne, he told Amil not to break Annie's heart by dying on some distant shore.

She didn't hear the unspoken words though; only what Du said. She cuddled against Amil. "Or me either."

"I'm glad you would," he whispered into her soft brown hair. "Though I would rather you stay here."

"Alright you two... Amil, give her a kiss... I need to haul her off to her room for some sleep. She gets cranky if she doesn't get enough rest," Duval teased.

Giggling, she tucked herself under the hood Amil always kept low over his face and whispered, "I'll miss pouncing on you!" It was her favorite way of greeting him; running up and getting a hug from him.

Duval looked away, up to the sky, the cobblestones, the water... anything to give them the illusion of a moment of privacy as Amil smiled to Anne, whispering with some small measure of humor, " Aye, I'll miss you trying to sneak up on me constantly."

"A quick kiss?" she continued to whisper as she rubbed her nose against his, "and we'll put Duval out of his misery, okay?"

"I can still hear you," Duval said dryly.

Annie giggled, then, without turning from her nose to nose embrace with Amil, she loudly whispered for him, "no you can't!"

"Come on, Squirt. 'Lex is going to start worrying about you if I don't get you home soon."

"Alright," Amil gave her a quick kiss, "You better get going."

"He is such a pain some days," she whispered, giving him a quick kiss back. Stepping back away from the scent of Amil under his warm hood, she struck a jaunty pose. "Better, Du?"

With a tight frown on his lips he shook his head no. "Yes, thank you."

Amil's warm hand settled against her back, giving her a slight push. "You better be off."

She grinned at Du's discomfort, but as they walked away, she sobered to look back and see Amil with an expression that made her think he would never come back.

Chapter Two
Homelands

Standing at the rail, Amilmamir Mor Nermakiir let the winds blow his cloak around him. His face however was tipped down, keeping the hood from pushing away from his face. His kin would know him by the bow he carried at his back and the blue plate affixed at his left shoulder. There would be no need for them to see the scars that marred his features.

High mountains ringed in clouds loomed into view. The undertow rolled beneath the boat, causing waves to bounce and jostle the small craft as it approached Tuarenlin. He hadn't been back in a very long time. Were it not for his honor and his respect for the Oracle, he wouldn't be here now.

Fishing and farm villages, as they drew closer, showed very few out working. This would be why he had been called home. There were plenty of younger elves that could hold up better for this duty, but he had the experience. The Oracle had asked for him by name. She only asked for people when she had something she both needed them for and needed to tell them. Now was his time.

With a few steps, he made the leap to the docks while men were still tying the ropes off. While his hood remained up, he would be nothing more than another of the Oracle's guards. There would be no questioning him, so long as they saw the blue shield on his armor. He would go straight to her, absolve his duty to her, and return to Lareah.

Whispered prayers followed him as he strode through the small town, looking at none of the hopeful gazes. He kept his eyes fixed on the far gates that kept the forest at bay beyond it. It didn't bode well to hear prayers so soon after landing. They could only mean dire trouble for his kin, that they thought he would soon be in need of such attention with the gods.

The wooden doors were pulled open for him when they saw the marks that held him as one of the Oracle's men, allowing him to pass through unquestioned. The sooner this was settled, the better.

"Uncle," a younger version of himself fell in step beside him.

He stumbled to a stop as he did a double take. "Elith?" The boy was the spitting image of him.

Motioning them onward, the young elf took the lead. "Aye. I've been sent to guide you back."

"You're serving then?" He fell in step, ignoring the pain in his knee as he kept up with the brisk pace set.

"As all Nermakiirs have before me," he said proudly.

Amil was proud of his sister's son. To serve the Oracle was the highest of honors with the heaviest responsibilities. It was what had earned him the right to the blue plate against his black armor. Purity, self-sacrifice, and allegiance to a higher good were what only a select few were granted in service to her. Every generation had seen one of his family line granted that privilege. And if it couldn't be a son of his own, he could certainly be proud of the young man now with him.

"She has been restless, uncle. The need to impart something to you personally is only one of the many problems she's been beset with."

Chapter Three
The Freezing Sorrow

The sun climbed high overhead as they brushed through the forest undergrowth, stirring the mist that covered no matter how hot or bright the sun shone. The birds chirped happily from their feast of bugs and worms. Dust danced in the beams of sun breaking through and leaves fell gently in the absence of the wind beneath the trees. The world was so calm, so peaceful. Amil breathed in the pulse of the forest.

He knew his nephew wouldn't speak more on behalf of the Oracle, so they had discussed family and duty as they quietly made their way further inland. Amil found a kindred spirit in the boy's view of duty and his single-minded training with a bow.

Into this, a noise in the distance echoed from tree to tree, shuttering through the very earth, sending birds to flee from their afternoon songs. Another great noise – a roar – as if the winds themselves howled through the forest in a rage, ran chills through the two men as they glanced at each other.

"Oh gods! It's coming!" A woman shrieked out of sight from them.

With no thought to their own safety, both men drew their bows and ran in the direction of trouble.

The woman fell, looking back to see trees shuddering at the weight of a beast cracking branches as it bore down on her. Crawling backwards, she was unable to let her gaze fall from her coming doom.

White scales gleamed like fresh winter snow and claws shaped as long and thick as icicles continued drawing closer, as if a blizzard was upon her, letting her feel the cold creep through her body as it gained on her, closer and closer.

What remained of her companions sprinted by, grabbing her by the arm. "Keep going!" they encouraged, practically dragging her to her feet, forcing her to run. Heart pounding in her chest, she could hear the cadence echoed in her ears with every beat. Her chest hurt and her breath gave out as she fell again.

She prayed. She prayed to the gods and she prayed that the Oracle might send aid.

As if appearing from thin air in the midst of her death, a dark object stood before her. With a hand above her eyes, she looked up at the dark ghost that became the figure of a man in a cloak. The cloak wavered slightly, though the air was still. She looked past the man and saw the open jaws of the great White opening as if to swallow them all. The man did not move in the face of the monstrous dragon, although she could feel the earth shudder as the great creature came down on them like an avalanche from the peaks of the highest mountains. Freezing air rushed past her, but she couldn't let her gaze turn from the beast's approach.

Frozen in terror, a scream still managed to escape her as she futilely threw an arm up to protect herself. The man before her moved quickly to the side as the dragon suddenly stopped its charge, roaring a challenge. From either side of the beast she saw the man and one other, both dressed identically in dark armor and black cloaks. Both had the shoulder plate of the oracle, edged in blue. But these... they were both Rangers by their mannerisms. Only those of the wilds could move with this ease, handle a bow as they were... and remain so calm before imminent death.

Perfectly still, they each held a long bow in steady arms. Arrows notched were held perfectly level and resting near their cheeks, flames sparking to life at their tips.

Almost in tandem the arrows flew, striking true to the creature's face. It roared now in pain and anger, swatting at the flames. It reared up on its hind legs as the men let fly with another set of arrows. A shriek of defiance declared the dragon's wrath as an arrow struck true in the throat. Its voice cut off as it began to hack and cough, swatting at its jaw trying to dislodge the myriad arrows. In fury, it swung its tail towards one of the men.

Amil saw it coming. This wasn't the first large creature he had ever battled. He just managed to roll out of the way as the tail sailed past barely over his head, colliding into a tree and shattering it into splinters. Leaves settled from the impact, falling around the area like a light snow.

The woman had the wind knocked out of her as the other man plowed into her, rolling her out of the way as the tail rushed past the spot she'd been in. Elith came up with his bow trained across the way. Following his gaze, she saw three small white wyrmlings perfectly visible against the forests greens and browns.

Lowering its reptilian head as if it were a plow, the frost dragon rent dirt and stone from the very earth as it charged the first man. Amilmamir fired a shot towards the dragon while he carefully jumped up on a fallen log. The bow was tossed aside as he pulled a blade. Jumping to the dragon's snout, he ran quickly up its head, driving the blade home at the base of its skull. His balance lost, he rolled down the dragon's sharply ridged spine and onto the trail to land on a knee.

She looked from the little ones to see the man roll, rising then to hold his side, blood dripping to the ground from an unseen wound. The dragon lay limp on the ground. His hood had fallen back, letting her see the long ears, blond hair, and blue eyes marred by a scar down his cheek. He picked up his bow and pulled the hood back over his head as he started towards them.

From the ground, he picked up a tooth from the great beast. Examining it for only a moment, he pocketed the item. Before he could start moving again, Elith rose, pulling the woman to her feet as well. "Move!" the younger man ordered, giving her a push in the direction of the gates.

Tears in her eyes, she looked again to the baby dragons and to the mother that now lay slain nearby. When she looked back, the two men were gone… vanished as if they had never been there. The forest was dark and silent but for the cries of the young that even now were sniffing in her direction. She ran for the town.

The two men had already moved on towards the base of the mountain.

Chapter Four
Don't Go Back

White dragons were known for their ice. What few thought about was the sorrow that followed in their wake. Too many had suffered loss to a dragon's appetite. Here in Tuarenlin it was no different. There weren't many, but every so often a large dragon, like the one they had needed to kill, came seeking a safe place for its young. They couldn't stay. Not if the elves that made their home here were to be safe and wanted to keep the Oracle protected.

Amil regretted the need to have killed such a magnificent beast; it wasn't good stewardship of the lands to kill, even if it had been necessary. Looking to the young archer at his side, he wondered if his nephew shared that thought. Elith's face was hidden beneath his own hood, his posture giving away nothing. That Amil could understand. He didn't care to discuss matters that were settled either. So he instead addressed what awaited them atop the mountain. "Has she been calling others home?"

A simple nod was his answer. "But your name has come up most often. She keeps asking if you've arrived yet."

That didn't bode well for him. He had served his time as the Oracle's guard once, too. That kind of attention from the Oracle could only mean a vision of some sort. She wouldn't have shared that information, so there was no point in asking about it.

There were no stairs up the mountainside. It was meant to be a challenge if the Oracle was to be approached. That meant a slope angling upwards at about forty degrees, spots with loose gravel, and no cover or caves to stop by. His lungs burned until he had made the climb. He had been tired after the battle with the dragon; it took everything in him not to ask for just a few minutes to rest. He refused to be seen as weak or old, especially on a visit to the seer.

Luckily the alabaster home of the Oracle loomed ahead. Large spiraled columns marked the entryway, one of the two guards standing beneath relieving his position to Elith as they approached. Alone, Amil entered the hall, taking advantage of the red cushions recessed into the wall. It relieved the stark whiteness of everything else, but this was the first time he had actually sat on them. They were quite comfortable.

It felt good to be back. He had spent a good part of his younger years serving either at the doors outside, or across the hall inside the doors to her chamber. The honor of watching her work above the small wisp of smoke that rose from the center of the floor was one he assumed Elith hadn't yet earned. But for all those years, he had never heard what she told others; he had only been sent to fetch them when necessary.

"Amilmamir Nermakiir."

He looked up at the slight woman wrapped in silk the same butter color as the walls in her room. She hadn't changed at all since last he'd seen her. "Lady." He rose, bowing to her.

Her milky eyes never saw him as she smiled, turning and going back into her room. It was the first time Amil had ever heard of her greeting a supplicant herself. His stomach lurched as he made himself follow and close the door behind.

"You lost your wife." She said softly, stating nothing new to Amil, as she turned back to him, "and your daughters. It's time for you to return."

Disagreeing with the woman went against everything he had been raised with. The Oracle didn't speak unless she had something important to share. He paused, trying to determine why he would need to come back. "I can't," he finally said.

"You can. And you will." Her voice was gentle, but brooked no disagreement. "You are on a path that will soon turn violent, and it does not serve our lands."

He knew she often saw futures no one else could yet fathom, but it wasn't something he saw for himself. He had given the fighting over to younger people. All he wanted now was to train others and enjoy the time he spent in entertaining conversation with Anne.

"It does not serve our lands," she repeated with more bite when he didn't answer.

"Lady…" He carefully chose his words, not wishing to argue with someone his people all held in high regard. Least of all, one he was related to, but he had chosen a different path. "I'm a simple ranger now."

The wisp of smoke rose between them, yet her eyes, despite not seeing this world, seemed to pierce straight through Amil. "You have never been such." Her head shifted to give the appearance of her looking at his bow. "That is not a bow given to simple rangers."

He kept himself from glancing at it, although his fingers clenched it a bit more possessively. Of course she would know about it; she knew everything. "Aye…" It had been given to him by the god he served. Since leaving Tuarenlin, Firnos had guided Amil's steps, sometimes quietly, sometimes by direct contact. The bow had been one of the few things he had been given directly. That had been during one of the wars many years back when his unit was near failure.

He had prayed the entire time he had continued to shoot a bow that was frayed and cracking. Without help, they would fail. A man had appeared at his left side, shooting with the same ease. The tide of battle had turned in those next moments.

Only after did Amil look to see his Lord at his side. Immediately, he had dropped to a knee, bowing his head. When summoned, he arose, only to be handed the bow. A look, a nod, and the god had moved off along the wall, unnoticed by others as anything more than another fighter that day.

But he knew.

And he remembered.

A look of displeasure touched her. "Then you will need to aid our battle." She came around, gently pulling his hood back away from his features.

He winced at having his disfigurement revealed, but forced himself to otherwise remain still. She was the only one allowed her secrets. And she had to have her reasons for wanting him to join their fight. "What battle?"

"The Northern Pass." She walked away from him, entering a chamber he had never been in further to the back of the room. By going into her private chambers, she had just concluded their conversation.

"You are on a path that will soon turn violent, and it does not serve our lands?" What path, he had to wonder. The only violence he could see was the battle she was committing him to.

Chapter Five
The Northern Pass

All the explanation he received was that Tuarenlin was next to face an invading army. The oracle had called home all those who had long ago gone out into the world to aid in the protection. It was a duty long ingrained in all elves from these lands... but he found it wasn't home anymore. Lareah had been his home for much longer, and while lands around Lareah had snow, none got as bad as the mountains around the island he had been raised on.

The wind whistled through the empty hills, snow pounded down at the foot of the few trees that had once grown in the area. On the horizon, smoke could be seen, black like a cloud of locusts moving with the wind. The snow was deep, making movement slow as they finally saw the gray stone of the fortress arise out of the blowing sleet. They could see the battle raging on and around the wall, ladders rising and falling.

"What are we waiting for?" one of the other commanders bellowed. "We didn't come all the way here to freeze!" He stepped out of formation, smacking his sheath hard to free its frozen grasp on the sword, drawing and raising the blade high. "I'm not about to let those animals inside that pile of stone!"

The men responded with their own cheers and yells, forming into a chant. "They may be many, but not true soldiers!" Swords glinted high, punctuating their words.

"Charge!" the commander finally called, sprinting towards the black mob. As if possessed by demons, the formation raced after him. Their yells were deafening, giving each other the power to continue through, no matter the obstacle. As if the wind itself was driving them like a sail across a frozen sea, they closed the distance.

Seeing the attack coming from their back, the enemy roared at the charging battalion. Forming into a loose mob, they shouted, rampaging towards the elves as if they brought the hells themselves at their back.

The clash was terrific, swords crashing and spears shattering against foes. Screams of pain echoed across the hills, barely countering the shouted obscenities as the elves slashed their way through to the wall.

A horn blew from within the swirling snow, seeming to call the foe away. They left their dead and dying, left their fighting, and simply vanished into the whiteout conditions.

The men were tired, their casualties heavy. Dark snow rose in steam over the blood of their fallen. A chain creaked and clanked, lowering a gate for them to enter. What met them inside was the remnant of the last army to be sent out; men battered, weary, relieved for the reinforcements. Too soon it was the shape of those who had come to help. Amil's archers dwindled in number on the battlement as the commander's men died outside the wall.

Days turned to weeks, the cold and the war unrelenting. Tucking his hands into his armpits, Amil huddled lower into his cloak. This battle wasn't good for man or bow. This land closest to the isle of Tuarenlin was nothing but mountains. Straight up from the shores, they had climbed into peaks blanketed in snow that never melted. It didn't even help to stretch his hands towards the meager fire.

"Bloody hells! Incoming!" the watch called from the wall, gaining everyone's attention.

The large stones were so small when they soared high in the sky, though they sounded like banshees when they descended. The loud whistle was followed by a deafening BOOM. The earth shook and rubble flew in all directions. Men ducked their heads for protection while others, like Amil, got to their feet. The concussion had left them all dazed, his ears ringing. Dusting the snow and frozen earth off, he looked towards the impact area and saw a few men on the ground crawling away, a trail of blood marking their passage.

No time, the thought to himself as he ran up the stairs to the upper wall, stringing his bow with frozen fingers. He hated this place. It always snowed and the wind was so cold it hurt to even breathe. The men they fought, or whatever they were, seemed not one bit affected by its teeth. He looked over the edge, watching a group of them in the far distance surrounding a fire. Dressed in the skins of wild animals, chanting to their gods, a small contingent of them manned a catapult, hurtling stones into the air towards Amil's own men.

He ducked as a stone collided into the wall with a loud cracking sound. Nearby, the watchmen loaded a repeating ballista and began to rain the lethal spears upon the men at their catapult. A few hit their marks, causing the others to scatter from their war machine. "At least it will be quiet for a little while," he whispered as he descended back down from his perch.

Two months he had been here. For two months he had led a unit of younger, less experienced men. He had done as the Oracle commanded. Now he just wanted to go home. Those he had trained were a fine unit, ready and able to attack – and die – for the protection of their homeland; even if none of them knew why they were being attacked. There was nothing, outside of the Oracle, that was worth possessing in Tuarenlin.

Who were these men anyways, he thought to himself as he dusted the snow from a bench, sitting back near the fire. Their bodies were brutish, massive, and their lower jaw jutted forth. They resembled some sort of mixture of human... maybe something that had been forgotten long ago, maybe something now returned. *Whatever they were, their blood still ran red.*

Watching the fire dance as it charred the wood black, turning to ash, he thought back to better times. Green fields, a teenage girl laughing and hugging him, a wife playing with a little girl, a home full of life and visitors. Life had been so much better back then. No worries, safe... WARM.

But that wasn't completely gone. Anne was making his house a home again. She had brought laughter back into his life. So unlike the bard that had once been his, Anne was a tiny fireball, full of mischief. When she smiled, it seemed to shine from within her. Something about it fostered a sense of home in him. He smiled as he realized he had fallen in love with her, chuckling to himself.

He must have fallen asleep watching the fire, now dead with frost covering what had been warm and comforting. He awoke to shouting, men running. He rose and ran with them up onto the wall.

The fortress had been constructed before his time, although it was long abandoned and showing age. It had once been a trading post. Now it was nothing but a few crumbling buildings behind an unsteady wall. "Of all the places," he whispered, leaning against the inner wall, stringing his bow.

Arrows whistled over his head as he crouched low. "Incoming!" he heard the watch yell again. A stone boulder hit nearby, breaking their own ballista, splinters and stone raining down over them all.

He could hear them; marching, grunting, chanting. They were close, intent on taking this last fort before moving across the straights to the land of elves, the land of his forefathers. It wasn't going to happen today. He grabbed an arrow from his quiver, yelling as loud as he could, "Make ready!" His archers followed his example and as one they notched and stood. "Aim!"

There were so many. It was like looking into an abyss. A mass of movement closing in on them swarmed below. "Fire at will!" he yelled, letting his own arrow fly to strike its target. Of their own accord, his fingers pulled another arrow. Long years with the bow in hand made it second nature to not even truly aim, to just fire out into the coming death.

A ladder smashed into the ramparts in front of him. The battle was on them. He tossed the bow off the wall, his archers doing the same, as he pulled dagger and sword. The first creature lunged up onto the rampart and Amil slashed, cutting its neck wide open. He flinched slightly as blood spewed at him, spattering against his hood and cloak. Clunk! And again, and again; ladders landed against the wall. More creatures ascended.

Throwing his dagger, he hit one in the chest, watching it grab at the blade before it tumbled back off the ladder into its fellows. A scream told him one of his archers hadn't been so lucky. His pommel to another's face sent it falling into the mob that was quickly surrounding them. Putting his weight behind it, he sent a ladder over. Fist to the face of an attacker, he moved on to land a foot to a knee, breaking it and sending the beast over the ledge. So many now on the wall, he gasped for breath, his lungs complaining with both the exertion and the cold.

Jumping aside as the scream again warned only a heartbeat before a flying stone struck the wall, his own foot slipped as he twisted and spun with his blade, trying to stay on the narrow walkway. In the trickery of light and shadow from the moon, he misjudged. His cloak and hood twisted around him, hiding his vision as the air failed to catch him. He felt his body hit something hard, heard cracking as stars exploded behind his eyes. Warmth suffused him, even in this cold place. His hearing became hazy, the sounds of battle fading around him. In his mind's ear he heard the familiar echo of a little girl's laugh… and a child's small feet running along marble floors…

Chapter Six
Home Again

Amil awoke as the wagon bounced across some pebbles in the road. It was warm; and the sun was out. *Was it a dream?* Again the wagon bounced and he felt the pain in his ribs, letting him know it wasn't. Carefully rising up on his elbows, he looked back down the trail, the mountain now small, barely able to make out the pass he had spent the last months at. *I'm certainly glad I'm not in that hell.* He looked back to see the wagon pulled by a horse, yet no one was driving. He was alone. He sat up slowly, flinching at the pain in his side, nausea washing over him. There were blood smears and arrows stuck into the side of the wagon.

One other wagon trudged along ahead of his down towards the point they had first landed on the mainland. No one held the reins there either. Several lay in the back, but he couldn't tell if they were alive or dead. Had they won? Were others still fighting?

His head was spinning, but he forced himself to look beyond the horses. He started to lie down before his mind registered what he had seen. On the shoreline stood a woman that shouldn't have been there. Heedless of the pain, he quickly sat up, unable to look away from the pale blond hair blowing in the same soft motions as the butter yellow silk gown. The Oracle never left her temple… yet there she stood.

He rubbed a hand over his eyes. When he looked again, she was closer, impossibly closer, almost near the lead horses. With a jolt, the wagon stopped. "Nephew." Her milky eyes continued to look down the path, past him.

She had not called him that since he had been a small boy. "Are you here as the Oracle?" His voice was gravelly, his mouth dry. "Or my Aunt Sithia?"

She ignored the question. "Why do you carry your wife's name in yours?"

He didn't need to answer it. She would know that they had taken each others names. He had never seen a reason to drop it. "What happened to the others?" he asked of his comrades.

"The battle has been won."

It didn't answer anything, and yet it answered everything. The wagon ahead of him held the only other survivors. Those who had been capable of walking yet had likely given their lives to send the wounded on ahead.

"Come home, Amilmamir." It wasn't a request, despite sounding it.

A warm bed would be welcome. Family would go a long way in healing his wounds. But a slow dawning spread across his face, gaining a sad smile from the Oracle. The Nermakiirs were family, whereas Cane and Malania – his animal companions – and Anne… were home. He needed the furred warmth near him. He needed to hear her laugh. He needed her smile, her teasing.

"If you return to Lareah, you will never see Tuarenlin again."

It wasn't a threat, but his blood ran to ice. There was something she meant him to understand in those few words, something about not serving his homelands, something about violence… but he had survived numerous battles in Kordathya, the lands Lareah lay in. He had survived the Northern Pass. And she was out of the temple.

Maybe she wasn't even real. Maybe this was all some nightmarish dream.

The rocking of a boat next woke him. After that was the small town in Atil, his home. The villagers there helped him across the isle to his home. Rest. Rest, and then he'd wonder on what his decisions meant… and what Anne meant.

Chapter Seven
Amil loves Annie

Coming across a few people visiting, Annie identified Ryl, a rather frail mage visiting with a woman she didn't recognize. They were discussing the acquisition of some sort of magic scroll. As she came up to them, their conversation fell to silence. "Was I interrupting something?"

Neither commented, nor did a male mage she'd seen around town several times. He simply continued to lean on the table outside the Inn, observing the interactions of the others.

Back home, mages were rare, but here in Lareah they had an academy to train anyone wanting to use magic. They were an odd lot, and often involved in studies, theory, or practicing new spells. This group appeared to have been involved in a talk about something of that nature. "Wow," Annie tried to lighten the now-somber tone. "Bet you guys have managed to quiet the crickets even."

"Amil's up on the plateau." Ryl pointed towards the west as he dispassionately made the comment. Nothing more than a raised stone area, the plateau was the city's main gathering spot. A few benches, a nice bubbling stream and plenty of nooks for groups to sit in made it the ideal centerpiece of Lareah.

Glancing that way, Annie turned back to the group, still in good humor. "Thanks? So Ryl, that your way of saying get lost?"

"No."

"Then what?" Annie laughed. "I need to have an Amil attached to me?"

The female mage scowled. Humor was obviously lost on her. "What's an Amil?"

"A bunny wrangler," she nodded. "Not to be confused with a tree hugger." It was a running joke that the rangers did not find very funny, but humored her with. She differentiated them as the guardians of the forest by saying they herded animals or people where they needed to be. The few druids that roamed the wilds were the protectors of nature; those she teased as being tree huggers.

"He is an elderly ranger," Ryl offered.

"Agh! He's not old!" Anne tried not to sound annoyed.

"Age is just a number," the woman said with a shrug, "if you're an elf."

"Amil's...like wine." Anne nodded, pleased with her assessment of him. "Gets better as it ages. Or something like that."

The mage leaning against the table muttered something under his breath, eliciting a shrug from the woman.

"I meant more that he could use your company..." The mageling Ryl trailed off before turning back to the woman again. He seemed strained to keep up with two separate discussions. Long pauses fell between his words. "...No..."

Continuing to lean against the table, the male mage looked at Anne as if she were unwelcome vermin. The woman frowned, her conversation with Ryl ending.

The silence stretched. There had obviously been some other discussion occurring before Anne came upon them. "You guys are um... sorry, but, boring." She smiled to take the sting out of her words. "I'm gonna take a walk." Her soft slippers made no noise on the cobblestones as she lightly made her way out the southern entrance to the city. She greeted several people with cheerful words or by name, including several of the city's Defenders, as she went.

She took a deep breath, enjoying the air outside the city. Stepping off the path as she whistled up at a little bird, she then looked down into a nearby pond, watching the small things moving in the water. She lifted a small turtle plodding towards the pond and set it into the rocks at the water's edge. This was part of the joy her father had instilled in her about the world around her; mindful meditation.

Once the turtle had submerged itself, she returned to the path. A battered signpost just outside the gates marked the different directions. The wind had blown the southern marker almost off the post and the paint had weather-worn away to almost nothing. She contemplated the illegible sign. "Which way today?" she asked herself. Closing her eyes, she happily spun in a circle with her arm outstretched. It didn't really matter the direction, but she was facing west. "This way then," she shrugged to herself. Before she could take a step, Amil seemed to materialize from the trees nearby. "Hey look! A ranger!"

"Hey look!" he mimicked her tone. "A monk!" She was a sweet little thing that didn't use weapons, preferring instead to use martial skill in hand-to-hand combat. He had seen her go through her forms and knew that the simple, graceful movements were much like her; they belied the inherent strength hidden below the surface and could be very lethal.

Her warm laugh rang out. He had to have been following her from the time she had spoken to the others near the docks. He had some talent that helped in the forest to make him seem to blend with his surroundings. He was just as quiet as she was, but with that strange ability to not be seen unless he wanted to be. "Someday that won't work y'know!"

When he asked "why not," she gave him her most shrewd look, ruining it with her cutest smile. "Cuz I'll be good enough to see you."

"Maybe."

"What d'you mean maybe?"

"Just that... Maybe."

Some days he could be downright annoying with his mysterious discussions. She chose to ignore it. "What're you patrolling today?"

"Where ever the winds take me." His tone was cool, his thoughts elsewhere. She couldn't know he was thinking of her and the conclusions he had drawn while he recovered.

"Are you grumpy? Not enough bran this morning?" She playfully pulled on the wood of his bow.

"Brain? Hm?" he teased.

"Bran!" she laughed. "A fibery thing. It helps old elves poo!"

"Bran," he smirked, pretending to just understand now. "Hmm."

"So what's up? Oh I know!" she interrupted herself. "You're hunting prunes!"

"Never used bran..." he stopped, giving her an odd look. He never knew what to expect her to say or do.

"Why not?"

"Never had a problem with such things. I guess I keep a good diet."

"So you shouldn't be grumpy then," she cheerily informed him.

"You said I was grumpy. I didn't say anything about me being grumpy. So who is really grumpy?"

"Uummmmm... you?" She grinned.

"Nope," he smirked, "I think you're being grumpy."

Bright laughter came from her. "I hardly ever get grumpy!"

"Whatever, grumpy pants." His smile belied the words.

Putting her fists up, trying to look grumpy, she declared "I'm no grumpy pants!" in humor.

"Mmmhmm."

"So where's the wind say you should go?"

He pointed down the path she had been considering, answering "I figured you were" when she asked if she could follow.

She shrugged. "Maybe you need some alone time with the trees or something. Look! I'm taller than you!" she declared, hopping on top of a low rock.

Amil smirked at her. "Only by a few inches." He moved off along the path, eyes watching for anything unusual. "So I've paid to have some things done to the house, Anne. I hope you don't mind."

"It's your house!" she said cheerfully, then added in curiosity, "What'd you do?"

"Well you have been helping me keep it clean. I think you'll like it. They should be done tomorrow hopefully."

"So what is it?" she asked in excitement.

"You'll see. It should be... more lively." He had noted her attempts to make the place more of a home. He would let her find out that he had ordered new linens and many other things, inviting more of the female rangers to stop by to visit her.

"What'll I see?" She bounced along at his side, a happy skip in her step.

"It's a surprise." He held a hand up to have her fall silent, seeing something unusual ahead. "There's a trap." He went into the crouch of a much younger man, easily blending to the tree line. A finger to his lips warned Anne to remain quiet, his eyes serious enough to make her mind.

Even with her eye on him as he crept forward, he managed to disappear in the blink of an eye. She wasn't sure how he did it, but remained amazed by it.

No birds or other animals made a noise here. There was a hum of insects, but that more made the hair stand up on the back of her neck than calmed her. Then again, maybe it was the twisted shape of the trees, or the wet moss and knotted vines hanging from them. There was something about the drooping of the trees and weeds that felt oppressive... like death was watching. She rubbed her arms to try to shake off the creepy feeling.

He stepped out of an area to her left, startling her. Not even a blade of grass had rustled in his passing. Wiping a gloved hand against the back of his thigh, he smiled at her. "Bad place, that. Men were warned not to build there. Hallowed ground once." He spared a glance back at the area that showed no sign of his passing, and then motioned her with a slight head jerk to follow him. "Let's continue the patrol."

She fell in at his side again, sparing a few nervous glances back at the strange glade. Even after they were out of sight of it, it bothered her. And she now found herself lost, since he hadn't stuck to the roads and she hadn't paid enough attention. They had cut through the forests by some path only he seemed to know. Since he knew his patrols best, she decided to try to put it out of her mind by going back to their previous discussion. "So what's more lively? More mice? Did Cane get a girlfriend?" Amil said nothing. "Not even a hint?"

"You'll see." He couldn't help a chuckle at the tenacity of the little ball of energy at his side. "We've gone over this."

"But you've never answered."

They ducked under a few low hanging branches and came out near a village. "I did. I said you'll see." He smiled and put a finger up to warn her from asking again. "Boat." He turned his hand to now point at the small dock.

He was given a short reprieve from her incessant questions as she turned to the boatman, badgering him about information regarding the vessel. Too soon the city of Lareah came into view. "Anne," he caught her attention, shifting his eyes towards the land.

Hers followed suit. She scooted so quickly to the side of the boat that it rocked wildly. "We're almost there! We're so close, you could just…"

"No," he interrupted. "We aren't on my isle yet. That's another boat ride." Trying to hide his smirk of enjoyment at this game with her, he turned to help the captain bring the skiff into port. With a hand on one of the pylons for support, he then levered himself out onto the low dock.

"How are the knees?" she asked as she clambered out after him.

"They are fine." No need to tell her that they ached. "I might be old; I'm not broken."

"Oh good!" She pounced him for a hug, laughing when he stumbled backwards, almost dropping her. "Did you lose your balance?" she asked in good humor.

He smirked ever so slightly. "My back gave out." He gave her a bear hug, lifting her off the ground and getting a squeak out of her. "There we go; straightened back out." He set her back on her feet as she laughed.

"Did you plant a tree in the house?" she teased.

"You'll see."

She leaned against him. "Just one hint?"

"Sure. It's nicer. Livelier."

"That's not a hint!" she laughed.

He nodded. "Aye. A really big one."

"Is it new friends for Cane and Malania? Oh! I bet it's a dollhouse! For the mice to live in!"

"All the floor plans and everything made my head spin so I just signed the contract."

"...a contract?"

"Well, aye." Humor touched his voice, almost giving it away. He had bought furnishings, but there had been no structural changes. "The gnomes and elves didn't want to do any work without one," he continued.

"What're you changing it for?" She bounced on her toes in excitement. "Are you getting rugs?" She gave him that pleased-with-herself look, hands on hips, grinning. "Did you go to the orphanage?"

"No, I haven't."

"Oh good. Cuz I'm gonna do that for you. Find just the right kid. Mysterious and with a hood just the same shade as yours!" She gave him her best playful smile.

"...Are you trying to find someone like me?"

"Why would I do that? I found you! But maybe there's a kid that looks like you," she teased. "Big bow, dark hood..."

"I doubt it; unless it's another ranger that dresses close to me."

"Well, if it's a kid, you'd have to teach them to be ranger-y." She shifted gears abruptly back to the previous conversation. "How do you make a house livelier?"

"Adding stuff to it."

"You mean secret passages and trap doors?"

"No, like objects."

"Like... you bought furniture?"

"You will see."

"I dunno..." She grinned. "That might mean you want company."

His smirk crept back to his lips. "I allow you over already."

"Maybe you're gonna invite Bo and Dwight over for dinner." They were a few of the rangers he regularly worked with.

"Are you going to come as well then?"

"Am I invited?" She pretended to consider it when he said she was. "I'll need my red slippers back."

"You're wearing your slippers," he pointed at her feet.

"Oh." She glanced down at them. "Well then."

"So then I guess you can make it. Excellent. I'll cook for four then."

"That's it! You got a new dining room table! Didn't you?" She bounced along-side him. "I figured it out!"

"Nope." He smirked.

"...oh." Deflated, she quietly walked beside him, trying to think of what else it might be.

"It's okay." He offered. "I still l... like you." He had almost used a word long out of his vocabulary.

Catching the odd stutter, she tipped her head, smiling up at him. "I l-like you, too."

Still walking, he canted his head, glancing at her. "Mocking me?"

"Nope." She smiled when his fleeting look passed over her again. "I think you changed a word."

"I changed no words," he answered, trying to sound haughty.

"Well, then you stopped from saying a word."

"Maybe."

Her delighted laughter rang out. "Being cryptic on purpose?"

That laughter was impetuous and he never knew when it would come, and yet he lived for it. Her joy made him feel younger than he ever thought he could again. He smirked, knowing how best to irritate her. "Possibly."

"You're doing it again!" She playfully punched him in the arm, aware that he was trying to get a rise out of her.

"I'm not doing anything," he stated innocently. "I'm just... you know: being me."

She bounced around to the front of him, stopping him from going forward. Hands on hips, she raised her brows, grinning. "Cryptic."

He smirked. "No."

Joyful laughter rang out. "What would you call it then?"

"Being me." He shrugged.

"Which is...?"

"Being me. You're just looking for me to say it and I'm not going to say it."

"Well fine." She leaned towards him, teasing. "Maybe I don't like the word IT."

He shrugged. "So you don't like the word IT."

"So you don't need to say IT."

He turned aside so she wouldn't see the smirk. Her excitement over this was reaching a point where he'd get a reaction shortly. He knew what she wanted; he chose to answer only what she said. "I'm not going to say IT."

A frustrated noise came from her. "Why don't you wanna say whatever the word was?!"

"I don't even remember what the word was."

She abruptly changed tactics. "Did you get new curtains?"

"You'll see."

"Bedspread?"

"You'll see."

"What was the word?" she tried to slip the question back in to catch him off guard. It usually worked for people not used to the way monks played mind games.

He knew the way her mind was working. "Don't remember what it was."

She laughed. "So this dinner party..."

"You're invited. And yes, you're wearing your red slippers, so you haven't lost them." There was no party; something they were both fully aware of. They were enjoying the game so much that he saw she had missed the change in direction he had taken. They weren't aimed for the boat to Atil. In fact, they were headed further inland.

"Formal uniform or daily uniform?" She asked with too playful of a grin.

"Formal."

With a bright "a-ha" smile, she informed him, "I don't have a formal uniform."

"You don't need to wear anything special. Daily is fine."

"But you just said formal."

"I said I was wearing formal, and it was only mocking your statements prior of how I only wear two different types. Daily is fine though."

"You do only wear two types," she teased.

"I have clothes though as well. They're all stored at home."

"In boxes." She had seen the storage bins labeled with both his name and that of his dead wife. She had simply dusted them, and moved on to other items. "How do you know they even fit then?" she asked with a laugh.

How could one woman be so vexing to him? Her innocence should drive him crazy, but he kept finding her, kept playing into her mental games. "I haven't changed in height or even that much in weight so they should fit fine."

"Well, what about them? What are you going to tell them to wear? Can you cook?"

"Of course."

"Do you need help?"

"Depends if you want to help." He continued walking casually.

"Maybe you have new stuff in the kitchen and need help with it."

"Maybe I do."

"Cabinets or cook wear?" she doggedly persisted.

"Maybe."

"Are you going to wear a non-uniform?" She teased. "Or should I get you an apron to tie over your leathers while you cook?"

"Maybe I'll just cook you."

Laughter rang out as she tucked her hair behind an ear. "Like some fairy story?"

He glanced back at her. "And you'll be in it. Literally."

"That makes you the...mean ol' witch!" she exclaimed in delight.

"And you're the meal," he offered with a smirk.

"I don't think I taste that good." She licked her wrist. "Nope."

Skipping up a little closer to him, she extended her arm to him. "Here, try."

"I'll be sure to tell the tale to the orphans when they ask what happened to you," he teased, taking her up on the offer and lightly licking at her arm.

"And what orphans?" she laughed. "Did you pick some?"

"I thought you were going to."

"Then you better not eat me yet! So what else besides roast-Annie will you serve?" she teased.

He loved this playfulness in her. This silliness was something that had long been missing in his life, and he found himself playing into it with her. "A side order of Roasted Anne fingers."

"Hm..." she nodded sagely, as if she were truly considering it. "That has potential..." Her smile bloomed again. "But what kind of sauce?"

He barely missed a beat. "Hot sauce. To spice them up a little."

Annie stuck a finger in her mouth. "Hm." She wiped it on her pants. "Yeah. Definitely needs something. So which of your blades you gonna chop me up with?" Mirth sparkled in her voice and eyes.

But the words bothered him. He paused, brow furrowed, perfectly serious as he reached a gloved hand out to touch her cheek. "I wouldn't hurt a hair on your head, Anne. You know that." The light fell from her as she went just as serious. He knew she could somehow read his moods, and he didn't want that grimness touching her. To lighten it, he smirked as he started walking again. "Besides, I hate cleaning swords."

"I know you l-like me," she said happily.

"Well you obviously know what I was going to say then." He stopped near the lodge, turning to look at her.

"Just now?" Her eyes were large and innocent, but her smile loudly told him she was playing.

"No, when I reworked my words."

"What makes you say that?"

"The way you have been saying it," he gave her a pointed look that said he knew her game.

She knew it as well, giving a rich laugh. "It's the way you said it." She tried to sound nonchalant about it, "But if you don't even remember what the word was... you don't have to say if you don't wanna."

He appreciated that her voice was still light and playful. She wasn't prone to some of the moods he had grown accustomed to seeing in women over the last years. "Well I was going to say I love you, but since you want to make a big deal out of it, I won't."

She smiled, taken aback with surprise. "I didn't make a big deal..."

"Did to."

"Not."

"...to."

"Do you?"

"Aye, and you did."

"Well you started it. Trying to cover something up and all that. So it wouldn't matter if I felt the same," she gave him an extremely happy smile. "Even though I do. But if you don't wanna say it, then I won't either." Her tone was still quite playful. "Unless you change your mind."

"I haven't."

"About saying it or not saying it?"

"Maybe."

"No," she laughed. "You haven't about saying it or not saying it? Not maybe!"

"I said maybe."

"Maybe doesn't count."

"Does in my world."

She grinned. "And I bet bunnies dance jigs in pink tutus too."

"You haven't seen that skit yet? You should go to the taverns more often on Maleiinar's Night."

"Maybe you should take me there for a date then," she teased.

"Maybe I have better places than taverns for dates."

"Like where?"

"Want to go on a date?" He held a hand out to her when she nodded. "Come." It worked perfectly into the plans he already had in place for their evening.

With her hand folded into his own, he walked through the city, through its poorest section and out into the cemetery. "And here we are."

She looked at him askance. Not that she had that much experience dating, but she was pretty sure dates were supposed to be less creepy. He truly had a strange sense of humor if he thought this was the kind of place to try to impress a girl. "...kinda dead, isn't it?"

He simply smiled mysteriously. With her hand still in his, he jerked his head ever so slightly for her to follow. Intrigued, she skipped up next to him again. In her usual gi, she didn't have to worry about skirts tripping her up and her soft leather slippers gave her just enough of a hint of the ground below to feel the changes from gravel to sand or grass.

A single row of trees met them, the ground changing underfoot. As they passed beyond the graveyard, the breeze seemed to blow differently. She knew it was the same as before, but here it was less ominous and freer, allowing a cleansing deep breath. A lake lapped softly against the shore.

Amil saw the wonder on her face and smiled, pulling her around to a small hill and up the gentle slope. "And one of my favorite spots."

Awe was the only word she could think to describe it. Everything about it was peaceful, untouched by the city, and very beautiful. "It's...stunning up here!"

"The full moon, the overlook, the trees, the lake; much more romantic than a tavern I would think. Might even say I l-like it."

She smiled almost to herself. "Mmhm." He tried so hard to act stodgy and unromantic. Then he'd do something like this... going to the most serene lake she had ever seen. The trees rustled softly, almost to a rhythm with the gentle shush of the water at the sandy shoreline. Logs had been placed in different places below their hill, near fire pits ready for campers to use them as benches. And in the middle of the lake... "What's on the island?"

"Nothing."

Annie looked at him askance. "You could just make up something."

He offered a small smile.

"I bet it's where someone fell in love," she said romantically.

He thought to himself, *twice. I've been lucky enough to fall in love here twice.* Looking at her now, he knew that's what it was. He had almost let the word slip on their travels, his heart overriding the common sense of his mind. She was too young for him. He knew that; and yet... he was finding he didn't care. He liked what he was with her around. "It's where a phantom roams and likes to eat young little ladies alive," he teased.

"Then it's a good thing I have an old man to protect me," she grinned. "It'll confuse the phantom."

He was confused enough. "Indeed."

"Maybe," she continued her fanciful idea, "the phantom is a heartbroken man... who lost his lady to the waters."

"It's possible." He set his bow gently to the side in a niche that seemed made just for his favored weapon. With a soft sigh, he pushed his hood back. "No one really knows. But if you ever wonder why I chose to be a ranger, now you know."

Peeking over at him, she couldn't help smiling at how handsome he was. The moonlight sparkled off his silver-white hair, his pale skin almost a reflection of the moon itself. He rarely showed anyone his features, not unless he felt they were truly trustworthy. Anne knew she was lucky; not only did she see his visage regularly, but moments like now were precious. He was, for the first time since she had known him, truly serene.

The soft click of the few metal bands on his armor made the smallest amount of noise as he settled down onto the stone, one leg dangling over the ledge, the other bent up for him to rest his arm over.

With her eyes closed, Annie lifted her face to the slight breeze, pure bliss on her face. "You can hear the trees and water sing up here." She folded down beside him, graceful and silent. "Monks are trained to listen and be in tune with nature. If everything sings in harmony... well, I won't go into the philosophy." A soft smile graced Amil as she turned to him. "It bores most people."

"Aye, but to actually listen to it is different than being trained to hear it." He wanted her to understand that difference.

She did. "Dad showed me it's different. Some people can learn to hear it, but it takes someone special to HEAR it. Not just the sound, but the way it sings, harmonizes together."

"And some people," he gave her a slight smirk, "like to just enjoy it."

Placing a hand over his, she smiled at the twinkle in his eyes. She knew his words were a way of telling her talk wasn't needed, that she should just enjoy it. It was all just too perfect, and she couldn't help herself as she looked out over the water. "Does it sing for you?"

Worse than a bard, he thought. *Always with the chatter.* "It more talks to me than anything. It tells me of what is around me, the breeze tells me if something is close or far, leaves crack or shift when something passes on or by them, birds chirp and fly if they are startled or don't like something." He let his fingers slide between hers as she peeked at him before both looked out over the water again. "But I always come here just to listen to everything, so I suppose I do hear it sing. Just in a different way. Or in the same."

"Did you always know you wanted to be a ranger?" she asked softly.

"When I was young, no. I was trained as an archer for the militia, then as an Arcane Archer while I served our Oracle. It wasn't til I was just over a hundred when I was trained in the arts of the woodsmen when I actually fell in love with nature. To help others, and still enjoy what nature has to offer, and be one who helps preserve what you see and hear now."

Chapter Eight
Echoes

He smiled at the rapt attention on Anne's face. "And that's how Amil became a ranger."

"And it never changed? Never thought about anything else?"

His thoughts ran back to that time. He had only known service to his people and the Oracle. But after a certain age, his time with her had come to an end. He had moved away, wanting to see what else was out in the world. Lareah had become a home to him, even before he met the woman he would start a family with.

Standing on the plateau, which had always been a center of meeting for the city, he had been listening to the conversations of others when a skinny elven man had approached him, a bow in hand. Looking Amil up and down, he had finally simply asked, "a ranger?" in regards to the bow Amil held and his soft leathers.

Dar'chaos, his name had been, and he had offered Amil a place in the newly formed High Council of Rangers, if he were to pass three tests. He had needed to hunt an ancient brown bear that had caused trouble. He had managed, with many bruises to himself, to clear that trouble.

The second had been to run from Lareah to one of the furthest outposts quickly and silently, avoiding all detection from the factions such as bandits and rogue mages. That hadn't gone as smoothly as he would have liked, gaining him singed hair from a mage's fire.

"Your third test," Dar'chaos had told him, "is to tell me why you are a ranger."

"To. be the watchful eye," he had answered without a thought. "To protect those who are innocent and to bring justice to those who do wrong; to carry the weak and ward off the wicked. I never kill for fun; only in need."

"Always be true to yourself," the elf had said, handing Amil a uniform, "and always help those in need. Wear this with pride." He had called in a young vidu woman then, announcing her as Auren and the panther at her heel her companion.

The three of them were the first of the Kordathyan Rangers.

As the years had passed, he now found himself one of the last again to have stood on the ramparts during the many battles Lareah had faced. They had defeated evil in all its forms in every clime, from frozen wastes to scorching desert. They had battled alongside the Gray Gryphons from their earliest formations to their current militia. They had killed in Hirath's name with the Truth's Light, and they had made a last stand with the Guardians (now the Defenders) at the gates of Lareah, spilling the blood of enemies along with their own.

Because of this, the Hall of Heroes in Lareah housed the statues of quite a few rangers. It had always been known that no matter where you went in Kordathya, the rangers would be watching, protecting and guiding. They always protected life, doing what was right, no matter the cost.

"No," he finally answered Anne, realizing that what he did wasn't a job; it was a way of life. "I guess I never really wanted to do much else."

She reached up with her free hand to run a finger along the scar that ran across his face. "Even after? Or did that make it stronger?"

He closed his eyes against the power in that touch. There was something more tender than earthly contact, and yet it was so...Anne. "Only then did I truly feel what hate was, and for many years I wandered the forests til I finally saw I had become more saddened and lonely. I had not the hate I had felt anymore, and decided to come back here. I remembered the joy I had doing it in these lands, so I got on the boat and sailed til finally I could find a ship that was going here."

"Can I ask you something personal?" At his nod, she went on. "You mention your girls. And I hear it in your voice when you talk about them... or like the feeling in their room at your house. But the only sign of your wife is the chair." She knew there was a closet with magically sealed boxes of clothing, but, "No paintings, nothing else that might have been hers. What happened? You never even talk about her."

He tapped a finger to the side of his head. "I keep her here. Talking of her is one thing, but the memories are what makes everything, of who she was."

"How did you meet her?" she leaned against his arm, lending him support for something she knew he wasn't comfortable voicing.

"I met her in Lareah. She was a very young bard, and I a young ranger, and we had started talking and found we liked each other a lot. She started to go into the forests looking for me." He looked to the hand resting over his knee, his thumb going to finger the area where his wedding band used to sit. It still stood out whiter than the skin around it. "We grew closer. She designed our home from gold we had saved up together. We married, had two children." He morosely fell silent at the memory of his daughters. It was something else he wasn't comfortable talking about.

Annie noticed it and lightly nudged him, teasing, "Did you have trouble saying the word to her?"

"She was singing on the plateau, if I remember, when we first met. Well I gave her a flower which I guess said enough to her." He smiled slightly at the thought, gaining one from Anne as well. "Though Tahlon wasn't too happy. After a few weeks we found Tahlon actually had a thing for her as well."

"Uh-oh! What happened?"

"By that time we had already fallen for each other and Tahlon accepted his losses."

"She must have been really pretty...to have more than one guy falling for her. Bet everyone thought you were quite the guy to win her." She smiled.

Very few women would be comfortable talking about a former love interest of the man they wanted. Anne was unique in the fact that she never seemed to be jealous. And after years of not talking about someone that had made his life complete, it was good to finally share some of the history he had had with the bard. "She was very pretty... Ah... I didn't pay much attention to the talks around town. She and I actually went to the arena quite a bit," he added with a chuckle.

"The arena?" Anne laughed. What little she knew of the woman, that was counter to it all! She had been a very non-combat person.

"Aye." He smiled at the memory. "Tobias and Michael of The Tzee Dojo always invited us. We would spar with fishing poles." He shared a laugh with Anne at the absurd image in both their minds. "Michael thought I was perfectly suited for her after we duked it out for a good hour."

"Did you agree?"

"Of course, although I cheated." He smirked.

"You? How?"

"I wore magical rings that helped withstand his blows and gauntlets made not to loose grip on whatever I held. So every time he tried to disarm me, wouldn't work."

She looked down at their joined hands. "You still have those gauntlets?"

"No, I lost those along time ago." He looked to her as she lightly squeezed his fingers. "Hmm?"

Returning the rare smile from him, she said only, "Nothin'."

His own smile grew slightly. "But aye, we would go and spar at the arena, although Oceania would never really cheer either of us on, being Michael was her foster dad and I her husband. Really, it was a lot of fun, especially since we were sparring with fishing poles."

A girlish giggle, unlike most of Anne's happy laughter escaped her. "That sounds silly," she said with true warmth. It was good to finally hear him speak openly about something from his past.

"It was, but a fun time. The arena was also located in southern Lareah and was an open arena back then. Not like it is today."

"Hidden away."

He nodded.

"So you never had a girlfriend after her?"

"No, I never had one after her."

"How come?"

"I have never really been attracted to anyone after her."

"Maybe the girls were too scared to blow on your ears," she grinned. She liked that his ears were just a little longer and a little more pointed than most elves she had met.

"Maybe," he smiled again. The last time he had felt this happy contentment had been with Oceania. "I never thought about it."

"And now?"

"Well, it seems one has gotten up the courage to blow on my ear."

A warm laugh of contentment came from her as she leaned against him. "Yeah... but why me? I'm a monk, who by your own admission is short, I don't sing." She paused, considering what she might do that would be so fascinating to him. "I'm really good at annoying you," she grinned, "but I dunno if that's a reason."

He shrugged. "Because you…interest me. You're different than most, and you have a great personality that makes me want to be around you more." He gave her a slight nod, the barest of smiles touching his lips and his heart too obvious in his eyes.

"Oh, okay." A mischievous tone matched the grin she gave him. "Can we still fool Bo?" Bodecia worked closely with Amil, as the leader of the local druids.

"Well I thought that was a given."

"And you'll give me a tour of your home soon? I won't come clean your place again til I get the surprise!"

"Hmm speaking of which, I should go and see how they are doing. They should be nearing completion soon. You'll have to come back in a few days to find out."

"If I wait a few days, your laundry's gonna pile up," she teased.

"I think I can manage doing my own laundry." He couldn't help a smile at the thought. He'd been doing it just fine for longer than her lifetime.

"Don't forget to feed everyone," she reminded with true worry. "Even the spiders."

"Of course I won't." Yet another thing he loved about her; she not only accepted that he had wild animals in his home, like mice and spiders, but she had learned how to care for them. And, to his humor, she had named them all. "Fred and his family will get plenty of food, and yes the spiders as well."

"And give Cane and Malania an extra hug for me."

"Of course I will." He smiled at her, thinking how special she was to worry about creatures most would find beneath themselves, how she had turned his old wolf and panther into lap pets when she was around.

"And make sure they get scraps when you make supper."

"Yes yes, they will get the scraps." He knew he was grinning, but couldn't help himself at the sweetness she showed everything that mattered to him.

She smiled back. "What?"

"Nothing," he said lovingly as he got to his feet. "I should be on my way. I'm curious myself on how far they have gotten. I hope the date was acceptable."

"Oh, it was! Can we do it again?"

One side of his mouth turned up. "I'll look forward to another one."

"Wait..." she called when he turned to go. He turned back as she got to her own feet. "Um..." Judging them to be too close to the edge, she didn't dare pounce him for a hug, but she didn't want him to just walk away either.

Rolling her ankle as she thought about it, she finally decided. Stepping quickly to his side, she leaned in and blew on his ear.

He tilted his head as if trying to protect his ear. "Not nice..." he smiled a chastisement to her. She had to know how sensitive an elf's ears were.

Not that she'd tell him, but she did. She grinned. "I l-like you, Amil."

He smirked. "I l-like you to, Anne." He folded her in a warm hug, breathing in the scent of her.

Closing her eyes where she rest against his chest, she could have stayed there forever. All too soon, he stepped back, scooped his bow from the rock and nimbly made his way down and into the trees, fading from view.

Chapter Nine
The Past is the Future

Once married to a beautiful bard, Amilmamir Mor Nermakiir had seen a daughter into very young adulthood, only to have her attacked and turned into one of the vile undead. Another little girl of his had died in an attack as a small child yet. Worse, he'd survived the loss of a wife. He was a survivor. And he was tired. A ranger by trade, he led the local grove, but was more than ready to pass it on to someone younger.

He didn't look his age, other than his now-silvery hair that many elves had been born with. Tall, slender and full of vigor, very few knew he had knees that troubled him, or that his eyesight was starting to fade. But he had earned those marks of age. He'd survived orcs attacking his homelands, three vidu invasions since coming to Lareah, two human invasions, as well as aberrations and Undead. He had lived through the nine hells, but had no desire to tell the stories about it.

"Amil!"

"There's a familiar voice." It was the one thing still keeping him young. Despite all he'd been through and all he'd lost, he had one thing still lending a bounce to his steps. The young Annelise Erickson had made herself the unofficial mascot of his Rangers, insinuating her insatiably bright and sunny disposition into the lives of all the men and women that served with Amil in the wilds. "Good mor…"

She wiggled her butt before she pounced, throwing her arms around him to give him a hug.

He staggered back a step as he regained his balance and finished his greeting. "…ning, Anne." He chuckled, returning her hug.

"How've you been?" she asked, sliding back to her feet.

"As well as one can be I suppose. Much better than I was before walking up here, at the least."

A teasing tone put a lilt in her voice. "Better air up here?"

"Yes; much more of a pleasant aura in the atmosphere." How could she know that she was that pleasantness? She was never negative or sad; at least not that he'd ever seen. She was young, a human with some sort of elven blood lending to her appearance which couldn't have been more than early twenties.

Her warm laugh sounded at his comment. "What's been less than better?"

"Been on Atil more often than here on the main land." More and more often, the days found him on the small island just off the main docks that he called home. It was quiet, peaceful. He could tend his fruit trees and manage the little wildlife that remained there.

"Tsk." She grinned. "Sitting in your rocking chair and acting like a stodgy ol' man again, huh?"

"Helping out the islanders a bit. I may as well use the money I've stock-piled over the years on some good. Better than it turning into a pile of dust in the vault." A volcano had destroyed a good part of the island many years back.

"So Atil is recovering?" Excitement put a bounce not only in her voice but in her heels as she bobbed in place. "Maybe I could put the dojo back out there sometime?" Her father had been the sensei of a dojo that had long ago made its home on Atil. She had followed his path in becoming a sensei of the Tzee path.

He nodded. "Possibly. It may be some time before everything is back to normal, but the volcano is settled to its quiet slumber again."

"Hm... maybe not a good idea for there then." She tapped a finger to her cheek, pretending to be deep in thought. "I know!" she teased. "I could use your dining room!"

"I think my wife's spirit would come and haunt you," he threatened in good humor, "if you were to break the plates."

"I could use them for balance practice," she said in equally good humor. "I could warn the trainees that they'll be haunted if they drop them."

A slight chuckle escaped him. "Hmm... Might work."

"Or I could have the fuzzies bite." She teased. The "fuzzies" were Amil's constant companions of a wolf and panther.

He chose to ignore it. "You know my doors are open to those in need..."

"Even those just needing a hug?" she asked cheerfully.

"Of course. There's more than enough..."

"That's me!" Annie interrupted him, pouncing against him for another hug.

"...food for just one elf to eat," he finished, returning her hug.

"You should move into the city." She grinned in bright humor. "Or a tree."

"Tried the city; too many people for my liking. And the tree… I'd end up falling twenty feet in my sleep."

"Use rope," Anne answered quickly. "Tie yourself in."

"I'm an elf; I'm hands on." He smirked, waiting for her to argue it.

"Be serious," she answered with a laugh in voice. "You hardly ever touch anyone."

"No," humor laced his own words, "but I do poke at them from afar."

"Like this?" She poked at his chest.

"Except with sharper objects. And usually farther than half an arms distance." He indicated the long bow he always had at hand.

She ignored that, thinking yet on a fun way to poke back. "Want me to chew my fingernail to a point?"

"I'll pass." He smiled. "I'd rather keep my skin in its delicate form, and my blood in my body where it belongs."

"You're not *that* delicate... are you?" She pulled at the neck of his armor, trying to see inside. "Is that why," she teased, "you wear all the armor? So you look all big and muscular?"

"Hey!" He tried to sound offended as he shrugged, turning slightly from her. "You can't look. That's top secret."

She laughed, bouncing back a step. "Then who knows the secret?"

"If I told you, I'd have to kill you." His voice was light, belying the words.

"I thought you l-liked me!" She smiled, nudging him playfully.

"Rangers walk a very sharp knife on liking and killing." A smirk touched his lips, his eyes dancing as he teased her, sounding serious. "Very, very dangerous we are."

"Oh, I know," she answered, pretending an equal seriousness. "The bunnies told me so."

"You should have asked the raccoons." His answer was quick while he tried not to smile at her silliness. "There's a reason they have black eyes."

She laughed in delight. "Yeah, right!" She switched to a loud whisper that was anything but private. "You could tell me. I wouldn't tell anyone."

"And besides," he ignored her plea. "Why shouldn't I wear my armor? After all, I am in Lareah."

"So am I. And lookit this... I'm in a froofy dress!" She swished the skirt around below her knees by swinging her hips. Normally she dressed in her white gi with the red vest that buckled over the top of it.

He liked it. Not that he would encourage her cuteness any further than she already took it. "Sorry. Family secret," he continued to tease. "Can't tell anyone except for family."

She crossed her arms. "So how do I get to be family?"

"Marry a Nermakiir, be adopted... or find some family line that makes us related somehow."

"Jeez," she sighed dramatically. "Like there's so many options there. My folks aren't related to you... you being elf and me being human and vidu an' all. And I like you too much to let you adopt me. 'Sides, my folks'd kill me. And I hardly have a ring to marry anyone. Hey!" she teased with a playful smile. "You got any sons?"

"Unfortunately no, I do not. I was gifted only with daughters." A bittersweet emotion chased through him as he remembered how much he had loved them.

"And I don't really go that way anyways." A mischievous, playful tone entered her voice. "So. How do I find out these secrets if you're the only option to marry and you're already in love with that bow of yours?" she asked as she motioned to it. Then, in a loud whisper, followed with, "Does the bow know?"

"In love with my bow." She really was a treasure with the way she could find humor in such strange places. "Hmm; never thought of my bow like that. Not to mention having a ring on it would make too much noise in the forest."

"You could paint one on it." She nodded to reinforce the thought.

He dismissed the idea with, "My artistic talent isn't that good."

Thoroughly enjoying the game, she offered, "You could hire someone."

"I suppose, but I don't love my bow enough to marry it. It's more of a tool than a lover." A happy smirk he had long thought he had lost returned to his lips. The girl was determined to be a joy to anyone she met.

"Darn it." Annie crossed her arms, pouting around a smile. "Ruins that idea."

"Not to mention," he said, getting her back to the original argument, "me marrying my bow would still not make you family, for you're not related to my bow."

"The fuzzies!" She exclaimed in delight. "I just need to get someone to translate their noises and maybe they would tell me in exchange for a good brushing!"

His "fuzzies" would most certainly not want a good brushing. His wolf and panther were wild things better suited to the wilds, not someone's lap with a brush taken to them. "Not even the fuzzies know. That's how big of a secret it is. And the ones that do know are too scared to talk."

"Like who?" she hedged, trying to find out.

"Those ones are all dead," he said negligently, "if not eaten."

She laughed and pushed lightly on his chest. You're making it all up."

"If you say so," he offered with a shrug. "Like I said, family secret."

Narrowing her eyes, she wrinkled her nose and shook a finger at him. "You're teasing me with that family stuff!"

Placing his bow on its bottom tip, he shifted his weight, leaning on it slightly. "Of course I am. I made it all up. You shouldn't worry about what I am saying about family stuff."

She wasn't exactly worried. She wanted to know. She crossed her arms, trying to look nonchalant and to sound uninterested. "I'm not worried." She couldn't help peeking to see if he was buying into her comment.

"Good." He tried to sound final on it, but couldn't help the humor creeping into his words. "Then we don't need to talk about the Nermakiir family secret or that only you marrying me would allow you to find out what it is."

Annie sighed dramatically. "Like you'd ever do that." She rolled her eyes as she grinned at him.

"Marry you?" He pretended to shock. "So you're saying you wouldn't be a good wife?"

"You," she teased right back, "probably have some rule

about rangers only marrying other rangers on the brightest moon night that shines in glimmers off the fur of a... a... white rat... or something."

He fought a smirk touching his lips. Clearing his throat, he shook his head. "Not at all. Most rangers never marry a fellow ranger, usually complete opposite of a ranger."

"What?" She grinned. "Someone that cuts down forests?"

"Dar'chaos married a scoundrel. I was married to a bard.... Auren was married to a cleric I think?" He wasn't sure why he felt the need to justify this to her, yet he continued. "Let's see, Bodecia married a ranger... soo... like twenty-five percent of rangers marry a ranger. So, rangers don't really marry rangers." He winced inwardly. It sounded like he was trying to sell her on marrying him! "...and the rest usually stay single." That should diffuse it. "

"So what are you trying to say?" she laughed as she teased. "Rangers don't like themselves?

"Your statement about rangers was false. And most rangers don't usually worry about themselves. After all, we are protectors of Her creation, and carry out His wrath. But then again, I am a Ranger of the Old Ways. Much has changed since my youth in these lands. The name Firnos is but a whisper in the wind."

"I know the name."

The smirk that tended to come when they spoke crept to his lips again. She seemed to impossibly always be in the know about anything he brought up. "And I suppose only in mention?"

"Lots of stuff in books. Lessee... skinny elven looking guy in green that loves his bow," she teased, "calls it sweetheart when they're alone." She saw the disapproving look on his face and fell more serious. She did know about the gods, after all. It had been part of her training. "He's the patron of rangers and sometimes druids. He is committed to protecting nature and all in it."

"He is the protector of the Hunt," he corrected. "He will guide your path to a successful hunt, his wrath to be carried out to those who do not respect what She has given. She the mother and He the father... though now those of the wood look only to the mother, and have forgotten their father." He paused, considering how things had changed since he had been a young elf. "I've only known one other who served Firnos in the recent century. An old god, forgotten with time... as I will be one day," he said in too morose a tone. "And I assume both of us will be nothing but what is written in a book."

"Hey no! I won't forget you." She didn't like to see him so sober. She'd never tell him, but it brought out the faintest of frown lines on his face. "I know!" Her voice was almost too bright even to her own ears. "You could become a teacher!"

"Mm. I could," he didn't quite sound like he was impressed. "Though a classroom never was a place for me."

"Adopt a dozen little Amils and troop about the forest with them, teaching them all about the old ways."

Amil chuckled as she warmed to her topic.

"Or!" She bounced a little on her toes. "Have a little Amil!"

He shifted his weight, readjusting his bow so the tip rested atop his soft leather boot and crossed his arms around it. "Can't see myself surrounded by that many kids; especially ones taking after me."

"Then just one."

"One I suppose I could handle. But not many are here who would learn the old ways. They are after newer and brighter things than the past. I am an antique in a new world."

"The past is the way to the future. Without knowing where your foot is coming from, you can't know where to place the other." She stopped, blinking owlishly at him in surprise. A grin lit her eyes. "Are you whining?"

"Maybe I am, maybe I'm not." He tried to sound mysterious, but his tone also conveyed a slight annoyance at her catching him in a behavior beneath an elf of his age.

She laughed. "You're whining!" Seeing the look in his eyes, the weight he carried of his past, his losses and the history of the lands that was slipping away, she assumed the posture of the monk she was. Shoulders back, feet planted in a relaxed stance but chin up with a slight challenge, she let the serious tone of order into her voice as well. "You can't go, you know. Who would take over for you?"

It was one of the things he loved about her. Her moods were ever upbeat, but positively quicksilver. In the snap of the fingers, she could go from teasing and joking, to ready to teach or give orders.
He smiled as a quiet sigh escaped him. "I am only telling you how I see the world; nothing more, nothing less. I cannot prevent change. Nor am I the one to try and stop it. Not even mountains scrape the sky forever, Anne."

A heavy sigh slumped her shoulders a little in defeat. "I know. But you're still touching it now."

"Maybe in spirit," he said gently. "If you caught me a few centuries ago, I may have been parting the clouds. Don't worry though, Anne. I'm here right now. I have no plans on disappearing." He tapped the tip of her nose with one of is leather-clad fingers.

Her delighted laugh rang out. "But you don't need to disappear now. The other rangers look to you for guidance on how to do things."

"And many of them have learned how to lead, as have others done in the past." He picked at an invisible piece of fuzz on his bow string. "My days of leading the rangers were a long time ago, and I had stepped down." He glanced to see if she was still intent on this discussion. He should have known. Anne loved anything about his job. "I only recently had taken back the leadership because of the lack of someone trained. But I was never meant to take them under my wing forever."

"Y' know, a kid or a wife'd probably cheer you up." She nodded, almost to herself. "Maybe you've got a great-nephew ten times removed or something that could come live with you?"

Amil chuckled. "They would be better off in my home land. Besides, they would rather be there than here."

"Why?" She clasped her hands behind her back, her left foot rolling her little blue slipper-shoe on and off her foot.

"They have no ties to this land, nor do they worry about the happenings here, they have no concern over this land."

"But you're here. Doesn't that concern them?"

His face closed down, the light fading from his eyes. The humor of only seconds before settled into weary sadness. "They know why I came to this land in the first place, and why I stayed. Besides, there is more for them there than here. Just because I am here, does not make me a concern over more important matters."

It bothered Anne to see this moroseness, but she couldn't help her own curiosity. She lightly reached to touch his arm. "Why did you come?"

A remembered past weighed heavy in his memories. "Long ago, we were interested in ties here for trade, which that interest has long passed by with the more prominent trade routes established back home. I ended up marrying and having a family."

"And now?" she prompted when he fell silent.

"Now? This is my home. It's where I've lived most of my life."

"Is Firnos still spoken of back home?"

"No, he is not. Not for many, many years."

She flashed an impish smile, well aware that she was annoying him. "What would make you happy now?"

It had the desired effect in gaining a slight smirk from him. "To find out why I am being interrogated, I suppose. Why are you asking?"

"Cuz I'm curious," she grinned. "And I like you."

Her sweetness always got him. She didn't flirt, she didn't carry on about how great he had been, but instead treated him as a friend her own age. "What would make me happy now...? Hmm... As it was with my family, so many years ago... That was happiness."

"Well how do we give you that now?"

"That now?" he asked. It was something long gone to him. "A family." He wasn't sure he could go through that heartache again though. "I don't see that happening anytime soon."

"Why not? I already told you, you could just adopt some," she answered hopefully.

Best to change her topic. "You know my wife was adopted by Michael Mor.... a Monk from the Teejee dojo."

"Nope." A bright smile made her positively glow. "Didn't know that. How come? And it's Tzee, ranger boy." She playfully pushed at his chest.

"She never had a family... Her father was an elven merchant whose ship crashed upon the rocks of her mother's island. That woman was a siren... she disowned Osh at a young age and she found her way here." He paused when she pushed him, winking at her. "I figured I would test you. You passed."

"So why'd Mikey adopt her? And what test?" She missed the obvious.

"Don't worry. Like an arrow over your head; no harm. And for her hand in marriage I had to duel Michael in a duel in the old arena... so, like I said, we fought with fishing poles as if they were staves."

She laughed in pure delight. "That was silly."

"I wanted her hand, and nothing was going to stop me."

"My dad isn't like that," she dismissed with a flip of her

hand. "He just wants to know he can get along with the guys we choose."

"Aye, Michael wanted to know she was going to be with someone who would defend her and keep her safe." Oceania had been strong on her own, but there had always been that something fragile about her that had attracted him.

Annie's chin stubbornly came up as a proud tone matched her posture. "I can defend myself."

"That you can." He nodded, returning her smile. "Sure won't see me running to your aid... would be more like a hobble anyways." He'd go to the ends of the world to keep her safe.

"Pfft. You could if you needed to." She thought about that comment then. Maybe he felt he didn't deserve love anymore. "Is that why you don't marry again? You think you couldn't defend them?"

"No... I am sure I could," He would always do whatever was necessary. He just wasn't sure he wanted to go through the pain and heartache he had suffered before. "I just haven't been searching, I suppose." It was a good excuse.

"Why not?" she pushed.

"Not really sure why not. Just guess I never have really found anyone, and being gone a lot doesn't help in that. Usually get close and I'm gone again."

A look of "a-ha" crossed her face. "So you run."

"Not at all. No one ever looks for me. I would go deep in the forest, and yet Oceania would follow even if endangering herself by doing so, just to find me."

Anne considered that. He liked that his wife had needed him, but had a wild streak. "So... she needed protecting, but she'd go gallivanting about the woods... and ... you want a girl that'll come after you now?"

"I guess it showed me that she actually really wanted to be with me." He smiled, in his own thoughts. "I suppose that's why I took a fancy to her quickly. No matter where I was, she would find me some way or another. Even if she was muddy and scratched up, she would still come through the gates of the hells just to sit down and talk with me."

A laugh escaped her. "She knew."

He smiled, nodding agreement. "Knew that I would hear her coming a mile away. Every bear in the wood would start to stir, not to mention she would wear perfume so strong a wolf could smell her ten miles away."

"She knew you'd come for her. And she knew you needed her."

"Of course."

"And that's the problem now? You want a girl that needs you?"

"Maybe... Though no girl needs me, anyways." It was an old fashioned idea, but he liked knowing that he would still be needed.

Anne didn't need anyone to look out for her. "What if a girl just wanted you to love her?"

"And what girl would ever just want me to love her? Put up with an old ranger hobbling around a house all day and out all night." He kept his tone light, but glanced sidelong to see her reaction.

She quietly looked down, glancing up in a shy manner. "...I would."

Amil gave her a slight look of disbelief. "And why would you?"

Anne couldn't believe he had to ask. She stared at him for a long moment, trying to determine if he were serious. "Because," she finally answered, "you're you. You're strong, independent, confident... kind, caring, funny... want me to go on?"

His tone was dry but the smile in his eyes and the corners of his mouth belied it. "My ego is not inflated enough, maybe a bit longer."

Her warm laugh made a few passersby glance towards them with a smile of their own. "You're cute," she continued, "when you let people see you." He always seemed to have his hood up. "You're eyes are expressive. You're a natural teacher."

A bit too much," he said, as if he were critiquing her words. "Now we need to let some air out...."

Happy to oblige him, she added in a teasing tone, "You lean on your bow too much."

"Aye, I do, have to replace the tips all the time. Hmm..." he really looked at the woman that had arranged to clean up after his bachelor ways in exchange for the occasional date with him. She had taken care of his constant companions, Malania and Cane... almost to the point of exasperation for the wolf and panther, giving them baths and constant brushings. "So why don't you?"

"Replace the tips?" She asked, as if she didn't know what he meant, keeping a light tone to her voice. "I don't know how." She grinned at his dumbfounded expression.

"I could teach you."

"So that's covered too." She grinned. "Or did you mean something else?"

"I meant why don't you get married?"

She shrugged one shoulder, trying to act as if it were no big deal. "Because the guy I'm interested in doesn't see it."

"Hmm... Well I tell you what: let me see your hand."

She put both hands out, palms up.

Reaching into a pouch, he pulled his hand back out, keeping it clenched closed. Gently placing what was in his hand into her left hand, he closed her fingers around the tiny object. "If that guy you're interested in is too thick skulled, would you marry me? Because I wouldn't want to keep a woman like you waiting forever."

Her disbelieving look slowly turned to a smile. "You ARE that thick skulled guy!" Still not having seen what he put in her hand, she threw her arms around him.

"I knew that already," he responded with a smile of his own, putting his arms around her.

She stood on her tiptoes, peeking over his shoulder to see what was in her hand. A simple gold band sparkled with the etched image of vines and leaves around it. "Oh!" She loudly kissed his cheek. "How long have you been carrying that around???"

"A few hours," he smirked, eyes sparkling in humor. "You know; not that long."

"No, really!" A delighted laugh escaped her. "Did you just think that up or have you been thinking about it?"

For too long. Her sweet, undemanding manner had won him over long before he had needed to return to his homelands for an emergency. It had been a long time since anyone had "intruded" on his personal space and cheerfully turned his world upside down. "Around the time you started watching my house, and cleaning it up, sooo I kinda started liking you around a lot. I fell for you awhile ago I suppose." He tried to downplay the emotional importance he felt about this. For so long he had been able to moderate his manner to appear aloof. It was hard to do around her; especially with her beaming and bouncing in his arms. "So what do you say?"

"Yes! Yes!" She hugged him tighter, pulling him downwards towards her petite frame. "You never act like it, so I never knew for sure." She cuddled her cheek against him, squeezing her arms tightly around him.

He chuckled, returning her hug. "You know me: I'm not one to show emotion."

"Me either!" The ecstatically happy look on her face belied her teasing words.

"Indeed." He smiled. "Completely emotionless. I would never even know you were happy."

If it were possible, her grin was even bigger and brighter. "Course not. I'm just as stodgy as you are."

"Aye, just as an eagle can swim."

"Right!" She laughed at his flummoxed expression before looking to the ring in her hand again. She squealed in happiness, hugging her clasped hands and the ring to her chest as she wiggled her butt, bouncing in place in a funny little dance.

"I'm glad I could make you happy." A grin had come unbidden to his lips at her enthusiastic joy. "Though I don't think I have ever seen you this happy."

Laughter bubbled from her. "I am happy! She pounced at him for a hug again as she babbled, "I'll try to be a good wife... even though I don't know how. I prob'ly won't be as good as your other one, but I'll try!"

"It's all trivial. You are a great person, and I couldn't ask for you to be anything more than whom you are." As he spoke the words, he realized the truth of that. He still loved Oceania, but that part of his life had been over for a very long time. Anne was nothing like her. She was a strong, resilient woman trained to be a Sensei at her father's dojo. She could take care of herself and he wouldn't need to worry about her as he had about Oce. "You are perfect, and I am sure you will be just as good at being a wife."

"And you'll be a good husband." She happily cuddled against him, unaware of his comparative thoughts. "Even if you go prowling the woods every night."

He chuckled. "Someone has to keep the things that go thump in the night kept in check."

"That's you, alright!" she laughed.

"Which one? The someone to keep them in check or the

thump in the night?"

"Um..." she grinned. "Depends on the night?"

"Hmm... Very good answer."

"Will I still get to be the ranger mascot?"

"Unfortunately we will have to find someone else. After all, we can't have you as a mascot if you're my wife." The last thing he needed was for the others to think he was favoring an "outsider" from their group. Spouses were fine, but she couldn't be both wife and mascot without some crying favoritism.

"Hmm... I wondered. Might be too long to introduce me. 'Hi. I'm Tzee Master Annie, Ranger mascot of the Kordathyan forests and married to Amil.' Yeah... kind of a mouthful."

He hadn't realized his time away had brought her up a rank to full master. It was just one more reason he loved her. She wasn't prideful the way so many currently were. "Aye. 'Tzee Master Anne, Mascot to the High Council, Married to Amilmamir Mor Nermakiir, Elder of the High Council' is a very long introduction. We would be standing at the greeting hall for an hour just for introductions by the town crier."

His home had pretty much been open to her since he had left for his homelands. She had wanted to air it out, get the dust out of the corners, and she had done an amazing job of keeping the place cleaner than he ever had. It looked as good as when Oceania had first had the home built ages ago. But for all that, it was still an old bachelor's home these last years. "Hmm... Suppose I'll have to change a few things in the homestead as well. The bed... the bath... let's see... most of it is setup as a single elf's home. Have to move the spare bows and arrows out of the closet." The bow he carried was the only one he owned, having been gifted from Lord Firnos himself. "Never know when this one might crack or break." She knew there were no others anywhere in his home.

"Well, I'm not like most girls. I don't have a bunch of clothes or makeup or stuff."

He nodded. "Though I'm sure you would want space of your own."

"Yeah." She brightened further. "But I know what's in all your drawers! I can just rearrange some of them!"

"True, I forgot you pretty much run the house anyways."

"I'll need to write home and let mom and dad know. ... Oh!" She realized she had never told him her mother wasn't human. "You won't mind that mom's vidu, will you?"

"No, that is fine with me." He had figured there was something. She had such a youthful face, rounder as human bloodlines ran, with beautiful flowing brown locks over warm eyes. But there were the points on her ears that had made him figure there was likely some sort of elven in her heritage.

"They're gonna be excited!"

He smiled as she impulsively kissed him. "I hope so. Well I shall let you write your parents then, And I have a few things to take care of in town, I suppose I shall see you later on tonight at home?"

"Yep!" she answered playfully. "I'll come and tuck you in."

He knew she wouldn't yet stay the night with him, but it felt good to use "home" and know that it wasn't just a building anymore. She had just as easily answered, already seeing it as their shared space. It meant more than he could express in words, so he simply wrapped his arms around her waist and kissed her softly on the lips. "I love you, Anne." As he turned to the merchants, a smile that only seemed to come in her presence was seen. Less a smirk these days, and more a true smile.

She sighed softly, a dreamy smile of her own as she watched him go. "Love you, too."

Chapter Ten
A Quest Begins

"Ho there," the king of Phaethredun asked. "Any of you direct me to the arena?" The appearance of the king was a rare sight these days as he worked to rebuild his island city, but he remained approachable as always. He walked the streets with only a few retainers in his shadow. Lord Dorbourne of Lareah must be ill to not make the now-famous tournament.

Amil bowed slightly. "Yes Sire, the arena will be straight to your right down the street."

"My thanks, good man." He inclined his head as he spoke in a booming, cheerful voice. He wasn't exactly the typical image of a stodgy king. "Hirath's blessings on you this bright morning!"

With little else to do that day, Amil followed the excited crowds that heard King Sigers would be hosting the tournament of arms. Many fine men and women from various backgrounds were represented. Armor ranged from a simple leather piece strapped over a chest all the way up to full armor. Weapons were in the same state.

Rather than testing arms against each other, as had always been done in the past, the king had wild beasties that had been plaguing the lands. "Three rounds each; each progressively more difficult," the king announced.

Amil took his place among the combatants, watching the younger people show off their skill between his own events. Large tigers and other creatures that had repeatedly menaced the new city were brought in for the event, ending with the best of the king's men going up against the champions until first blood.

Among them was a petite elven woman in forest-green leathers. Her eyes were hardened with a past Amil could only guess at, but still she offered a dainty little curtsy at the start of each of her rounds. Her well-wrought rapier flashed in practiced style, aided as needed by quick bursts of magic. "Hunph. Well." She brushed her light blonde hair out of her eyes after her last round. "That was impressive." She was still standing with only minor scrapes and didn't sound impressed in the least.

It humored the king, whose booming laughter echoed inside

the arena. "I have to say, this certainly helps with some of our problems."

"Glad to be of service," a deposed knight from another land offered.

The elven woman's tone was dry. "Motley assortment of problems you have, highness."

"In the eyes of Hirath, you are both noted as champions. Name your reward from Us," the king announced to the small group before him.

The knight asked to again be a landed noble, earning a place in the king's cabinet. Others asked for random gifts from gold to weapons.

"I could use a better set of leathers.... or a better rapier," the woman asked. "Both of mine are... basic."

She was given a finer rapier with the comment, "May you be served well in its use." And then the king turned to Amil. "And is there anything for you?"

"I need no reward, Sire," he bowed respectfully. "A service to those in need is plenty a reward for me."

"Then may Hirath bless each of you and your days continue to be a success." With that proclamation, the king departed with his retainers, the new cabinet member among them.

Working through the press of bodies, Amil made his way to the plateau in the center of the city, leaning against the tree to enjoy the fresh air. He really disliked the stink and press of that number of people in a crowded area.

A few others milled around, discussing the events of the day. Double-checking small pouches on her belt, the serious elf with the new rapier lightly stepped into the area.

"Nang," Amil called her by the name the king had addressed her as. He respected anyone that handled themselves as well as she had, and he wanted to pass along something. "Do you use daggers?" It was common for those favoring rapier to often hold either shield or dagger in their left hand.

"From time to time," she answered, watching him almost suspiciously. She could use one, but most times she kept her off-hand free for the use of magic.

In a sheath, he extended a dagger to her. "It's been some time since I've seen that kind of skill." He offered it a little closer. "In appreciation."

She took it, pulling the wickedly curved blade for inspection. She was about to ask what he wanted in return when a gnome in construction gear approached. "Heyo! I'm looking for the right dock to Atil."

"Len, down on the far dock," Amil indicated the boatman's name with a nod of his head in that direction.

"Oh good! I hear there's work out there. New factories going in. Thanks!" The little man waved and hurried off.

Atil had been Amil's home for almost too long to remember. The last generation had turned the little island upside down with a volcano destroying most of it, along with the peoples that had made it their home. They had suffered and come back from too much, now looking to Amil and the few other rangers to help them bring the place back to habitable. Factories were not something that would belong there. Giving Nang a confused look, he moved to catch the next boat.

Curious, she fell in beside him. Maybe whatever this was would be a small way to pay back the dagger. Atil was not even a full hour from the mainland; at the very least, she could follow to see if he needed a hand with anything.

The boat was about the size of a yacht, just enough room to move around. The only other person was a tall vidu with deep scarlet hair. Nang noticed the dark, handsome man wearing an open white leather overcoat. The wind caught at it, exposing a scarlet interior. The way he leaned indicated he was very proud of his build, which showed with the glint of sun against the light fitted chainmail he wore under the coat.

For the first time in her life, her stomach did a funny little flip. She caught herself staring and snapped her jaw shut, intentionally looking away as the man smirked, raising a flask to his lips.

Amil stepped from the boat, offering a hand back to aid Nang down. Her brows went up as she smirked. "Hmph." She wasn't some silly girl in a dress. Her leathers were practical, functional... And she hurried down the ramp, brushing past him, to let him know she was the same way.

The vidu watched the elven woman in appreciation. Nice face, nice form. He approved. If she fought as well as she looked, she just might be awesome enough to be at his side... for a little while. Curious at their purposeful steps, he followed after the two of them.

She couldn't believe the discrepancy of the isle. Charred mountains with no sign of life warred with the lush landscape where they docked. Small granite flagstones had been fitted together to line the walk through an orchard of still-small trees up to Amil's home. But they never made it to the structure that could have been a fortress.

"...What the hells." Amil stopped short, looking out over the trees and past a wild lawn to where a few of his own sheds sat near an overgrown line of trees. Eight halflings with red swords were guarding a ramshackle mess of supplies. None of it belonged there. A camp was being set up! And the way the men were moving around, acting as if they owned the place... "What the hell are they doing on my land?"

Hearing that, the men turned their way, charging towards them. Amil didn't wait for Nang to respond to his question. Striding through the area, his bow was up and ready as he came to a stop. The first arrow flew before he had even taken the time a lesser archer would need to site it.

Amil had no idea why they were here. They kept getting attacked as these trespassers on his land defended their camp until finally they captured one of the mages in charge and began questioning him.

"What's going on here?" a stringy young man said as his partner was hit. He was dressed in unfamiliar clothing with a device neither Amil nor Nang had seen before. With angry steps, he started towards the duo.

"Stop now," Amil warned. The quiet creak of his leather didn't cover the sound of the arrow sliding against the bow as he drew it back, ready to fire. He had already had enough. "I'll put the next one in your heart. What are you doing on this land?"

"We have permits," He held his hand up in the signal to wait and rummaged one from a nearby chest. "We were told it was void of habitation," he said, holding it up for them to see.

"This land is owned. And where did you get permits? Who authorized this?"

"Queen Lutheria."

"What queen? Atil has no queen; they have a governor of the island. I ask again," he sited down the arrow, "why are you here on Atil?"

"To build. There's a volcano that can be harnessed for steam power."

Intrigued, Nang looked to the stoic ranger. "I'm no druid, but that doesn't sound like a good idea. Couldn't that muck up the volcano?"

Amil gave her a terse nod, never looking away from the man or the few warily moving around behind him. "It just recently fell quiet."

Further questioning drug on before it was determined that they planned to use the island's volcano has a power source for factories, designing a number of seemingly worthless trinkets. None of the names put to the items were things familiar to the questioners.

"It was determined there is no ruler of this island." The man held the permit scroll out to Amil for inspection. "Very official, from our lands, signed by the queen. You're the first we've seen."

A tense moment passed before Amil released the draw on his bow, setting the arrow back in the quiver. He took the form, looking it over with Nang just over his shoulder. "That's because the people are just starting to rebuild. Have you even talked to any of the survivors at the village?"

"Oh, we'll buy them out, if we find any. Or put them to work in the factory."

The flippant tone of the man astounded Amil. "You haven't even talked to them?" he asked in outrage. "And why is your stuff on my land?"

"A staging area; nothing more," he shrugged. "We'll be moving it inland soon enough. Is that your home?" he motioned back to the building. "You're out of venison," he went on at Amil's affirmation. "You'll want to restock that."

"...You invaded his home?!" Nang asked in shock at the exact time Amil stated the same words in a monotone.

The man shrugged one shoulder. "I'm sure someone knocked."

With a shocked look, Nang glanced at Amil. The corner of her mouth started to twitch as she reached for the dagger at her thigh. The man acted as if he owned the place, like he had every right to be here. What was worse, he completely ignored the fact that one of his companions had been killed just a short time ago. There was no emotion.

"You're not building anything on Atil, so pack your stuff get back on your boat and get the hell off the island."

"I'll have to wait for the next boat. And then they'll have to unload their cargo so we can load this up." His tone indicated he had no intention of leaving.

"Do you know how to swim?" He didn't try to hide the threat under the words.

"Well.... yes?" The man looked at him in confusion, either not hearing or believing the danger in the question.

"I think," Nang offered in translation, "he means you should start swimming."

"I actually came up through a cavern." He offered, as if it were the most normal thing in the universe. "The queen has been setting tunnels across the world for ease of transport."

"Tunnels...?" He wondered how stupid these fools could be. "You're digging tunnels around an island with an active volcano?"

"That *really* doesn't sound good. Can I just pop his eyes out of his sockets?" Nang asked with just a little too much enthusiasm.

"Of course! We'll need to tunnel dangerously close," he answered quite happily, ignoring Nang, "so we can harness the power. But the islanders can help in the digging."

"I am not going to let you place them into any more danger. They have gone through enough already and they just want to get on with how their lives were before all this trouble."

"How about his tongue?" Nang interjected.

The vidu smirked behind his bottle from where he watched a short distance away. He was intrigued enough that he had to come closer now. Knowing how tense the situation was, he didn't make any attempt at remaining quiet. Instead, he tucked his thumbs at his waistband, strolling towards them with a whistle. There was just enough of a breeze to make his hair and coat billow the slightest amount. He was fairly certain it gave him the awesome appearance of a hero approaching.

"Oh, but it will be so much better," the fool went on, "once our empire changes things."

"Your empire can establish trade routes through the proper channels; not just come here and set up shop nor will I have your empire threaten the lives of the people who live here." Amil shook the man to make his point.

"We'd never threaten them," he pacified, picking at Amil's arm in a terrible attempt at removing the ranger. "We'll give them purpose, jobs....Which way is the village?"

"What kind of jobs?"

"In the factories." He kept an eye on Nang and the vidu that had joined the other two as they looked about the area.

"What kind of jobs?" Amil repeated with another shake.

"Is this thing back here one of your 'inventions'?" Nang tapped a chest mounted with a strange mechanical device on its lid with the tip of her bow.

"Digging, working the bellows, tending the fires, the assembly lines..." he glanced over to the woman. "Yes, but it's defective. There was some wolf sniffing around it earlier."

"Defective? It became defective after a wolf sniffed it?" Amil couldn't believe the gall of this man! If Malania, his wolven companion, had been in contact with it, trying to move it, it had likely been pegged as a danger. He narrowed his eyes, leaning a little closer to the interloper. "Exactly what are these things for again?"

"Well, I do believe the wolf tried to pull it away by the teeth. You'd almost think the beast was intelligent. That particular item aids in clearing tunnels of debris."

"And what happened to the wolf?" His voice had dropped to a low hiss of danger.

"Singed a bit, I do believe," he cheerily answered, "but it ran into that house over there. Oh, we set a few traps in amongst the books too. Mice, you see. They'll never do if we have wires running."

He wasn't sure which should offend him more. The mice he had purposely welcomed in some time ago, and a true man of the land would never allow any kind of technology to despoil his home. "You set traps in my house? Wires? There aren't any wires in my house."

"Not yet of course; they're coming on the next ship." He offered flippantly.

Nang looked to Amil, starting to pull her dagger. "An eye and his right thumb. You can have the rest."

The interloper eyed Nang. "Good dexterity, hm? We could use you in the higher places for connecting wires and tubes."

"I'm not really interested." Nang's voice dripped with venom.

"Look, I'll make this VERY easy for you," Amil growled as the man gave him the "I'm listening" look of boredom. "You go back to your queen and tell her she isn't allowed on Atil, nor any of her little minions, and she will pay me full compensation for damages and lost time. Or else."

That same look of disdainful boredom continued in his voice. "Do you have papers claiming you to be the king here?"

"Aye," he got out through clenched teeth. "They will be written in your blood if you stay."

"So there aren't any." The man's posture and tone smacked of smug righteousness.

Nang would never beg, but she was spoiling for a part of this fool. "How about an eye and his right hand? I'll even hold him down, if you want," she offered.

Amil spared a warning glance at her. "You said the wolf ran into the house?"

"I think that's where the blood led, yes," he answered with no emotion.

Anger overtook Amil, now deaf to any other words. If Malania were injured… It was this man's fault! He would not lose anyone else important to him. The man was unwanted, unasked for, interfering, uncaring… The ranger decided he had no more time for this. Faster than the others would have expected, a short dagger emerged from a sheath at Amil's hip, flashing in a bright spark and leaving a crimson trail as the workman's throat slit open. The man fell to his knees, the gurgle of blood and air coming through the clean cut the dagger made. He placed his foot on the man's chest and pushed him over, keeping his daggers unsheathed as he turned and walked towards the house.

Impressed, Nang fell in behind Amil as he started looking for signs of his wolf's passage. To any other, the path in the grass would have been negligible, but after years of working with the old girl, he knew her step as surely as he could track his own.

Chapter Eleven
An Unwelcome Greeting

The vidu from the boat had finished a bottle of wine, leaning against one of the chests. He wasn't sure what was going on, but as he wiped his mouth with the back of his hand, he watched the two elves make their way towards the building that was either a home or a guard house. Both had their eyes on the ground, like they were tracking something.

Across the wide yard and up the stone walkway, they entered Amil's home. From either end inside, they could hear talking and partying. Amil frowned to think of strangers invading his private space. This home had been built to the design of his Oceania. His daughters had grown up here. His eyes narrowed as it registered that some of the people were in the wing where his late wife's library was and where the girls had shared a bedroom. He growled and raced across the entry, taking a sharp right past the four throne-like chairs that his family had once met those with nature's complaints on.

Adjusting the collar of his fine white coat, the man outside crossed quickly to the entrance. Blood spatters littered the area that was also piled with odd construction supplies. There was no considering if he'd be welcome or not; it wouldn't be a question. He was amazing, and they would see that. He pulled a large scythe from its place at his back, tapping it against his silver-tipped boots to rid them of mud and went in to find the woman just going around a right-hand corner.

Short dwarven men and women, six of them, lay between Amil and his destination. He came to an immediate stop, his bow up in automatic memory action, firing off two volleys before Nang could catch up.

She and the man following her came a little more cautiously, but ready none-the-less. They saw the two men fly backwards off their feet, flaming arrows jutting from their chests. The other four dwarves, shaking off their surprise, were just coming forward when the red-haired vidu roared past in joy. He pushed Nang back, letting her know this was his battle. Just as quickly, he elbowed past Amil, who pulled back, readying another arrow.

There was no time for it. The heavy scythe that looked so unwieldy, danced through the air around the man, his white coat elegantly fanning around him as the blade hummed a whistle on the backstroke, the wet slide of meat on the fore stroke. In seconds, those remaining lay in pieces on the floor.

Pleased with himself, the vidu grinned... and took a congratulatory drink.

Amil let him have it, not asking about the newcomer, as the ranger took a few running steps, bounced a foot off the wall to help jump him over the mess, and landed far softer than the others would have thought of the old ranger. With barely a sound, his soft boots touched down on the far side of the bodies and he was off at a run again.

Around a second right turn, he paused before one closed door, briefly setting a hand on it, and then moved on to the end of the hall where the library lay. Immediately visible were several mousetraps that he triggered while Nang looked for any others to destroy. "Ah," he sighed in relief to find the little house mice hiding under a bench. "Stay hidden, little ones. It will be over with soon." From a pocket, he carefully pulled several small pieces of bread, laying them near the mice.

Content they were safe, he went back out and down the hall. "Name's Vicarious Val'Sadar," the vidu was saying to the woman as Amil rejoined them.

"Good for you," Nang answered dryly, not returning the favor. She wasn't about to let him know she was in the least bit interested in him.

Amil moved past them to the door to the room that had belonged to his daughters. His steps slowed just enough for him to check the latch on the door and find it still locked. Around the corner, he found the dead bodies in front of the guest room... and a mess of junk and spilt food in the room. A noise very like a growl escaped him as he strode across the entry and into the other wing of his home.

Several short, stocky fighters tried to bar his way, but he was having none of it. They were destroying his land, his home... and now they met him with naked steel in his own abode.

As his bow came up, Nang ducked under his arm. "I've got this one."

Not to be outdone, the vidu flashed in from the other side. There was little battle before the four usurpers lay dead. Blood was thick in the air. Bodies laid across tables, in hallways, over piles of books, a once peaceful home now rich in blood and bodies.

Amil moved on to the bathing pool at the end of his wing. He could hear someone in that room, moving about as if they belonged there.

"Oh good!" that stranger joyfully exclaimed from where he rested in the shallow pool. "They finally hired someone." He waved an arm dismissively at the three. "Quickly, get me a fresh towel in here."

They shared a look before Nang asked of no one in particular, "Are you kidding me?" At the same time, Amil wiped his face of the blood and sweat, and aimed an arrow at the man's head, asking why he was in the ranger's home.

"Tch," the bather chastised. "That won't get you a payment."

Nang thought to use a little diplomacy before there was more bloodshed. She kneeled at the side of the water. "You know you don't belong here."

"Actually I think you have that backwards," he said, full of self-importance, adding a little sniff of disdain. "I'm in the middle of a bath."

That did it for Amil. He very calmly un-nocked the arrow, sliding it back into his quiver. Just as calmly, he checked the tension of the bowstring. Quicker than anyone could react, the bow slipped over the man's head between the lower leaf and string. A quick flick of his wrist with a sharp pull jerked the man's balance, turning him in the water, half-rising up over the stone ledge. Amil's right hand shot out, the palm crashing into the back of his skull, driving the man's head into the side of the bath.

Letting go, Amil stood and stepped back in the same second the crack of bones breaking resounded and the man fell back in the water, bloody bubbles rising to the surface.

Nang gave Amil a slightly disapproving look. "That won't do. He'll drown."

With a frown at her, Amil grudgingly grabbed the naked man by the arm and drug him out, slapping his broken face.

"Hold up," Nang stopped Amil as the bather groggily started to come to, his broken nose running with blood. Her rapier flashed quickly, and with too practiced a move, dragging across the back of his ankles. "There; no running for him."

The vidu wasn't sure what he had come upon, but he was impressed with the speed and efficiency of the two elves. What didn't impress him was the sniveling man screaming like a little girl, "wha u wa?" over and over. "Gosh," he said to himself, resting the end of his scythe on the ground, "this looks awkward."

Nang glanced back at the scarlet-haired man. If this was awkward for him, he could easily go. Or, he could quit with the niceties and help them find out why Amil's house and lands were being overrun.

"That's the payment you owe for taking a bath in my house." Amil grabbed the man's broken, bloodied nose, pinching hard and violently twisted it around, ignoring the elf's painful gurgling of blood and air. "And that's for being uninvited." He ignored the high pitched screams. He'd been through wars with worse treatment of prisoners. "Now answer!" he demanded. "What are you doing in here?"

He sniffed blood loudly, unable to speak clearly. "Wai'ing fo o'dews."

Amil had always welcomed rangers and druids to his home. And Anne. Anne had free access. Firnos forbid! They had only just made some decisions, however tenuous, between them. His heart constricted to think she might be in danger. He needed to know where this was all coming from. "From who?" He drew his fist back in a warning to speak honestly.

"Keen Luthe'a," he whimpered.

"Where is your queen?" Nang asked.

"So you think you can just do what you want!" Amil growled.

"No no! To'd to wait he'e." He gagged on his blood, coughing, causing Vic to make a face at the noise.

"Answer her question," Amil demanded as Nang tipped him forward to keep him from further gagging. "Where is your queen!"

"I do' know! On a ship!"

"Coming here?"

"Mebbe!"

"Then where! Why is she on a ship?"

Nang took hold of his left arm and bent it around his back,

wrenching it out of the socket. "Answer his questions."

He let loose a high pitched scream that made Vic need to try to cover a smirk. "To obersee the co'struc'on. She'd neber use tunnels. Too duddy."

"When will she get here?"

"Dunno!"

Nang tugged a little harder on his arm. "Who knows more than you do? Do you have a supervisor?"

Vic leaned on his scythe, drinking from a bottle in his free hand. He had the appearance of a man thoroughly entertained as the captive man squealed like a stuck pig.

"Jeff!"

"Where's Jeff?" Amil asked.

"In da hole!"

"Where's the hole?" Amil demanded as Nang tugged his arm up further.

"In da te't!"

"I'm pretty sure I didn't hear that right." Nang stated. She tugged on his arm a little more. "Where is it?"

"Da te't! da te't!" he squealed.

"Tent?" Nang asked.

The man nodded vigorously as Vic giggled gleefully.

Nang looked up at the men. "We should find this Jeff of his."

"I agree," Amil said while Vic nodded agreement.

"Otherwise..." she shrugged. "Do you want to kill him?"

The man whimpered. Amil took out his dagger and slit the squealer's throat. Nang let him go has he gagged, twitching. The body fell dead as the blood continued to spurt and ooze.

Vic muttered "ewww" as Amil flung the blood off the daggers.

With things quiet for the moment and no other strangers around, Amil now glanced at the red-headed interloper. "Who are you?" he asked as he moved out to the hall, looking for something…or someone.

"I came here for; well that ain't really important, but I saw some blood trailing in here and I thought maybe somebody was in trouble… so I was kind of right. I'm Vicarious! Maybe you heard of me before."

"Ah," he responded distractedly to the man, following a flash of dark gray fur into his bedroom. "Welcome to my home…

Excuse the mess..." He glanced over the room, then knelt beside the bed, looking beneath it. Relief coursed over him to find Malania alive, but anger flashed just as quickly to find her muzzle roped shut and a bleeding gash on her front leg. "It's okay, hun. Come on out," he coaxed. "Come on, girl."

Vic watched silently for a moment, impressed that someone so cold-blooded just one room ago could be so tender with an animal. It deserved a toast. He pulled a flask from some unknown pocket, taking a long drink before asking, "So who was that guy anyway? There's two dead dwarves at the front..."

Nang watched the ranger gently convince the wolf to come out into his lap for a good rubbing while he spoke soothingly to it, scratching its head. She smiled that such a sober, serious man was being so worried and concerned about an animal that he hadn't heard the question. "Someone that thought Atil was up for some... renovations," she answered Vicarious. "Factories, using the power of the volcano."

"Oh right! That's why I came here." Vic snapped his fingers as if a revelation had come to him. "A gnome said there was some construction going on up here and I was bored... Also, I needed to catch a gnome, but never mind that." He absent-mindedly pulled a flask, taking another drink.

"What did they do to you?" Amil muttered as he cut the muzzle from her snout and examined the wound on her leg. He lightly touched his forehead to the wolf's as her tail thumped quietly against the ground. He stayed like that, almost in communion, for long moments while the other two visited.

"We're looking for their queen," Nang informed Vic. "Apparently 'Jeff', who's in a hole, knows more about her."

"A gnome queen?" Vic sounded impressed. "You mean like ants have a queen? Is that how they do it? Of course...!"

"Err... I don't know." Nang had to wonder if his mind was addled with the alcohol she'd seen him consuming. "We've seen gnomes, halflings, dwarves and humans so far."

"So what's this about construction? Ya made it sound like it ain't supposed to be going on."

Amil wrapped the wolf's leg with cloth he carried for medical situations and gave her a final pet on the head, earning him a lick on the face. "Good girl," he said, getting to his feet. "Guard the house and stay safe." He turned to the others. "Ranger Amilmamir, High Council of Rangers and Druids," he said by brief way of introduction. "Nang," he waved vaguely in her direction. "Malania hasn't seen Anne or Cane in some time. Neither was home when she found that box." He rested a hand on the wolf's head in affection. "At least she bit the fool that cut her. She said the short ones tied her mouth closed."

Both looked to him like he had lost his mind. None of the names meant anything to them and he didn't bother explaining that rangers learned to communicate with their chosen companions over the years. There wasn't time for that. "Let's find this Jeff."

Vic cleared his throat. "It just so happens I'm pretty bored right now, so I'll help you! Free of charge even!"

"Very well then. Another blade will be welcome. Hmm," he muttered as he saw the full extent of the mess as they made their way back to the center of the building. "Anne is going to be pissed... House is wrecked... Blood... Bodies everywhere..."

"Hey Fred, got anymore of that chicke...." Another stranger came from the kitchen, eyes intent on the chicken leg he was pulling the last meat from.

Vic pointed. "Hey it's another one. He said Fred!"

" ...You're not F... gllackk!" he choked as Amil grabbed him by the throat.

"No, I'm Amil, the man who owns the house you're in, and the owner of the chicken you've been eating."

"Ohhh busted!" Vic smirked and took another drink from his bottle as Amil tossed the man back.

"Good chicken," the man said breathlessly before side-stepping in the direction of the door. "I'll just... go ...over ... um... bye!"

Five human men with old, pitted weapons poured from the kitchen. "We've claimed this!" they cried, and "No room! Find your own space!" They didn't want any new people staking space in the area.

Too bad the home's owner felt the same. "This is my space. I want it back."

They didn't hear it. They continued with comments yelled to get out, reminding Vic of small yappy dogs. Nang rolled her head in sync with rolled eyes. The men were in poor shape with bad weapons. If they were smart they would have backed down.

Stupid, she thought. They rushed at the three, swinging wildly. It was hardly worth the effort of countering. Yet, they had little choice since the intruders were set on protecting what they thought was theirs.

Quarters were too tight for his bow, so Amil crouched low long enough to set the bow to the floor and give it a good shove clear of the fight. He came up quickly, despite a sharp pain he was long-used to in his left knee. It didn't stop him from being annoyed at the mark of age, and he channeled that into the situation in front of him. That irritated him too. The man faced Nang, giving Amil the chance to quickly grab his head and jerk, breaking his neck. He pulled a small hunting dagger from his belt. Into his left hand, blade facing back, he spun counter-clockwise to give him the momentum needed to land the blade in the gut of the man approaching from his right.

"Reinforcements!" one cried out, running further into the building. "Outside! Outside!"

"There's only one door." Amil raced after, grabbing the man's short cloak and jerking him back towards the fray. Vic was ready. Holding his scythe like a baseball bat, he swung at the man now stumbling towards him. "Fore!" He called out as he connected, severing the head while the body rolled limp across the floor.

Two remained. One had grabbed Nang's sword arm. She drove her dagger into his forearm, forcing him to let go. As he screamed, backing up, Amil settled his dagger into the man's kidney, twisting enough for the man's knees to give out as he squealed.

Vic bounced in readiness as the last man ran at him, shouting some incoherent noise. His scythe went high overhead, his grip tight and in control. The man raised his sword overhead, leaving himself wide open, closing too fast for the long reach of Vic's weapon. Still, he maintained the pose. At the last second, he let the scythe clatter to the floor, his fist landing square in the man's face. "Ske-doosh." He grinned as the man stopped, body stiff. His eyes rolled back in his head and he fell to the floor. "Well," Vic grinned, "that was unexpected. But then, I *am* amazing." He nudged the man with a toe. "Seems dead to me. Too bad..." He looked around at the carnage. "Ya suppose one of them was Fred?"

Amil retrieved his bow. "Guess we have to find the gnome then."

"I thought," Nang wiped her dagger clean on one of the

bodies before sheathing it again, "that we were looking for the tent and the hole?"

"Nice house by the way." Vic was obviously used to battle. The blood and the mess didn't distract him from noticing the building style and the décor. "I'd look good here."

Amil managed a tight smile of appreciation. "Thank you. Hopefully that was all of them." He stepped over the mess, heading for the door.

Chapter Twelve
Cane

The other two followed as they crossed the yard, back out to the sheds by the tree line. Men, probably their hirelings, climbed up and down a ladder into a hole while others moved around, erecting pavilions and unpacking trunks coming up from the tunnel.

"Scuse me," Vic offered after a hiccup. "Whazzat?" He pointed with a bottle down past where they had first encountered these rude interlopers.

Looking around where Vic indicated, Amil found a collapsed tent with a small breeze blowing up through it. Amil started to pull the canvas away while Nang took a place opposite him to aid in its removal. Vic sauntered closer, taking a strong pull on his bottle. He leaned forward as they heard movement below. "Ya don't spose?" He interrupted himself with another hiccup.

"Fred! You down there!" Amil called.

"Jeff," Nang quietly corrected.

"Free chicken!" Vic offered as loudly as Amil.

From below they hear the distant answer of "Fred's in the house! Waddaya need?"

"Is this Jeff?" Nang asked.

"Sommat killed the bugger! Threw him on the junk heap!"

"Is this Jeff's boss?" Nang pushed, giving Vicarious a look to stop "helping" with the stupid comments.

"Nah, with Jeff... incapacitated... I'm the boss. You the gnomes?"

Vicarious took a quick drink, trying not to giggle. "Yeah, we're the gnomes. Pffsh!" He started laughing, only to have Nang rush at him, covering his mouth with her hand.

"We need help," Amil called down in a flash of inspiration. "This stupid contraption its acting up again!"

Grumbled mutterings finally settled into the man below, answering that he was coming up.

In fine linen clothes, the man arrived at the top of the ladder. "All you need to do is twist the..." he looked up as he his feet hit level ground, just in time for Amil to grab his callous-free hand and jerk his arm up behind his back.

"Whoah..." Vic offered in appreciation of Amil's speed. He raised a new bottle in salute while he swayed where he stood.

"Now what's in the hole? What are you working on in there?"

He had barely answered that they were reinforcing the tunnel when Nang asked when the queen would be arriving. "Hellfires and fiddlesticks! She's coming here? I didn't hear she was coming! We aren't ready!"

With a dry look and an even dryer tone, Nang turned to Amil. "I think he needs added incentive."

"I'd tell me what you know and quick," Amil advised in a low, lethal tone. "She's not nice." It was the one thing he had determined about the woman in the short time since the tournament; she wasn't afraid of doing what needed to be done.

Nang grabbed the man's soft white hand, taking her dagger and pressing it against his wrist. "Care to keep this?"

"Please, I wasn't supposed to be the supervisor yet..." he whined.

"You came here without rights." Nang let the blade bite into the man's skin.

"No! No no... we have the permits."

"Your queen does not give you the rights to come to an island inhabited by people and just set up camp," Amil shook the man.

"Think this idiot actually knows anything worthwhile," Nang asked Amil, "or do we turn him into a blood smear on the forest floor?"

"Do what you please," Amil nodded to Nang, then jerked on the man's arm again. "So your permits are false, which means..." he jerked on the arm again, "you don't have permits."

"They're from the queen!"

"Not my queen," Amil threw back. "Not anyone's queen on this island. So again, they're fake, means you're invading an occupied island. Which means we have *every* right to kill you right now."

"They said they'd checked; that Lareah had too many people, but that no one really lived here anymore."

"Really lived here? But there are people who live here. If you and your boys wish to keep their lives, I'd suggest," Amil said in a low, threatening tone, "that you pack your things, along with everyone else illegally on my property and leave this land."

A haunted look crossed the man's face. "She won't accept that. There will be more coming."

"Then I guess you'll all die. Starting with you." Nang showed no emotion as she tightened her grip while her razor sharp blade cut into the man's wrist, sawing slightly.

The man tried to pull free. There was nowhere for him to go, held tight between Nang and Amil. The pain made everything go white, sweat standing out on his face, as Nang gave a grim smile, tossing the now severed hand off to the side.

Vic blinked, watching the hand go. "That sucks…" Rather than sounding concerned, Vic actually was more intrigued at the clean job Nang had managed of it.

"There'll be more coming… and some of the dwarves are already here." His breath was shallow, his skin white as a corpse now with pain and blood loss. His eyes were glassing over. "The big ones," he answered when Amil pressed as to which dwarves.

"I think he's being vague again," Nang said in irritation. She knew torture. She could do better and slower methods if she needed. "What do you think, should I take his other hand?"

Picking up the severed hand, Vic came up next to Nang. "Wait, wait! Watch this…" he cleared his throat, placing the hand on her shoulder. "Can I give you a hand?" He dissolved in laughter at his horrible joke, gaining a look of irritation from Amil.

"No no!" the man started to say when Vic came over. "In the hole, they're…" He stopped in shocked horror, unable to believe he was being mocked like this.

"They're what?" Amil reminded.

"…big." He wavered on the edge of passing out. "Juiced up."

Still enjoying his morbid sense of humor, Vic couldn't help adding, "They got a hand then." He followed that with a small laugh and apology when both Amil and Nang gave him a dark look. "Heh, sorry."

"And why would you change dwarves?" Amil pushed.

"I didn't do it! She did! They make better warriors!" He wavered, unable to maintain under the torture any longer. He collapsed, either unconscious or dead.

"Aw," Vic tossed the hand on the victim's body. "Well that was fun." He sounded disappointed, but took another drink to counter it.

"Down the hole then," Nang said. She went first, then Amil, trying to ignore the ache in his leg.

Vic watched from above until they were clear. "Amazing approaching!" was the only warning he gave before jumping in. The other two looked at him in bewilderment as his loud thump vibrated down the tunnel.

More ground-shaking thumping sounded towards them. Nang slowly turned from her surprise at the idiot not using the ladder to face the long path now before her. It was blocked by the sight of what at one time might have been dwarves. Now three figures stood even taller than Vic, their short legs stocky while their upper bodies had swelled in muscling masses to over four times what would have been normal, almost brushing the sides of the tunnel. Changed, twisted by alchemy, they were no longer anything of their dwarven ancestry, nothing but soulless brutes the size of two full grown ox. Oversized and over-muscled, their tenuous hold on what it was to be a dwarf now gone, they were nothing but power, strength... and death. How they stayed upright was impossibility. Yet their skill with the massive hammers they carried rang true as they attacked in the tight quarters.

Exhaustion left their arms shaking as the battle drew out. Multiple wounds marked them almost as badly as on the dwarves, not just from enemy weapons, but from each other as they learned to fight as a group, or from the walls as they crashed into them.

"What in the hells..." Amil circled around the bodies once they had been dispatched. "I've never seen anything like this."

"Those were some bad-ass dwarves." Vic pulled a bottle, looked at it. "I prolly should be a bit more sober." He tucked it away again.

"Might be a good idea." Amil nodded.

They could hear people moving what sounded like crates and supplies around off a side tunnel; something to be dealt with later. Amil wanted to find out where they were coming from first. And that would be ahead of them. "Two on the other side," he warned, motioning into the depths of the tunnel.

Vic, for as drunk as he had seemed only moments ago, changed his stance, no longer swaying. "No problem."

"Hellzabells," Nang's jaw dropped. "Geezes, four of them."

"Mebbe I can do somethin'..." Vic started pulling things from inside his coat. Bottles emerged and disappeared, scrolls came out, getting tucked under his arm as he checked them, stuffing some back inside. "Right! I can maybe hold one with my spells!"

"Where do you keep all that?" Nang was stunned.

Moving his coat to the side, Vic patted a pouch hanging from his belt. "Magic bag." He grinned at her in a bad attempt at flirting. "It's as amazing as I am."

Nang rolled her eyes again as Amil gave them a disapproving look. "I have a few spell scrolls as well. Not sure if it will affect them though." Not everyone could read the magic in the scrolls created at the mages enclave, but a few – such as himself – had learned over the long years.

"Worth a try." Vic unrolled a few, getting them in order.

Nang nodded, stretching each of her fingers in turn where she gripped the handle, her index finger resting comfortably against the quillon. "Ready when you are."

Nang was slammed to a wall by a casual flick from one of them, knocking her momentarily unconscious. Vic set aside his liquor, focusing all his intent on the abominations before them. In their confusion, one of them backed up, pinning Vic to the wall, crushing the air from him as it swatted at what it thought were annoying flies.

Blinking back the fog and stars from her concussion, Nang managed to strike out with her newly acquired rapier while Amil's arrows started striking true. Vic's scythe bit deep in the creature's shoulder, thrusting the beast forward in surprise. The vidu was back in the game in the same moment Nang found her feet.

In short order, three were down. Vic spit blood. He had taken a blow by one of their fists to the side of his head. "That's brutal!" He hoped it hadn't damaged his good looks.

Two more. "One more," Amil warned after that. Using skills he had learned of the wilds, he called roots up from the floor and walls. They stopped the creature from moving, twisting around the body, squeezing, while others pulled at the limbs, eventually tearing it apart.

"Bugger!" Vic offered in appreciation. "Remind me not to upset you."

They quietly made their way down the tunnel, each nursing the random injuries they had incurred over the last few hours. Nang had never seen anyone so full of themselves that they thought they could just take over an island without checking with anyone. And to send people that were so devoted that they would die for her was near crazy. "This queen," she said with venom, "needs to pay for what she's done."

"Yeah," Vic said with incense, "I got bruises now!"

They were saved from commenting on that as they came into a larger cavern. There was no one around, but a portal sat in the center, sealed shut.

With no obvious way to work it, Nang made the jump of logic to assume. "I'm not really all that gifted with magic. Either of you?"

"Hm," Amil shook his head, looking around for anything like support beams. "Not much."

"Wellll..." Vic offered, "I've blown some things up from time to time. I have the incantations too! ...But sometimes it just stops someone's heart instead."

Nang gave him a dry look. "Handy if we had a heart to stop." She turned back to the pillar, finally spotting a few magical inscriptions of some kind sealing the portal tightly shut.

"Hey! Hey!" Vic stepped closer, leading with an ear as if he were listening to something. "I hear a... uh..." he snapped his fingers several times, "uh... cat! Yeah! A cat."

Amil's head whipped towards Vic while his heart clenched. Cane... "From where?"

"Really far away," he offered vaguely.

"That doesn't help," Nang informed him acerbically before going back to trying to dispel the wards. "A hunting cat?" she tried to clarify.

"Right. Those huge black cats. Well, I was just saying... it seemed strange to hear a cat here. I think it was one of them panthers that are so popular."

Then Amil heard it. It was Cane. And he was trapped somewhere. "CANE!"

Nang knelt down, looking the portal over as the men heard the panther's answering call from some distance away.

"Hey, he's calling back again. I think he heard ya." Vic wandered around the area, trying to determine where the cat might be calling from.

"CANE! Come here, boy!"

"Er…" Vic looked back at the portal. "I think it's actually coming from that portal. Definitely not over here." He moved from the far side back over to the portal.

"How did he get on the other side?" Amil asked, almost to himself.

"Most of these portals have a trigger of some kind. A word, an item…"

"Open sesame?" Vic offered.

"Was just thinking that," Amil muttered.

They tried several words with no result before Nang surprised them by speaking in gnomish. Small pieces of the stone portal twitched.

"It did something." Vic poked at the stone with his scythe.

"What are you saying?" Amil asked after several attempts.

"I'm telling it to open," Nang explained. Then, going on in gnomish, "Open for the queen, to further construction." Several glyphs lit up on sequence, only to fade out again.

"I thought the poking was working." Vic poked at it a few more times, randomly pushing at different marks.

It was a few choice words, Nang was sure of that. But what was the *right* word? She tried words in ones and twos with no result.

Vic grew bored, and pulled his bottle while Nang tried several more combinations. "Maybe if ya say the right phrase involvin' the words you used?" He tipped back, draining what was left in the current bottle and tossing it away.

"Maybe if you lay off the liquor and help," she muttered. Words like open, construction, queen and factories seemed to cause the glyphs to shine or flicker into sight, but the right combination just eluded her. She let out a deep sigh, rubbing her temples. "Any suggestions?" She and Amil tried several other combinations with no luck. "I hate these things," she grumbled while Vic "helped" by pulling another bottle and pacing.

From some distance away, Amil heard Cane offering his own suggestions in the tongue of animals. "Cane says it's something with what they're doing here… what they're creating."

"This is getting us nowhere," Nang grumbled in frustration. "I think we need to regroup on this. Think it over."

"Cane," Amil called, "If you hear me, we need some more information. We are having trouble with the wards. You remember what they said at all?" The situation wasn't funny, but he couldn't help a chuckle when he heard his panther's response of "I was a little busy not being turned into a fur pelt at the time!" He shared it with the others, but only got blank looks. He sighed, the humor fading, and kicked the portal base.

"Maybe I should poke it with something else," Vic offered. "I know! We can ask that gnome back in Lareah!"

In frustration, they decided to return, leaving the glyphs and Amil's faithful friend Cane. As much as Amil hated to leave, it was useless to stay in the tunnel if they couldn't find a way through. Help would be needed. They didn't yet have the answers to solve this riddle...

Chapter Thirteen
Ground and Center

Amil stood on the plateau contemplating what the answers could be. What would he tell Anne about the mess in the house? What would he do to stop these crazy people from taking over his land?

Anne stopped, cheerfully berating him for such a ridiculous mess. And what did he think he was doing, letting Malania get hurt like that? By the way, the pantry was empty. With a happy hug, she was off to get more cleaning supplies, heading back to Atil.

It did bother her that she had seen him returned with wounds and ripped clothing. He had wanted to simply brush it off, not telling her what had happened. She worried; but she knew he was a private person. A time would come that they could talk about all this.

First matter was to make sure his home was secure yet and that no further intruders had made it inside. Hard to do when he believed in an open door policy for his rangers to come and go. He had never barred the door in the past.

She had barely returned when a dark robed woman entered, looking for Amil. Outside, the sounds of pounding and hammering came. Malania limped into the front hall, growling at the stranger. Anne turned to see what was wrong with the dear fuzzy... and was hit on the back of the head. She turned, her weight settled over her right foot, striking upwards with the heel of her right hand, pushing up into the woman's nose on instinct. Dizzy, she could see the dark-robed woman crumple to the ground, nose broken and pouring blood.

Ground. Center. She had learned to work through pain. She dropped into a ready stance, finding her balance. Anne didn't need panic, didn't need her eyesight behind the stars that still danced in them. Movement. Four people, then. One approached from her left, arm flying to punch. Anne focused on the moment, letting her body react, her right hand grabbing the attacker's left wrist, jerking hard towards her as her own left hand came up, level to the ground. The force of her pull drew the woman off-balance, her chin meeting the heel of Anne's left hand at high force. It caused her to snap back, dropping from the impact.

Both feet grounded, weight balanced slightly back on her right foot, as the next came at her from the front. Her hands came up, palms facing outward, close to her chest. Wait. Let the woman inside Anne's guard. At the last possible second, she pushed outwards with a snap in both hands as she released the spring waiting in her right leg, using its force to knock the woman back away from her.

Spinning towards her right, her foot swept low, knocking another off her feet. That left one more. Steel. A dagger. She twisted in a quick spin, trying to hop back out of its reach, but had forgotten the mop bucket behind her. She landed hard. The woman pressed her advantage, moving in towards Anne.

Malania lunged over Amil's intended. If Amil accepted her as family, so did she. Malania's jaws clamped around the woman's sword arm. The dagger clattered as it landed, the woman's free arm balled into a fist, landing hard against the wolf's cheek and forcing her to let go.

The woman moved to claim her blade. Anne saw it in the same moment and had a choice: she wasn't ever to touch a weapon, not as a sworn Tzee Divine. But if the woman got to it first... Anne grabbed the dagger. She was able to block the blow coming at her, but just barely. Her divine gift was now temporarily blocked, because of her touching the weapon. She threw it away from them, returning to her monk skills... although everything was off now. Her balance, her timing...

"Fred! Alice!" she cried, seeing the house mice scurry up the intruder's robes, biting at her wrists, trying to help. Malania was back in the fray. Anne was disoriented. A sharp pain in her side knocked her to her knees. Sticky wetness met her hand when she touched her ribs. Malania cried out in pain.

Pulled to her feet, Anne stumbled along for a few steps, felt fresh air, the grass... She was so weak, couldn't hear Malania now, darkness was claiming her... Something was very, very wrong.

Chapter Fourteen
Malania

Frustrated over her inability to figure out what vital activation word or phrase was needed for the portal's glyphs, Nang met Vic and Amil at the Inn to discuss matters over a drink. She had witnessed the abilities of both men to make use of magic scrolls and while Nang had a few spells at her disposal, she wasn't that gifted of a magus. As much as she hated to admit it, they would probably need a full mage to decipher the glyphs.

Fortune seemed to favor them, as two mages joined them while they were discussing their next plan of action. They were in talk about the portal until they met up with some mages who offered to help; Felicia Windsong of Kron'tir and Siril Te'lie. Amil certainly seemed to know the woman, while the other was a Defender of Lareah who had volunteered his services when his offices had heard about the problems.

Looking over the man, Nang had to wonder at the wisdom in having yet another vidu join them. Vicarius, while quite skilled with his scythe, behaved as an idiot. This guy claiming to work for the city looked frail and didn't even carry a weapon. Just a stupid walking stick with a blue crystal placed on top. But he was in a professional uniform and his white hair was braided at the temples, used to neatly tie the rest of his hair back away from his face.

Amil didn't care what they looked like. A defender wasn't given their position on corrupt merit. He had asked for a reference, and if the city's general counted Siril as competent, "He's in. I don't think he'll be spouting off incantations and burning us alive with fireballs anytime soon."

Vic and Nang filled Defender Siril in on what they knew, which wasn't much at this point. The woman listened, but said nothing during the telling. "Sounds like you need mages," she offered when they fell silent.

Nang wasn't sure this woman would be any better fit for their needs. And if she were a mage... well, Nang didn't see anything to say she was. Most mages she had seen wore robes, had their hair pulled back and smelled, like Siril did, of musty old tomes. She smelled like a campfire, her dark thigh-high boots were form-fitted, her hair hung loose, and her clothing didn't.

"I'm not sure what we need at this point, Felicia." Amil shifted, resting his bow against the ground again. He hadn't slept much in the past weeks. And it bothered him to think that Anne had gone out to his place with the intruders still around. He had to remind himself that she was a sensei. She could handle herself. But if she couldn't... if he failed...

"Any one of us could help you," Nang tried to ease Amil's mind. "You could even find other people, if you needed."

"Everyone needs Vic!" Then, sputtering in the middle of a drink, "What!? No one's better than me!" he indignantly informed a man near him that he had obviously worked with before. The friend had implied with a happy smirk that perhaps Vic was less than adequate in his skill with the scythe. "I'm the man! Never! Not in a million years!" he slurred the words together. "Impossible I tell you!" He narrowed his eyes, purposely speaking quite clearly. "Has someone been telling lies about me? Where are they?"

Nang frowned. Cute though the man was, there were issues at work in him. "I think you have a problem, Vicarious."

"Well, hey," Vic grumbled. "Who's watching yer house right now? Maybe they came back."

"No one, really. Malania is there though; she should be on watch. Unless Anne locked her in the room..." Amil considered while Vic took another drink from his ever-present bottle. "Think we should go back and do some more interviews? Waiting on this gnome to appear seems to cost a lot of time." Too much time, with not enough in the way of reward. Almost two weeks of searching for the little bugger had turned up nothing, and still no solution to save Cane.

Vic shrugged. "Might as well. I doubt he's coming back here."

They had gone as far as the open air markets when a woman approached. "Atil?"

"Who's asking?" Amil assessed the fine quality of her black dress beneath her hooded cloak. Ankle length, it was a durable fabric, fashionable yet suitable for travel.

"Me." She was obviously of few words, not caring to speak.

"Why are you on your way to Atil?" he pressed. The isle

didn't have a tourist trade anymore. And the rapier and dagger at her hip were at odds with the choice of clothing.

She noted his gaze, narrowing her eyes beneath her hood. "I need to remove a problem."

"Wow, so do we!" Vic threw out there.

"Indeed," Amil gave Vic a warning glance before turning back to the woman. "What problem do you have on Atil?"

"Interlopers." Her tone was flat, trying to shut down the conversation.

"Really?" Vic cheerfully added. A warning went off in his mind, but he kept up the appearance of stupidity. "Oh hey, she sounds like one of those guys. Maybe she knows a password? That would be really convenient!"

"Interlopers." Amil wondered aloud. It was already sounding like the problem was the people that belonged on the island, at least according to these people. If she were part of them. "Do they belong to an empire?"

"Not really," she answered with a dry tone.

Nang did her own quick assessment while Vic took several long drinks from his bottle. This woman carried herself in the same manner she had been trained, right down to the pairing of weapons. It was the first female they had seen that might be in league with the others, but why a dress? And the last fool they had "interviewed" had claimed that the people on the isle were a resource they intended to use. "Are they people that live in the village of Atil?"

The woman sighed quietly. "I'll just ask at the shipyard." Annoyance was clear in her voice as she turned and strode off.

"Well hold on..." Amil started to say as the stranger went down the cobbled ramps to the lower docks.

They raced after her, but found no sign of her and no boats just leaving the docks. "Where did she go?" Nang asked.

Confused discussion followed as they milled around each other, trying to determine the direction before Vic stated the obvious with "I bet she'll be at this guy's house!" as he indicated Amil.

They were barely ashore when they found new developments in front of his home that involved more equipment piled everywhere and fresh blood at his doorstep. "What in the hells..." He rushed the last few feet, slamming the door open and calling for Anne.

"They've been busy." Nang followed a little more cautiously, eyes sliding around the entryway looking for would-be attackers. Siril and Felicia came just as carefully as Vic casually sauntered behind them.

The home had once again been breached by the minions of the queen. It was eerily silent, devoid of any sign of life. Nang carefully stepped over a broken mop and overturned bucket. The mages stepped further to the sides to avoid the soapy water mixed with blood all over the floor. Amil turned in circles, panicked. No Anne, although her supplies were all there. And no Malania.

With hand signals, Siril indicated they were to spread out, look for anyone in the building. While they moved like rogues stealing through the night, carefully entering rooms and verifying they were clear, Amil went to one knee in the front hall.

Two little mice scurried across to him, squeaking and bouncing their story to him of how they had seen Anne attacked by women in black and taken towards the docks by several other women that had come in behind her. Due to their diminutive size, they hadn't been able to see far enough when the captors gained in distance to know the exact path.

"Thank you, you two." Amil gave each a soft stroke on their velvety heads. "Very helpful. Now please, stay safe. Anne would kill me if you two got in trouble." Most women would have run screaming in terror at mice or tried to kill them. Anne had declared them "cute," and had insisted on spoiling them as badly as she did his wolf and panther.

He called for everyone to regroup. "They took Anne and Malania. They say she was taken towards the docks." He gained strange looks from the mages when he informed them that new information had come from the mice. He didn't care. Mages had familiars; it shouldn't be that odd to them. And this was more important.

Siril's curiosity was piqued. He scooped one up as Amil gave him a dark look. "Don't hurt her."

The defender turned it in his hands, examining it to see if it was in any way magical. "I have no intention of hurting it." Uncomfortable, as most animals, with being on its back in the defender's hand, it squeaked, twisting and bit into his thumb. In surprise, Siril let it fall from his cupped hands.

Amil glared up at him from beneath his hood as his hand shot out to gently catch the mouse and scoop in towards his chest in a fluid motion that would keep it safe. Once secure, he put his hand back to the floor. "It's okay, Alice," he gently soothed, stroking once down the mouse's back.

"Oh yeah," Vic decided to add to the discussion that wasn't happening. "I think they're his houseguests that live in his library." Pleased that he had somehow furthered the conversation, he strode outside.

Following, Amil put his tracking skills to use. He knew Anne's foot size. She was such a dainty little thing, and had so often rolled her ankle in habit or playfully kicked at him. He had always caught her foot, often stealing her slippers; her favorite red slippers... the color of the blood on the ground. His mind raced to figure out this newest riddle. Why would they take Anne?

"Amil, up!" Nang jumped to defend his back as a band of eight halflings moved in on them with murder evident in their drawn blades.

He spun as he rose, bow slipping to his fingers and arrows nocking almost of their own will. Vic took a last swig, tossing a half-full bottle out into the grass as he shrugged, settling his scythe into a ready stance. With a joyful bounce, he let the battle take him over. "Hee Hee!" he giggled, enjoying the freedom of the moment with his best partner.

Blades flashed in the battle while fire bolts flashed from Felicia. "My my, they wanted to play," she purred with the sharp crackle of fire behind it before setting her hands, covered in blackened gloves, on the arm of the nearest little man, severely burning his arm in the simple touch. She tossed him away from her with a strength not apparent in her slight form.

Siril caught the man in a hold spell as he stumbled, locking him into place. "Maybe we should take one for interrogation instead of carving them up like a roast." As he readied another spell, an arrow from Amil whizzed through the space, striking true and laying the man low.

Another noticed Amil being carefully aware of his steps around two small mice that scurried about underfoot. "Fred, Alice, inside," Amil warned the little white balls of fur. It came seconds too late as the man's rusty blade came down full force to break the backs of both tiny squeakers.

Furious that one more thing had been taken, Amil threw

himself into the fray, bow forgotten as he pulled his blade to finish someone that would so heartlessly take innocent lives. He let the others dispatch what remained of the attackers as he dropped to kneel beside his little friends. Amil gently picked them up, a deep sadness etched in his features. They had been part of his family this last while; something that made him think of Anne.

Nang was surprised to see how hard Amil took the deaths of the mice. They were mice, after all, not like they were especially useful animals. But she rolled her eyes when Vic tried to offer help by suggesting that maybe the mages could put them back together again. She let them explain matters as she determined to find the source of trouble, searching the ground for any signs that might remain of the path yet. Unfortunately, there had been too much activity of late to determine which direction the kidnapper went. That left them with one option – to go back into the tunnel system and investigate the portal.

Siril had agreed to come along after hearing the overview, but this looked like much more than a routine situation. A portal or a missing animal was no problem, nor was a case of squatters needing to be removed. "Would anyone care to fill me in on some of the details? I don't really like walking into a situation blind."

"Sure!" Vic announced before taking a swig from a dubious bottle he pulled out.

"Halflings, gnomes, elves, humans and alchemically enhanced dwarves have decided to take ownership of Atil," Nang tried to cut it to the basics of the problem.

"See," Vic cut in, "there are these people that are trying to take over the island. This queen ordered them to clear it out, and they invaded his home, see."

"All in the name of a queen of some empire," Nang interrupted.

"Really..." the defender asked dryly, not quite sure yet he believed them. "And who is Anne?"

Amil didn't need to tell them everything about her yet. Less was more. "She helps me tend to the house when I am away."

"The attackers?" Siril pulled a small pad and quill to make notes, waiting for further details.

Vic nodded vigorously. Nang only slightly. "They plan to use the volcano to power factories."

"Makes sense," Felicia added, "using the volcano to power

the factory."

"Except the volcano is still very unstable," Amil added as he rejoined the group. "The house is clear."

"Those dwarves are pretty mean, though. "They're like giant chest muscles with arms poking out. And twice as tall as me!"

Nang had to admit Vic was right on with that assessment. She nodded agreement. "Pretty much."

Siril nodded, not sure how his superiors would take this information.

"They have been deforming them with chemically enhanced drugs; deformed and pretty bad." Amil frowned, his mind still worrying on where Anne could be.

Siril watched the ranger. Everyone knew who Amil was; he even had a statue in Lareah in honor of all he'd done in past wars. Whatever this was had to be bad if the ranger was this distracted. "Any weaknesses?"

"Stab them enough." Nang smirked, setting a hand on the basket of her rapier.

"We never had magic at our disposal, so maybe. Otherwise, stabbing. But they leave the worst bruises... I still have one. See?" Vicarious pushed one sleeve of his white coat up.

Siril glanced at the arm, then up at the man. It was damn near impossible to see a bruise on vidu skin. Vidu were known for white hair; this one apparently dyed his for some odd reason. Now this; Siril questioned the sanity of the other vidu. "Mmhm..." he offered dubiously. "If they attack again, allow me to try to catch one."

"Bad idea," Nang quickly answered.

Vic followed with, "They're kind of suicidal like that."

Siril sighed. Amil agreed with the others, stating that they had proven relentless. In the background they heard further sounds of intrusion, machines running loudly, trees cracking and falling amongst others in the forest.

"But what are we doing?" Vic wanted to get moving again. "Going to the portal? They got hostages now, right?"

"My near sight isn't as good as it used to be." As hard as it was to admit, Amil met the stare of impatience the others were giving him. "I could spot a target a mile away, but if its close..."

Vicarious frowned. "Tracking really isn't my specialty."

"Maybe we need another pair of eyes." Unimpressed with

the drunk's apparent disinterest, Siril called in his familiar. A small green dragonling winged into their space, sniffing at the different members before perching on Siril's shoulder, her tail wrapped comfortably his neck. "Ulth... take a look around."

Between them, they were able to determine steps coming into the house, but none leaving. There was sign of some stumbling, then Anne's footprints abruptly stopped.

"Picked up." Nang said with a nod. "She was dragged around and picked up."

"Huh?" the drinker asked. "How's that?"

"Aye," Amil glanced up as the little dragonling's head snapped up and she darted towards he trees. "Female tracks, though to this point we've only ran into halflings and men."

"Well, what now?" Vic questioned at the same time Nang asked what the dragon had found.

Siril, noting the dour expressions, fought a small smile. "A squirrel. She said it was tasty."

Nang gave him a blank look while Vic let out a small laugh. "Heh, sorry I asked!"

"Did the female who grabbed her come this way?" Amil chose to ignore the familiar. "I'm only seeing Anne's tracks over here." He was still just a short ways off to the side from the front door.

Nang felt bad for his frustration, but there was only so much she could do. "Too many tracks for me to follow," she shrugged. "I'm guessing they picked her up."

"What about the boatman?" Siril tried to get them to look outside the crushed grass as the only option.

"I don't think he would ferry someone carrying a hostage..." Vic said dubiously.

"Especially if she comes here often." Nang added.

"All the same..." Amil led their party back down to the docks. The regular boat was long gone. It hadn't been there when they docked with a second boat, but it was worth looking around anyways.

"Oh wait," Vic pointed out a prone body some distance down the beach. About the same time, the others started noticing that the boat was in smashed pieces and, as they got closer, that the ferryman was covered in blood. "Well!" Vic unnecessarily announced, "At least that means the kidnapper didn't leave the island."

"What other buildings are here?" Siril glanced around. The only home he'd seen so far had been Amil's. "Any barns or sheds of any kind?"

"This one," Amil nodded back towards his place, "there's a small stable in the far corner of my land. And the village, though some current volcanic activity has cut the village off."

Oblivious to the emotions attached to the situation, Vic cheerfully, albeit callously, added his own thoughts. "That doesn't leave us with much option then. Looks to me like you gotta choose to go after yer girl, or yer cat." An uncomfortable silence fell amongst the others while Vic took a long drink, breaking the silence with a burp and a happy sigh. "Well… you still wanna try that portal after this?"

Chapter Fifteen
A Family Visit

Unhappy with it, Amil had to be content that at least they would be doing something. Stiffening his resolve, he determined to deal with the holers first. Then Anne. She always swore she could take care of herself. He'd have to trust that now. "Seems like we have no other choice but the portal for now."

Nang gave him a sympathetic look. "That really is the only real option."

"Cut it off from most people," Felicia agreed.

Amil tapped the defender's arm as they approached the tree line, pointing out the mess of mechanical bits and pieces scattered across the area. "I think those are more of the contraptions they build at these factories they plan to make."

"Oh. I was gonna say, you must spend a fortune on furniture."

Everyone ignored Vic as they looked around. There hadn't been horses in the stable since Amil's wife Oceania had kept a few, but now there wouldn't have been room for the animals. It was full of timbers and equipment for building. Chests both solid and broken or with broken locks littered the area. Those that were looked into held more supplies for building.

Nang shimmied down the ladder into the hole they had checked into just a few days before, Siril following close behind. Amil extended his fingers, the leather of his gloves stretching with soft creaks, before swinging down onto the ladder. Letting his feet slide out just far enough that his hands could guide him down, his feet loosely broke his momentum by bumping against the rungs. Felicia chose to avoid the ladder altogether, creating a small amount of heat below her, letting it magically lift and carry her down to the others.

"That looks fun." Vic rummaged through his spell scrolls, not finding what he wanted. "Up, up and fly!" He hadn't used anything magical, but somehow thought it would work. He landed, ungracefully, on his rear in their midst.

Nang rolled her eyes and offered a hand to help him to his feet while Siril asked details about where they were. At least this time around the group didn't encounter the horribly altered dwarven minions.

"These are the tunnels they have been carving beneath Atil," Amil told Siril as they all cautiously made their way to the portal. "We killed the unnatural creations we found down here last time. And the portal..." He stopped as they entered the dim chamber with the huge obelisk standing in the center.

"So this is the thing that poking doesn't work on," Vic announced as though giving a tour, then proudly took a drink.

"And the gnomish words trigger things to flick or flash," Nang added.

"They sure look pretty," Amil crossed his arms, still upset from the loss of his little friends and others still missing. His voice came across more than a little snarky. "Now what do they mean?" Hopefully the mages would have better luck.

Siril carefully set about closely examining the portal and any of the writing. "Seems that the words read in a spiral around the pillar."

Leaning on a staff, Felicia idly looked the pillars over. She wasn't a puzzle solver. She was a doer. They could figure this out; she'd help with any trouble that came along after. Besides, the tall brute with the scythe was likely to cause more trouble with the way he was poking about at the large stone.

"What do they say?" Nang ran her fingers along the pillar. "Wait... these were glyphs the last time we were here. This looks like a sentence."

The same sarcastic tone laced Amil's words. "So we don't have to play the flick flick game?"

"Too bad," Vic took a long drink. "I wanted to win that game."

Felicia cocked her head to the side. "Flick flick game?"

"But the words weren't there before, right?"

"They weren't?" Siril glanced at Vic before turning back to the odd writing.

"Glyphs before," Nang repeated. "They flickered when we had a near right guess."

"Somebody say something in gnome-ese," Vic prompted.

Ignoring Vic, Amil picked up on what Nang had been saying. "And when you would say certain words the glyphs would flicker and dim again; as in the flick flick game. We spent a good amount of time spewing words at it." He picked up a pebble and tossed it at the portal, feeling useless and stuck.

"It wasn't as fun as it sounds really." Vic didn't want the two mages to feel like they had lost out on a great time.

"More annoying than anything." Amil scowled at the pillar.

"I have it." Siril said with some thrill. They were perfectly clear to his mantic sight; he should have tried magic right off. He went back to the top where the words started to wrap around. "It says 'construction is the way, factories a must; industry, whatever will become of us'." As the words left his mouth, each mark on the pillar lit up, stone grinding against stone as it started to twist, shrinking to the width of a thin rope. A bright light flared, consuming that spot with a thunderous boom.

As they blinked their vision back into being, a swirling portal now stood before them. "Sweet deal!" Vic exclaimed.

"Just make sure you're not walking into a trap," Felicia said just as Amil stepped into the portal. Considering his age, Felicia thought he was behaving much too impetuously. Even if all this was over a girl, the ranger needed to slow down and think his actions through.

They came out in a dark, shadowy plain. The call of buzzards and wild cats on the hunt sounded from the distance. Moans and screams cut through the hollow sensation as trees rustled, dry wood creaking in a wind they couldn't feel. Underneath it all was a faint heartbeat, more felt than heard.

Felicia cast light on her staff and Siril did the same with a small wand he held aloft. Even then, the light only vaguely filtered through heavy fog that made noises resound thinly through the cool mists that whirled lazily around them. Slow figures passed through the shadows, just a little darker than their surroundings, unphased that a group stood so near their path.

"Helloooooo?" Vic's voice sounded muffled as though wool lightly plugged their ears.

Nang shivered, wrapping her arms around herself. Normally she wouldn't show fear before others. This wasn't normal. "I can feel the chill in the air, the sense of death. This... this is Romx."

"No way!" Vic exclaimed. "For real?"

"What are these foreigners doing with the land of the dead?" Amil frowned.

"If they are looking to take over your island," Siril offered, "what better army than one of lost souls?"

While the others stood around discussing the whys and wherefores of the situation, Vic decided to attack the situation head on. He stepped confidently over the crinkling susurrations of the crisp grass in the direction of one of the shadowy figures until it resolved itself into a young female with red hair. "Say," Vic waved a hand in front of her to get her attention. "You didn't see any gnomes or other people around did you?"

She stepped closer, the mist shifting like smoke around her, yet her features weren't quite clear to them. Her body posture and the tilt of her head indicated some confusion, to which Amil asked, "Why the look?"

Felicia considered all the lands that had different languages. If their dead all ended up here... "Perhaps it does not understand you."

"Pfft!" Vic made a dismissive noise at her. "Oh! I know! I know! Cuz we aren't ghosts! Right?"

The woman's left hand came up slowly, so slowly, index finger pointed vaguely in Amil's direction while the other fingers hung limp. Her voice came as a breathy rush of air escaping a tomb. "Yyyyou're aliiiiive..."

Siril gave a small snort. "Kinda obvious...a small group of alive beings in the land of the dead..."

"Living beings don't belong here." Nang's voice sounded too fearful to her own ears, even with the overlay of strange noises around them.

"I got it!" Vic crowed, doing a victory arm pump, then took a drink. He may act stupid, but he was far from it.

"Aye," Amil ignored the idiot, talking instead to Nang while focusing on the ghost. "But a portal to the land of the dead... I would have thought more than just us would have been here. Not to mention Cane is here somewhere. So her thinking we are odd in this place... it just doesn't seem logical somehow."

"Oh! I bet this was the trap! That was pretty sneaky of them." Vic nodded, sounding impressed with the plan he figured had been laid out by the intruders.

Shaking off the creepy feeling, Nang forced herself to step a little closer to the ghost. "Are there other living creatures here?"

"Ooooothers coooome.... ooooothers taaaake..."

"Take what?" the defender asked.

Her head turned so slowly. "Uuuuusssss..."

"Do you know where?" Siril didn't scare easily and there was a job to do. He intended to keep this professional, regardless of the odd circumstances.

"Slaaaaavemaaaasters staaaay..."

"I wonder if they use souls to make the mechanical devices work," Amil wondered aloud. "I know they do that to some golems..."

Siril considered, giving a small shrug and nod in tandem. "It's not unheard of to use lost souls to power things."

"I knew combining magic and mechanical things was possible," Felicia added dubiously, "but souls?"

The ghost looked directly at Amil. "Earrrrrlyyyy... yooou..."

"Early for what?" A chill raised down Amil's spine at what he thought she might mean. He wasn't ancient, but by Firnos, he wasn't young anymore either. And the oracle in his homelands had offered something of a warning herself. He narrowed his eyes, trying to get a better look at the girl.

"Oh, she's saying you ain't s'posed to be here yet."

Amil didn't need Vic putting his own thoughts into words.

"Wait... so some stay?" Nang fished around inside the neck of her armor, pulling out an ankh she kept around her neck at all times. "I want you to listen and obey." The ghost slowly turned to Nang as she kept the holy symbol out. "We need to know if they brought other living beings here. A panther and a woman."

"Paaaanther .... yeeeesss.... the Guaaaardian ooooof the Daaaarknessssss haaaass..."

"The panther is still here," Nang confirmed. "What about the woman?"

"Maaaany wommmmmen heeere."

"The living one," she pressed. "Anne."

"Noooo..."

"What about a Wolf?" Amil worried. "Malania?"

"I reeeememberrrrr heerrrrr." She smiled. "Yeeessss... buuuut the woooolf cannooooot leeave. Sheeee protecteeeed the giiiirl..."

Vic looked between the ghost and the ranger. The silence stretched out. "So?" he finally asked.

Amil looked down. He didn't want to show emotion. He hated that despite his best attempt at sounding monotone, his bone-deep sadness still crept into the few words he had to say aloud to make it real. "She means she's dead..."

"Oh. Ohhhh."

The same wind-in-the-reeds sound echoed through the ghost's continued slow speech patterns. "Iiii'll taaaake care of herrrr..."

A sad smile touched Amil. "I know." The others gave him a strange look that he would say that to a ghost, but he had reason. He knew this particular young woman. It was someone he had never thought to see again.

When Nang brandished her ankh with a little more authority, demanding to be taken to the panther, Amil gently pushed her arm back down to her side. "We don't need to force her, Nang." There was a sense of loss and wistfulness in his quiet words.   Between them, and with care for what seemed a fragile moment for Amil, they continued their questions with a little more respect. They learned that some kind of "slave masters" and a "darkness" had beset the landscape, wreaking havoc and disturbing the peace the dead longed for. The unwelcome ones were threatening to overtake portions of Romx by removing ghosts and souls at a quickening rate to be used for some unknown purpose. Further questions revealed other living beings, something the ghost called Defilers of Nature, were the ones actually taking the souls.

They needed to find the ruler of Romx. B'ho was rumored to be ferryman, ruler, eternal guardian. "Apparently there's a Darkness here that needs to be destroyed." Amil set his shoulders, rolled his neck and settled his hand on the bow grip. Everything from his posture to his tone indicated he was ready for business. His eyes still watched the female ghost, seeming to wait for something further.

She solidified for a moment under his intense scrutiny. Beautiful porcelain skin beneath brilliant red hair made her eyes shine the same blue as Amil's. The ghostly echoes of her words disappeared long enough to say, "I'll watch Malania...... father....."

She gave him the same sad smile he had given her before the strange fog rolled up over her, making her disappear as if she'd never been more than a wisp of smoke.

Siril shifted his weight from right to left foot. He looked

askance at the others in question. "... she just say what I think she said?"

"Father?" Felicia made the question sound like she might have been confirming Siril's thought at the same time she was asking Amil to clarify.

"I'm pretty sure she did." Vic considered. "Yeah, she did."

Nang simply watched Amil, who stood silent for long moments, looking to where the ghost had faded away.

He had let this daughter down in life, never there as he should have been. He hadn't protected her in life the way he wished he should have. Now she was about to be used again. Not on his watch. Not this time. He finally pulled an arrow from his quiver. "Let's find B'ho."

The guardian was true to what they had read in tales of him. Shadow black empty eye sockets looked deep into their souls. B'ho listened quietly, the sound of air rushing around him like a fierce storm, though nothing moved.

His hand came up almost as the girl's had, pointing some distance off in the dark. Faster than they would have expected, they found the Darkness the spirit had been talking about, along with the slave masters who accompanied it. Two metal creatures stood with an ebony hound-headed creature. They asked no questions of the trio but quickly attacked them. Felicia brought her fire elemental to hand, the flames burning strangely in the odd atmosphere, its attacks hindered but still effective in aiding the heroes. And so the fight ensued, living to living, destroying what the dead could not. The lands of Romx were free from their captors.

"What was that thing?" Siril asked.

Vic shrugged, stating the obvious. "Fast."

As they stood catching their breath, a large panther bounded playfully over to Amil, as healthy as any and happy to see someone living again. "Cane!" A broad smile touched Amil as he knelt, not feeling the pain in his knee, to give his companion a good scratch behind the ears.

"I assume this is what we were looking for?" Siril smiled ever so slightly to see the old ranger acting like a boy with a favored pet.

Everyone's joy turned to confusion when Amil went still, looking across the field. They could hear a child's singing, a little girl in a sundress and sandals fading into view as she skipped closer.

She squealed in delight. "Daddy!" She sprinted the last little distance to Amil, throwing herself into his arms.

Exchanging looks, the party wondered if this was a different version of the previous ghost. But it couldn't be. The child had white-blond hair flowing loose around her shoulders, where the other had been crowned with red locks.

The tiny spirit pushed back Amil's hood, giving the group their first clear look at Amil's visage. Always hidden from strangers, they now watched as the child reached a hand up, running her palm over Amil's right cheek. "You got hurt."

"A long time ago, baby," Amil whispered. He remembered the day the scar had been earned. Every day he looked in a mirror, he had been reminded since then of that day. Little Marie and Oceania had left that morning to enjoy the day, fully expecting him to meet them for a picnic. He had raced closer, spotting first his beloved lying broken and dying. She had taken her last breath in his arms as he rocked her, begging her to hold on just a little longer.

Bandits had laughed gruffly, pulling him from his misery. He had looked up in time to see a blade coming at his face. That impact had run through his perfect elven features, down his brow and across his cheekbone. The only thing that had saved him had been quick enough thinking to throw an arm up, covered in his leathers, to block it from going deeper.

He had attacked at their barbs, so lost in grief he hadn't considered his little girl. The bandits had; and used her against him. She was sobbing, eyes covered with the pretty blue sash from her waist. When Amil had tried to step closer, to stop it... He had been helpless to save his family.

His injury had been nothing compared to that pain. As much as he had hated the reminder of his failure, that scar was still with him. And a little girl long gone to him now ran her fingers along it. She absently pushed her long tresses over her shoulder. "You should have that tied back, Marie," he said softly.

"I lost my hair tie," she pouted.

"Of course you did," he smiled at her. He had pulled the bloodstained ribbon from her tied hands that day and had never let the small blue ribbon leave him. All these years, and now it was time to return it. He turned her to face away from him, out of practice with a child's hair. Pulling it into the high ponytail Oce had always given their child, he finished it with a clumsy looped bow. "There you go. All better now."

She turned, kissed him quickly on the cheek, giving him an equally quick hug. "Thank you, daddy!" Marie ran off as any child might to play, but disappeared.

Standing back some distance from them in that same direction was the ghost of the young woman, a large wolf sitting calmly beside her. Amil took a step towards them, then reconsidered.

"So uh..." Vic came up beside him. "You wanna talk to it – er, her?"

Amil saw the uncertainty in the girl's face. His hesitation had made her question where things had been left between them. He made the decision in that moment to close the distance between them. She was still his daughter. "Juniper." He reached one hand for Malania to come to him and the other for his wayward daughter to get a hug.

She watched Malania quietly rise, padding over to bump her head against Amil's palm. He scratched the head of his trusted friend, lowering his head to sit forehead to forehead for a moment. "I'll miss you, my friend." The wolf whined once, licking Amil's hand before going back to the girl, giving her a slight push towards Amil.

An eternity passed in the space between them. So many things that had been left unsaid. So many choices that had driven a wedge between them. He had been gone at the time, off at war, and had come home to find his nineteen year old had Turned to the path of night, when she had become a vampire. He had never known if it was of her own free will or not, but she had followed him, begging and needing a father's love he wasn't sure he could give anymore.

In his early years, he had been like most people in wishing the vile undead destroyed. They were a scourge that endangered nature. But she was his child, his oldest daughter, and although he couldn't forgive her, he couldn't turn his back on her either. He had done what he could, short of allowing her under his roof. And that was her undoing. She had found other ways to survive the night, ways that led to her demise.

Shame at his failings had brought back his old ways. Rather than simply remember the good in his daughter, he had become more furious with the undead than before. He blamed not himself, but all undead for what had happened to his daughter.

Only as the years passed did he see the perspective. Marie's birth had engendered all those fierce feelings of protectiveness, reminding him that no matter what, his daughters would always be his children. The disappointment in Juniper transferred to himself. He blamed himself for not being there for her, to help guide her in life and her decisions, or watch her and protect her as he done for Oceania when she had been younger.

That feeling of failure was something he had carried these last many years. He had never told her how proud he had been of her, or how she had managed such a terrible affliction. He had failed as a person, and he had failed as a father. Her death – both of them – had been as hard as knowing he had failed his daughter Marie when a bandit held her life in his hands.

He had been given a chance to find closure with this child. He had never had a chance to tell her it had never been her. Never. It was what she had become, but it had never been him hating her. Just the choice. "I forgive you, Juni."

She closed the distance between them, becoming solid enough for him to put his arms around her, holding her one last time. "Thank you," she whispered, although the land made the words carry. "... father..."

Painfully aware of his company at his back, Amil didn't want to speak of emotions and prove he wasn't always detached and aloof. But he would never have this opportunity again. Speaking as softly as he could, he hoped it only reached her ears. "I wish I could have been there more for you, and am sorry I was not there for you as a father."

Her body was cold against him, no scent at all. But for the moment she was solid and real as she hugged him in return. "I've always loved you, daddy."

Tears pricked eyes he had long thought dried of tears. "We all pick our paths, baby girl," he said against her ear, voice gruff with emotion. "My regret is that ours was not closer together." He felt her solidity sliding away. He didn't want to let go, but was losing anything to hang on to. "I love you. I *will* see you again."

"We still have that whole empire business," Vic interrupted the touching moment.

The ghost stepped away, turning incorporeal again as she glanced around in worry. "Theeeey taaake the Iiiiinfeeested Briiiidge somewhere... Iii caan't heeelp moooore..."

The girl was obviously Amil's daughter. And the wolf had died defending Anne, now needing to stay in Romx. But if the ghost could just give them a little more information... "What's an infested...?" Nang started to ask.

The spirit startled, the wolf's ears going up. None of the living heard anything, but it was enough to send both rushing off into the darkness. And then she was gone. What clue was it she had given them? What did it mean? Where did they have to go next?

"Man-made bridge or natural bridge?" Felicia asked what they were all thinking.

"Perhaps," Siril offered, "we should find our way out of here. We can figure out details later."

"Let's find B'ho again." Amil started walking back the way they had left the guardian. Grateful for their assistance, the keeper granted them transport back to the mortal world again.

"Wheeeeee-ah..." Vic looked around in disappointment as they all reappeared, a real wind blowing strongly around them now. "Aw. Are we in a cemetery? I don't like cemeteries."

"Back to the plane of ashes," Felicia dismissed her elemental, seeming as unbothered by their encounter as Amil was shaken. Siril was still focused on the task. "This is the Lareah cemetery, if I am not mistaken."

"That it is," Amil answered. "Your eyes don't lie."

"That's kind of inconvenient." Vic actually sounded like he was pouting. "Now how do we get back to the island?"

Nang couldn't help but shiver at the feeling of having been in the land of the dead, even with her connection to it. "Sounds like we have a new task ahead of us."

The only bridge any of them could think of that might apply was one Felicia had seen in the snowy reaches of Aloria. Strange creatures kept the frozen passes from most visitors. "And just for the record," Felicia gave each of them a dark look. "I hate the cold."

Chapter Sixteen
An Epic Story

It had been another routine day, as near as Nang could tell. Vic sauntered up onto the plateau, bottle in hand. "Huh, I thought fer sure they'd be here, partner," he mumbled to his scythe. "Hey there!" he called as he spotted Nang.

"Evening. Seen Amil?"

"Isn't he over there?" He pointed towards some buildings on the level below them.

"Where?" Nang didn't see anyone in the drizzle. Just the buildings.

"See?" He leaned in close, the alcohol on his breath enough to make her eyes water as he sighted down his arm, pointing at the end of one of the market stalls.

"No, no I don't. How long have you been drinking tonight?" She looked at him from the corner of her eyes, then rolled them as she saw the intense thought he was putting into trying to remember. "Let's think about physical bridges for now. Do you know of any bridges in Kordathya? Any that might be near Atil?"

"I'm not very great with riddles... Ummm..."

Nang sighed, resisting the urge to thwap him alongside the head. "A bridge, Vic. This isn't a riddle. It's a problem."

"Alright! I'm not very familiar with Atil, but a couple bridges come to mind. Not near Atil though."

"Where at?" Nang turned the collar of her cloak up higher, vainly trying to keep the water from slipping down her back as the light drizzle turned into steady rain.

He tucked the scythe into that strange magic bag at his side, muttering to it, "You wouldn't like getting soaked anyway. Bugger! Not the hair." He pulled an umbrella, shaking his hair out before patting it to be sure it was still in perfect order. "Well, I think there's one leading up into Val'reveran... Or did they take that down?" he asked himself. His family and their people were high in the mountains, away from most other groups of people. Several bridges had been built to make travel through the passes easier. There had been talk once of cutting the main bridge away, becoming more reclusive. "But there was one there at least. And another separated Aloria and the desert! Although that one ain't a wooden bridge, it's more of a land bridge and it's kind of gloomy. Plus, I think there are huge snakes in the water. Like really huge ones."

"So," Amil pulled his hood a little lower against the rain as he joined them, "any idea on the bridge?"

"We were just talking about it."

"Very well then." He motioned them to follow him out of the city, thinking to at least rest in the forest's grove. "So what bridges come to mind... the only bridge I can think of is the one to get to Val'reveran, which is a stone bridge and crosses a cut high in the mountains, though not very big."

"Right!" Vic answered Amil. "I said that one too! But I don't really think it's infested..."

"Infested with what though?" Nang thought out loud to herself. "And how are they taking it?"

"Termites? Trolls? Fairies?"

Nang gave Vic a dark look. "Don't be an idiot."

"I know all about trolls and fairies." A man in bright, fancy clothes joined them near the city gate. "Edward the Fabulous," he said with a formal, flourishing bow, "at your service."

"Obviously this is getting larger than just Atil." Amil got them back on track. "Seems their entire operation is spread out through the world. Atil's their starting point."

There was discussion that the bridge may not be a physical one at all, but a purely metaphysical or metaphorical one when a distinctly elven woman made an appearance.

An earthy woman of auburn hair threaded with flowers and a soft loamy green dress twined with vines and leaves met them just inside the grove. Poised and calm, all nature seemed to bow to her. Amil knew in a glance, as did the bard Edward from all the ballads. They bowed to her, giving her the deference she deserved.

But not their Vic. "What's wrong?" Vic looked to the admittedly pretty girl, then to Ed, taking a drink. "Your shoe isn't untied." He considered who it could be, then spoke to no one in particular. "Who's she think she is? More important than me?" Vic whispered less than quietly. "Ow!" Nang had reached over on that to thwap him on the back of the head. Vicarious had failed to take note of the goddess that stood before them – Maleiin, the goddess of nature.

"Trust me," Edward said from the corner of his mouth to Vic, "you are not that important. Read a book sometime." He pulled a book from the satchel at his side pushing it towards Vic while Nang tried to cover a laugh behind a cough. "Here."

"Child, why so formal?" Her voice held the gentle zephyr of spring's first warm breezes.

"Formality is my nature," Amil said, fully aware that the goddess of nature stood before him, "especially in the presence of you, m'lady."

Her soft smile alighted on each as she gazed over those assembled. "I understand you've asked Firnos for aid."

"If he hears not my plea, at least the plea of those who have died by these foul intruders my lady, and for him to allow me... us... to carry their revenge upon those who made such destruction upon your creation. To retrieve those who have been taken from the gods, and allow them their freedom as they so rightly deserve."

"He has heard, my child. And he pleads your case with another of our kind. Our sympathies are with you in this time of loss. Your daughter spoke true to you. Go deeper inland." She nodded once, gracefully.

"Thank you, Lady Maleiin, I can only hope He shall soon help us, and for us to be His spear."

"I'm pretty sure I'd recognize some kind of god," Vic muttered, flipping through the pages. "Nope, she ain't in here... and this book has no pictures." He handed the book back to Edward and he took a long swig from his ever present bottle.

"He said her name!" Nang thwapped him on the arm again, horrified that he would be so stupid before a goddess.

"I am the mother of all, child," the goddess smiled to Vic.

The wizardess Felicia joined them, her gaze stopping on Maleiin for a moment with a look on her face somewhere between awe and horror. Seeing a god...dess... was a high honor, and it usually meant trouble of some kind. She didn't want to think what kind of chaos would come to their small group now.

Then she looked to Edward as he berated Vic. "In the chapter 'the Life'...did you even read any of it?"

"Oh! Oh that one! They should have said so! Wow! Neat!"

Edward shook his head at the stupidity of some of the common people while Nang shook her head with a face palm at

Vic's density. "I think those 'roided up dwarves hit you in the head a few too many times." She was rewarded for the comment by Vic reaching up to feel his head for bumps.

"But what direction, m'lady?" Amil asked. "We hear of a bridge, and now deeper inland..."

"They defile the lands by touching Death's domain, as well as the abyssal realms." Her gaze passed over them while Edward couldn't help playing a calm, earthy tune, the combination leaving a warmth inside each. "It is a heavy burden we place on you. We know this."

"A burden I shall carry til I cannot carry it anymore," Amil answered solemnly. "Too many count on it."

"It's time you decide your legacy, ranger-mine. What is worth living for... and what is worth dying for. You have a destiny," the goddess said to Amil, "and hard choices to make. Firnos has heard your prayers. We do as we can for you, but this will not be an easy path. Your honesty alone will save another. Your sacrifices will save others. Speak truth for her to be returned to you. Go further inland to seek your path." A gentle smile warmed her face, giving everyone that sense of summer's glow. She inclined her head ever so slightly before turning on her bare feet, taking a few steps away from them, disappearing. As she departed, small vines grew up, providing Healing Leaves for those that would travel with Amil.

While everyone else stood in quiet awe, Vic took a drink, belched loudly and grinned. "Does this mean we get to be in an epic story?"

Chapter Seventeen
Go to Hell

"Well," Edward the Fabulous cheerily announced. "I must be off. This has raised a few questions that I need to poke around for the answers to."

"You don't even wanna come?" Vic asked in surprise.

"Sadly, I have a performance I've already committed to." Ed gave them all a jaunty little bow before taking his leave. "I'd ask the gods to be with you... but it seems they are!"

"Lady Felicia," Amil asked, "would you know anything of the abyss?"

She didn't like having the others overhear that she might know something of the dark arts or how to access areas better left alone. But this was for a good reason. Even so, she gave Amil a cold scowl to let him know she didn't like him announcing something like that in front of people she was just getting to know. "I only know of a portal that may or may not work anymore that leads to the first and second layer of the nine hells. Last I knew it used to require a book to activate."

"... A book? Like... this one?" Nang had any number of odd trinkets she had picked up over the years. Maddeningly, Nang's research had only turned up books about the subject. Actual knowledge of where to find the blasted portals across Kordathya was guarded more closely than a king's counting house. However, she still proved to be the key, as she had recently come into possession of a book specifically created to allow passage into the abyss.

"That would be the one!"

"Then it seems we shall be going to the Abyss," Amil announced.

"Actually, I don't think I'm going to like it there very much," Vic scowled.

"There is plenty to kill," Amil cajoled.

"I didn't say I wasn't going! I'll mow them all down!"

"Really not looking forward to the cold," Felicia muttered.

Back to Atil and further inland, they found another clearing that had been made and now housed more supplies. Some sort of entrance or portal stood at the ready. Their path led them down into the abyssal realms where siege equipment was being built. Tunnels and pathways ran everywhere. The first layer they arrived in was blisteringly hot. Flames leapt from magma on either side of the stone causeway that they crossed, as yet more creatures were slain with Amil's advance.

"It looks pretty unholy to me." Vic had nothing to base it on, but figured it sounded good.

"Around the corner." Amil warned quietly. People could be heard moving around.

"Do we talk first?" Nang wondered at the same time Vic asked, "Should I take them out? Suppose we give them a chance to talk, right? Hey! Hey! Can one of you come here! I need some help moving this stuff!"

"I'll get the dwarves," one of their priestesses said in a very annoyed tone.

"Oh, no! Not them!" Vic groaned.

"I don't like how they have siege equipment."

"Yeah," Vic stepped around Felicia, checking things out. "I don't like them. Oh neat." He looked in the barrel of a cannon, then in curiosity went around to the fuse.

"Don't touch that," Nang warned as, of all people, Amil noted its aim in the direction they would need, and struck a flint against the fuse. A boom resounded through the chamber, dampening Amil's hearing as he waved a hand to clear the smoke.

"I hope they didn't hear that... but they probably did." Vic threw his hands up to show he was well away from the explosion. "I didn't touch anything!"

"NO, I DIDN'T SEE ANYTHING," Amil answered. Hindsight told him that might have been a bad idea. He had heard of cannons and the ease in which they worked; he hadn't thought about the extreme noise problem.

"Oh heh, he went deaf..." Vic couldn't help a laugh that cut short as more arrows flew in their direction.

"STOP SHOOTING ...Damn..." Amil ran into another fray.

Felicia called on her elemental to help dispatch the women in dark clothing that swarmed around Amil with knives. He continued speaking louder than necessary even after their death. "Okay," Felicia had had enough of it. "I won't have you yelling anymore." A muttered spell cleared his hearing, leaving Amil rubbing his ears.

"Look," Nang motioned ahead. "A bridge."

"Two more," Amil indicated women ahead.

"Take them out!" one of the women demanded, seeing them at the same moment.

"Get over here, wench," Nang demanded at the same time Amil ordered, "Drop your weapons and surrender."

"Not an option!" They both drew their daggers.

"Want me to cripple her?" Nang asked quietly.

Vic, of all people, found another way. "We're confused. Can you answer some questions? We're lost here."

One of the women gave them an assessing but wary look. "You're new recruits?" Many came with the confusion of the newly "converted" when they hadn't adjusted to the fact that their minds now belonged to the empire. Some needed a few extra sessions of hypnosis… or torture… to convince them.

"Yes," Nang quickly bluffed. "All hail the queen."

"Right!" Vic followed. "I love the queen!"

Both became jumpy. One hissed, "Don't say that! You'll be called to serve her directly!"

"Sorry," Amil apologized, "he's really new."

"Defilers, priestess or mechanic?" one of them asked, trying to determine their earnestness.

Vic nudged Amil, whispering in just about a normal tone of voice. "Put me down for the defiler."

"Ah, mechanical here." Nang partially raised her hand.

The lead priestess before them eyed Vic. "You might be able to handle the dwarves. The priestesses are the hardest. We get lucky to get the right kind only rarely."

"Why is that?" Amil tried not to get defensive, fought his instincts to cross his arms and look more imposing. It paid off.

"They need to be god-touched first." The priestess was overly delighted, clasping her hands together before herself before continuing. "Our newest positively reeks of the gods!"

"I'm sure she does," Nang offered. She could care less about the inner workings of this organization. "Look, we're trying to find the infested bridge," Nang attempted to bluff. "Our… supervisor told us to go there next." It wasn't her best job. She could only hope it had sounded convincing enough.

"He's always saying stuff!" Vic sighed overly-dramatically.

"He really doesn't say enough of the right stuff though."

Her nose went up, her mouth turned down in disapproval. "Who doesn't?"

"That supervisor guy... what's his face..."

"Jeff," Nang said in irritation. "Jef-f."

"I don't know any jefifah" the robed woman said in a tone that was part disdain and part dismissal.

"Thought it was Fred," Amil muttered.

"That's a stupid name," Vic muttered in regard to the woman's interpretation.

Nang gave both men a look warning them to shut up. "No, our supervisor is Jeff. Pronounced Heff."

"Pfff!" Vic fought a laugh. "Really?"

The joy the woman had just displayed as she mentioned some god-touched person disappeared as she sobered, really looking at them now as she realized they didn't know where they were. "You've been crossing it."

"Oh," Nang looked around, "so the abyssal plane is the infested bridge."

Pointing off to her side at a bridge, the woman dryly stated, "No, that's a bridge." Her tone had become much colder.

The group continued playing stupid, engaging in dialogue about who told them to come here and what the name might be, much as they had done when first calling someone up out of the hole in Amil's yard. Unfortunately, this woman was much smarter.

"Man..." Amil tried to act dumber than he was, "I am sooo gonna get yelled at for not remembering his name..."

"If you listened closer, you'd know these things." Nang nodded, trying to act like she assumed these women would... just a little too much disdain to her voice, as if she might be in charge of the situation. "Anyway, we'll be going over to the infested bridge now for further training."

Extremely annoyed now, the woman was frowning. Something didn't sit right with the priestess. True ire and annoyance laced her posture and voice. "I don't know how you got in here, but I think its time you were removed." She motioned to someone out of sight in the room behind her.

As she turned, Nang mouthed to Amil, "Want me to shank her?" getting a nod from Amil to go ahead.

"Dwarves!" Felicia warned as Nang took out the priestess.

"Again?" Vic eyed the oversized, over-muscled abominations as they readied themselves at the doorway, but found the large creatures to have trouble with their shoulders fitting through to attack them. "Can they fit through that door?" Vic asked, pushing in between them to be at the front of their group. "See! I don't think they can fit! Blehjhhh..." he made faces at them, angering them further. "Heehee," he giggled in glee. It only angered them, forcing them to push through the doorframe, cracking and busting the mortar that might have otherwise held them in.

"Ah!" He jumped back as they started turning sideways, ducking through the entryway.

"Can't fit, eh?" Amil asked.

"Vicarious..." Nang gave Vic a dirty look, a warning in her voice as she lay in with her dagger and rapier to the creatures, "Keep your ideas to yourself next time!"

"They didn't look like they should fit!" he shouted back, bouncing around with his swinging scythe. "Damn, these things are fast!" Three had been felled, but four more had surrounded Vic. "Bugger!"

"Get out of there, Vic!" Amil hollered, firing lightning arrows from the rear.

"You know," Vic whirled, ducking, trying to keep from letting them hit him. "I'd love to. Find me an opening!"

"The one with the sword," Nang drove her dagger into the lower back of one opposite from Amil. "Strike him!"

"They've all got swords!"

Felicia sighed in frustration. "Ashes, go." Her elemental appeared in a swoosh of flame, rushing to the fight. At the same time, she cast a singe spell that would leave further damage every two minutes the creatures remained alive.

As the last of them fell away, Vic put his hands on his hips, breathing hard and glaring at Nang. "The one with the sword?" He was not humored. "Daft woman."

Chapter Eighteen
Teamwork

It was on yet another bridge that they discovered they had found the infested bridge and that the Queen's minions had taken yet more from Atil. Gaunt, hollow-eyed men seemed pulled about as though they were marionettes. Forced to attack, they tried to pull back, failing. Amil's group had no choice but to go on the defensive. One held himself at a distance, jerking against unseen strings, fighting whatever was forcing him to come closer, yet he begged for death. "Please Amil, for the love of Atil, end this for me. They won't release us."

"Hey," Vic said cheerfully, "This one knows you!"

Amil did know the man. He was one of the good folk from the village on the far side of Atil. They were simple men and women, living off what they could coax from the land. They didn't deserve this. "Do you know where your captors are? Why are they doing this to you?"

The bound man shook his head with a crunchy bone-on-bone sound. "The Priestesses of Suffering. They make us pay for trying to protect our women. They've taken our women, killed men, taken some of us to live like this. Save our village. They talk about the one they took from the big house on Atil; your home. Is that…?"

"Anne," he nodded. "They are the ones that took her…" Priestesses of Suffering were behind this. And they admitted to having Anne. It destroyed something in Amil to see villagers from his island in this plight.

"She's with the queen. I don't know where. Please; don't let me suffer anymore."

"I swear I will avenge you. If I have to trudge through their legions, I will release you all."

The Priestesses of Suffering had taken the men, women and children from the island and turned the men into undead creatures under the control of the empire. One of them retained enough of their past self to beg Amil to slay him, so he could pass on into a more peaceful life. "You're a good man. Save our women. Set us free." He opened arms, letting them get a good aim at him.

"So… he wants us to hack him to pieces?" Vic asked in

shock. They were supposed to do in the bad guys, not the villagers. But when whatever was controlling the man went back into play, they had little choice.

It took more work than they had counted on, but the man finally went over the side of the bridge into the lava roiling below them. "Thank you…" he sobbed as he burned away into cinders.

Amil sighed. "May Firnos welcome you home," he offered in parting to the man. He had been a simple farmer. Amil had purchased goods from him in the past. He didn't deserve this kind of ending, but Amil had to content himself with the knowledge that the man had at least given a better idea on where to find Anne.

"There must be more of those priestesses here," Nang glanced around. "Let's get moving."

"Or," Felicia added, "they may have moved on to a lower level of the abyss?"

Amil nodded. "There's more to the abyss than a few rooms and passages." He motioned the others to fall in and follow him. He had no idea where he was going, but listened for any movement that might give him a clue as they walked along.

The lava rivers bubbled, the heat making all but Felicia wipe their brows. The stone was too hot to touch, yet the floor remained amazingly and impossibly cool. The fires cast a reddish glow over the area, leaving passages beyond the first turns in darkness.

Nang crept around, checking various nooks and crannies. Too many hidey-holes and corners for her liking. "There must be more of those priestesses here."

"It was harder than it looked." Vic looked down into the lava pit. "Considering he wanted to die." He frowned, turning away. "How 'bout that way?" He motioned to the path Amil was looking down.

"Dead end." Amil shook his head. "Umm what?" he asked when Vic made a snorting noise.

"Maybe are they free yet?" Vic asked. "Or do we need to kill more priests?"

"That is, if they didn't progress to the second level." Felicia frowned.

"Can't say," Amil muttered. "Nothing has really happened in this abyssal place."

"Aww." Vic sounded disappointed.

"Sorry Vic," Amil smirked. "You have to kill some more. It's a rough job, but someone has to do it." He looked down the different paths. "Left or right?"

"Wait." Vic dug in his bag, pulling and holding up a scroll with a grin. "Something to cast light." He looked at his options, eyeing Amil's bow or Nang's rapier. The thought crossed his mind to light his scythe, but it might just have outshone his own amazing awesomeness. Instead he moved quickly, casting light on the rear end of their pretty little Nang.

She gave him a murderous look, but before she could give him some ascorbic comment, she spotted something large moving down one of the near passages. "Three o'clock," she pointed with her rapier. "I thought I saw something."

"That way," Vic pointed down the other direction, seeing other trouble, then shrugged. "Or that one then," he pointed the way the girls were looking.

"Demon," Felicia said as they fell in back to back, only then realizing that the light was attracting the creatures. "Balor," she clarified, then looked where Vic was pointing. "Demons both ways then." Felicia called her elemental to her side.

A balor, two demons, and four halflings, despite outnumbering the heroes, were soon dispatched. The short men were the first down. Vic harried them with the scythe, taking no few marks from behind by the demons, while Nang worked the opposite side. Felicia fired spell after spell at the demons, trying to keep them distracted. The soft thunk by Amil's bow sent discharged arrows flying overhead to the demons that towered over their party.

"Trouble!" Nang announced, racing onto the forward-most path to take on the four running from that direction. "Halflings at twelve o'clock."

"Demons at nine," Amil added.

Several of the vicious little men spilled out around the demons that thundered in the paths. "For the queen!" was called more than once as they charged at the party. Either they were zealots or they had been brainwashed to be so single-minded in their attacks.

Amil took up his place in the rear, bow rapidly firing into the mix of large and small while Felicia sent a spark of fire into the nearest demon to set her elemental on it. Its claws of fire slashed at the creature, distracting it long enough for Nang to rush in behind. Hitting her knees, Nang slid under the reach of the monstrous creature, her dagger slicing through the tendons on the back of its ankles. She rolled, pulling her rapier as she came up, skewering one of the halflings. Vic's scythe spun underhanded, catching the demon as it toppled down, biting deep into the neck.

"Nang!" Amil called. "Duck!"

Without a thought, she followed the order by grabbing the arm of one of the short ones, pulling him off balance and to the floor with her as a volley of arrows shot past where her head had been.

"Hold that," Vic gave one of his bottles of alcohol to the fire elemental, keeping an eye on it as it heated, starting to bubble, the glass melting. "Throw it!" He pointed towards the back of the enemy.

Felicia followed the line of sight, mentally urging her Bound companion to do so. Ashes let fly with the super heated bottle which broke on impact. Amil set an arrow aflame, releasing it to land at the same time. Heated alcohol and open flame ignited, setting the two demons to the rear on fire.

Pleased with the result, Vic wished he had time to drink a toast to it. Instead, he spun, the tails of his coat flaring below as the scythe whirled high above. At its height, he shifted his grip, sliding a hand to a better position on the snath. The weapon gained momentum on the arc down, coming up with the scythe's toe facing upwards, implanting deep into the demon's chest. Not losing any balance, Vic's raised foot came down in a hard slam, his weight shifting quickly to the front, then back to the planted foot behind as he pulled, the weapon ripping free in a bloody spray that left the creature's chest open. The wooden end, already aimed slightly down, landed in the skull of one of the halflings. "Two in one!" he cheered himself.

Dancing around the arrows flying from Amil, Nang nimbly made her way amongst the few remaining, rapier to the chest, dagger to the neck. A spell uttered from Felicia set the one approaching her on fire. A last spin and strike landed Vic's scythe in a dwarf, toppling its still twitching body to the ground.

And then it was quiet. They looked to each other, breathing hard in the scent of scorching flesh, giving each other slight nods of approval to the way they worked together. Vic pulled yet another bottle, taking a long pull on it before tucking it away and kicking clumps of meat off the scythe around the body it was lodged in.

"Um... okay... Let me just..." He put a foot up on the beast, trying to duck the swinging claws while he pulled on his scythe and pushed with his foot. "You're not helping here," he admonished the demon.

"Like he cares," Nang shot back at him, wanting to be angry at him, but too impressed with both his moves and his nonchalance about the whole thing.

Vic had the temerity to wink at her with a broad grin. He knew she was mooning over him – which was fully expected, considering the levels of amazing that made him up. Didn't mean he intended to act on it though. There were forces in his life he didn't really care to share with the others, like the fact that he was in truth next in line to rule his family's lands. Or that he might actually care a little bit for the feisty little elf.

She opened her mouth to make some remark, but Vic cut her off. Purposely looking at his scythe as if it were a lover, he took a tone to match. "You only make me more amazing."

It's not that he wanted to hurt Nang, he considered as she prepared to rage at him again. It was more that he wanted to discourage her. He liked women. But there was something about her that bothered him. Maybe it was that she could be more to him. Bah. Better he just not return her wartime flirtations. He purposely kissed the tang.

Fists clenched, she glared at him. "You... self-absorbed..."

"Focus." Amil's tone brooked no further disagreement as he sited, letting another arrow go to land in the eye of Vic's troublemaker. "Only demons one way now."

"Fireball!" Felicia warned with just enough time for the others to turn away and shield themselves from the primary blast right behind the demons as she cast it.

The creatures roared and howled. They dealt with fire in their environment and could handle the heat. But even they didn't walk about in the flames. It was enough to have the explosion right behind them burn into their thick leathery hides, continuing to burn deep into their tissues.

Vic struck deep, driving his weapon into the beast. It started to go down, turning as it did so. "Oh hells!" Vic jerked hard, not about to let it snap the haft. "Your fat ugly hide isn't keeping this! It's mine!" He had just enough force to keep it from falling away from him, instead buckling to its knees. There was just enough time to rip the blade from its body before it crashed backwards.

"Besides," he negligently brushed loose hair from his face with a shake of the head and flip of his hand before posing with a playboy grin, scythe firmly planted at his side and one foot resting victoriously on the body, "you just made me look even more amazing."

Nang stared at him for a long moment before rolling her eyes. "You are such an idiot." She turned to follow Felicia who was walking with the Book of the Abyss open to a sketchy map. The path took them in a fairly straight line, wavering only as much as a road might rather than in the maze some of the other paths had been. Whatever Nang had expected to find, an actual door was not it.

"This leads to the floor below." Felicia tapped the door lightly with her staff.

"Whattabout this one?" Vic asked about a second door right next to it.

"Back to the material plane, our plane."

"Oh good! We have a way out!"

Amil gave Vic a look that said it wouldn't be happening. "We have to go this way. Make sure they haven't gone any further." He tried the door, surprised to find it unlocked with no traps.

Chapter Nineteen
One Good Deed

The shock in the change of temperature was immediate as they stepped through. From the dark red glow in extreme heat, still sweat-slicked, they walked into a vast white landscape of eternal ice and snow. Felicia braced herself as they passed from heat into cold, quickly slipping off an amulet and trading it for one that burned as bright as fire. She was ill at ease with the plane, shivering at the intense cold. Nang was also bothered by the abrupt change, likening it to being back in the realm of the dead. Nang shivered. "Aaalmost as bad as R-r-romx."

"Awwwww... it's c-cold! And it was so warm before." Vic added.

The crack and groan of ice shifting around them echoed in the crisp bite of the air. Thundering steps formed into ice giants lumbering towards them with monstrous clubs. Amil wasn't going to have it. He had a path to follow and they were in his way.

He fired arrows one after another, imbuing fire into each. When they closed on their range, he let loose a shout of frustration, tossing the bow aside and drawing daggers. Following his lead, Vic and Nang issued their own challenges, following Amil into battle. Felicia held back, knowing her spells would be most useful now, but trying in vain to counter the effect of the cold on her elementally charged form. "S-stu...pid... giant." She stuttered. Her anger finally fueled enough to fire a few moderately powered flames into the two creatures.

"Heh, not immune to my blades, are you?" Nang mocked, easily striking small blows over and over.

"Whooo! Victory!" Vic gave a victory arm pump as the beasts finally fell.

Through yet more of the empire's minions and native ice creatures they fought, following a trail of clothing they found strewn about. In quiet sadness, Amil started picking them up.

"That's weird." Vic picked up a lacy bodice. "I'm pretty sure those things were a few sizes too big for this."

"What is it?" Nang asked.

"Looks like something I wouldn't mind seeing on a girl with

me." Vic held up the embroidered silk for them to see. "My awesome factor would definitely go up."

"My wife Oceania..." Amil said quietly. "These were hers. They went through my storage." His wife had been dead for many many years. He had never been able to part with the items, but had safely packed them away. The heartless usurpers had violated the last boundary with Amil.

Nang shouldn't have been surprised to find that if he had children, he had likely been married, but he was so taciturn about everything that she was amazed to think there had been another like Anne that could see past his moods. She was even more surprised to discover he had kept all of that woman's things, and that they were now scattered across the landscape. "What would those be doing down here?" Nang snatched it away from Vic, giving him a look to behave.

"I have no idea." Amil fell silent as he picked up each item with the utmost care. Each box of her belongings had been magically protected. Anne had known about the boxes, and had treated them with the same respect she did any of his belongings. These foreigners had disrupted his home, upset his life, taken Anne... and now they'd taken his memories.

Oceania had been part Siren. He wasn't sure where, or if, they were welcomed to a home by the gods. It was believed that Sirens didn't have a soul. That meant that unlike Juniper, Oceania's belongings and the music she had created were the only thing left of her. "She died almost a hundred and fifty years ago now..." he finally said quietly.

Felicia had known the woman once, when they had both been young. Her voice had been the stuff of legends, men captivated by the dulcet tones, but Oceania had only had eyes for one: the ranger that now sought to protect her memory.

"They just threw her clothes around..." Seeing this blatant disregard was almost harder than having faced his daughters. This was like they had gone straight into his thoughts, all he remembered of Oce, and said none of it was worth a tarnished copper.

Nang respectfully started picking things up and folding them as well. The boxes were nowhere in sight, leaving them with no option but to simply stack everything in an orderly pile. Vic surprised them when, after watching quietly, he started carefully picking up the folded piles and gently setting them in his magic bag with the same care he would give any bottle of booze he carried.

As annoying as the pompous vidu could be, Nang actually felt a moment of softness for the idiot. Rather than dwell on that, she left him to do his good deed without drawing attention to it (he'd just think it made him a more amazing person if she did), and turned to Amil. "Then they made it this far?"

"They must have taken it from the house. So, yes. They must have come this far as well."

Teeth chattering, Nang stood a little closer to the natural heat Felicia was giving off. "I guess we go on then."

Every so often they would come across another article of clothing or what remained of a box of clothing. No one said anything at that point about it anymore. They quietly picked up, and just as quietly handed them to Vic. Nang had to reassess his self-importance yet again when she handed a slightly larger pile of velvet skirts to him.

There had to be a limit to what he could put in that single bag and it seemed to have hit its limit. Vic frowned, looking into the bag, then to Nang's stack of clothing. He glanced around her to Amil, who was single-mindedly focused on finding every last garment. He looked back at Nang, giving a lop-sided smile.

She could see the pain in his eyes. He understood this situation and was being respectful enough for once not to make fun.

What he didn't say was that he *did* understand. It was one of the many reasons he never wanted to be in a relationship. Most importantly was because he couldn't stand the idea of anyone looking better than him, but almost on the same level was the very real fear of having to face a pain of loss like Amil obviously had.

Man to man, *that* he understood. And to have had a love like that was rare indeed. Despite knowing that Amil now loved Anne, this was part of his history and obviously his first and greatest love.

It pained him to do it, but he sorted through his own things in the bag, pulling out several bottles of the cheapest wine that he carried. His eyes barely met Nang's before he looked away, almost ashamed to be caught doing such a good deed, and set the bottles behind a snowy rock.

When he silently put his hands out to accept them, Nang handed them over in stunned silence. As much as he probably hoped otherwise, it didn't go unnoticed.

"Thank you," Amil clapped him on the shoulder, words quiet and choked with emotion. A tight smile, a nod, and another clap on the shoulder, and Amil moved off to lead them onward again.

Chapter Twenty
Cushy Rooms

Attacks from ice giants and ice demons came at regular intervals. Massive beasts of pale skin and hairy bodies, or leathery skin with ice at their call, both seemed to rise up from the snow itself, lumbering or flying into their paths.

"No-no, demon," Nang chastised every so gently before running it through, aided from the far side by Vic's own strike.

An arrow flew past Vic doing a little victory dance, causing another demon to roar as the point struck true in the beast's eye. "Pay attention," Amil said, but with less annoyance. Vicarious' action with Oceania's clothing had earned him a few marks with the ranger.

"Right way again," Nang picked up another delicate looking cloak. She noted the unhealthy bluish color taking over Felicia's normally fiery presence. The wizardess already had a thick cloak on, but still was obviously very out of her element. Rather than give the cloak to Vic, Nang hesitated only long enough to look at Amil first before settling it over Felicia's shoulders.

"Thank you," she chattered, pulling the elven fabric tighter around her shivering form. She let the others be her wind break as her core temperature continued to drop, leaving her stumbling and trudging behind them.

Amil led the vicious attack against several other beings that thought to block their way. With Vic at his side, the two men fought through what were rapidly becoming white-out conditions. There was no reason for the groups of creatures in this area to attack, especially when none could stand against the mighty party. Creatures fell while the two worked heedless of the cold. Amil's cloak whipped up and away from his body, driving the freezing air in around his leathers, making it stiffer and less pliable. Vic's coat tangled about his legs then blew away from him only to have the toe of his scythe catch in it. Swearing, they moved further from the girls.

With an arm around Felicia, her cloak now wrapped around both, Nang was more focused on keeping the woman from falling over. Even with three cloaks and body heat, the wizardess was still fading fast. She looked up into snow that had started swirling in howling winds. "Where's Amil and Vicarious?"

And then... a portal. A pale blue light pulsed around it, but couldn't be seen until they were almost on top of it. "Th..th..this is n..new." Felicia's words shivered and stuttered as badly as her body did.

Random articles of clothing had continued to show up in this direction, although they were fewer as the blowing snow covered the path. "T-t-trail of c-c-clothing... L-l-lead h-h-here." Nang tried to spot the men again. Taking a deep breath, she coughed as the cold hit her lungs. She put an arm up over her face, trying again before shouting, "AMIL! PORTAL!"

The men barely heard her over the wind, but immediately turned and sprinted back through the growing drifts towards Nang's continued calls.

"Does it work?" Vic asked as they caught sight of the glowing object. He kept attempting to straighten his hair back into order, despite the wind's icy fingers twisting it into impossible knots. "We need to get out of this wind."

She had read something about this kind of portal before. But she was getting tired and her mind just wouldn't bring that memory entirely to the surface. "It's going t-to hurt t-to use," Felicia got out around lips going numb, "but anywhere's got to be warmer than here."

"Any idea where it goes?" Nang eyed it suspiciously. She didn't really want to deal with any extra pain if it wasn't necessary.

Seeing the bad shape Felicia was falling to, Amil agreed with the wizardess. "Well, I guess we find out if we can go through it." He dusted as much of the snow off his clothing as best he could and reached to touch it, intending to see if he could step through it. "Ahh!" He jumped back as it sparked out towards him. Pain shot through his leg, the knee almost giving out. Sparks and lightning flared outward, wrapping around and grabbing him.

"You have to pay for passage." Felicia pushed away from Nang to go stand before the portal while Vic tried in vain to slash at the ethereal bonds Amil struggled with. "I've done stupider things so..." Almost stumbling herself, Felicia tried to call some measure of magic to her hand. "Just a small fire..." she grumbled.

Nang came up beside her, linking arms with her as she pulled flint and tinder. It took both of them huddled over it to get the barest flicker. It was enough for the portal to flare towards them, wrapping around them in electric shocks and pulling them in, taking them from the depths of an icy hell to the hall of a luxuriously opulent home.

"Oh thank the gods there is no snow!" Felicia exclaimed. They beat the snow off each other, stomping it away from their feet.

From the other side, Amil saw the girls disappear into the sparks after giving an offering of fire. "Find an offering!" He shouted at Vic as he pulled one of his magical arrows. The powers reached for it, pulling at him. He used the momentum to add to his own run at the energy, adding a jump at the last second.

"Any clue where we are?" Felicia was already feeling better, her body temperature starting to go back up.

"Not a one. At least it's warm and there's no immediate threat." Their conversation came to a halt as Amil dove into view, snow blowing in behind him. Nang watched the blasted woodsman get to his feet while a strange pang of concern for the idiot vidu touched her. Shadow and hells, she was actually worried about him! "Is Vicarious comi...?"

At that moment he calmly walked through, running his fingers through his hair, casually shaking the strands back into perfection. "Had to give up a perfectly good bottle of scotch." He walked past Nang, taking in her wind-blown hair and frostbitten cheeks. "Eesh," he pulled back slightly as if she were infectious, making a face. "Clean yourself up; you look horrible." Not giving her time to comment, he looked around at the well appointed, rich furnishings noting that opulence reigned. "Where is this?" No time was wasted before he started opening drawers, chests and cabinets. "Not so bad except there's no booze." Giving up, he turned back to the others. "So is this the plane of cushy rooms?"

Chapter Twenty-One
Come Back

"I'm not sure where we are now." Amil shook the last of the snow from his woolen cloak.

Embarrassed that Vic's comments had bothered her, Nang fussed with straightening her own clothes and hair out as she added, "I don't know either."

The ranger went back through the entry hall the portal had moved them into, trying the door. "We're locked in."

"Let's make a sweep of the house then." Nang quit fussing, pulling her weapons out instead.

Several doors opened into bedrooms or sitting rooms, all with trouble. Fights ensued, Felicia's magic aiding as effectively now as Amil's bow. More men and the proclaimed Defilers filled the hallways. A final bedroom opened onto a great many of the Priestesses chanting... and a woman on the bed.

"At least twenty," Amil said as he peered around the doorframe. He had a terrible feeling it was Anne, resting in death. His throat closed on the panic that caused. He didn't want to have failed her this way. "Go get 'em, Vic."

He made a joyful noise, making Nang laugh, as he rushed in. Amil was right on his heels, the two women right behind.

The chanting of the women stopped as the party attacked.

"Ha ha!" Vic exulted, bouncing around in graceful sweeping forms, cutting the women down quicker than they could defend themselves. Amil went in close with his daggers while Felicia stayed back.

Nang rocked her neck, rolled her shoulders. "Payback time..." She lowered a shoulder and plowed into the nearest woman. The point of her rapier pierced the woman's breast as she hit the ground.

The slaughter of the dark robed priestesses continued. Each one seemed intent on protecting the female form hidden under a veil on the bed. Only after the last of the vile women had been cut down were they able to truly take in the sight.

There were no decorations in the room but for a single

cabinet and the massive bed that rested in the center of the room with no headboard or footboard. Only the barest rise and fall of the woman's chest let them know whoever it was to be still alive. The veil covered the body but for the feet – one bare and one wearing a battered red shoe. Beneath the body, scattered across the king-sized bed, was an assortment of naked steel. Blades and daggers of all sorts had been laid carefully with the woman centered in all of it.

Vic busily wiped gore from his chest and weapon, looking at the bed. "That looks dangerous."

"Strange thing to see," Nang agreed.

Amil carefully approached the bed. Anne loved her red slippers. He started to lift the veil starting at her feet. He glanced back at the others when he realized there was nothing on the woman's bruised and battered legs. If it were Anne, she would have been wearing her gi.

He smoothed the veil back over the legs and braced himself as he moved around to the far side where the woman's head was. Seeing the soft brown hair tumbling over the side of the bed from beneath the veil, he carefully reached for the end, pulling it back only to uncover the visage of the stubborn and lovable woman he had fallen in love with. "Anne!" he cried out in horror. She was bruised, pale, and very near to death.

"Double hooray!" Vic came closer. "Is she okay?"

He took care in not uncovering her body to the others, but inspected her for other injuries. Had she been well at all, she would have giggled in ticklishness, smiled as she tried to be still... but there was no movement. He frowned, worry lines creasing his face as he found a deep gash in her side. "Not at all..."

"...Oh." Vic, unsure what to say, backed up and pulled his bottle.

Amil leaned closer, listening for her breathing. It wasn't perfect, a slight hitch on each intake, her face contorting with the pain it must have caused to the bloody wound just under her ribs. He pushed his hood back, leaning to touch his forehead to hers. "I'm so sorry, Anne," he whispered.

Continuing to check the hallway, Nang worried that they just might be in this queen's home. With the number of attacks they had already encountered, she fully expected more. This Anne wasn't looking well, was obviously comatose, and they still needed to find the queen. She debated telling Amil this, but changed her mind when she turned back to him.

Eyes never leaving Anne's face, he set the bow off to the foot-end of the bed, heedless of the sharp slide of steel against steel as the bow pushed weapons around. He adjusted his shin guards to be sure they were properly in place. With all the care and grace he had learned in the long years he had spent in the woods, he made his way onto the bed, crawling across the daggers and blades. Leaning over her, he carefully worked his right arm across her body and under her left side, rolling her slightly towards himself. "I'm sorry," he kept whispering. "I'm so sorry."

With her shoulders lifted just far enough off the bed, he slipped his left arm under her neck. Her head rolled back limply as he scooted closer on his knees. The tiniest whimper escaped her when he had to bounce her a little, adjusting his hold on her. Trying to keep the veil about her, he put his right arm under her knees, lifting her into his embrace.

Other than the brief moments she had hung on him after one of her pounced hugs, he had never held her weight in his arms. At just over five feet, she was only slightly smaller than Amil, but she was so light, so fragile seeming; not at all the strong personality he had become accustomed to.

In slow, steady movements he worked his way from the left to the right side of the bed. Trying to slide forward as slow as possible, not wanting to jostle her, Anne's petite form became heavier as the pain in his knees seared through his legs. He damned the age that continued to take small things like this from him. He damned himself for not having saved Anne before this.

"Vicarious, help him out," Nang ordered when she saw the strain.

He had already seen it, and was moving forward as she said it, meeting Amil at the edge of the bed. A look passed between them; Amil not wanting to relinquish what he saw as his responsibility and Vic not willing to let the ranger's stubbornness rule. Vic gave a slight nod, indicating they would work together on it. He wouldn't deny the man his dignity in this. Facing Amil, Vic made it look as if he were only putting his arms near the place Amil had his own beneath the girl. In truth, he braced his arms directly below the ranger's, clasping the elf's elbows. Without making it obvious to anyone else, he had just managed to take half the girl's weight.

When he went to step off the bed, Amil's knee tried to buckle, drawing a hiss and a wince from him. Vic was right there, not letting anyone else see the weakness. He held Amil's arms steady below the girl.

"Lay her down carefully," Amil said when the pain passed, nodding his thanks to the vidu for his discretion. Together they set her on the floor, Vic then backing up a few steps while Amil went to his knees again to look over her wounds. "I'm sure she will be needing a healer...." Her breathing settled into something more normal, with no hitch in it as soon as she was away from the bed. Even her color seemed a little better now that she was on the floor.

"I could probably bind that for now," Nang offered.

"I'm actually a pretty good field medic!" Vic had earned plenty of experience in his time serving with the Arms Masters Guild in Lareah, as well as his time in the forces back in the mountains.

Nang gave him a disbelieving look. "Ah... no. I think I'll take a look at it."

"What?" Only then did he realize they must think he was only a stunningly handsome man with little actual skill. "Well, okay."

Felicia hovered nearby while Amil and Nang looked over the cuts and bruises on the girl. "...and I.. am useless in this situation. Hmm..." Not wanting to waste time, she went to the cabinet, opening small doors and drawers.

"Let me know if you find anything to drink in there," Vic directed at her.

"Only things here are a pair of bracers, some gold coins and two keys."

"Hang it all," he swore.

"The keys might get us out of here." Amil mentioned over his shoulder. "Vic, I need some of those clothes."

"Anything?" Vic rummaged around in his bag.

"Anything." He had told Anne once that he had Oce's memories. Her clothes would never bring her back, and they could be used for bandages right now. And clothing for his Anne.

Yet he hesitated when Vic let a silk dress spill into Amil's hands. The image came unbidden to his mind of the day she had sung in this performance gown. The rich burgundy had only enhanced her red hair, her beauty second only to her voice. He had known that day that he loved her with everything in him.

He cleared his throat and purposely ripped the fabric into long strips. This dress... was not going to bring her back. He had never thought to love again, that anyone would want a jaded old elf. But Anne had won her way into his heart with her sunshine and smiles. He wasn't going to let her die on him now. He had failed Oceania and little Marie. He hadn't been there for Anne; he had assumed she could see to herself, just as she'd sworn. He should have known better. Carefully looking over her head for bumps or bruises, he then set to work on the other wounds. The gash in her side had quit bleeding, allowing him to wipe away the wet blood and bind that as well.

"Well, the wound at her side is clotted fine." Nang sat back on her heels. "I don't know why she isn't awake."

Felicia considered if it might be something magical, noting the marks on Anne's body. She looked to the bed, back to the girl. "Might want to put those weapons away," she said at long last. There was something about the blades that was aggravating the situation. "Vic, come help me." The two of them loosened the sheet and carefully folded it up around the blades.

Watching them, something niggled at the back of Amil's mind. He had taught Anne how to use a bow shortly after meeting her. He smiled, remembering what a terrible shot she had been. "The great chair hunter" she had called herself. He had made her the promise that if she could learn to hit the battered wooden chair he used for a target, she could be a mascot for his rangers.

He had loved the excuse to be close to her, much as he had used the same ploy so many years ago for Oceania. But where Oce had smelled of the sea, Anne smelled of fresh sunshine. He had a feeling that both women had continued to be bad shots for the same reason he had loved showing them over and over again how to use the bow.

Then came the day Anne had told him she had earned the right to be a certain kind of healer, that she had taken a vow. Seeing the shapes of the blades almost burned into her flesh now, it finally occurred to him what the true problem was. Anne was a healer-monk. She had told him some time ago that her father had been Gifted by the gods, and that that had transferred down into her birth.

He wasn't sure how that all worked with her, but the other

thing she had been really excited about had been taking up the mantle of something she called a Tzee Divine. *"That means,"* she had told him, *"that I can't touch weapons at the risk of losing my god-given gifts. My hands should only wield healing instruments, never steel weapons."*

"It's the weapons," Amil said, the full impact of the situation dawning on him. "They're keeping her unconscious." He hurriedly pulled the bandages away from the wound in her side. "Damn." The blood may have finally stopped, but from the inflamed skin around the wound, a blade may have been lodged within her side for some time.

Someone was going to pay for torturing Anne. That someone was going to be the queen they hunted. He looked around at the people that had committed to helping him in this endeavor.

High on a wall, Vic had found something he was tapping with the heel of his scythe. "Neat thing here."

"Vicarious, that's a mirror." Nang shook her head at his stupidity.

"Are you sure?" Vic peered into it, turning different ways as he gazed into it.

She rose, stretching before going to his side. "Yes," she said, standing on tiptoes to look into it.

"Okay. Explains why they had a less than amazing portrait of me." He proceeded to fluff and adjust his hair. "Perfect!"

Nang rolled her eyes. "Right. We should definitely get out of 'here'; wherever here is, of course."

Amil agreed as he carefully pulled one of Oce's dresses onto Anne. The veil covered her, but not well. And if he needed to carry her anywhere...

"You've done well this fight, my children." The voice of Maleiin came softly. "Ranger-mine, it is for you to find the truth you need to speak to save her. Until then, to safety with all of you."

In a blink, they found themselves once more in Amil's home. Anne lay positioned on the floor exactly as she had been at the other home.

"Back to Amil's," Nang said in confusion. "Which means, at least for now, this place is safe."

"How did we...?" the wizardess looked around, baffled.

"I'm confused." Vic didn't get it, but figured it was as good a place as any to empty the clothing all over the floor.

"I think that's your natural state, Vicarious." Nang couldn't help a smile, earning a frown from Vic.

"Then I join him this once in confusion in how we got here." Felicia held by her magic. She didn't stand much on the gods and wasn't sure what to make of this now.

"Leave it to the gods for bringing us here." Amil picked Anne up, gently laying her in his own bed. "None the less, we are here."

"But I thought we were gonna waste the queen."

"Apparently not yet," Amil answered Vic.

"And now we're back to square one," Nang put out there in some irritation, "unless Anne can give us some information when she comes to."

"You gonna leave her here?"

If he had it his way, Amil would never let her leave. He'd convince her to move into his home; it was big enough for a crowd of people to live in. She could have the guest room near the library. But first she had to recover. He nodded to Vic. "Hopefully she will wake soon. I think I may wait this time." There was no think. Amil wasn't going anywhere until Anne was well. And he intended to tell her how much she meant to him.

"I think that's a good plan." Nang nodded. "We'll see what we can find in the mean time."

"I was gonna say, it doesn't seem smart to leave her where they abducted her the first time." Flopping into a nearby chair, Vic made himself at home, propping his feet on the end of the bed. "I'll wait too then!"

"So thinking I never want to do that ever again," Felicia grumped. "Travel to the abyss, the frozen hells, and get lost in the frozen path."

"Time to mull a few things over, I think." Nang tweaked Vic's ear. "Let's go." Even if the idiot couldn't see it, Nang saw that Amil needed some time alone with the woman that obviously was so much more than a housekeeper to him.

"While you mull over things I am going to warm myself a bit more." Felicia followed them out the door.

Amil didn't hear them go. He had almost lost Anne before truly having her. He had done a disservice to her in having become engaged, but not saying anything. He should have let the world know how she mattered to him. And yet the woman had gone along with it, playing by the rules he unconsciously set.

He took her cool hand, pressing the back of it to his cheek. Things were going to change. He made that promise to himself and to the gods. If Firnos and Maleiin would just bring her back, he would be the kind of person Anne saw him as. He would love her… with no reservations.

***

Setting aside his cloak, Amil ran fingers through his hair and picked up a hairbrush. "Let's clean up a little," he said as he carefully moved to sit near Anne's head on the bed. He gently pulled her limp form upright, settling her in his lap so her head could rest against his shoulder. This had been a ritual every day for the last week.

"You have to wake up, Anne," he said conversationally. "I need to be able to go after the woman that hurt you. And I don't plan to leave until I know you're okay." The whole time, he drew the brush through her brown hair, carefully pulling the tangles out. Until this past week, he'd never noticed the red highlights that kept her hair from being a plain wood brown. "There we go." He had asked Vic to bring him red hair ribbons a few days ago, one of which he now tied her hair back with.

Next was using a basin of water at the bedside to wash her face and hands. Careful of both wounds and modesty, he then changed her gown and tucked her back into his bed. "Come back to me, Anne," he whispered, pressing a kiss to her cool brow.

Chapter Twenty-Two
Random Ruminations

All of them had been exhausted from their recent journey and had split up to find their own peace. Nang had returned to Lareah with mixed feelings in her heart. It bothered her that this queen had such free reign to move her minions about the planes and the world. While fidgeting with the pommel of her dagger, she mused that death would no longer be a stranger to the queen's empire.

She couldn't help but think of the home in Atil as a staging ground for the upcoming battles. In what was becoming routine for her in the next few weeks, Nang and Vicarious patrolled the lands around Amil's house in Atil. Despite what she thought of his drinking habit, he was a powerful warrior and more than capable of dealing with their various foes. It surprised her to realize that, despite him always acting the fool, she trusted the tall vidu at her back.

Finding nothing new, they returned to Lareah and went their separate ways again for the time being. He most likely to the lodge for a drink, and Nang to the raised meeting area at the center of town. Maybe someone had heard something new.

What she found was the city defender standing duty. With the helm on, she couldn't tell them apart, but he did have one difference not common to most in his profession. "By your staff," Nang indicated to him, "I would guess you're the defender that was with us before?"

Siril Te'lie nodded. "I am. Has the ranger found the woman he was looking for?"

"Three weeks past," she said with a slight inclination of her head. "She's probably still resting in Atil yet."

"Good." He gave a single nod. "I trust all is as it should be then?"

"It seems like she's in a coma, and we still haven't tracked down the queen yet... but the island seems like its safe for now."

"A coma...perhaps Chessi, the priestess could help her?"

"Maybe," Nang answered. "I'll tell Amil about the idea next time I see him. I just hope the next place we need to go to deal with the invaders is more temperate than the last two."

"Less than hospitable environments?"

"Two layers of the abyss; one like a flame blasted inferno and the other a wind-swept arctic tundra. Neither of my favorites."

"Hmm… and you tracked this 'queen' through both of those places…perhaps she is of a demonic origin…" he thought out loud as he pulled his helm off and tucked it under his arm.

"We've tracked her minions there," Nang answered his thoughts with a nod.

"Interesting," Siril said thoughtfully. It wasn't usual to go into the abyss, but it wasn't unheard of either. The holy order of Truth's Light had many such cases recorded in their files. But for a foreign queen to move so easily across not only the lands, but the other layers of existence spoke of added layers of danger. Demons perhaps? Wizards of evil intent? "One would think that if her minions are in a dwelling like that, then it would make sense that she herself has some sort of tie or allegiance to such a residence."

"They didn't seem to be from there… they were definitely using it as a training place."

"…Memories fade…" a young elf added. "Minds go blank… people change…"

Siril studied the figure for a minute. He seemed a little on the malnourished side, a little too pale, even for an elf, to be considered healthy. The black leather armor he wore was very lightweight and extremely worn. Siril could only guess that either the strange man was a traveler… or from the slums. Either way, he was odd.

"Rain," Nang looked up in annoyance. "At least this isn't freezing or hotter than everything."

"It's still annoying though," Siril answered her over his shoulder.

A young woman standing under a tree put an arm up, using her shield to block the rain, listening to the group under the patter of raindrops.

" …in the very shadows of time…. I stand still."

"A poet," Nang said in a snarky tone. "How different."

Pale skin under dark hair with equally dark clothes and eyes, the young man studied them all carefully. He finally settled on Defender Siril who stood completely motionless, returning the study. "Is there something I can help you with?" The vidu asked, trying to keep from looking too authoritative in his uniform.

"No." The rain quit and he laid a worn cloak over one of the benches, taking a seat. He didn't seem very interested in visiting.

"Very well, then." Siril turned back to the others. "So is anything known about this queen?"

"What queen would that be?" the young woman said, lowering her shield and flicking the water off it.

"Greedy for land, no matter what the cost," Nang said. "No name that I can recall hearing, no descriptions... she lives like royalty. At least I assume she does; we may have been in her home when we found Anne." She considered. "Not that we can be certain. We didn't see her; just crazy women that attacked on sight to keep us from Anne."

"I see..." Siril's brows came together.

"There was a portal that led us there, then we were teleported away by a goddess." Nang shrugged.

"By a goddess?" Siril couldn't quite believe that. The gods weren't known to make appearances for just anything, especially for something like helping people leave a house.

Nang nodded. "Maleiin."

"...Tell me," the young elf in black said in the same strange far-away voice. "what flies when it's born, lies when it's alive and runs when it's dead? Anyone? A... guess...?"

"No idea, stranger," Siril finally answered after a long pause.

"A snowflake..." A small smile touched his lips. Several commented on how clever it was. "Then... onto the next riddle. I'm lighter than a feather, yet no man can hold me for long... what am I?"

"Breath," Siril offered.

"Sand," the woman under the tree said.

He nodded. "Breath. Have you heard that one before?" When Siril shook his head he added, "Good. Your mind is strong indeed."

"I have been told that before," Siril told him, wondering at the odd behavior, "it is my greatest asset." Noting the man's features in case it would need to be reported later, he turned to Nang again. "I would hear anything you know that may be of help on your case. Any detail, no matter how small could be the key to why this is happening, and more importantly how to stop it."

"You were there when we went to Romx." Nang thought back on the time that had passed. "That was only the second trip with Amil. The first one led to tunnels below Atil. I know for a fact that they have priestesses, assassins, arcane magi... maybe rogue druids with them. They seem to know how to affect creatures with alchemical potions to bulk them up."

"Sounds like this woman has assembled quite an army." Siril considered the facts, wondering how Atil had become so insular that none of this had really affected the mainland yet.

Nang nodded. "I'd guess the four of us have slaughtered at least a legion's worth of troops. They've stolen souls from Romx..." She paused to think about it. "Kidnapped people and turned them into undead servants... no summoning of demons or devils yet."

"Perhaps a priest or a few members of Truth's Light should be brought in, just in case things get really ugly." Siril had worked with the holy warriors on more than one occasion. They could be a little single minded, but their intent was for the greater good. "Or maybe a few of the bruisers from that mercenary village east of our town? For pure brute strength?"

"I thought I saw some of your fellows going out there," Nang nodded agreement as the woman under the tree wandered off.

"General Amraphel sent a few men."

"...oh, what are you talking about?" The frail looking elf turned his dreamy look to the conversation.

"Strange man," Nang whispered to Siril.

"Indeed," Siril whispered back with a slight inclination of his head. "Obviously unhinged mentally."

She returned the nod. "He's weird, to say the least." She raised her voice to a normal tone again. "I think that brings you up to speed."

"I'm hungry," the elf said out of the blue.

Siril looked over at him. "Simon serves a fine meal at the lodge."

" ...that made me think of another riddle..." he said. " "I'm not that big on riddles." Nang was a little too dry and sarcastic, but couldn't quite help herself. Nang was not going to play at these silly riddles all day. "You should certainly get something to eat if you're hungry, though."

"Guess so..." He seemed almost at a loss. He didn't look in the direction of the lodge, or any of the market stalls. With a somewhat blank look about him, he wandered off. "...I will be back..."

Siril adjusted his cloak and shrugged his shoulders to settle his armor. "If you will excuse me," Siril said when they had both watched the young one go, "I should make my rounds."

"Of course. Safe journey." Where Siril went west in the direction of the food courts, Nang took the opposite path to see if she could find any of the others. A quick check of the lodge didn't find Vic, but he was on the plateau when she returned. "Have you seen Amil lately?" she asked as she approached him.

He waved drunkenly, his arm loose. "Er... no. He's probably still at hish house takin' care of the lady."

"How much have you had to drink?" She crossed her arms, frowning in disapproval.

"A lil... lil... bit."

"...he drank a lot... from a bottle..." The strange young man was back and thought he'd add to the conversation.

"That," Nang said dryly, "doesn't surprise me. He seems to have a pretty high threshold."

Shaking his red locks back from his face, the vidu tipped another bottle back, almost missing his mouth. "Mehhh. I fight better win... when 'm drunk 'nyhow."

Giving him the most disapproving look she could manage, she added a frown. "I'm hoping you can sober up, if need be."

"Pfft, I kin shober anytime I want." He took another deep drink.

"I'm sure you can." Nang reached up and took the bottle from him.

"Right." He pulled another bottle from his magical bag. "Sho, that Amil never said nothin' ta me... Not to you either then?"

She shook her head. "Nothing yet."

"We could... we could... We could visit 'im!"

Before Nang could agree, the young elf interrupted. "Who the hells is Amil?"

Vic eyed the kid, squinting slightly. "Who in the hells 'er *you*?" He took another swig letting the youngster know he didn't really care.

"He's the Elder of the High Council of Rangers," she answered the elf while taking the newest bottle from Vic. "And probably one of the oldest elves in Lareah, if his story is right."

Another bottle found its way into Vic's hand as he looked to Nang. "Who'sh this guy?" he thumbed in the direction of the elf.

"Really?" She gave Vic a disapproving glare, pointedly looking at the bottle, before answering. "I don't know; only saw him for the first time earlier tonight."

"Mebbe he's one of them... them... empire folk...?"

"...I am part of no empire."

"Somehow," Nang looked over the rag-tag appearance of the young one, "I don't think so."

Vic glanced over him as well. "I shpose not..." Then, with the bottle almost to his lips, he pointed with the same hand holding the booze. "Hey! Hey I know you.... Yer that... yer that guy! The weird one." He had seen Anne talking to this guy before her kidnapping. He had been strange then.

The youngster let out a sigh as Nang smirked. "The weird one... that doesn't tell us much."

"Hee hee!" Vic pointed at him again. "He was all 'I'm no one' and 'No' and... he's creepy kind of! Shee-see?" He pointed vaguely in the direction of the elf.

"He speaks nonsense," the boy said with no humor.

"So were you earlier," Nang reminded him.

"Not nonsense." Vic shook his head. "I speak perf'cly good common... an... and.... other shtuff..." He nodded to punctuate the thought before downing another mouthful of the strong drink.

"Even if you would know my name, what would you do with it? I am no archivist, no history book... though some might remember me, but as I said before... memory fades, minds blank..."

"Pffffft!" Vic didn't appear to be talking to anyone in particular. "Heh." He drunkenly trudged over to a bench, dragging his scythe behind him, making a horrible chalk-board scraping sound across the cobbles that made Nang cringe. A loud hiccup punctuated his sitting down.

"Was that entirely necessary?" Nang gave him her most disapproving look.

"Whut...?" He grinned, perfectly aware how much he was annoying her.

"He's drunk..."

"I think that much is obvious." Nang spit out sarcastically.

"He can't even walk straight. What are you trying to get out of him?"

"Waiting to see reason."

"Do you have any artifacts of value, miss?" The young man changed topics, listing several items he desired, all of which would have served dark purposes.

Wary, Nang backed away some. "Why would you even want to ask for an object like that? If I came across anything like that, I'd destroy it." She narrowed her eyes at him, crossing her arms. "What did you say your name was?"

Nervous, the young man finally said, "Just Nyhm. No other name."

He seemed a little sad about that, but Nang had had enough. Between the "weird one" and Vic's drinking, she threw her hands up. She was frustrated that someone like Vicarious could be so intriguing but for that one fault. "I'm going to bed." Maybe things would be clearer in the morning.

Chapter Twenty-Three
Not an Alchemist

Feeling much better about things the next day, Nang made her way back out to Atil. She had looked around the docks, had made her way through Amil's home, and was just starting to check the area around the front. Anne had been quietly sleeping, and she hadn't wanted to ask where Amil was.

While she was nosing around, Vic appeared, whistling merrily – Nyhm at his side – and quite sober. "Hey! He inside?

"At least you sobered up for this." She glanced around. "Isn't Amil with you?"

"Guess not. Nope, I ain't seen him."

"The house was empty, but for Anne, and didn't show any signs of forced entry or other problems."

"You don't suppose," Vic said, "that he ditched us for another group?"

"And have to tell everyone the history so far? I can't imagine he'd want to deal with all of that all over again. Besides that, we work well together."

"Sure we do!" Vic said, "He must be out for some other reason..." He looked around, rocking on his heels. "So... You wanna play twenty questions? It's a game!" He added at her confused look. "We can play it while we wait for him!"

She sighed, pushing a stray bit of hair out of her eyes. "I know what it is. I thought you had something else in mind."

"Eh? What else would I have in mind?" At her blank look, he shrugged. "Alright then... wanna ask me a question?"

"I'm not really thinking about anything at the moment."

"... That's not how you play twenty questions."

She sighed and asked Nyhm why he had come along.

"No reason, really. I'm just following the other woman."

"What other woman?" Nang frowned, looking around in some concern. "And why would you decide to randomly follow someone?"

"Oh yeah." Vic had apparently not considered it. "Why?"

"Didn't she venture this way? I thought I'd find out who she is."

"He's creepy, right?" Vic grinned at Nang, jerking a thumb towards Nyhm, obviously pleased at being right in his initial assessment.

Nang was surprised he even remembered his earlier observation. "Are you," she demanded, "here as a spy for the Queen's Empire?"

He gave her a baffled look. "...I am part on no empire and I follow no queen. Unless the woman I follow happens to be a queen."

"So," Vic asked with a grin, "on the condition of her being a queen, you *are* a spy?"

"I guess I am, because spying is mostly what I do. So...yes."

Pitching her voice loudly enough for anyone nearby to hear, Nang called out for the hidden person to show themselves.

Felicia dropped her magic that had kept her invisible. "Just when I find a nice spot to sit, too."

"What were you gonna ask her?" Vic leaned towards Nyhm.

"Ask?" Nyhm questioned in surprise. "Why would I ask? That would reveal my position."

"You should hide then." Vic grinned. "See? She sees you now. And she isn't happy."

Nyhm frowned. "Are you afraid of me leaking vital information?"

"Vital information?" Felicia laughed. "Hah! I am too paranoid to reveal much of anything."

Nang was appreciative of the assistance both Vicarious and Felicia had given so far to Atil's plight, no matter their strange mannerisms, and hoped that the newcomer would shape up to be able to lend the same sort of aid. Either that, or he'd end up dead from stupidity.

Still considering that, Nang noticed a man eavesdropping on them from behind a tree. He wore the rich silks that matched the others planning to build factories. "I'm more worried about the guy that thinks he's hiding." She motioned with her chin in the direction of the trees across from them. "Maybe he'll be kind enough to step out from behind there." She intended to help him make that decision by pulling her rapier.

"I could smoke him out so to speak." Felicia grinned. "Well, more so burn him. Ashes," she called her fire elemental to her. "Want to go play with someone?"

But when they got to the spot they'd seen him, he appeared to be gone. "Where'd he go?" Nang asked, looking around quickly.

"I dunno," Vic offered while Nyhm looked around all perplexed, adding, "He was just in front of me."

"Everyone," Nang ordered, "spread out, but stay in sight of each other."

Vic shrugged, still trying to find the stranger behind trees. "Like he vanished or somethin'."

"Where'd the other guy go now? The one in black?" Nang meant Nyhm, who had also seemed to have disappeared.

"Right here." He emerged from the shadows.

Nang frowned at him. "I said stay in sight."

"Whoever we're lookin for is pretty sneaky," Vic put in. "Let's check the house. Wanna?"

Nyhm agreed to go with. Nang added, "Go in pairs and let us know if you see something. We'll search out here." She sighed. "I wish Amil was here."

"I don't like the fact one of them was hiding here," Felicia commented.

Nang nodded agreement. "Nothing to be done with just standing around." They carefully searched the nearby trees, around the house and moved out to the area with the outbuildings. "Stables look as empty as before."

"A lot of places one can hide here," Felicia said with a sigh.

Staying within shouting distance, the two women split up to cover more ground and search for any signs of activity. Quickly back together, Nang mentioned, "Trees, old buildings... Even the backside of a house... been used, but not lately. Anything on your side?"

"Crates and chests. A few tents. Nothing new."

"I wonder if the men found anything yet." With Felicia on her heels, Nang went in to find the boys. "Anything?"

"Nothing inside," Vic and Nyhm both said.

"Nothing at all?"

"Well, except for Anne," Vic shrugged. "She's still unconscious."

Rather than admit defeat, Nang suggested they return to the hole they had first went in so many weeks ago. It was in her estimation that you needed to return to the beginning to make headway... sometimes. "May as well check over there."

"I thought we were done with the hole business," Vic whined to Nang. "It's murder on my hair."

She gave him a look to not be stupid while Nyhm pointed ahead.

An overturned cart and a dead body lay near the hole. "A corpse?" Nang went over, kneeling to check the body. "Dead... and I don't remember seeing him before." Several arrows jutted from the man's back. "Hmm..." Nang looked around. "There was a horse pulling a cart."

Vic found the damaged wagon, but came back shaking his head. "Nothing."

"He must have had something."

Felicia agreed with Nang. "Could be anything depending on the person or race of said person. Dwarves value ale, for example." She shrugged.

Nang carefully rolled the body over. "Human. And his throat's been cut."

Vic wandered around, fishing out another bottle to drink while they talked.

"Something of value then," Nyhm added. "Gold?"

"Looks like it's been a couple days," Vic took a drink after noting the color of the man's skin and the dried blood around the wounds. "Those Amil's arrows stuck in him?"

Nang wrinkled her nose. "Two days... No, not his." Nang looked them over. "These are poorly made; definitely not Amil's."

A noise made all of them wary. Vic closed his eyes, tuning his hearing for the direction, as Felicia prepared a spell and Nang readied her rapier. "Four... five of them, nine o'clock," Nang whispered.

"Yep," Vic whispered back. "It's what I thought."

"Perhaps kobolds or such..." Nyhm bent down to look for traps, then took up a handful of dirt and smelled it, looking to see what kind of being had done it. "Small feet; probably goblins or other lesser humanoids."

"There have been halflings with these people. And right now they're invisible," Nang explained. "They don't think they make noise. Ready for this?"

"Oi! You guys over there!" Vic shouted. "Surrender and we won't have to maim and or kill you!"

"He means it," Nang added as a warning. When they didn't respond, she glanced at the vidu on her left. "Vic, sick 'em." Then, as Nyhm struck the last one, Nang added too late, "Keep one alive!"

Without warning, the small people all tried to hide under a cloak of invisibility and Atil's heroes went to work, taking care of them with relative ease. Nang's request for "hold" went unheeded and all were cut low.

"I didn't do it." His mock guilt was totally ruined by his grin.

"This time." She gave him a sidelong glance.

"Hey! I didn't do it the other times either!"

"Who do they follow?" Nyhm checked a body for any emblems or badges. "There," he pointed to a symbol on the shoulder of one, showing a shield with a whip snapping in the center. "I'm not familiar with this symbol."

"That empire of course," Vic waved his hand dismissively, "and that's a goon symbol. I know!" he announced. "Let's raise one!"

"You might not like this..." Nang told the others before tugging an ankh necklace from beneath her armor, pressing it to the lips of the dead person and using necromantic energy. "I command your soul to return for questioning."

"Heh... hey, welcome back pal!" Vic squatted before the man who looked around, more than confused. "You're a scary zombie now! Ohhhh." He wiggled his fingers dramatically.

"He's not a zombie, Vic," She explained. "Just temporarily reanimated. We need answers," Nang demanded then of their prisoner. "By the covenant that I formed, you are required to answer any question we ask. Understand?"

The dead man nodded as Vic took another drink.

"Are you part of the empire trying to take over Atil?" Nang continued when he nodded agreement. "What is the name of your empire and your queen?"

He tried to speak, then pointed to this throat, which had been slit.

"Ohhh," Vic said in mock sadness. "That's bad luck. Not much you can do for that."

"Should I heal him?" Nyhm asked, unsure if he was even welcome to try.

Nang sighed. "You can't heal him; he's a corpse."

"Well then," Nyhm quietly asked, "can you write?"

With an offended look, the man nodded.

"Good." Vic took a drink as Nang demanded, "Write down the name of your empire and queen."

Nyhm lowered his rapiers, taking out a sheet of rice paper with the watermark of a restaurant, a quill and a small pot of ink. He handed the items to the man.

He wrote down two words: Sirenia and Oshiania.

"Did you kill that man?" When he shook his head no, Nang pressed, "Do you know who did? Did you see who took what that man had?"

With a guilty look, he nodded, pointing into the forest.

"Are they in the forest too? Do you know which way they went?"

Again there was a nod and he pointed into the forest.

"Hey, Amil!" Vic cheerily greeted the ranger as he joined them. "We caught this guy... and uh... those guys too, technically," he indicated the corpses.

"No direction?" Nang pushed. She looked over her shoulder to Amil. "Someone killed that man." She indicated the corpse by the wagon behind Felicia.

He had been trying to find out what had happened to the farmer now lying with the arrows in his back. He didn't like knowing that still more of the people that counted on him were dying. "And who is this man?" Amil nodded towards the one being interrogated.

"Someone that tried to jump us." Her voice showed how annoyed she was with the idea.

The dead man turned while they were distracted talking, and tried to shamble into the forest. He hit a tree, his helm spinning around backwards as he continued to pinball off trees. Nang sighed, catching the corpse by the shoulder. "You are released, spirit." Only after the body dropped to the ground again did she tuck the ankh back under her armor.

"Impressive," Nyhm said to her work, gaining a smile from Nang.

"Hey Amil," Vic nudged the ranger. "Wasn't yer wife named somethin' like Oceania?"

"Aye, she was."

"...beautiful name, if I may say it myself..." Nyhm said

almost to himself.

"I mean, that's a coincidence right?" Vic gave them a cheesy grin.

"Maybe." Nang didn't want to add to the idiot's ego.

"Oh right," Vic went on, "and their empire's name is Sirenia. We can finally call them stuff!"

"Assuming that's the right name, sure." Nang gave him a look, letting him know she wasn't going to let this go to his head.

"Huh..." Amil considered. He hadn't told this group about Oce's bloodline; only Anne. "Odd coincidence, as Oceania was part Siren..."

"Really?" Vic asked in surprise as Nyhm gave him a blank look.

"No lie." He didn't want to get any further into that right now. Best to focus on the problem at hand. "Obviously I think it's in the forest... for answers." He set off into the tree line, following a game trail that was barely used. After a short time, he looked around to see if he could spot anything broken or disturbed by passing people. It was hard to tell much of anything with the mist twisting amongst the trees. "See anything?" he asked Nyhm. The young man was definitely odd, but seemed to have a knack for astutely finding almost hidden tracks.

"No, unless my eyes deceive me." Nyhm finally felt like part of the group and wanted badly to prove he belonged with them.

"Does anyone feel like climbing a tree to get a better look?" Nang looked upwards.

"I can," Nyhm immediately offered.

"I don't tree climb," Vic said at the same time. "Yeah, let him do it..." He took another drink.

"But in this fog I don't think it would help so much, though I will give it a try..." He unstrapped his belt and threw it around the tree, climbing with it as a safety.

Vic hopped up on a nearby stump with his bottle while Felicia offered in her dry humor, "If you fall, I'll have the fire elemental catch you."

Scanning the area from above, Nyhm only spared her a thought on it. "...Very thoughtful, miss..."

Felicia had no reason to really trust him yet and enjoyed pushing him. "You're welcome. I'm sure you won't mind his warm fiery embrace!"

"Something moving... can't see though the trees..." Vicarious squinted out into the fog, "but I'm guessing we are going to have company..."

"Well then," Nyhm slid down, taking care with his grip, and restrapped his belt around himself as he reached the ground, "Carry on?" He motioned the direction he had seen from above.

"Hee hee..." Vic hopped off the stump as he spotted Siril coming down the path to join them. "Hey buddy!"

"Hello again," the other vidu in their group said on joining them. "Seems our work isn't yet done. I passed a human corpse a little way back; anyone know what that is about?

They quickly filled him in on the discussion they'd had and the strange circumstances surrounding it. While they did, they moved further into the forest, gaining only an "I see," from Siril on it.

"Weird things ahead," Vic warned.

Strange looking dwarven figures were around a small fire, rummaging through random packs of food, tossing away things they must have felt smelled or looked bad, while devouring what they thought was good. Amil frowned beneath his hood, thinking that these ... dwarves... were eating the delivery that should have made it to his home.

"I've seen those," Siril put in. "Not them exactly, but like them." He considered. They were short humanoid figures of stocky build. Not quite dwarves, but not halflings either. "Why would they be in the light? I've only ever seen deep dwarves in caverns far from the light..."

Vic grinned. "We're vidu, man." He saluted with a near-empty bottle, took the last drink and tossed the bottle aside. "They always like a fight." The vidu were nothing more than a version of elf. Some said they had always been dark. Some said it was to match their black hearts – a reference that they liked to fight. And for elves, they really were the best of the warriors, with blood just as red as any other elf.

"So Vic," Amil picked up the empty bottle, handing it back in an attempt to keep the forest natural, "You want a fight?"

"Always." He took the bottle, handing it to Nang. "Make yourself useful, huh?"

She frowned but took it from him. "Keep one alive."

He advanced, scythe at the ready. "Hey," he called out, "surrender and stuff!"

"Don't kill him!" Nyhm hollered at him as he cut down the last one. "...her." He corrected when he saw it was a really ugly woman that fell.

"Damn! They looked so harmless."

"This usually happens," Felicia said in disgust. "One says don't kill it and the rest do it anyways."

"Up in the ruins," Amil said and pointed up ahead after some time of walking again. Several of the massively muscled unnatural dwarves stood some kind of guard duty over things they couldn't quite make out yet.

"I'll go check," Nyhm volunteered and disappeared in a rustling of leaves.

"No need," Amil tried to cut him off. "I see them plain as day."

Nang rolled her eyes. "He's going to be paste."

"I have a spell that may be of use," Lieutenant Siril Te'lie offered, "but the subject has to be alive."

"Use on the dwarves?" Amil asked.

He nodded. "That is, if you wish to catch one. Otherwise, I have several that are useful in destroying them as well."

Nyhm reappeared in a rustling of leaves. "They don't seem to be guarding anything that I can lay eyes on."

They moved closer, all crouched low and creeping. Ancient ruins had been taken over by equipment that seemed to be aiding some sort of gruesome experiment – several alchemically altered dwarves ambled around and three cages held the remains of different races within. Nang gave Nyhm a disapproving look. "Rather strange looking stuff. How did you miss this?" It was hardly the nothing Nyhm seemed to think it was.

"Just those beefed up dwarves running about the forest is strange enough for me," Amil said. "Isn't always a good idea, and I wouldn't want them to be called for backup in battle."

"Felicia," Nang asked quietly, "when we deal with them, can you look into it?"

With her nod, the others started to creep forward. Four of the odd deep dwarves moved into their path. Battle ensued, hindered by the close quarters in the trees. Still winded, Nang groaned. "More deep dwarves! Eleven o'clock."

A few more of the beefy dwarves stood atop the ruins as they came into the small clearing. Not only were there cages, but hanging baskets near the tables of strange equipment housed skeletons of various creatures (most of which were dwarves) that hadn't survived whatever tests had been done on. But first was the need to eliminate the creatures that shouldn't have been created.

"Stand back," Nyhm called.

"Nyhm!" Nang hollered as a massive dwarf fist came at Nyhm's head. That was followed by calling "Amil!" as the ranger dove at Nyhm, rolling as they both hit the ground, bumping into Felicia.

"Keep one alive!" Nang called, again too late.

"Screw it," Amil said in disgust as the second one went down in a shower of magic.

"Again," Vic felt it necessary to add, "I didn't do it. But for future reference," he looked at Nyhm, "let's not have all of them run into me. I had my hands full with the drugged dwarves."

"Whoever used magic to move me," Felicia warned in high irritation, "do it again and I will kill you."

"Calm yourself," the Defender pacified. "I simply needed a clean line for my magic."

"Alright, Felicia," Amil motioned her towards the supplies. "Should be everything on the surface," he indicated the dead bodies. "You can look through the stuff."

Felicia studied a box of mechanical paraphernalia beside one of the tables. Only a moment of looking over the various bottles, flasks and fluids was enough to anger her. Amil watched as she started kicking around and shattering supplies and a strange tank at one end. She utterly destroyed the apparatus that had been used to create the misshapen creatures. "I can't let that exist," she said much too calmly for the amount of anger she had thrown into the destruction.

On top of the ruins, Siril and Nang found manacles worked into the stone – a clear indication that the dwarves were being changed against their will. "These look waaaay to small to be for those monstrous dwarves." Nang knelt beside them. "Unless..."

Siril nodded. "Much too small."

"Unless," Felicia looked up at their perch. It looked way too much like a sacrificial altar for her tastes. "Unless they were being created here."

"Considering the track record of these Sirenians," Nang asked, "what if the dwarves were being altered against their will?" She glanced at Nyhm, who had sat down to check a tear in his clothing. Letting her gaze drift out into the trees and over the rocks, she looked to see if she could find signs of people living nearby. "What are the odds that this is the extant of them in the woods?"

The Defender agreed. "We're most likely somewhere close to a deep dwarf encampment."

"The equipment was alchemical in nature with the exception of the mechanical equipment which was a part of it. So it's apparent they might have either extensive knowledge into alchemy, or the possibility of the combination of mechanical and alchemical combinations."

Amil looked at Felicia. "So the dwarves are part mechanical?"

She shrugged. "I'm a wizard, not an alchemist."

Chapter Twenty-Four
Two Queens

As the group deliberated where to go next, a human gentleman approached them. "Hello the ruins!"

"Seems we have company." Siril rose from his search on the manacles, pulling his tunic back into order.

"On behalf of Queen Lutheria," the man formally announced, "and her nation of Sirenia, I welcome you to Siren-two." He bowed with a fancy flourish of his hand.

"... Siren Two?" Amil asked as Nang quietly nocked an arrow.

"Can't very well have two Sirenia's now, can we?"

"But you just said you do." Vic grinned at the stranger.

"Last I checked we are on Atil. Not Siren Two." Amil crossed his arms.

The stranger eyed each of them, running a thumb and finger over his long mustache. "That is being changed. Are you going to be joining our forces then?"

"Vic," Amil leaned his head in the tall vidu's direction, "should we join their forces?"

"Does it pay well?" He grinned, taking a swig of his booze. "I like being paid."

"I'd say it depends on the benefits," Felicia added dryly.

"If we play this right," Nang whispered to Siril, "we can get to their commanding officers." She disliked this guy instantly because of his pompous and smarmy attitude.

"Well, of course you'll be paid! All our ... employees receive just rewards." When Amil asked for examples of such awards, the man added, "Enhancements. Upgrades."

"Ohhh," Vic shook a finger at the man, "you mean like those big dwarves."

"Of course! You know, our finest accomplishment was giving a spider an extra eye," he bragged.

Nang narrowed her eyes. "Don't they already have several eyes?"

"Indeed. And we found room for one more."

Nyhm couldn't quite believe what he was hearing. "...they mechanically enhance your body..."

"Now," Siril stroked his chin, "had you given it legs....that would be something to brag about."

"Ahh," Felicia interjected, "but do you know anything on the theory and practice of combining machine and magic or alchemy?"

The man really studied the wizardess. "We do not add mechanical parts to anyone. Alchemy, yes. Do you, my lady, know the mystery of adding machine to man?"

"No," she answered abruptly. "Just to magic."

"The queen would enjoy speaking to you." He nodded as if to reinforce that idea.

"We get to meet a queen?" Vic was practically giddy at the idea, forgetting for a short time that the queen was their nemesis. "I always wanted to meet a queen!"

"I've spoken to a king..." Nyhm was off in his own thoughts again. "Oh wait... two kings."

Felicia gave them both looks of disdain before looking back to the newcomer. "It should be interesting to meet her then."

"And you," the man wiggled his long handlebar mustache as he looked to Amil. "Your home..." He made a kiss to his fingertips, opening his fingers up then. "Divine. As is the female. She'll make a fine addition."

Nang narrowed her eyes, carefully easing a dagger out. "Can I just stab him now?" she whispered to Siril.

"Well is there some way we could possibly speak to someone higher up then you?" Amil purposely ignored the comments about Anne and his home. He knew Anne was safe in his home; he had just checked on her before joining his group. "After all, you seem to be more of a scout or someone of that stature."

"I am hardly a scout," the man spit out, more than insulted.

"Who are you then?" Siril demanded. "What is your rank?"

"I," he puffed his chest out, wiggling the long mustache again, "am head of the takeover of Atil and I am queen's consort."

"Oh," Amil said dryly. "Like a jester."

It set Vic off in a fit of giggles. The man, on the other hand, was now highly offended. He made a tsk noise, then seemed to drop straight through the ground, disappearing.

"Heyyyy," Vic said with a flick of his head, shaking his well-quaffed hair from his eyes. "I wanted to meet the queen."

Siril smiled at the idiocy that lent humor to the frustrating situation they were in. "I'm sure we will soon enough."

Amil stepped on the spot the man had been standing on. "Guess they didn't want us to join their cause." He kicked some of the leaves about, jumping on the ground. Solid.

"Maybe he was wearing some sort of artifact," Nyhm offered, "making him able to do what we can't."

"Or it's magic." Felicia pushed through them, giving Amil a look to get out of the way. A concentrated burst of fire propelled from her hands, hammering into the spot. With the sound of tumbling rock and dirt, a hole opened up. "Like that." She stepped back, adjusting her gloves as Nang peeked down into the inky darkness below.

Vic's brows went up, corners of his mouth turned down as he nodded, letting the others know he was impressed by the action. "Wanna go down there then?"

"What do you say, Amil?" Nang asked from her cautious perch above the hole.

"Well... Suppose we go down and end up finding more of those dwarves and deep dwarves coming down on us from above."

"So let's continue," Nyhm motioned onward with one hand. "Take the lead."

Amil agreed with a nod. "Maybe a quick sweep to make sure nothing will get us right away when we are down there." At his direction, they all ranged out a little, searching the forest as they moved.

"Hold," Nang said after they had walked for a short time.

Nyhm had knelt to inspect the ground. "Small feet up ahead. And a few large. Not animal."

Slightly narrowing one eye, Nang looked to the others in question. "Are we dealing with two groups?"

"I'll look ahead." Siril cast invisibility on himself and crept in turn in both directions Nyhm had noted the footprints. A few men with close fitting clothing and staves with crystals atop them stood off to the right in quiet discussion with each other. Mages.

The other direction held a party of halflings twice his group's number. "All have blades," he warned the others just before the little men burst from the trees and attacked.

"Weren't you silent, Defender?" Nang angrily hollered as she countered a blade.

Siril spared her a dark look. "I used invisibility, not silence."

Spinning to the side to avoid a magical spark, Amil then had to duck the burst of flame coming from Felicia's hand. "Focus! You two can fight later."

"We're having fun fighting now!" Vic cheered as his scythe cut low, striking yet another.

"Mages!" Nyhm called as the ones Siril had warned them of came at the sounds of battle.

Both Siril and Felicia called "Silence!" as they directed their spells at two of the four mages.

The other two Sirenian casters sent wind and water, hitting the group with an icy spray. "For Queen Lutheria!" one shouted. It was the only spell they got off before the two were silenced by the wizards. There was no stopping them, though. They wielded their staves as expertly as any weapon, charging the group and attacking.

The last of the little men cried, "For Queen Oshiania!" and charged at Amil from the rear. The ranger's blade reversed at the sound, pushing back behind himself. The point hit home in the other man's throat. Gurgling as Amil withdrew the blade, he collapsed to the ground bleeding his life out.

Three of the mages went down. Nyhm spotted the fourth, a halfling, standing back and charged him.

"Nyhm!" Nang shouted. "Hold your blade or I swear I will put mine down your throat if you can't control your blood lust."

With a slight skid, Nyhm came to a stop at the side of the mage.

"Nang, would you please interrogate our friend here?"

Flipping her dagger out, Nang grinned at Amil. "I would love to. One of your friends told me that you work for Queen Oceania."

Nyhm drove the tip of his blade into the ground, moving to tie the man's hands behind his back as Siril lifted the spell of silence.

"Oshiania. Yes." He sidestepped Nyhm's attempts to get his wrists.

"And now we know of Queen Lutheria. Are they both in control of the same land?"

"That wouldn't work well, would it?" he sniffed, offering the question a little too smug for the group.

"Then who," Amil demanded, "is Queen Lutheria and who is Queen Oshiania?"

After a long drink, Vic offered, "Maybe they wanna make one queen of this place while the other rules the other place."

"I've never heard that Lutheran name. Queen Oshiania is the most beautificous woman," the mage said in an adoring tone. "Sings like an angel and has curves that don't stop..."

"Curves that don't stop you say..." Vic said thoughtfully, running a hand through his red hair and giving his head a little flip to make his amazingly perfect hair more amazing.

"Vic," Amil couldn't help a small smile. "Brain above your shoulders, not below." It gained chuckles from the others and a long suffering sigh from Vic before Amil turned back to the questioning. "And she wants Atil as part of her empire? Do you work with magi that can turn dwarves into deformed giant-like creatures?"

"Not me," he said too quickly. "No sir. I'm magic through and through," he answered when Nang asked if he knew any that did. "Told if I do good here though, I'll get promoted! I'll be learning that there alchemy then!"

Amil frowned. "You never answered why the queen wants Atil."

"To take over Lareah, then Kron'tir, then um...those other places... She says the volcano here will do just fine to start with."

Felicia laughed. She had served as an official in Kron'tir. It was a city of darkness and too often of evil. She knew how hard it could be to overthrow people that could be darker and more threatening than anything coming at them.

"To start with?" Siril asked, catching that tacked on.

A sudden thought occurred to Nang; that perhaps these other people they had been fighting hadn't been born into the empire. Maybe they had been taken in through other conquests. Their prisoner confirmed this with a nod. "We get to join and learn stuff or, you know... die."

Further pressing him about who the queen was didn't help much either. "I don't know this Lutheria," he shrugged. "But there's this guy... he's kind of a problem."

"Yeah," Nang asked sarcastically, "a ranger?"

He gave another shrug. "I guess so. We're supposed to keep an eye out for him, in case he comes after some girl."

A moment of panic made Vic look to the others, Amil in particular. They all knew which girl. Maybe word just hadn't reached the outlying Sirenians that the girl had already been saved. Unless she had been taken again. Vic couldn't be sure, but offered, "I'm pretty sure Anne was still at the house..."

"Someone bind this person's arms and feet please," Nang ordered. "Just in case."

He had been trying; Nyhm gave her a withering look until she finally held the man still so he could tie the small man's wrists back. The dark haired elf asked if the queen was of human bloodlines. When he was answered with a lascivious grin and a comment of "man, I'll tell you, she's not halfling, but… hey!" Nyhm tied off the rope extra tight, not liking the intent.

"I don't care for your view of women." Nang broke the pinky finger on the man's left hand, gaining a scream from him. She knew what she was doing and knew the permanent damage she had just caused. "Now you'd better focus," she added with a cool smile.

"That'll cause trouble with some of my spell casting!"

Siril watched in a detached, objective manner as Felicia added in a tone to match, "Don't forget to keep the wound localized."

Nang nodded to the wizardess before giving the man an icy, toothy smile. "I know," she informed the others before giving her attention to the man again. "Where's your queen... and if not here, where is your top commanding officers?"

"She's not here! They're everywhere! Moving around! I just do magic, man!"

"Where is your commanding officer? Think fast, it might cost you another finger if I don't like the answer."

"In the grove!"

"Which grove?" Nang demanded. "In this forest?" She had to push for every nod the man gave her, letting her know it was past some overturned carts sitting northeast of their current position.

Vic started wandering in the general direction of the carts. "That's northwest, Vic," Amil said with a grin under his hood.

"Oh right. I knew that!" and he wandered off in the right direction.

"And the caves below the ruins?" Nang asked. "What's down there?"

"Vidu," he gave the two in the group a dark look. "Dwarves."

"How many? Are they part of your army?"

"I don't know. Not yet. They just tunneled that deep the other day. Sir Roger needs to convince them to join us."

"Enough time wasted," Amil ordered in irritation. "Seems we have to find the commanding officer and this Sir Roger…" He considered a moment, and then waved his hand dismissively. "Dispose of the halfling in a fitting fashion."

Felicia grinned. "Cooked or ashes?"

Nyhm barely muttered, "Just kill it," before the wizardess reduced the little man to cinders.

Ahead they could make out the sounds of movement in an old grove. The area was set in a shallow depression and framed by ancient oaks. Within were robed figures moving about while intoning dark chants. Making haste, Amil lead the charge. Cages, cells and other signs of enslavement profaned the quiet grove in the middle of the forest. "Halt or die!" he ordered as his daggers flashed amidst the magic flying from the necromancers.

"That's for you, mortal!" One of the women let loose her magic in the direction of Amil and Nyhm. Both rolled out of the way, the heel of one of Nyhm's boots getting scorched in the process.

"Okay," Amil rolled to his feet, drawing his bow as he found moderate cover behind a tree. "Let's try halt or be completely obliterated to the point not even the god you worship will find a finger bone of yours for praise."

"Fine." The last one went still, tucking long boney fingers into her sleeves. "I've halted."

Tending to the cages had been a group of dread necromancers that Felicia recognized instantly by their garb – that of the Cult of Cadav.

Chapter Twenty-Five
Memories of Blue

"I know their group first hand," Felicia said quietly. This group had followed the path of the dead, raising and using bodies as they wished. "We had an understanding until they resurrected something evil." She raised her voice to the woman hiding a weapon in her sleeves, adding command to her tone. "The mace – drop it."

"The queen is quite convincing," the necromancer smirked, taunting them. "Lord Dorbourne and King Sigers will fall before her."

"Highly doubtful," Siril answered in a dry tone.

Tapping his foot, Vic impatiently kept busy with drinking while Nang interrogated their captive. They found that the woman meant Lutheria, but did indeed know of Oshiania. They were from the same empire, but when Nang asked if they were the same person, the mage smirked. "I am Oshiania. There are two lands. And two classes of people."

Something wasn't right with the statement to Amil's mind, but he couldn't quite put his finger on it. "So... two lands united to conquer Kordathya as their own?"

"Wait... two different classes of people..." Nang narrowed her eyes as the woman smirked again. "How much of your land is undead?"

Siril had had enough. "You're a lying sack of bull droppings." He looked to the others, his tone asking them to believe him. "This is no queen."

Felicia agreed. If the woman was part of the true Cult of Cadav, certain names would be known. "Where is Thommi?" No matter what this one's local group was, Thommi was of such a rank that he would have been known regardless.

"I don't know that name," she said in complete disinterest.

Vic smirked around his bottle as he took another drink. Even he knew that was the wrong answer to give the wizardess.

"Oh?" Felicia feigned interest, albeit dry. "Cadav's leader knew him... and I knew him quite well."

The woman looked down her haughty nose at Felicia. "I'm not from your lands."

Nyhm quietly spoke up. "You... still have a soul... yes?"

"If she does," Vic ignored the woman's snide answer of yes, "my scythe says she wants her." He pat the haft lovingly.

Nang's jaw dropped for a moment as she stared at Vic. He now said his weapon talked to him? He'd had too much to drink, obviously. She shook her head to clear it of that thought. "All I want is her head," she told him. "You can have the rest."

"Her soul would just go to the god of the dead and by chance," Felicia added, "may come back as undead."

"No," Nyhm agreed. "It won't." He worried too that the person may just be raised by the other members of her order.

"What were you doing here specifically?" Felicia demanded.

Amil stepped in closer to the wizardess, presenting a unified front. "And who are you?"

"Ruling," she smirked at Felicia. "And I told you: I'm Queen Oshiania."

"You are no queen," Siril said as Nang pushed her rapier harder against the woman's back. "That much is obvious. So, try again. Who are you?" he demanded.

"But I am. Of Siren-two." She turned to Amil, giving him a pointed look. "Isn't Oshiania a pretty name?" Her voice was full of sugar, trying to cover the maliciousness of her intent.

For a long moment, Amil merely watched her, a muscle ticking in his jaw. This wasn't just an attack against the lands. They were personally targeting him. This queen had researched him and his family, had taken his memories.

"Say the word," Siril spoke softly at Amil's side, his back to the woman.

"You mispronounced it," he finally said to the woman. His wife had pronounced it OSHenEEa. He purposely turned his back, walking away from the situation. "Kill her and let's be done with this nonsense."

"Fair enough." Nang plunged her steel into the woman's back, gaining only a small flinch and shudder before the body collapsed.

Seeing that Nang had the situation in hand, Siril calmly walked over to stand beside Amil. Neither was looking at anything in particular, just out and away. "Does that name hold special meaning?" Siril quietly asked at long last. He knew only of Amil's reputation; nothing about his personal life.

He glanced at Siril, then back out into the forest. It wasn't the trees he was seeing. It was that day well over a hundred years past; the one that had continued to haunt him ever since.

The morning sun was well above the horizon, Oceania walked quietly down the wagon road while her young daughter ran in front of her, skipping happily along enjoying the world around her without any cares. Oce carried a basket and was dressed in a simple blue dress; her daughter a white dress though she had a blue ribbon in her hair and a blue sash about her waist, tied in a small bow on her back.

"Well, look at this... seems we've stumbled upon two helpless girls lost in the forest," a rough male voice said with a chuckle. "Maybe we should bring them back home," another man said.

"Oh, I'll bring them home alright." Another man smirked stepping out from behind a tree and started walking towards the two, the little girl now hugging her mother tightly.

Having been out late the night before, dealing with bandits that had tried to take up residence in his forest, he now woke suddenly, the sun instantly glaring into his eyes and making him squint. He looked to the empty spot on the bed next to him. He was supposed to meet his wife and youngest daughter for a picnic today. "I slept in.... Damn... I'm going to be late!" He quickly dressed and hurried out of the door.

He made his way past small houses and stores to a simple dirt road that took him past the ripe grain fields and back into the forest. He followed it awhile until he came to an opening into a field dotted with a few trees here and there. It was a place he had long come for picnics with his family, ever since his oldest had been born. The clearing was halfway between the village nearest him and one on the far side of the island.

Something wasn't right... He looked across the clearing, noticing something lying where the path picked up again. A woman... in a blue dress. He started to jog, and soon broke into a sprint towards the figure.

He knelt, quickly turned her onto her back. He saw her... his love... lying in the middle of the road. She was still alive, though fading fast. Her cough brought blood to her mouth, spraying over the face he knew so well, her eyes looking at him in a plea of help.

He could do nothing but look back with his own pleading eyes. "No... NO. Don't die love... stay with me... god, please..." He was holding her close to his chest, rocking back and forth on his knees, his hand holding the wound which pierced her chest. "Don't leave me..." he whispered softly. She coughed trying to speak but only more blood flowed and bubbled slightly before he felt her body go limp in his arms, he carefully ran his fingers across her face, softly closing her eyelids, heedless of the blood on her beautiful face. He continued to hold her in the middle of the road rocking her softly, trying to control the shaking consuming his body. His heart felt as if it froze in its beating.

"Hm hm hm... Well looks like the hero's late." He started to turn to his left just as a sharp pain sliced across the right side of his face. He let his wife's body slide to the ground as he instinctively rolled up to his feet, one hand over the bloody gash on his face, the other on his own blade. He felt warmth flow down and into his eye as his good eye took in a man in simple clothing, wielding a short sword. Starting to run at Amil, the man thrust his blade towards the ranger's chest. A quick step to the side allowed the blade to pass between his arm and his chest. His own blade parried as he pivoted back, quickly twisting the man's grip on his sword, allowing the weight and momentum to break the murderer's hold on the blade and force him to the ground. Amil's longsword sliced the attacker's side before the man let go of his own blade, stumbling forward to fall face first into the graveled road.

"He fights better than the girl; maybe he'll give us a run for his gold." Another man said in humor as he stepped out into the open from the tall grass that surrounded them.

And then another. "Oh she was a fun little thing to play with; a real fun thing to play with." The newly arrived man grinned from ear to ear.

They were trying to goad him now. "You bastard..." He stood looking at the two men, their third slowly getting up from his fall, still trying to catch his breath while blood dripped from the wounds Amil had inflicted. The ranger took his sword by the blade, heedless of the sharp pain lancing into his hand, and threw it towards one of them.

Reaching up, the man grabbed futilely at the blade, now lodged in his throat, before collapsing to the ground. The second drew a small dagger and started to run towards him.

He started running as well giving the man a sharp kick to the kidneys, knocking the wind out of him, before running past. He quickly snatched the sword back up yanking it out of the fallen man's neck and thrusting it forward, stabbing the man in the stomach. The man dropped his dagger, pulling the sword out with a shout of pain before doubling over; hand on the gushing wound as he fell sideways to the ground.

"That's enough!" a shout from behind made him sharply look back, it was the man who had been on the ground. He had a dagger resting at Marie's neck. Her blue sash was used to silence her and her hands where tied behind her back with her hair ribbon.

"I'll slit her throat, elf; I swear to the gods. Give me your gold and get out of here... and I'll think about sending her back in one piece." The man growled at him. "You're more of a pain than anything. Drop the gold"

He looked at the man and then the little girl. Her eyes watered; he could see she was terrified. "Alright... Take it easy..." He pulled out a small bag and slowly knelt down placing it on the ground in front of him. This was a situation he had been in hundreds of times before. Never with his own child, but he had stayed the hands of others.

As he pushed the pouch forward, he reached with his other hand for the dagger near the dying man. The one holding his daughter started to relax just as Amil quickly stood and flicked the dagger to strike the man deep in the eye.

But instead of falling forward or to the side, the man fell backwards. The dagger still near the little girl's neck was sharp, cutting deep. A single spray of blood came from the sudden wound as she fell back with the man.

"NOO!" He ran to his child, too late to do anything but see her small lifeless body lying there... He placed his hands around her face, seeing tears that had not yet dried on cheeks now void of emotion. He began to weep tears that rolled off his face and dripped on hers; he bent down, kissing her on her forehead, he slowly removed the tie from her hands and the sash from her mouth before touching his own forehead to hers, trembling again as he wept.

But that wasn't something he really wanted to talk about. "We need to find Sir Roger before he barters with the dwarves and vidu." He efficiently set about a quick search of the woman's body, looking for any other odd devices.

Felicia checked for anything magical, finally kicking the body with disgust before showing them a small disc. "Transport token. We have a way out."

"So," Nang queried, "the commanders of the halflings were the necromancers?"

"Seems so." Amil was abrupt as he stood, glancing around. "The underground next, to find this Sir Roger."

"Perhaps a place to rest a bit first?" Siril offered. He understood Amil's hurry. But that had to be tempered with reason and tactics. He and the wizardess would be no good if they didn't get a chance to rest and study their spells.

Agreeing, Felicia used the token to transport them all to a place near the tree line on Amil's property.

"Maybe I should check the house..."

Amil nodded. "Good idea, Vic. Don't want Anne in danger again."

"Right! And not at all because I need more booze." He paused, realizing that came out aloud. "I mean, forget I said that. I meant about Anne."

Nang shook her head with a smile. He was such an idiot at times.

"Of course not," Amil gave him a tired smile. "I mean, there is a lot of wine and liquor in the pantry, but... you wouldn't want that."

"Not at all!" Vic agreed before sprinting off in the direction of the house, the others following at a more leisurely pace.

Chapter Twenty-Six
Sir Roger

A few days had passed again. Returning to the main hall of his home, Amil found the others gathered and deep in discussion. Their poses all spoke for their personalities, from the vidu Defender leaning against a wall to Nyhm sitting cross-legged on the floor. Only Vic was missing.

"This group's knowledge is where the problem is," Felicia finished talking about the necromancers as Amil came up.

"Time to stop this Sir Roger," Amil informed them, pulling his bow from its resting place near the door. "Ready to go underground?" He may not be able to conscientiously go after the queen while Anne was in this state, but by Firnos, he could take out those that added to the problem!

"Lead the way," Defender Siril said, standing straight.

"Right behind you!" Nyhm got up from his spot on the floor.

Felicia sighed, lacing her fingers together only long enough to settle her gloves more comfortably. "At least it's not frozen down there," she complained.

"Or blistering hot." Nang took her leg from over the arm of the chair and rose from her seat in one of the four throne-like chairs that graced the entry. "I like my temperate zones."

Despite the grousing, they were committed and easily followed Amil down into the tunnels once again. They had told that the deep elves and deep dwarves had been hesitant to accept Queen Lutheria's regency. Keeping that in the back of their minds, they stepped cautiously from the tunnels into the cavern system. Deeper and deeper, through twists and turns, the soil walls finally opened onto marble and stone ruins. The odd smell struck them first. They had expected musty, moldy air, but the scent of fear and unwashed bodies twisted in amongst that... and death. Nyhm worried that traps may have led to earlier accidents.

In agreement, Siril took point, moving slowly and carefully. His eyes should have been more suited to the dark, but it was Nang that shouted, "Behind you!" at the same time Nyhm called, "Ambush!"

A group of deep dwarves moved against them with their heavy hammers and pick axes. What they thought were only three fell beneath their skill, only to be replaced by another and another of the groups. Without Vic, their arms all grew heavy in the continual combat.

Nyhm cried out as a hammer slipped past his guard, landing heavily against his arm. Nang's blade came up underhanded, catching the dwarf near his armpit, taking away the force of the hammer. It was enough of a pause for Felicia to let loose a focused fire spell, finally dropping the last of their attackers.

"That," Amil said, breathing hard, "was painful."

"And possibly too strong for just the five of us," Siril added.

Felicia snorted. "We have six, if the need arises." Nyhm's slack-jawed expression of confusion made her impatiently roll her eyes. "Ashes. My elemental."

Amil had moved ahead across the odd chamber, footsteps echoing off the walls. He had stopped, barely visible to them, and called them over. A hand out stopped them from moving out over a ledge he had barely seen himself. Digging a copper out, Amil let it drop down into the dark. The time ticked on as they all leaned forward, listening for the faint "sploosh" that finally hit water far below.

"Great," Felicia groused. "Just great."

"This… looks daunting." A deep sigh escaped Nang as she put her hands on her hips. "Do we go back then?"

Amil was about to agree with that suggestion when Nyhm noticed movement across the distance. "Something over there." He nimbly made his way along a very narrow ledge he noted on their left side. A few pebbles dropped, sliding off and into the depths below.

Knowing they were about to be spotted now anyways, Siril cast light to help them all make their way across. What came into view were the dwarves that had begun to make up their nightmares.

"Oh, hell," Nang commented. "And no Vicarious."

Four of the beasts could be seen ambling about, still unaware of Nyhm moving ever closer. Yet he was steadily gaining on them. Siril and Felicia shared a look and a nod before each touching their respective genders, the defender to Amil and the wizardess to Nang.

With spells spoken in unison, they transported the group across, meeting Nyhm at the same moment the dwarves noticed them.

A quick battle ensued.

"Hold still, you misformed beast!" Nang shouted at the last of the four as it moved with more agility than its misproportioned body should have allowed. "We have a person that needs to be deadified now."

As the body finally fell, she took a deep breath, letting it out slowly as she looked around in the dim light of the mage spell. "Where's Sir Roger? Shouldn't those things have been protecting him?"

"...He must be down here." Nyhm moved about, keeping to what shadows he could find near walls and outside the light of the spell to see if they were missing anything. "Over there," he whispered, pointing deeper into the cavern. "There is a guy with a really ugly floppy hat on."

"Sounds like the man from before."

"Must be our Roger," Amil agreed with Nang.

Giving a thumbs up expression, Nyhm started moving forward. "Let's get him."

The faint light started to wink out. The time for secrecy and care was past anyways. "I've got this one," Felicia told Siril. She called her fire elemental to her, its light suddenly blazing the room into bright clarity.

A man with his back to the wall gave a polite clap, the fingers of his right hand to heel of the left hand. His expression was dry, bored, and at odds with the foppishly large hat perched on his head.

"Sir Roger." Amil approached him with care.

"Ah, got my name, did you?" He watched them with equal care. "You'll excuse my protecting my back."

Amil informed him that they had actually managed to get someone to stay long enough to give them details. Nang interrupted with "Called herself a queen." She held up a helmet. "But I'm afraid she lost her head."

"Aren't you the clever one?" Roger asked, not meaning it in the least.

"I can't be the pretty one," she answered in humor as she put the helm away again. "That's Amil's job."

"And now I say you will have to pay for your war crimes

against these lands and its people."

"War crimes?" he laughed at Amil.

"Aye." He backed up the seriousness of his words by crossing his arms and planting his feet solidly. "I'm not laughing."

" ...pay with your life, and soul..." Nyhm said in his far-away voice.

His smile faded. "Oh dear."

"Unless you have information that can pertain to our mission here. Then we may let you have a fair trial in a tribunal in the city of Lareah."

When the man asked which mission it would be, Nang was quite pleased to speak up. "To remove you from Atil and all lands we call home, of course." Circling to the man's left, she added, "Right after you tell us who your commander is."

"I answer to the queen. All others answer to me."

"You answer to him." Nyhm pointed at Amil. "Or you answer to my blades."

Striding forward, Amil's left hand flew out, twisting in the man's hair, pulling hard. "I ask the Firnos-bedamned questions. We could just execute you now if you prefer. Now tell use what you are doing down here."

Running his fingers nervously over one side of his mustache, twisting it into a fine point, his eyes darted over the group. "I hold this land for the queen. She is yet to come."

Considering the truth of the man's words, it didn't quite satisfy Siril's need for answers. They still needed to know where the queen was. "Where is she?"

"Travelling in state. On her way here." He continued to fidget with his mustache, lip to tip, endlessly twisting and turning it to a tighter point, claiming he didn't know when she would arrive.

"And for the love of the gods, quit playing with that thing on your face!" Siril demanded.

"Nyhm," Amil spoke in a calm he didn't feel as he strode away from the man, purposely showing his back to him. "Think he's lying?"

Nyhm looked at him with wide eyes, surprised to have been called on. Siril spoke before the younger man could. "He's not lying."

"The queen is everything," Roger said as if it was something memorized and oft quoted.

"...I believe he is under a charm spell or such," Nyhm finally said, "but not a simple one."

"I think he knows more about the queen's plans," Nang announced just before firing an arrow off at him, missing intentionally. "Next one hits something vital. Do you have battle plans, troop displacement, building plans?"

A tell-tale wetness spread down his pants. "Of course we do!"

"And you have access to them?" she pushed.

"I'm in charge of them, you silly twit!" he spit at Nang, pulling his sword.

"Siril, you wish to take him into custody?" Amil stood relaxed, but with crossed arms indicating his intent.

"I do," he nodded as he pulled a set of iron manacles from their spot on his belt. "I think you're coming with us. Maybe a few days in the defender stronghold will make you a little more helpful."

"Sir Roger, surrender your weapons." Amil had taken on a tone of order, acting within the full rights of the High Council of Rangers. "You are under arrest for war crimes against these united lands, planning alliances with enemies of all cities and towns in Kordathya."

"What!?"

"You heard me." His voice went from conversational to yelling, punctuating each word. "Y O U. A R E. U N D E R. ARREST!"

"Drop the sword." Siril readied a spell of immobilization just in case the man tried anything stupid. "Now." After only a small hesitation, the man complied. "Ranger, if you would be so kind... pick up his weapon."

Amil kept an arms distance away, carefully reaching his leg towards the blade. Nudging his boot under the blade near the cross guard, he kicked it up into the air, deftly catching it as Siril came around to clamp the manacles on tightly.

When Roger struggled against them, Nyhm, in his strangely dreamy voice tried to threaten him. "...I could rip your heart out of your ribcage and feed it to pigs..."

"You know what your problem is, weird guy?" Nang pushed Nyhm out of the way. "You aren't convincing."

"I gave you the weapon!" His voice rose to a higher octave

while he wiggled and thrashed. "Besides, how do you intend to get me out of here?"

Nang didn't like the snotty tone of righteousness in his voice. "Search him," she ordered Nyhm and Siril. "Strip him if you need to. He has to have some sort of magical device."

"I'll drag you out like a sack of moldy potatoes, if needs be." Siril started patting the man down on one side as Nyhm took the other.

"Well then," Nyhm pulled a smoky red stone out of a small pocket inside the man's shirt. "What have we here?"

"Probably something Amil should hang onto." Nang leaned a little closer to get a look. "And did your men attack an Atilian in a cart? About two days ago?"

"If he was going to report to that troublesome ranger, yes."

Nyhm clenched his fists. "Now can I knock him unconscious?"

"He had something," Nang addressed the prisoner while shaking her head at Nyhm. "What was it?"

"Supplies. Food."

Siril took a pointed interest, making notes for his reports later. "Anything else?"

"Chemicals, most likely." He then claimed he didn't know what the chemicals would have been for, no matter their course of questions.

Nang's patience wore thin. Her hands quickly flew to grasp either side of his head, bashing it back against the wall.

Amil worried that they'd lose a chance at answers. Setting a gloved hand to Nang's shoulder, he stepped around her to face the man. "What was he going to report to the ranger?"

"Transformations." The man's eyes were dilating and pinpointing as he tried to focus on Amil. "The ranger would come and stop it if he found out."

"For transforming people into those... monstrosities?"

"No."

"Then what are they for?" Siril ordered. "And where are these transformations taking place at?"

Amil had grown tired of the discussion. He wanted the information now. "Three." He held up the same in fingers, letting the man know he was almost out of time. Nang followed the intent with a nod, putting her hand against the side of Roger's head again.

Whimpering, his eyes showed white as he rolled them in Nang's direction. "We need the girl back."

"Tell me why. Two." He dropped a finger.

"She's got abilities. A ranger can't have any use for something like that," he cajoled. "She's god-touched."

"What are you going to use her for?"

"Remember?" Nang glanced back at Amil while she tightened her grip in Roger's hair. "That's how they make the Priestesses of Suffering."

"Aye." Barely controlled rage came out through Amil's clenched teeth. "I remember."

None seemed to notice that the manacles were no longer keeping Roger's hands behind his back. "She'll come to me," the man, despite the dire situation, squeaked his mustache with a smirk, "for her first lesson in pain. Then she'll be given to the other priestesses for further training."

Nang bashed his head against the wall on principle, a loud crack resounding as Siril backhanded him a second later with a loud smack. "Don't be an ass," the defender spit at him.

If Amil could have gotten between the two of them, he'd have lashed out as well. What this man implied shouldn't be done to any woman, least of all his Anne. "What makes you think she would even come to you?"

Dazed and blinking stars back, he fought nausea as he informed them, "She'd be chained down... Weapons do something to her... we can use that against her."

Nang flipped out her dagger. "I'm going to make you a eunuch."

Siril agreed. The race he had been born to was known for violence, but he had lived among humans and elves too long. This was not something he could morally allow. He made a judgment call, fully aware that his general may not like it. It was time to play hardball.

"Don't kill him yet. Sheesh." Felicia had always taken a "do what you have to" approach to her life, but even she had to wonder about Nang's overwhelming obsession with violence. "I don't think even I've tortured anyone like this before."

"Oooh," Siril smirked, "She's gonna cut off your cluster. Might wanna play nice."

"Nang," Amil warned, "Don't go off and kill Siril's prisoner."

She gave the ranger a hopeful look. "He'll only bleed a little. I'll make sure the wound gets cauterized."

"No no! The queen needs me like this!"

"Why does she need you so bad?" Amil asked.

Again, he ran his fingers along one side of his mustache, pulling it outward and twisting it between a thumb and forefinger. "I'm the best."

"Okay, that's it..." In irritation, Nang grabbed one side of the handlebar and ripped it off.

He screamed, bleeding profusely as Felicia smacked him with her staff. "Stop being so full of yourself."

Siril pulled a small rag from his pack and tossed it at Roger. "Clean your face off."

Covering his mouth with the cloth, he put his free hand over his family jewels. "Just don't touch the boys."

"Then you had better be very... friendly... when the Defenders put you away," Nang warned. "And very, very informative."

"I'll go with them," he agreed with a panicked tone, allowing Siril to once again put his hands together and clamp manacles around his wrists. "Just no more of this!" He quickly added, when questioned, that they didn't know what was further below either, since they hadn't tunneled through yet.

"We were told you came here to barter treaties with the deep elves and deep dwarves," Amil pushed. "Said you broke through. Don't lie to me!"

Dazed and confused, he answered with "Yes?"

"Are you telling the truth about not breaking through further?" Nang set her foot at the instep of his left knee."

"No no! No further, I swear! Call it off!"

"You know," Felicia put out to them, "he's just going to be replaced once they know he's gone or killed in his cell."

"True," Amil agreed, "but he's Siril's prisoner, and that allows us to have information spread to the Defenders in Lareah and fellow states in Kordathya of their threat."

"Is there anything else you wanna tell us before we haul you out of here?" Siril asked, motioning for Nang to step back.

"I'm a good guy, I swear it!"

Amil highly doubted that. Anyone that could be that gleeful about bringing pain to another was not what he would consider good. "We will let your trial decide that."

"If you're good," Felicia said with a snort, "then I'm a priestess of Hirath." There was no way she'd be caught following the patron of the holy city Phaethredun.

"*If* that's the fact, you really have nothing to worry about," Siril informed him. "However, if you lie... Well then," he considered the worst fate he could really think of at the moment. "I'm gonna lock you in a room with Nang over there and let her have her way with you."

His eyes widened again, his hand nervously reaching to squeak his mustache before he remembered it was gone. Nang gave him a very, very grim smile. "I can make you last a very, very long time before dying."

"Smart choice," Siril said when Roger stated he'd rather take his chances with the defenders.

"There's a narrow tunnel along the back wall. Goes back to the surface," Roger added in a defeated tone.

With a smirk and a snarky tone, Nang glanced to the others. "Look at how cooperative he gets, all of a sudden."

"Aye," Amil agreed. He turned to poke Roger in the chest with a finger. "I'll beat you to within an inch of your life if you try anything. And tell the guards you resisted."

"Lead the way," Siril ordered, jerking the chain between the manacles like a leash.

Moving in a hunched position, they couldn't quite stand two abreast and needed to watch for tumbling pebbles from those moving ahead, but steadily they grew closer to the surface again. Instead of finding themselves on Atil, they found the tunnels had again grown and spread, now branching far enough to bring them up into the forest outside Lareah's walls. All commented on how interesting this turn of events had become.

"Come on," Siril yanked on the chain, pulling Roger towards the city while the others stood guard behind and to the sides.

Once at the Defenders Stronghold, Siril left the group long enough to secure their prisoner deep in the bowels of the Spellhold, a specially designed area that prevented any type of magic from being used, just in case. Carefully latching and locking all doors on the way back up front, he fought the need to knuckle his eyes in exhaustion. "I will have one of the higher ranking officers question him, unless there is anything any of you wish to ask him still." He looked to Amil and Nang, getting simple headshakes as an answer. "Very well then. Once he has been thoroughly questioned, I will send word to you, Ranger. We will see what happens from there."

All three thanked him and offered their services in the interrogation. Siril nodded, chuckling. "I will give your names to the officer in charge of the questioning. If he needs you, he will send word. Now, if you will excuse me, I have reports to write up on this."

"And for the love of the gods, Siril," Amil added in exasperation, "stop calling me Ranger. Call me Amil, guy, person... If people called you Defender all day, don't you think you would get tired of hearing it?"

As they all shared a laugh, a young vidu woman stepped in, looking around. Finding a small bell on the desk in the front hall, she lightly tapped it three times.

"How may I be of service, miss?" Nyhm separated himself from the group to ask.

"I'm looking for someone. Annelise Erickson," she went on when Siril asked who in particular it was.

Amil studied her, noting that while Anne was fair skinned and darker haired than the vidu girl before him now, there was something in her face that was similar to his Anne's. "And who might you be, miss?"

"I'm one of her older sisters. Dad said he felt her in trouble."

Anne had often commented about strange happenings in her family. This solidified for him that she had indeed been truthful about all of it. She had said that her family was a mix of human and vidu and something she wouldn't name. She had said her father could sense the safety and well-being of his children, no matter the distance.

She had said a great many things that he had taken in jest over their courtship. Not once had she complained about it. And now the proof stood before him. It could have been a shadow copy of his Anne. "She was in trouble," he finally answered. "But she is now safe in my house on Atil. She is not to well at the moment, but is recovering slowly."

"Was it natural? Or weapons?"

"Weapon wound, though it clotted and the bleeding stopped." Just like his Anne, this girl had jumped right into details, forgetting something as small as naming herself. "I am Amilmamir, usually called Amil," he offered. He pointed out the others that had been helping him, gaining a wave from Siril as he left for a back office and from Nyhm as he went out the front doors.

Delighted, she exclaimed, "You're the Amil!" She took a moment to look over the dark-clothed man that had won her sister's heart. Letters home had mentioned how serious her ranger could be and how rare a smile was to come from him. "Always look so... stoney?" She grinned.

"Sorry," he couldn't help a smile coming to his lips. She really was like Anne. "Better?"

She nodded. "I'm Leslie. And you need to make sure she's purified."

"Purified by what means?"

"Didn't Annie ever tell you? She's a Tzee Divine. She's not to touch blades out of deference to the gods. She needs holy water to bathe the wounds in."

"Ah... She left that part out... Not much knowledge on the Tzee Divine... or monks. She shoots a bow good enough..."

Leslie laughed. "She takes after dad. I heard you trained her on the bow."

"Holy water, you said?" Nang cut in.

"I did!" she answered with a nod. "Otherwise, her strength is gone. It's a trade off." She smiled. "Like dad's Gift; that's how I knew to come. Anyways, could I get an address to find her?" She held out a sheet of parchment.

"Is it wise to send someone out to Atil right now?" Nang asked in concern. "They don't need another person to kidnap."

"General Amraphel sent a few Defenders to guard my home," he said, taking the parchment. "That way any refugees can make their way there. And," he added, drawing a map of the path from dock to his home, "at least the home won't be ransacked and there will be food for those in need. Besides, Vic's at the house. Don't see why it would be too dangerous." He turned his attention from Nang as he finished the sketch, scribbled "first large house you see," and handed the parchment back to Leslie. "It's pretty much right next to the docks."

"I'll look into it. Thanks!" Leslie gave him a quick hug and kiss on the cheek. "And welcome to the family! I got the letter from her about the ring!"

"Ah." Amil called after the woman's retreating form. "Well thank you!"

Nang grinned at the sly ranger. "Your maid, hmm?"

Chapter Twenty-Seven
Holy Water

Nang had stopped by the temple in Lareah, asking for a vial of holy water at Amil's request. They had looked at her strangely, but then, it couldn't be the oddest thing ever asked of them. Carefully carrying her treasure on the boat ride out to Atil, she knocked briefly before announcing herself as she entered.

"So there you are." She offered it to Amil on finding him in the bedroom. "If those women were as dark and evil as we think they might be, maybe this would help."

"Hmm...Well." He took the holy water out, looking at it. Anne's sister had told him it should work, but not for the reason Nang thought. "I suppose. Let's see if it works." He popped the cap, sliding the blanket off Anne.

Nang leaned against the column, her hand going down to her absent blade. Sighing, she fumbled around as she looked for pockets, anything, that would do to keep her hands occupied. She finally just crossed her arms, watching Amil's tender ministrations. For such a hard-ass demeanor, he was certainly extremely gentle with Anne.

He had dressed her in one of her own nightgowns once the others had left before. Just like everything else in her meager wardrobe, it was practical; plain cotton with a single tiny red bow at the neckline to dress it up.

Pulling her gown up so he could uncover the wound dressing, he tried to ignore the presence of Nang in this one thing. It seemed almost too private a thing to have someone watching.

Her bare feet were first, slowly moving up her body. The wound was going to be bad, even if she wasn't awake, so he saved that for last. Her hands and arms were done after her legs, then her face and hair. Carefully lifting her upright in his arms, he did behind her head, her neck, then dipping inside the top of her gown to wash her chest. While he was still holding her, he pulled the back of her gown up to wash over her back. That done, all that remained was the wound. He gently laid her back into the pillows again, and took a deep breath.

The last thing he ever wanted to do was cause her any pain. Even though this was necessary, he winced against doing it. Lifting the gown up, he forced himself to keep steady hands as he poured the holy water over the wound.

Her body arched as the water washed over the angry gash, dissolving the scabs that had formed over it. Anne's face contorted as the water soaked deeper, the infection bubbling up to the surface. A scream tore from her as she thrashed on the bed.

"It's okay," he tried to assure her, hating the pain he saw her in, hating that he couldn't do anything about it. "It's okay."

For the entire span of a candlemark, the water worked at her, drawing from her the poisons that steel had become to her system. Then all went still. Her breathing calmed.

He held his own breath, waiting for something to happen. Taking a deep breath, Anne's lashes fluttered, her eyes slowly opening. Looking around in some confusion, she finally saw the only person she was truly worried about. "Amil." She gave him a soft, warm smile.

"Anne..." He smiled back to her, placing a hand on her cheek. "You have soooo much cleaning to catch up on," he teased with a slight smirk.

Nang couldn't help a smile at the odd thing he'd choose to first say to her.

Anne tried to laugh, ending on a cough. "Silly bunny wrangler."

"How do you feel, besides wet?" He set the empty water bottle off to the side. "Better than when those bi....ummm women... were here."

"Who were they?" Nang stepped a little closer. "Did they say who they were working for?"

"Good," he said softly at the same time. "We had to go through two planes of the abyss to get you back. Nang complained about the heat the whole time, and Felicia the cold..."

Anne gave another tired laugh, then looked to Nang. "No... she seemed surprised to see me here. Two planes, hm?" She looked back to Amil with a smile. "How'd your ol' back hold up?"

"My apologies for the questions," Nang gave a sheepish shrug. "Amil's home has been rather invaded and I don't care for this queen of theirs."

"So, it's really my fault." Amil's guilt crept into his voice. It had probably been the dark-robed woman that had asked direction that day on the plateau. She had said something about removing a problem… "I should have guessed something was amiss when she came here. I should have stopped things with that first gnome."

A very dark, angry un-Annie look crossed her face. "I don't like them either!" Instantly, she became herself again, taking his hand. "It's not your fault."

"If I'd stopped her sooner, you would have been fine..."

"And then," Nang interrupted, "we would have been set back in learning more about these invaders and their queens."

"I was fine until they started harassing me with weapons. Stupid women."

"Well they aren't stupid anymore." He smiled. Her hair had come loose of its ribbon during her thrashing, and he now reached to tuck the soft brown locks behind her ear. "We... enlightened them."

"That we did." Nang smiled, cracking her knuckles.

"That's my bunny wrangler!" she gave an exhausted laugh, then looked around in concern. "Where's Malania?"

Nang pushed her hair back from her face, very glad she wasn't the one needing to tell Anne that "people" she had loved were now dead.

"She…" Amil ducked his head down, not wanting to look at her as he said it. "She didn't make it. Fred and Alice didn't either."

"Nooo!!" A deep sadness resounded through her drained voice. "I told them to hide!"

"They came out to tell me what happened. We were caught in an ambush." He leaned forward, resting his cheek against Anne's lap. "They didn't even have a chance."

"If I'd only had you teach me Mouse..."

Anne was so dejected over something Amil couldn't have taught her. Only long years in the wilds had allowed him to learn the language of the animals. It wasn't funny, but she looked so heartbroken. "They fought to the last tooth..." he said with a smirk she was all too familiar with.

"When the time comes," Nang promised, "there's going to be a copious amount of retribution handed out."

"Aye," Amil agreed. "On top of the about two legions we have killed so far."

"What about Cane?"

"He is fine." He gave her hand a squeeze, this time giving her a warm, humoring smile. "I am sure right now he is raiding the pantry…and watching Vic drink the wine. He somehow accidentally found safety behind the portal to Romx."

Anne blinked, shook her head, thinking to clear it. That caused the room to spin and a pounding to set up behind her temple again. She still wasn't sure she had heard them right. "The dead lands?"

He nodded, deadly serious. "Well… we did go to the dead lands... then to the abyss.. then finally found you."

"Two layers worth," Nang reminded.

"How're you holding up?" Anne said quietly, really looking at him as she reached to touch the scar on his face.

He winced away slightly from the attention to the old scar since Nang was still in the room. "I'd have gone through every layer of the Abyss to bring you back." He leaned in and gently kissed her. "I'm glad you're alright, Anne." He smiled then, wiggling his rear end from where he sat, trying to mimic the way she had so often done before moving to pounce him. Instead of that, he simply pulled her in close for a hug that he hoped didn't hurt her newly healed wounds. It was enough to make her laugh and hug him back.

Raising an eyebrow, Nang asked, "Would you prefer that I give you both some quiet space?"

"Oh no!" Annie quickly responded, then in a loud whisper to Amil, "Who is she?"

"Nang Teglen," she answered for herself. "I've been assisting Amil since the beginning of this."

"Nang has helped me out for awhile now, even helped save you." He nodded. "Very trust worthy. And a good blade at ones side."

"Then please," Anne pat the other side of the bed. "Pull up a rock."

"I'll stand, thank you." There was a slight coloring to her cheeks. "We must remain ever vigilant."

Anne's laugh filled the room. "I didn't embarrass you, did I?"

"Compliments are few and far between for me," she shrugged. "I work and expect little in return."

"Well, if Amil trusts you at his back, that's a pretty high compliment!" she smiled.

"Nang's right about being vigilant, Anne. They are looking for you now. They wish to find you and make you a priestess."

"But why? I'm nothing special." Her dad, maybe, but she was just Amil's Anne.

He smiled, tucking a strand of hair back behind her ear. "They called you God-Touched."

"Oh," she made a face. "That."

"I understand if you don't want to stay here now." He squeezed Anne's hand again, his mind screaming at him to demand she stay. He wanted to know she would be safe, and he had taken measures to protect this house now. But ultimately, it had to be her choice. She didn't like being told what her only choice was any more than he did. "But if you do, there are a few Lareahan Defenders stationed at the door helping refugees from the village and to provide security of my home." Amil hoped she could see how serious he was about this, and what he felt he would lose if anything happened to her. "I'm not losing you again." He thought of another thing that might convince her. "And Vic – another warrior – I am sure stumbling drunk somewhere about the house. Just so you know who is in the house at least."

"Hm... Amil asking me to stay..." she gave him a playful smile as she tapped a finger against her lips. "Hm hm hm..." She drew out the moment, pretending to think about it. She wanted to be close to Amil, but didn't want to seem too anxious to know he was safe too. "Do I need to clean up after that guy?" she asked instead.

"At this point," Nang said dryly, "he's probably passed out." She gave it a moment's consideration. "Although he does seem to have a rather high tolerance level for alcohol."

"He usually finds the alcohol in a clean fashion, though there may be some bottles here and there that need picking up. But he's a good fighter, even when drunk."

Nang nodded her confirmation to that, gaining a smile from Anne. Nang looked like she was very regretfully conceding on that point, very exasperated.

"S'pose this means I'm moving back to the guest room?" Anne let Amil know in her own way she wouldn't be leaving. There was an unspoken challenge in the way her chin tipped down a little in stubbornness as she crossed her arms. "Or is this Vic guy in there now?"

"You are staying in this room. I won't have you sleeping in the guest room." He smirked, winking at her. "Vic can sleep there. This is the most secure room in the house."

She brightened. "If you're insisting." A little of her playful spunk crept back in. "And you can sleep right here next to me! ... On the floor!" She gave him a mischievous smile.

"So long as I know you're safe, I will." He'd go without sleep if it meant she wouldn't be taken from him again. "And I am insisting." Not to mention he would be able to know every move that was made by or against her. And Cane was still available to aid him.

As if knowing he was being thought about, the panther surprised Amil by doing something he'd only heard Anne say he did. In all the years Cane had been his partner, he had always been a wild thing Amil had respected. Anne had reduced him to a very large lap cat that now curled up at her side.

Anne buried her face in Cane's fur for a minute before looking to Nang in question. Amil followed with his own expression of inquiry.

"I have my own apartment in Lareah," Nang said when they looked at her. "No need to worry about me either."

"Is it safe?" Anne worried.

"There is plenty of bed space here, Nang."

"I don't want to put anyone out."

While his daughters' room may be off limits, Anne knew he still had three other guest rooms, plus a dorm style room for his rangers to use when they met for large gatherings.

"Have you seen all the beds in this place?" Amil nodded agreement with Anne. "You are more than welcome. Besides, there are plenty of beds in the barrack room for Vic to pass out on," he added, making Anne laugh. "The second bedroom is plenty comfortable. But of course if you prefer your apartment..."

"Only keep what I can carry." Nang carried her weapons and a single change of clothes. It was easier to move around that way. "I won't take up much space at all."

"It'll be fun having another girl around! Just like having my sisters again!"

"Er... I'm not that much of a girl." Nang was not about to start doing hair and nails in lieu of wading into battle.

"I met your older sister, by the way," Amil added.

"Which one?"

"Lei.. Lehil... L something.. More vidu showing then you... I was more focused on the holy water she told me about."

Nang nodded. "She said it would reverse your ailment."

Anne smiled at Amil. "All my sisters are darker than me. I'm my dad's only daughter."

That caused Amil a moment of concern. Maybe they had magically done something to her head; maybe she had been injured worse than they had thought. It didn't make sense to say "all" and "only" in reference to her sisters. He knew she had a big family; she was very proud of them.

"Why was she here?" she interrupted his thoughts.

"Holy water," he reminded her.

"Leslie, I think," Nang offered.

He nodded. "Leslie; that was it."

"Yep! That's my sis."

"Details." Nang tapped the side of her head, nodding. "Very focused mind for things of that nature."

"Yeah, she checks on things for dad these days. Oh!" Worry overtook her as she looked between them. "He must've been nuts over this! How long've I been out?"

"Three weeks, maybe four," Nang answered. "At least since you were brought here."

Amil shot Nang a look. He had wanted to ease her into knowing it had been almost a month of unconsciousness for her. Focus on something else for now. "I told your sister where you are, and an address to find you."

"Holy cow!" she giggled, making an invented religious symbol in the air and muttered, "Blessed by thy moo-juice." It turned into a tired laugh when she saw their baffled expressions.

"I'm not sure I follow," Nang looked to Amil who shrugged.

"It's a joke. Cows aren't holy." An uncharacteristic giggle escaped her.

"Riiight," Amil humored her, a little worried yet for head injuries he might have missed. "Now, I did have a conversation with a cow once. He even worshipped Big D," he teased, using the common term for the patron god of Lareah. Even though she was still weak, it was good to see her trying to be like herself. "Seemed pretty holy to me."

"Well, if you shoot'em full of arrows they are..." she settled back in the pillows, pleased with her comeback.

He smiled. "Like I said; I was talking with him, not shooting him."

"Neato!" Anne looked to Nang. "Have you seen how cute he is under his hood?"

Nang blinked in surprise at the strange turn in the conversation. "Beg pardon?"

"Amil. Not the cow." She looked to Amil. "Did your cow wear a hood, too?"

"Most of my time has been spent in dangerous situations." Nang's tone was dry as she answered. "With him, that is."

"No, the cow didn't." Amil smiled at Anne's conversation bouncing around. The trauma must have involved a head injury he hadn't found. "But aye, we have been in some pretty tricky, dangerous and life threatening places." He squeezed her hand. "When you've got strange, juiced up dwarves the size of four stacked oxen swarming over you, there's not a lot of time to bring down the hood for a chat."

"S'pose not," she laughed. "But how 'bout now? Hm?" She held up a finger, giving him an "a-ha" look.

He ignored it. "Or those little imp things in the Abyss."

"What imps?" she asked in worry.

"Little buggers would sting back if you hurt them. Or anyone around them, for that matter."

"Along with all the priestesses, magi, halflings... The list really does go on. I'm not sure which was more of a pain."

"Aye, undead warriors," Nang added. "Demons."

"Jeez louise!" Anne's spunk was coming back as she managed to actually sound outraged. "Sounds like you've had all the fun! All I got was some crabby, mean, pruney women that've been suckin' on lemons or something. They kept talking about harnessing my skill."

"Well," Amil lightly kissed the top of her head, "a few prunes are better than the couple hundred we have battled."

"I would tend to agree," Nang added, then motioned to Amil. "How is your stock of arrows, by the way?"

"Empty." He didn't see a need to add that he had been gifted his bow by one of the very gods that seemed to be watching over them now. All he had to do was sight along his hand and basic arrows would magically come to hand. "Don't worry about it. My bow can handle the magic of what I need."

A deep frown cut across Nang's features. "Sir Roger made mention of such things."

"Indeed, he did."

"Siril took him to the Defender's hold to be dealt with later." Amil was so glad to have a defender on their side with this. They didn't need to explain why someone like Roger needed to be locked away.

Nang smiled as Anne yawned. "You must be exhausted from your recent ordeal."

"Sorry," Anne said with an apologetic smile.

"And I'm sure Amil would be rather upset if you didn't get rest."

She gave a bright smile. "Gotta get well so I can plan the wedding."

"Of course." Nang inclined her head to each, offering them a good night.

Chapter Twenty-Eight
This is My Fight

While the plateau in Lareah was the easiest place to wait or meet each other, they had taken to either meeting at Amil's out on Atil or in the grove that resided in the forest to the west of Lareah. Sitting in that grove with her back against a log, Nang ran a whetstone over her dagger while she awaited the arrival of several of her newfound allies. Nyhm and Vicarious appeared in a relatively quick fashion, and while they visited, Amil joined them.

Speaking amongst themselves, it came as something of a shock when a man in hunter's leathers approached them. Soft doeskin boots masked his footsteps as easily as the hood hid his face and the green helped camouflage the brown he wore. A longbow and quiver at his back and the short sword and dagger at his hip marked him for one belonging to the forest's hunt.

Amil tensed in surprise for a heartbeat only before bowing low. It had been long since this god had walked the lands. "Lord Firnos."

Raising his flask for a long drink, Vicarious used the time to study the man. The clothing was drab, to his way of thinking. And just like Amil, he was keeping his face hidden. *Ah well*, he thought, *at least he can't look better than me this way*!

He let his body language convey that, even while he shook in his boots. It wasn't often heard that someone had met a god, let alone to see two of them personally. Vic could admit – at least to himself – that this was an omen to the importance of the task they had undertaken.

"My son," he addressed Amil directly, sparing only a glance for each of the others, "the hunt is afoot. They've unleashed hounds to find the 'troublesome' ranger in Atil."

This was the god, Nang realized, that Amil had committed his life to. Nyhm came to the same conclusion, finally realizing how large this adventure had become. He was part of something that wasn't done every day; not when the gods themselves guided one of them. He was awed and very quiet.

They were allowed to ask one question and a single word from Siril stayed Vicarious' tongue. Debating amongst themselves,

Amil finally chose to ask Firnos about any weaknesses the queen might possess, as they had virtually nothing to go off of besides her seemingly endless desire to have men with her. That, it seemed, was it, according to Firnos. Queen Lutheria's power came from the ability to bring men to her side and without them to guard her, she was powerless.

"There are sacrifices," Firnos went on, "one of yours will need to choose."

While the others wondered what the choice would be, Amil had no doubt. "I choose," he said quietly. "This is my fight."

"Hey, if it's something amazing..." Vic started to say before Nang smacked his arm. "What? Maybe I want it."

"I'll choose," Nang offered, still unsure what it involved. But if it came to needing to be clear-headed over Anne or this queen, she wasn't sure Amil would be able to make a solid choice. She knew she could stay detached.

The god inclined his head slightly after glancing over them all. "Hunt well, my children." Moving as if he were tracking something, crouched somewhat and blending with the shadows, Firnos moved away from them, gone between one blink and the next.

A long silence lay between them until Amil finally took a deep breath. "You can all back out if you wish." He knew what had been asked. One of them may not make it to see an end to this. He couldn't ask it of any of them.

He didn't have to. Nang simply told him that she saw all her missions to the end. Siril said much the same, as did Vicarious.

They made their way back to Atil's vast forested land, intent to discover the tunnels beneath the ruins. They did find them, and killed several vidu warriors. Again, Nang sighed as she repeatedly called out a "hold" command to question one of their attackers.

In what Nang assumed was his drunken state, Vicarious slipped and fell down a crack in the ground. He had actually found the space, just wide enough for someone as big as he was to slide down into, and had seen movement. Letting the others assume as Nang did, he surprised the queen's men by dropping into the middle of them.

Sounds of combat could be heard, and soon all of them had followed, carefully dropping down into the large chamber. What might have been overwhelming for just Vicarious was short work for them as a unit.

Scattered amongst the rubble, Vicarious had found several weapons lain out. Soon, he was carrying on what seemed like a conversation… only it was with someone that Nang and the others could not see. The conversation went on for sometime, and it escalated when Amil picked up an apparently rusted blade. It had seemed that a distant relation of his had been captured while trying to locate him, and imprisoned in the blade itself. Whether truthful or not, after being freed, the young elf escaped out through a crack and the others followed her.

They found themselves in yet another chamber, this time with a vast underground pool in the center of it. Ahead of them, they could hear the sounds of fierce growling. It was the hound that Firnos had warned them of – a great mangy beast with two snarling heads above an incredibly agile body.

Intense combat broke out and the foursome had a difficult time in piercing the creature's thick, coarse fur. The few strikes Nang was making hardly countered the gouges the beast's claws were leaving in her, but she didn't back off. Neither did Amil as, from the far side of the pool, his arrows continued to sing between his companions reach, striking true only enough that the one side was starting to look like a balding porcupine.

Vic's scythe danced with him in and out of range, the hound finally grabbing the snath just above the blade as he swept it towards the legs. Both sets of jaws clamped tightly as it growled and pulled, shaking the whole front of its body.

"Hey, you're…" he stumbled, "…making me look bad! Bad dog! Bad!" More growls answered him. He growled back at it, finally shoving forward, the chine biting deep into one of the creature's forelegs.

A surprised whining yip came from it as it let go and danced back a step. Snapping at arrows and Nang's blade, the other head stayed focused on the vidu. Now angry not only at its quarry, it started biting at itself as well.

Throughout, Nyhm stayed back, keeping an eye on the beast, but also checking for weak points in the walls. "Over here!" he finally called to Vic, pointing up at a section of the ceiling that ran with fissures.

Balancing on one foot, kicking with the other, Vic spared a glance, noting what the short one wanted. "Are you insane?"

"Do it!" Amil hollered back.

"You got a death wish?" He spun, clocking the beast on one head with the heel of his scythe. "I'm too good looking to die today!"

Nang abandoned her spot, fishing out flint and tinder as Nyhm readied some sort of narrow container he added alcohol to. Working quickly together, Nyhm pulled back just as Nang twisted a piece of cloth, shoving it in the end. Nang let the sparks catch fire just as Nyhm let loose, his aim striking true at the same moment Amil sent a fire arrow to join the impact.

That section rumbled, dust and thunderous noise filling the cavern as loose rock fell over the beast. Coughing and waving the debris from the air, they found the beast was no more.

A stockpile of equipment had been protected by the hound, and the group took it up themselves. Nang reasoned that the Sirenian Empire needed to be hit down a few notches. Vicarious, on the other hand, helped himself to the stores of alcohol that had been hidden in the chambers. The lake itself provided an exit this time, via a massive geyser that shot them up and into the lake just outside of Lareah's walls.

Amil was not impressed that the lake he found the most peace at had been compromised. This was where he took Anne for dates. This was where he sat to enjoy a small piece of undisturbed land. It was one more thing he added to the charges against the false queen.

Nang left the others, hoping that Siril would have his chance to ply information from their captured Sirenian noble. There needed to be an end to this destructive campaign, and Nang only hoped that she could help see that end.

Amil didn't need to hope. There would be an end to this, and it would come by the name of Amilmamir Mor Nermakiir.

Chapter Twenty-Nine
The Foundry's Core

Replacing arrows that had been used up on previous missions with Amil and restocking other sundry supplies, Nang kept the end goal in mind: that of removing any and all forces for the Sirenian Empire from Atil and Kordathya's shores. The last step in her routine was to return to the plateau in Lareah's city center and await the rest of her companions.

She didn't need to wait long, really. Vicarious made his usual appearance from the south, already reeking of alcohol. Amil usually arrived from the west. Nyhm approached from the east, slightly more unusual than normal. Claiming the need for sleep, the young tracker ventured back in the direction of the inn, leaving the three of them to discuss the past matters.

None of them had heard back from the Defenders with information regarding Sir Roger. If it wasn't for her respect of the authorities, Nang would have broken into the stronghold and taken the information from the pompous fool directly. As it was, she was willing to give the Defenders just a little more time to return with information.

As they were about to leave for Atil, a runner from the Defender's Stronghold brought them a message from Siril. A female from the Empire had made her way to him and claimed to want nothing more to do with said peoples. She wanted out. So much so that she had been willing to inform the defenders of the newest tunnel to reach the surface. They had dug directly into the Hall of Heroes in an attempt to catch the city's guards unawares. Siril's note said he would be along shortly, if they wanted to take the advance guard in looking into matters. With that firmly in mind, they made their way to the hall, killing the invaders with brutal efficiency.

Only three men had been present. From their clothing, they seemed to have been more of the Defilers that came ahead of an actual attack against the people. Amil left the bodies for the defenders that came in the next moments.

Much to Nang's surprise, there was a statue of Amil among the others… and a hole directly behind the statue. Amil's statue had been chipped and paint spattered across it in a deliberate attempt to destroy it.

Ignoring the defacing that had been done to it, Amil leapt into the hole, followed quickly by Vicarious and a cautious Nang after him. It was dark enough that even their elven sight didn't penetrate it. None of them spoke as they made their way along the damp path, the only sound their breathing and the crumbling dirt that would fall in their passing.

Just as they all started to feel that the walls were pressing in on them and that their sight might never return, the tunnel opened into a sprawling city. Large buildings were spaced at regular intervals. Smoke wafted into the twilight sky from what looked like steel barrels atop the stone structures. Narrow rivers had small foot bridges crossing. The cobbles they found themselves on held no dust or dirt. What grass and ferns grew appeared to have been purposely planted in particular sections. Everywhere was a strange order and cleanliness that was surreal.

Moving in slow steps, they kept their weapons at the ready, not trusting to the quiet. "What is this place?" Vic asked, getting edgy with the waiting, let alone the fact that they had come on it so quickly. Strange magics seemed to rule the tunnel passages.

"Keep your eyes open," was all Amil answered with.

Only moments later, strange bird creatures attacked, coming from behind many of the buildings. A cross between the head of a raven and the feathers of a chicken, they moved like people, but fought with beak and taloned feet. The group tried to speak with them, but words went completely unheeded. Amil even tried using hand signals to display peace.

It wasn't until they crossed over a large bridge that they encountered a single semi-peaceful member of the odd creatures. It seemed to want to communicate via... martial arts? It posed in strange positions, making stranger noises that might have related to a chicken... or not. Nang was mystified, but Amil had seen Anne move in many of the same poses the creature was using.

She had told him there were names for each position. Amil couldn't help wondering now if maybe those names would have helped them understand what the beast wanted to tell them. He would have to have Anne teach him once things settled down.

A late appearance by Felicia helped them communicate with the bird creatures. She recognized them as intelligent bird-men, and pointed out that the empire's mark was branded on his beak, as well as on a band around his ankle. Slavery and mind control seemed to be what kept them in service to this empire the group sought. Nang bit her tongue back, angered with the treatment of creatures in the Sirenian realms. *They would pay*, she thought.

Moving swiftly, they located several mages and priestesses. One of them had to be a leader, they surmised. Attempts to talk were rebuffed with a magical attack, and they found a Priestess of Suffering that apparently enjoyed suffering to an extreme. When Amil plunged his blade through her shoulder into the ground to hold her steady, the woman nearly gushed in pleasure.

Even taking the woman's right thumb did nothing to loosen her tongue. It required a change in tactics that Nang resented, but found necessary. She took out a light blue topaz and lied, telling the woman it was a soul stone. That brought the desired reaction, as the woman thought she'd be painfully sucked into some state of trapped existence. It was a strange sort of brainwashing.

Nang pressed the woman for information, learning that "Shangsani" was the true leader of the empire's goons in this land called Vunak. More searching led them to find the race, only to learn it was some sort of froglike creature.

The group fought it to a standstill, and then it mentioned a man by the name of Remy and started to flee. The creature never escaped, never had a chance, given the foursome's skills. Further searches in the city lead them to confront two strange wandering swordsmen, both of whom vanished when Felicia attempted to magically harm them.

Most of the buildings yielded nothing, but one doorway transplanted them into a cavern complex as they stepped through. A single hardy soldier stood in their way and attacked them fiercely. Built like a battleship, his bare chest flexed with overly-muscled threat as a greatsword swung at them with intense precision.

They managed to kill the man, but with wounds taken by all. When they followed the tunnel network further, they discovered a huge foundry, heat blasting them all. Following two more protracted battles with strong warriors, a woman called their attention.

Her low, sultry voice carried a hint of hypnosis to it, drawing the listener in, making them want to come closer to her. A small jeweled crown sat atop her styled hair, marking her as the possible queen they had been looking for. At odds with the smoke and flame of the cavern, she was dressed in a floor-length gown of sheer material, barely hiding what she looked like beneath. She was as curvaceous as Sir Roger had mentioned and was calling out to get Vicarious' attention.

Nang notched an arrow, only waiting on Amil's word. Vicarious, on the other hand, decided to play "stupid," ignoring the woman's attentions. She likely only focused on him as he was the tallest, strongest, and most awesome member of their small group.

Unfortunately, this only seemed to upset her further. She wasn't interested in facing the annoyance of the ranger; she merely wanted him gone. She would have liked to have the tall one, but if they weren't responding to her magic, and had already caused this much trouble... she called for more guards to attack.

Dozens of men, all experienced fighters, all fully armed, seemed to pour from all the dark crevices and shadowed pathways. Turning back to back, each could only focus on what was coming at them. Now used to fighting together, they knew how they each would move. Nyhm struck low, letting Amil and Felicia fire arrows and magic over his head while Nang and Vic used rapier and scythe.

They worked outward, forming their own groupings, Nang and Vic finding themselves in the familiar position of protecting each other's backs, her blade lower while his struck high. Nyhm slipped beneath the heat of the battle to roll and make his way to the wall. Slipping amongst the flickering shadows, his dark leathers looked like little more than another cast image dancing along the stone. As the enemy would slip close enough, he would dart in to strike, then quickly find another area to await the next hit.

Amil tried more than once to advance towards the queen. At every turn, he found his way blocked. Had he been given a clear shot, he'd have taken the woman out, but he found himself unable to use the bow. Sword and dagger came to hand. Felicia stood cornered to his back, ready to attack to either side with both magic and a blade that had appeared in her hand.

A cold laugh of joy rang through the area. A flash of light with accompanying noise made them all blink back the white sparkles left in their eyes. Amil growled in frustration as he looked to the wooden stand the woman had been standing on. She had disappeared, leaving them to deal with the last of the guards she had abandoned.

Bursts of flame came from the few cauldrons, causing smoke to drift through the area. "I've got it," Felicia muttered, striding through the area as if she owned it.

The others found fewer and fewer facing them as the wizardess reached the fires. "Ashes," she called her elemental. "Flames." The creature appeared, devouring the flames within the blackened iron pots.

When the smoke cleared, the four had managed to kill every warrior in the foundry. That, however, left them with the question of where they were. Nang investigated one of the pits below a smelting pot… and saw what looked like magma. They were beneath Atil and directly above the volcano's core! The Sirenians were using the volcano itself as a source for their war machine, and they knew it had to be stopped.

The bitch had beat him this time. Amil was furious to have been denied an ending to this mess. And now to see the state of the volcano's core… It was unstable, thanks to that woman's stupidity.

Amil launched an enchanted arrow directly at one of the supporting columns of stone. The four retreated into a tunnel as the roof began to collapse. Impossibly, the ash and searing heat followed them out into a winter land that shouldn't have been so close to Atil. Yet again, the Sirenians magic had managed to shorten the distances along the tunnels.

In silence, teeth chattering, they made their way to the docks of this far off island. They traveled in equal quiet, looking to each other in shock. The very core of the island had been breached. The volcano had been harnessed. Things had gone far beyond what they had ever expected.

A dark cloud of ash was visible as they stepped foot off of the boat in Lareah, obviously coming from Atil. The volcano's wrath had been awakened and it rained down upon all the land. Soot and ash mixed with rain, coating everything in a charcoal film.

Bone-weary from the ordeal, Nang separated from the others and returned to the lodge. She didn't have it in her to see how Amil's home had fared, but she trusted the gods wouldn't let his ancient home come to harm.

Amil didn't have that same trust. Something odd was at work that had nothing to do with the gods. This queen meant only to use what she could before moving on, leaving destruction and desolation behind her. The volcano, luckily, was far enough away from his side of the island yet. But at the rate this was going, how long would he have before the bursts of ash became rivers of lava?

Chapter Thirty
A Trap?

    Still nothing from the Defenders and Sir Roger. Nang was beginning to suspect that Vicarious may have had a point in trying to either break in or get arrested for a minor crime, just to give them the opportunity to speak with the man themselves. With that in mind, she and Vic made their way to the Defender's Stronghold to speak with Siril.

    "We let the man have some time to cool his heels," he was telling Amil when they arrived. "Nothing has been done about this supposed consort of Queen Lutheria yet, but," he smiled behind his helm, "the time has come." He led them to where the formerly moustached man was waiting for them in a cozy meeting area, flanked by a nameless guard, hidden behind his helm.

    Part of Nang quivered in anticipation of the work to be done; she was good at coaxing information out of unwilling people and Roger would certainly not be the last. The only stipulation given by Siril was to keep the amount of blood to a minimum. That was fine with Nang; she knew countless methods to harm a man without a hint of bloodshed. Taking his wrist in her hand, she wrenched back on his hand. Roger screamed in pain and proceeded to give them some of the information he had promised.

    With a little further coaxing and breaking of his wrist, Roger began giving them the information Nang had hoped he held. Sirenia had four to five "troops" stationed around Kordathya. Further clarification and a dislocated shoulder later, the group discovered that a "troop" contained several thousand individuals. There was also a twin to Roger named Remy and another higher ranking warlord simply known as 'Betrayed.'

    Roger made a number of rude and insulting comments about Nang, prompting her to send necromantic energies into the man's dislocated arm. Rather than heal what they'd done, the death magic caused the muscles to atrophy and the injuries to create patches of dead skin around them that flaked or festered.

    Siril finally called her off and guided the man to a couch, calling for a healer. Nang stood quietly in the background while the

Defender proceeded to use gentler means to further extract information from him. Remy, it seemed, was addicted to a drug of some kind that the Queen gave him. If he missed a dose, even for an hour, he would begin to get debilitating cramps.

Roger was more than willing to talk to Siril, who had shown himself more sympathetic. With a wary eye on Nang, he swore to the defender that he would do everything he could to free Remy from the Queen's clutches and the group quickly put together a plan to swap Roger for Remy. The major catch in this plan was the lack of a known location for Remy, the Queen, and her warlord. Roger still had tricks up his sleeves, producing a scroll case that could travel between the brothers by the use of a simple word. That, Roger claimed, would return with Remy's location.

There was nothing to do but wait until the enchanted scroll case returned with Remy's location. Each took their leave for various needs: Vicarious for his alcohol, Siril to prepare magical aids, Amil to see to his home (if it still remained), and Nang to resupply with goods. As she passed into the streets, Nang hoped it wouldn't be the case, but couldn't help but suspect the whole situation was a trap.

***

Idle chatter filled the time between Nang and Vic outside the inn until the magi, Defender Siril, joined them. None of the three had seen Amil since the interrogation of Roger. It disturbed Nang that a few days had again passed with no word from him. She hoped that he had finally gotten word from Roger's twin, but to be sure she proposed a trip to Atil to once again check on his home.

As they were about to leave, a water animal came up on the plateau, bearing a scroll case that looked very much like the one they had sent from Roger.

Burnt in bands wrapped around the otter's four legs, exactly like those the bird-people wore. As they were attempting to figure out how to speak to or get the case from the otter, a delicate elven woman approached them. She raved about how they were torturing the little animal and that it was typical vidu behavior. Nang immediately discounted the woman, thinking of her as less than intelligent. Unfortunately, the otter used the time in an attempt to flee from the group.

Vicarious and Nang went after and herded the otter back up by the plateau. The little animal was naturally distraught, but finally allowed them to take the scroll case. Inside, the note told them that a cache of booze had been left at the bottom of Lake Amanalu, most likely for Vicarious. With the added late assistance of Nyhm, the three men and Nang went to the lake and dived deep down.

Roger's brother had come through. While he hadn't been able to tell them much, he had gotten word to them about more than just the alcohol. They found a large crystal ball that showed the queen going about her business… and a tuft of black hair. Carefully packing it all up to take with them, the group went back up to the surface and split up, eagerly awaiting the appearance of Amil.

Chapter Thirty-One
A Strange Orb

Siril sat alone in the Defenders meeting room. Staring at a candle flame, he made all the mental preparations he would need; which spells to commit to memory, a list of supplies, both magical and mundane. After this was done he took out a quill and a blank scroll and set to writing. When the quill left the parchment for the last time, he called for a runner. "Take this to the chief or the captain of the Gray Gryphons in Garrison. Return their answer to me as soon as possible. Time is of the essence." The runner simply nodded and dashed out the door.

Several hours later, as Siril sat studying a musty old tome, the runner appeared in the doorway, out of breath and followed by a young man dressed in red and black... the colors of the mercenary unit stationed in Garrison. Rising from his seat, Siril motioned the two young men in. "Well?" he said to the runner he had sent, "their answer?"

The blue-clad recruit looked at him a moment, then to the man standing next to him. At this point the young man dressed in red and black spoke up. "Sergeant Te'lie, I am a messenger sent by Captain Ironfist. His answer is this: When you need us, you may call upon us with this horn." He produced a bone horn. "If and when you sound the horn, the Gray Gryphons will come to your aid."

Smiling to himself, Siril took the horn and tucked it away into a pack after thanking the young men and sending them on their way. Now that he had secured a few allies, besides his fellow Defenders, he could rest a bit easier. There was still much to do, and less time than he would like to do it in.

He returned to one of the small rooms inside the Stronghold, letting the magical catches recognize him before he opened the iron locks with an old key. Upon a roughhewn table in front of him sat a large crystal orb, its surface swirling with a strange mist. It had been retrieved from a hidden chamber below the lake outside the city, showing different scenes within. He could spread his hands wide and almost cover the surface, although he wasn't sure yet he wanted to touch it.

The Defender concentrated on the object in front of him, watching as the scenes played out within its depths. He watched for any detail that could help him and his compatriots in their endeavor. He saw men come and go. He saw a copy of Roger's familiar face on another man as he wandered past on regular intervals, looking for his ration of whatever drug it was that held him to the queen. Siril watched the queen herself as she thoroughly enjoyed her male company and all the attention they lavished upon her. But he didn't see anything that helped. For three days and as many nights he watched, breaking only to find meager meals.

The morning of the fourth day produced something. Not the weakness he was hoping to find – or a way to win – but it cleared up one mystery that he had mulled over more than once. The queen came into view, much like she had countless times over the last few days, only this time she wore a cloak. As she turned to speak to one of her slaves, Siril saw that it was not a cloak wrapped around her, but an animal skin. He watched closer, trying to see the details, making out that this was clearly the skin of a large cat...a black panther. He also noticed that the skin was missing a patch of fur that looked like it would be somewhere around the base of the creatures neck. Siril pulled the tuft of black hair from his belt and laid it out on the table; roughly the right size and shape. He shook his head a bit and went back to watching.

Siril turned his attention from the Queen and concentrated on the other aspects of the scene. Watching the faces of her slaves he began to notice a pattern. When she wasn't looking at them or talking to them, all the men seemed to look tired, worn out... sad even. But the moment she looked in their direction, their faces changed, they went from looking down trodden to an almost euphoric look. Could it be that they didn't want to be there? Or could it be that they were so "hooked" on this woman that the only time they were happy was when she was looking at them?

He watched as Remy wandered around in his drug induced stupor. He watched in amazement at how many times a day he needed his fix. *Truly amazing,* he thought to himself.

Once again Siril's eyes roamed over the scene, looking, searching for anything that might help. He looked at the windows in the background, noting snow falling so heavily that it obscured the view of anything outside. "If that snow would stop for just a few minutes, maybe I could see..." he muttered aloud, then stopped short. Snow. The mage laughed to himself. *Sometimes you make things too complicated, Siril.* Snow... constant snow. Now he had something they could use.

    Siril stepped outside of the room that he had occupied for the past four days and called for a runner. The exhausted vidu gave the young man Nang and Vic's descriptions and sent him to look for them before going back to the orb. If the key was there, he would find it. And when he did, they would need to see this for themselves.

Chapter Thirty-Two
Cil Loves Amil Too

"Showing a bit of skin tonight." Amil had never seen Anne in a skirt so short. It was stunning on her toned figure, but the only time he'd seen so little on her had been while she was recovering and needed bathing. Seeing her supple little form in motion now was almost more than he could handle.

Anne jumped in surprise, turning. "Amil!" she pounced against him for a hug.

Fully expecting it, he took her in his arms. "Looks amazing."

"Thanks," she answered as he put her back on her feet and she tucked a lock of hair behind her ear. "Mom sent it. Said I should look like a girl once in a while."

He chuckled. "Unfortunately, I think you're stuck looking like one unless, well, some mage changes you into an otter or something."

"That would be silly!" she laughed.

"Okay. Suppose so. How about a mouse?"

She tried wrinkling her nose up, pretending to be one. "How's this?"

"No," he laughed, "I don't think a mouse fits the description either."

A young elf, not much older than Annelise could have been, walked up with her quiet grace, soundlessly placing one bare foot before the other as she found a place for herself on the plateau. She glanced swiftly to the sound of familiar voices before narrowing her eyes suspiciously, even jealously, at seeing Annelise with Amilmamir.

About then Anne noticed her, waving her over.

Hands still at Anne's sides, Amil looked over his shoulder. "Cileria." He nodded to her. He had always harbored a small attraction to the girl, although he would never have taken it anywhere serious. She was the niece of a fellow ranger he had always counted as a good friend.

Anne tugged at the hem of her red skirt as she smiled at Cileria. She was one of Amil's rangers, and one Anne had once thought Amil in love with. "Haven't seen you in a while."

Terrible at acting, Cileria still pretended not to have noticed them. She had been watching them from the corner of her eyes though. And now, with them addressing her, she couldn't ignore them. "Oh, hi." She turned towards them, putting a smile on as if she had only now seen them.

"Is she mad at me?" Anne whispered before raising her voice for Cileria. "You okay?"

Amil tilted his head curiously at the idea, but waved off the thought of Cileria's odd behavior. "Looking well Cileria, haven't seen you in a... hmm in a few months or so... maybe a bit longer."

"Sure." Her eyes shifted between the two of them, her voice a moderated monotone. "Are you?"

Looking to Amil, then to Cileria, Anne told her, "Malania died."

"Months..?" Cileria ignored Annelise, focusing on Amil's comment, her tone more than annoyed. "I stopped counting the days ages ago with you."

Anne blinked her eyes at the odd reaction. It was something to expect from a lover, not someone he'd always held dear to him. "Cileria?"

She blinked, looking to Annelise. "Malania died?" She was confused, but sympathy for anything dying did touch her.

"And Cane is missing," Anne said with a nod.

"Who's Malania? And Cane?" she demanded.

"My Companions," Amil said quietly. "The wolf and panther."

She tilted her head back, eyes going wide as it dawned on her. "Ah." Then the full import hit her. "Oh, that's horrible! What do you mean missing? They just left?"

"Malania died trying to keep me from getting taken. Cane is just... missing. Again."

"He died?!" Finally realizing the enormity of the situation for Amil, a deep look of sadness spread over her.

"She," Amil corrected. "She died." He returned the squeeze to his hand that Anne offered while he continued, "She has passed on into the land of the dead, where she is happy. She has no more concerns of this world. She has others to watch over now."

Anne tried to smile for Amil, to let him know she was there for him, but she failed at not showing her worry as she glanced up at him repeatedly. "You should tell her what happened, Amil."

"Which?" he asked. "The story of how you were captured, nearly killed, and how we had to go through the land of Romx, save the souls from slavery, and travel through the nine hells to prevent them turning you into a blood priestess?" The bitterness and anger he felt towards the queen for all of it raged through him. "That story?"

"All of it. Things you were told. Or about meeting Firnos." Her eyes and voice held all the love and concern she felt for him. "Or who you said was with Malania now. Or Oceania's clothes." She turned to Cileria. "People have attacked his lands, the people… it's terrible!"

Her green eyes stopped aiming daggers at Anne as the details piled up. The jealousy she had first felt again that night vanished completely, overcome by concern and sadness. She couldn't help feeling a little like she had been living under a rock the past months, rather than simply working a distant patrol route.

Cileria had taken that patrol to get away from the anger she felt towards Anne. She had wanted to be with Amil. She still loved him, even if she wouldn't admit it aloud. But this… changed things. They had been through something awful together and looked even stronger for it. She didn't want to admit they belonged together, but she did feel compassion for what Anne must have gone through.

"Sounds like a lot of bad things have happened," she said to Amil, wanting him to know how much this mattered to her and how worried she was for him. "Are you okay?"

"Aye." There was no disguising the exhaustion he felt. He was too old for this anymore. "Atil is under siege by a queen trying to enslave the people and use the volcano to fuel her factories of war."

The young archer was amazed that they could mention meeting a god and not brag about it. She wanted to ask for more details, but saw the pain in Amil's eyes as he continued with his story.

A hint of bitterness crept into his voice. "Besides the killing of literally hundreds of her soldiers, losing a good wolf and friends, almost having my house destroyed, traveling through realms of fire, ice and death; oh and exploding a volcano… I'm doing alright."

Anne leaned against his arm, squeezing his hand in affection as she smiled up at him, her voice soft and quiet. "Thank you for coming for me." She had never doubted that he would.

He smiled down at her from under his hood. "Couldn't have done it without some help. At least you're safe now." And he fully intended it to stay that way.

"Welladay," a young elf greeted with a wave as she joined them. Her pretty dark hair was tied back in a loose tail, her dark robes simple and elegant with silver embroidery.

"Good afternoon to you as well," Amil offered with a slight nod.

Anne offered her own exuberant hello with a tug at the hem of her short skirt while Cileria was merely silent and thoughtful, casting glances over at Amil and Annelise. Typical "how's the weather" and "how fares the day" questions led to Anne finally explaining, "We were just catching up on all the... bad stuff that's been happening."

"Bad stuff?" Her voice held genuine soft-spoken concern, but there was something behind it that seemed to speak of a strong, proud ancestry. "Things have improved, I hope."

Cileria shrugged, remaining silent, now enviously watching the dark haired elf that had joined them.

"Of course," Amil answered with the barest of nods. "With each arrow and every blade swing, things tend to improve."

"There's good too!" Anne added. "I'm gonna get married to this guy." She nudged Amil with an elbow, grinning at the woman.

"A wedding?" Her green eyes lit in happiness for them. "That is truly a joyous occasion!"

"Thanks!" Anne said excitedly. "Not sure there'll be a home 'til all this other stuff is done, but hey," she grinned at Amil, giving him a playful push. "There's always a tree, right?"

"Though not until things settle down," Amil amended. "There is too much on my mind, and too much to be done right now for a wedding."

"Yep. Told my parents to keep my dress safe until we knew Atil was safe again. Then they'll come here with it for the event."

"A very wise decision. Home is where the heart is," the woman smiled, touching her blue bodice over her heart. "I'm sure wherever the two of you end up will feel comfortable." Realizing a lapse in manners, she added, "Forgive my rudeness... I am Vilmalia E'limion, priestess of the Lord and Lady."

Cileria continued to study the ground at her feet. Anne pressed her palms together, stopping from her formal bow just as she realized the skirt would be too short for that. "Tzee Master Annelise Erickson."

"Pleasant to meet you, Priestess." Amil introduced himself, and putting a gentle hand to Anne's back, her as well. "And the one who is so curious about the cobbles is Cileria." He looked to his left as Nyhm seemed to appear from nowhere. "And this is Nyhm."

"Hey there, nimblebutt!" Anne cheerfully teased.

He bowed deeply as the woman put a hand to her side where she might, in other clothing, carry a sword. "Blessed Father!" Vilmalia exclaimed. "How is such a thing possible?"

"He is a walker of the shadow plane," Amil offered by way of explanation. He had known many over the years that were so good at hiding and tracking that they seemed to be one with the very shadows. Nyhm had proven himself one of the best.

The young priestess signed herself over her heart with a circle, back tracing a crescent moon within it. "That is the way of evil... you should not pass through such places."

Nyhm looked to his companions with the same far-away expression he always wore, only now slightly confused. "A way of evil? A shadow hurts none who knows the ways of it."

A frown marred the female elf's features. "Shadows are servants of the Dark One." Vilmalia shook her head. "Perhaps it is not so in these lands... but I would prefer we change the topic to a lighter tone." She looked at the darkly clothed elf. "Have you lived in Lareah for some time?"

"Well," Nyhm said after some time, "Lived and lived." Another pause. "I'm more of a drifter. I sleep when and where I like. I go where I want to be and none can really do anything about it."

The young priestess wasn't pleased with that notion at all. "You have no greater direction or purpose to your life?"

He shrugged, unwilling to elaborate. He'd been on his own too long.

Noting Cileria looking rather upset yet, Anne hooked her arm with Cil's and casually started to wander off. "We'll let the boys explain things to the priestess. We need to chat a minute."

With a start of surprise, Cileria didn't put up the resistance she normally might have, letting Anne lead her away from the others. When asked what was wrong, what was bothering her, she pulled in a shaky breath through her nose. She shook her head, but her eyes belied the truth of her words. "No, nothing."

She smiled in understanding. "C'mon. We're both grown girls. What's wrong?"

Still looking down, avoiding eye contact, she tried, "Noth..." She swallowed against the lump in her throat. She wouldn't cry. Not over this. "Nothing."

Annie knew it wasn't "nothing." Cileria was a tough girl. She could be rude rather than admit weakness, she could be snide rather than show emotion. Cileria was the kind of ranger Annie would have thought a better match for Amil.

Looking up in admiration to where Amil visited with the priestess, it came to her. "Is it all this with Amil? Cileria," she said when the other still refused to look at her, "I know you've been a close friend of his for years. He needs us to be strong for him now."

Bitter skepticism grew in Cileria's eyes as she met the other girl's gaze. "What's that supposed to mean?" She wiped her nose on her sleeve, then quickly brushed a few tears from under her eyes.

She couldn't believe this monk could be so disconnected as to not know how Cileria truly felt for Amil. All she thought this was, was worry for this current threat? Angrily, she wondered that the girl could not know how many battles Amil had been through that had been far worse. This wasn't about Amil. It was about how she felt.

"He's lost his friends," Anne told her in worry. "His wife's clothing was strewn all over the nine hells, he almost lost me, and to top it off, he had to see his daughter in the land of the dead." She knew Cileria was bothered, but Anne had to make her see how bad it had been. Amil didn't need drama. He needed support from those still around him. "He's got to be a wreck. He needs people like you in his life now. Or is it... ohmigosh..." It suddenly dawned on her how long Cileria had been out on patrol. "Is it about the wedding? You didn't know?"

The last question hit a nerve, causing Cil to concentrate on holding her mask of uncaring, looking away again.

"Oh Cil..." Anne hugged her, despite the girl's stiff unwillingness to it, finally realizing what the situation was. "You love him too, don't you? Gods, I'm so sorry!" she said sincerely when Cileria nodded reluctantly, swallowing hard once more.

She looked up, away from Anne, not wanting the sympathy

of someone that had the only thing she wanted. Amil had always been some unattainable goal to her. She had thought he was untouchable to anyone since he'd been alone for so long. It hadn't stopped her from trying. She had gotten him alone many times over the years. She thought she had been making some progress with him. "Mmhm," she offered noncommittally.

"I didn't know." Anne tried to touch her shoulder, only to have her pull away, turning slightly from her. "I'm so sorry! I thought for the longest time you two were together." She moved to stand in front of Cil again. "I tried to stay out of your conversations and everything. I was surprised when he admitted his feelings. I thought you were the same then: just friends." She moved again as Cil tried to turn away once more. "You don't... hate me? Do you?"

A hurtful glare met her. "I did not know what we had, and I did not know that..." she took a moment to collect her thoughts, "...it was over." Cil's thin, bitter smile lasted only a moment before she shook her head again, slow and sad.

"How can I make this right with you?" Anne gave her an honest look of concern. She got a bittersweet smile from Cileria, followed by a sniffle. "I know you've always been close to him. I was going to have you stand as my witness." She offered a rueful smile, afraid of hurting Cil's feelings even further. "I don't suppose you'd want to?"

Taken aback, Cileria wasn't sure what to think of the proposition. Emotions flitted across her face as quickly as they raced through her mind, mostly bitter and hurtful.

"Is that a no?" Her tone was light, almost teasing. "I mean, I could always ask Bodecia, I suppose, but I know he likes you better." Anne smiled, absently tugging at the hem of her short skirt again.

"I..." She set fingers to her forehead, shaking her head. "I can't possibly answer that now. I am not sure... I can..." Bitterness crept back into her tone. "Not like this."

Anne blinked in surprise. "Like what?" She heard Amil telling the priestess about the city, where things were located; heard him mention the location of the museum called the Hall of Heroes. "Amil's in the Hero Hall!" she couldn't help yelling over to them before turning back to Cil, who was now giving her an astounded look.

Trying to take a hand Cil pulled away from, Anne tried again to make amends. "Please tell me. I don't want us to not be friends." Honestly worried, her features looked even more young than usual. "I know this with him isn't easy. But I'd like to have you as a friend. Can we try? Will you think about standing as my witness?"

A heavy sigh escaped Cil as she glanced over at Amil, knowing she had to let him go. "I know he's gone often; takes his trips. But I feel as if he's held me for a fool. It's not like there weren't signs that we shouldn't be more than friends…"

"I know!" Anne agreed with a nod. "He was friendlier with you sometimes than I could deal with. It almost broke my heart. I don't think he ever meant to hurt you though." She followed Cil's gaze to Amil, smiling softly. "I don't think he could. Not to people he cares about." She had to smile at Cileria then when a snort of disagreement came from her. "Okay, maybe he can be daft that way once in a while."

Cileria wasn't ready to let it go. "I'm not sure I should say this, but friends don't kiss, do they?"

"Sometimes. And maybe he does love you, too."

"Or let girls sleep in their…" She stopped with a frown as Annie giggled. "Why are you laughing?"

"I've slept in his room, too." Amil wasn't the kind of guy that had casual company in his room. She trusted that about him. He avoided any kind of complications, especially something like sex that could be an emotional mess. Anne knew Cileria was only trying to hurt her now. "I think we both know Amil doesn't give his heart away easily. We've both got a piece of it." Time to turn the tables on Cil's hurtful little game and let her know that Anne was above it. "Maybe we should see about both being with him."

Her jaw dropped. "You're making jokes out of this! You can't possibly be serious."

Anne shook her head. "Why not? I mean, are there laws that say we can't? Could WE stand each other?"

"Are you for real?" Cileria asked, completely baffled.

She shrugged agreement. "I can't lie." And she hadn't. She had asked a question; not made a statement of fact.

"What do you mean," Cileria narrowed her eyes, "that you can't lie? Everyone can lie…" she glared towards Amil, wishing daggers in his direction, even while he continued to be oblivious to her anger. "Or at least keep the truth for themselves."

"It's part of my dad's heritage to me. Ask me anything. I can prevaricate, but I can't lie."

"Love is between two people," Cil spit at her. "Only filthy human and awful vidu have relationships with multiple partners." She had a moment of glee as shock registered on Annelise's face. "I can't believe you're willing to share your lover. I'd never do that." She tried a few calming breaths, trying to get her rampaging emotions back under control as a longing glance took her back to watching Amil. "I'd give my lover my whole heart and my entire devotion."

Annie's shock at Cileria's insults settled as she took in what Cileria had otherwise said. Cil loved Amil, but it wasn't the everlasting, "do anything" kind of love that she had with him. It wasn't about sex. "He's not my lover," she explained. "Not yet. But I understand love. My father loved my mother so much, that when she wanted a child before me, and he couldn't give her one, he was willing to let her be with another to conceive. I know that some will die to protect their Heart when it isn't this," she put a hand over her own heart, "but another person; someone that will do anything to be sure you are safe and happy." And she knew it was true. She would die before she let him suffer any more in his life than he already had. He had come after her, saved her from certain death. He was her whole world. And truly, she had no desire to share her Heart with anyone else. "Love," she smiled, "means making the other person happy; about not being selfish."

"In true love," Cil shook her head in disagreement, "there wouldn't be desire for anyone else." She was baffled that Anne couldn't see that.

Anne did see it. And felt it. Somehow, somewhere along the way, Amil had become the other half of her heart. She could see that Cileria didn't want to believe it, that the elf didn't want to let go of her own dream of having Amil, and that she would say almost anything to try to ruin things for Anne. But Annie trusted Amil. She knew he would never have "slept" with Cileria the way Cil was presenting, not after swearing his love to Anne. She just needed Cil to see it. "I don't know that I could love anyone else." She looked over at Amil with her heart in her eyes a moment. "But if he loves both of us..."

"Clearly he doesn't..." bitter hurt laced her words.

"Are you sure? Maybe he thinks there's only one choice as well."

"Too late to find out, isn't it?" she asked acerbically.

Not in her mind. She smiled mischievously, then turned to yell over to Amil. "Amil! Got a question!"

"You wouldn't dare!" Cil gasped, grabbing her arm.

"Wouldn't I?" She grinned at her as Amil looked their way, excusing himself from his conversation. "I meant it. I can't lie."

"Don't!" Cil pleaded as Amil came their way. She was furious that Anne would have such an impish grin about this whole thing. "Go back!" She called to Amil, waving him away as if he were a small animal. "Shoo! Shoo!"

With a confused look to each of them, Amil slowly turned, walking back to his conversation with the priestess. Once he had turned away, Cil smacked Anne on the arm. "You're clearly not taking me or my emotions seriously."

"I most certainly am! If I'd have known you loved him before this, I might not have fallen in love with him. I can't NOT be in love now, but if we both are... then why not find out if he feels the same?"

"He doesn't. He wouldn't. It's..." she sighed, "not even a question." Her head drooped. "Maybe I've just been fooling myself all this time..."

Anne crossed her arms, smiling. Finally! Cil was starting to understand. She had to make sure Cileria saw it though. "Isn't sharing him better than hurting like this?"

A stunned look met her. "I don't want to share him! Go back to your future husband and I'll wander off with my tail between my legs."

"Not a good answer." She needed Cil to let go of the jealousy, to see that she was important to Amil yet. "You're part of his life."

Chapter Thirty-Three
A Wedding is Planned

Amil watched the two walk off, but knew enough to stay out of the affairs of women. It would only lead to misery for a man if he were to interfere. Instead, he turned back to the woman. "Is there anything you have questions about, Priestess?"

She asked about the holy city, and if it were true to be a bastion of light and good.

"Aye. Most paladins train and live there. Though it's had its short falls, it is being rebuilt since an invasion destroyed it many years ago. Indeed," he went on when she asked about the holy order of Truth's Light being in residence there, "they now stay on Arindia."

"Then the building here is simply an outpost?"

He nodded. "For the people of Lareah, aye. It's a safe haven for those of the order and those looking for 'salvation' or help. Arindia has been wanted by many over the years, but always it has gone back to the Sigers family, and always it's been protected by Truth's Light." Until now. If he failed, the queen could take all that away, make it a bastion of darkness. He had to stop matters before they reached that point.

Eying the symbol hanging from Vilmalia's neck – a copy of the motion she had made earlier in signing herself – Nyhm asked what higher power she followed. She touched the symbol in response. "I follow the Lord of Day and the Lady of Night. I believe here they are called simply Hirath and Charys." She turned back to Amil. "A further question, good sir? Would you know who may lead the holy orders, both here and in Phaethredun?"

He looked to where the two women were deep in thought, a little concerned at the manner. Both could be very stubborn, which left him a little worried. "Unsure if there is a High Priest or such," Amil turned back to the little priestess before him. "But I know the king is usually dealing with such."

"A liege?" A small gasp of surprise escaped her. "The king deals with such things?"

He chuckled beneath his hood. "He's in charge of rebuilding

the City of Light, though you cannot take my word for it. I do not keep up much on the doings of the king. I have only seen him in regards to other matters."

It made him feel a little old to stand with someone likely Anne's age, so fresh-faced and excited about the world. At least Anne's training made her seem a little older to Amil. Vilmalia was full of questions about the lands and the different islands nearby that housed small communities, such as Atil and the holy city. Then it turned to Lareah, where she was making a home for herself. "It's split up into the impoverished section, the residential," he pointed northeast and east of where they stood, then south. "Southern district has the official buildings: library, Defenders Hall, Hall of Heroes..."

Anne caught the last, hollering back, "Amil's in the Hero Hall!"

He smiled at her wanting to brag about him, but he pretended to ignore it. "And the main docks of the city where you are now, where most of all shops and work is to be held," he continued. "The inn is down to the east," he pointed off the plateau and past Anne and Cileria, then pointed to the west "and opposite is the market. Just beyond that the temple."

Nyhm, quiet up to that point, stretched and smiled at Vilmalia. "I'll be at the um..." he pointed in the direction of the lodge and disappeared.

The little priestess signed herself with the circle/moon symbol again. "Such a talent... I frown to think how that would be treated at home. You said there was a pauper's district here?"

He smirked at both her upset over Nyhm's strangeness and that he had known that the poor would touch her. "Aye, northeast. And an orphanage." With a tone too dry to convey his humor, he answered her question about whether they were given sustenance by saying, "If they are not working, they're on their own."

"Please tell me that is a jest of some ill kind," she responded with a deep frown.

"Life is not always as simple as some wish it can be. Many turn to thieving, murder; many crimes to make a living."

"In a place that seems as established as this, there is no effort to give aid to those less fortunate?"

"There is always an effort. People give coin to the children, try to keep crime to a minimal occurrence and the temple..."

"Hey Amil!" Anne shouted, interrupting his conversation. "Got a question for you!"

He excused himself for a moment. "Aye?" He asked in some trepidation as he approached them. Anne had a look in her eyes that was much too mischievous for him to think any less than that she was up to something.

"Go back!" Cileria waved intently as if she were chasing away a bug or a small animal. "Shoo shoo!"

Unsure, he turned, catching a last glance of Anne looking like a happy version of trouble while Cileria only looked relieved. "As I was saying," he returned to the woman, "they try to help, but the relief is not always enough unfortunately."

Her concern led to him telling her of the orphanage and giving a simple parchment map of the city. "My thanks to you again, Ranger Amil. Truly, the Lord and Lady have blessed me to meet such an established figure in this land."

Uncomfortable with the praise, he brushed it off. "Only because I've been here so long; you manage to remember things that happen around you with enough repetition."

She reached towards him as if to touch his arm, stopping just short of it. "Is there some way I can repay you for your kindness?"

"We'll need someone to do the ceremony!" Anne called when he tried to dismiss it.

"I suppose there is that," he conceded with a chuckle.

She smiled warmly. "I could, if such would be your desire; although I do admit ignorance to your own religious affiliations."

"We follow different gods, so a neutral ceremony would probably be best."

Down the ramp, Cileria searched Annelise's face, trying to find some sense of humor about the monk. What she got was open honesty watching back with focused concern. The offer to share the man was preposterous. "You just… it's just… you seem to take this so lightly... It's confusing."

"Not lightly." She had fallen into the role of teacher again, master of the philosophy she had been raised to. Primary lessons had taught her that nothing could "belong" to a given person. Everything was the property of the world. "I was raised on the concept of the All."

To walk in meditation, ever mindful of what gifts were around you, to share what you could... whether Anne liked it or not, it was an honest option. Not one she liked, but if it would suit the needs of all involved, it could be done. "Whatever I do, will return to me in time, usually three fold. I wouldn't willingly hurt another." She kept her voice pitched low, as they had throughout their conversation.

"I'll leave that to her," Amil answered the priestess' question about writing their vows. "I'm not much of a writer." Even with Oceania, she had just known his feelings. He had never been much for talking about them.

Seeming to sense the same thing, Anne glanced over, raising her voice again. "I'm a monk, not a bard!" As the words left her mouth, she winced, just realizing how painful that comparison might be to him.

Cileria flinched for a very different reason. All this talk of love and marriage and happy vows... "This is painful for me, you know," she said quietly to Anne.

"I know," Anne gave her an understanding smile. "Which is why I want to straighten it out between us. Somehow."

Unaware of what the girls were quietly discussing, Amil turned back to Vilmalia. "We will just go with what's on the tip of our tongues."

She smiled at Amil, glancing to Anne. "They need not be works of poetry; only an expression of your feelings."

Anne's eyes wandered towards Amil a moment, then back to Cil. "I'm not generally sad very often. I look at whatever positives I can find."

"I can't find one right now." Cileria acerbically threw out.

Shoulder's drooping slightly, Anne felt like she was repeatedly walking into a wall. "I'm tired, Cileria. This is so hard. And I need to stay up for him. He's lost so much..." She glanced over to Amil again, hoping he wouldn't notice her worry. Not while he was so calmly and contentedly discussing details they had already decided on for their wedding day.

"Go to him." Cileria told her in a friendly, if sad, tone. "You and I had no relationship, and you do not owe me anything."

"And we can try to be friends then?" She gave Cil a hopeful look.

"An overlook on the cliffs near Lake Amanalu," Amil went

on. He couldn't think of a better place to marry than at the one spot where they had spent so many quiet evenings. "Not a lot of people. As it goes for good friends…" Respect he had in good measure, but, "Mine have long gone or have passed on."

Anne glanced back at the conversation again before smiling at Cil. "I know who I'd like," she said in a soft, kind tone.

Genuinely confused at all the strange twists and turns she couldn't understand in Annelise's discussion, she asked, "Why would you want to be friends with me?"

"You mean something to Amil. That means you're important; to him and to me. And I have a hard time seeing suffering of any kind." Sparing a glance back, she then smiled encouragingly at Cil. "What do you say? Which option? Stand with me or stand beside me?" She needed Cileria to say it, say that she knew she couldn't have Amil. At Cil's bafflement, she added, "Do we find out about sharing him, or will you stand witness for me?"

"This isn't as simple as that." Her voice was more than a little waspish.

She crossed her arms, smiling. "Yes it is."

Cileria looked down, a deep sadness weighing down on her. "To me it isn't."

"Life isn't made of easy choices," Anne offered sympathetically. "We have to find our own ways to move mountains; one grain of sand at a time."

"To me it's not an option. I am not about to share someone who doesn't love me. And I do not believe in the possibility of loving two people equally. Not in a romantic way."

Anne didn't doubt Cil's belief in that. She also knew it wasn't really true. Plenty of people could love more than one person. She called over to the others to get their attention, earning a nudge from Cileria. Smiling at Cil, she nudged her back as she addressed the others. "Is it possible to love more than one person? At the same time? C'mon!" She called after Cileria as the girl abruptly walked away. With a sigh of frustration she went up and explained to the others, "She's in love."

Vilmalia considered. "I don't see how that should be such a difficulty, unless the object of her affection is spoken for."

"Sort of. Yes."

"That is rather problematic."

Anne nodded. The priestess didn't even know how convoluted it was.

"Well to answer the first question, aye it is possible. And two, aye. I would have to agree with Vilmalia." Amil considered how love had put such strange twists in his life over the years. "I loved a wife and two daughters. I would still defend them, even if it meant my own death. Or that I had to kill a cleric, if it came to it. No offense." He offered to Vil.

Chapter Thirty-Four
A Tough Choice

"Life is made of complicated and difficult choices," Priestess Vil offered magnanimously. "We each go our own path."

"Speaking of which," Annie smiled at Vil. "Would you mind if I borrowed Amil for just a teeny tiny... longish... moment? I promise I'll bring him back."

"He is your intended. I don't see that spending time together would be a poor idea."

"C'mere, Bunny Hugger," Anne used her pet name for his title of Ranger while tugging lightly at his arm as he excused himself from the priestess. She lowered her voice when they had moved out of earshot. "Did you know Cileria is in love?"

"She's never really spoken to me of anything of the such."

"Of course not!" She playfully hit his arm. "It's with you!"

Blinking in surprise, he looked down to the cobbles in thought, then glanced at her from under his hood, his thoughtful eyes shadowed by its darkness. "That's why the question? And her leaving so quickly?"

"Yep. I was going to ask you something earlier but she got embarrassed. So," not at all hurt by the thought, her curiosity came through quite clearly. "Do you love her too?"

"I... I don't know what to say... I didn't know she had such feelings." To him, she had always been the niece of a good friend. Pretty, definitely attractive, but he had never considered her as a potential mate; not seriously. Sure, he might have indulged in a few kisses over the years with her, and she had stayed in his home, sometimes in his bed when she needed to be protected or watched over while ill. But she wasn't Anne. "I don't know if I love her. I never really thought of her like that; more of a good friend. We would do a lot of patrols with each other." A lot of patrols. He had helped train her, keeping his friend Tahlon from the prejudice of training his own blood. "She's one of the rangers I suppose I was around the most."

"Okay." Anne smiled. "Cuz I told her I'd ask. If you said you loved both of us, I'd be willing to share you... But she says she couldn't do that." It broke her heart just a little to even speak the words. She could do it, if it was what he really wanted, if it would make him happy, but she wanted to know he loved her and her alone.

"And what do you think of all this?" he asked, sensing the truth. He wasn't going to make the decisions alone in this relationship. She needed to speak her mind, as she had always done, right from the start.

"She thought I was lying about the offer, even after I told her I can't lie." She thought about it, unable to lie, but unwilling to lay her heart out to possibly be crushed. Better to focus on Cileria. "I think she's hurting. Badly. She didn't know we were that serious."

"She is? I... Hmm..." He had never told Anne about the kisses he had shared with Cileria. They had been back when they were just getting to know each other. He didn't think they had affected Cil that deeply. "I didn't know she had such strong feelings about me," he offered honestly.

"I just want to know your thoughts, especially in light of everything that's been happening." She gave him a smile she hoped was understanding. "If you can manage to love two people, after all this time alone, I think that's amazing."

"That would indeed be odd," he answered slowly, weighing his words. "And having two... indeed different and unheard of."

"Do you love her then?" She tipped her head enough to see under his hood, to look for the truth in his eyes. What she saw was a man caught off guard and a little surprised.

"I... I'm a little lost at words at the moment."

"Why?" She grinned playfully. "Because I figured something out, or because you thought you could only love one, or because... what?"

"I have to say I do care for her." Not love. Not like Anne was expecting. "But I don't wish to see her hurt, especially because of me." Anne had offered an excellent solution to the problem... if he wanted it.

He had only recently adjusted to the idea of letting Anne into his heart. He hadn't wanted to fall in love again. And now the idea of two women... "I am a little off-set by the idea of having two people to love in such a way. And how one could even go about doing such... I'm feeling a little lost and unfocused now; as if I'm in the midst of emotional turmoil between two people.

"And you thinking like a monk, in calm serenity, almost makes me feel as if you would go to all ends on trying to make everyone happy." He shrugged more to settle his leather armor that suddenly felt much too heavy. "I don't know what is going on anymore, and I feel like I'm sacrificing my own beliefs as an elf when I don't even know what you really want."

"What I want?" She blinked in surprise, offering a serene smile. "And what beliefs would you sacrifice?"

Amil pushed his hood back to the crown of his head, allowing his blue eyes to give her a penetrating gaze. "Aye, what you want." He loved this crazy, bubbly woman and she needed to realize how much. "It's a bond of two people, to become one in life, to share each other's emotions even, to know how one's emotions are, feelings." His heart constricted as he remembered how much he had loved Oceania; how much he loved Anne now. He had lost part of himself once before. If anything happened to Anne…

He had never, not in all the long years since Oce's death, talked about how that had felt. As hard as it was, now was the time. Taking a deep breath to steady himself, to remain as unflappable as always, he went on. "When you lose your mate, Anne, you feel the very world tear itself apart… as if you lost half your soul."

With absolute concern and worry, Annie admitted her own fear about that. "It's crossed my mind with everything that's been going on. I worry you won't show up after chasing this queen. I worry that something bad will happen, that I won't have you to bring joy into my life."

All the joy she always carried fell away, leaving her more serious and solemn than Amil had ever seen her. She set one small hand on his chest. "You're the other half of my heart," she said quietly. "I don't want to share you, but if it meant the greater good is served…" With her fingers barely touching him, she turned her gaze away from the deep look on his face.

The quiet stretched between them. She knew he was waiting for her to make the final decision. She knew he had likely made up his own mind, but he wasn't the kind of person to demand things go his way. This was one of those things. He wanted her to know her own mind and be content with the decision that would ultimately affect the rest of their lives. "Okay look, here's the thing," she finally said, the spunk back in her voice. "I don't want to share you. I want to be there to help pull your boots off when you're too old to do it. I want to curl up with you at the end of every day and hear what you've been doing. I want YOU, Amil. I love you. And I'm going to marry you." Her heart shone in her eyes, tears threatening to fall with the power of the emotion she felt. "Is that what you wanted to hear? That all my training is crap when it comes to you. I want you, Amil. My job, my training… it can all be damned if I don't have you."

His gaze softened as she spoke, a smile returning as iron bands he hadn't felt around his heart released again. "That's exactly what I wanted to hear."

Pulling her into a kiss, she threw her arms around him, kissing him back. He broke the kiss as a laugh welled up from inside himself with the joy of knowing he was more to her than her duties were. Picking her off her feet, he hugged her tight, absently noting one of her dainty slippers falling to the ground from her foot.

Chapter Thirty-Five
Kiss Kiss

"I'm so scared I'll lose you." Anne kissed Amil. "I've never been so worried about another person." Another kiss. "It feels like my heart is ripped out every time I find you've lost something."

"As long as you are here with me," he continued her kisses, "I do not feel as sad as I should, you are the light and happiness I feel." Another kiss. "You fill my life with joy." He kissed her again, smirking just a little. "Don't expect anything to poetic... I am a soldier after all," he offered as an apology for his frank words.

A joyful laugh escaped her before she kissed him back. "So what," she kissed him, "do we tell Cileria?" A kiss. "I'll share you," she kissed him, "if it's what you and she really want." She rubbed her cheek against his, her nose tucked under his hood with him, taking in the warm scent of leather and that "Amil" scent that had come to mean home to her. "But I don't want to. And I don't mind the no-poetry." Another kiss. "I like the way you look at me."

"Anne," he held her safe and secure in his arms, "I am not one to be shared. She does not wish to share me, as she said to you. Such things happen, and cannot always be resolved. For the other party, things just cannot be as they wish."

Her heart soared to know he was hers. She rained kisses over his face, her arms tight around his neck, not paying attention to the press of the armor against her. "Promise me one thing." He murmured some assent to her. "Before you go after that queen, marry me. Even if it's just a quiet little thing with only a few people. I don't need the big thing. That's more for my mom anyways."

At his nod, she squealed like a small girl and squeezed him tight in a hug. "Should we see if we can fix things with Cileria then?"

Anne challenged him to a race that was more a game of keep-away to try to catch her. Laughing and kissing, they finally found Cileria, far out at the end of a dock. Her eyes flashed in anger as she slowly turned to the happy couple.

Cheeks flushed, Anne couldn't quit smiling, even knowing the difficulty of the conversation they needed to have with her. "So um..." She looked up at Amil.

"I do not believe Anne's idea of sharing is worth it to either of you." Amil wanted to get right to the point and have this matter settled, despite Cileria looking uncomfortable and uneasy with suspicious fear in her eyes. "And with my love to Anne, it's not fair for you at all. I know you have feelings for me Cileria, but I cannot change them."

"Oh, gods," Cileria put her hands over her face, embarrassed.

"Nor do I expect you to change them," he went on gently. "We all love and we cannot help what feelings we have for another."

"I gave him the option." Anne sounded sincere, if not a little too apologetic.

"I told you not to." Cileria sighed and shook her head behind her hands.

"He deserved to know," she offered in a kind tone. "And you deserved the truth from him, too. You two have been friends too long."

"Well," Amil said into the silence that descended on them. "I don't expect anything to change. I still need an outstanding ranger and a dear friend to drag me around on patrols."

When Cileria put thumb and forefinger to the bridge of her nose, eyes closed, and inaudibly muttered to herself, Anne whispered loudly to Amil, "I think that's her way of saying I'm irritating her."

Equally mixed between frustration and sadness, Cil finally answered, "I didn't need your excuse or explanation; nor," she directed at Amil, "did I want what she proposed we could try."

"I didn't mean to embarrass anyone. I just want to make everyone happy."

Strangely, Cil knew Anne was being honest about this. It didn't make this easier. And Amil wasn't exactly helping matters. But Anne was trying, in a very odd way, to help. "You have a strange sense of it," she offered dryly.

Amil smirked when that gained a confused look from Anne, her gaze going back and forth between Cileria and him.

"What?" Anne gave a half-smile, nudging Amil. "What's so funny?"

Amil shook his head while Cileria insisted there was nothing.

"So what now? Do we find you an Amil-ish guy? Are there any?"

"Is there anything else the two of you want?" Cil cut in, her tone sad. "I'm not really in the mood to see anymore of either of you right now."

Noting Anne's concern and truly worried about Cileria, he motioned Anne to go back up to the plateau, perhaps to visit yet with the priestess. "Would you excuse us, Anne?" His voice was low, soft, but he conveyed in his look how important it was he speak to Cil alone.

Chapter Thirty-Six
Walk Away

Amil watched Anne go up the short ramp, hearing her greet someone in her typically chipper tone. Only then did he put a hand on Cil's arm. "We need to talk."

It was the last thing she wanted, but Amil had that pitch to his voice that indicated he wouldn't take no for an answer. She simply nodded, following him to a bench.

"You know I don't take this attitude while we're working," he put out there immediately. He hated drama, refused to have it around him. This would be settled now. "And I don't want it in my personal life either."

She scowled at him. "You should have thought of that before you kissed me."

"Cil..." he sighed. Those few kisses had been years ago. He cared about her, always had, but not the way she seemed to have understood it. "You knew I never wanted to marry again."

"Then what is this?" she demanded, fury in her voice. "For not marrying, you sure seem to be planning one."

"Cil..." There were larger problems that needed his attention now. He pushed his hood back, letting it slide to his shoulders. She was one of the few he willingly showed his scarred face to. He hoped this would let her see how important it was that she understand this; that by keeping his voice soft, low, she'd appreciate what he was saying. "I never expected to fall in love with Anne."

"But. You. Did!" she got out through clenched teeth.

"Aye, I did," his resigned tone reflected in his slightly slumped shoulders.

"You let me stay in *your* room. *You* kissed *me*!"

"I won't deny that," he agreed. "But that was some time ago. And you merely slept there." He looked deep in her eyes, his blue ones blazing with the importance of the discussion.

He had wanted to love her, had tried to convince himself he could...or did. They would have made a good match, especially as she was related to a man he had served alongside for many, many years. "You're Tahlon's niece, Cil. That means something to me."

She shook off his hand when he tried to put it on her arm.

"So I'm good enough to kiss and keep in your home, but not to marry," she spit at him.

"Aye!" He said vehemently, then shook his head. "No… Cileria…" He sighed, fighting the desire to roll his eyes or shake her. "You're good enough for anyone."

"Just not you."

He forced himself not to look away from the accusations in her eyes. "I watched you grow up, Cileria. I couldn't…" he shook his head.

"But you can with her. And she's younger than me!"

Amil reached out like quicksilver, grabbing her arms and shaking her. "Aye! And I told you I never meant it to happen. You know…" it hurt to even say it aloud. "You… know… how much it hurt to lose Oceania."

Cileria's jaw set in stubbornness. "She's dead, Amilmamir. She's been dead a long time now."

A muscle pulsed in his jaw as he fought the anger that brought up. He knew she was hurting, that she was only trying to lash out at him, but it didn't stop her words from affecting him. His voice was low and deadly, coming through clenched teeth. "I died that day. And I swore I would never get that close to anyone again."

"You mean to me," she spit out.

"I meant… to anyone. Cil…" He forced her into a hug. "You're like family to me. I'd never do anything to hurt you intentionally. I do love you… just not the way you want." Her stiffness told him louder than any words that she didn't want to accept facts. "I tried, Cil. I did." He stepped back from her when she wouldn't relax. "I wasn't ready to fall in love a few years ago."

She ignored the scent of home he evoked for her. The leather, the forest, the underlying scent of him… "That's why I had to go on patrol in the farthest sections of Kordathya?"

The sigh that escaped this time was only part frustration. The rest was sadness; sad that he had never told her to go on patrol. She had chosen that. But the deepest distress to him was how she claimed love for him, but knew nothing of what had happened. Worse, that she didn't seem that affected by it.

Even in the light of that knowledge from Anne, she was barely touched with the losses he had faced. She hadn't internalized the pain he was dealing with; not like Anne had taken the losses.

Cileria loved him, but not the way Anne did. She was more in love with the idea of being in love.

That wasn't the first time for him, either. Because of his long history in Lareah, many had looked up to him, tried to win him, or wanted him for their own. He wasn't a prize. And he hadn't asked for the attention. "No one made you go, Cil. You chose."

"And I'm choosing now." She put a hand up to stop him from saying anything else. "I'm walking away. I'll see you at the next council meeting."

"You'll always be family to me, Cileria," he called after her. If she heard, she didn't respond, but continued to walk stiffly away from him.

He knew she would eventually calm and be able to talk about it with him. The question was: did he have the time to wait?

Chapter Thirty-Seven
A Promise

Anne found Vilmalia still waiting, with Nyhm back visiting as well. "Hi!" she called out to get their attention. "He's gonna be a little longer."

They glanced at her before Vilmalia continued talking to Nyhm, sincerely interested in what he wanted out of life. He looked up at the sky, that strange distant look in his eyes. "...I don't know. I make a living by stealing treasures. But," he hurried on, dropping his gaze to the girls, "then I give it all to the orphanage."

Annie saw the look of consternation on the face of the priestess. The monk gave Nyhm a bad time whenever she saw him, but she knew he wouldn't be at Amil's side if he was nothing more than a simple thief.

"What do you feel compelled to do?" Vilmalia asked when Anne mentioned her thoughts.

"...Um... protect people... make people happy, and safe. I think," he said after a moment of vacant looking thought, "it's what I never had; safety and happiness; that's how I ended up like this."

"Compassion for others is an excellent value, Nyhm. But you must be careful not to give too much of yourself." Vilmalia lightly touched his arm. "Giving until there is nothing left of you will certainly bring you to poor health or other injury. Life is a commitment to balance." She waved an open hand out across the stars. "Even the Lord must give over to the Lady at sunset."

"So for everyone I save," he asked in confusion, "I should kill someone else? I guess that is balanced, but unfair... I don't want to end an innocent life."

"I never said you should kill anyone!" Vilmalia looked aghast at the very thought. "Killing is not an act done lightly. I was referring to a balance within yourself, not in a morality context."

"I'd wouldn't kill a man who have done nothing wrong," he worried aloud, using the street vernacular of the poor. "At least, not intentionally..."

"Have you ever given thought to what will happen to your soul when you die?" the elven priestess asked him.

"My... my soul? ...when I die?" He looked up at the stars again. "I guess I will be reborn as something else... maybe a star or a tree." Doubt drew his gaze back to the women. "What if I am judged unworthy by the gods?"

"If you worry about such a thing, then something must be in your past to cause such concern. My advice would be to find a noble and just cause, one that is selfless."

"Oh!" Anne interrupted. "He's got that!" She nodded at Nyhm.

"I am mostly unsure about the judgment of the gods..." he added, still concerned.

"Have you spent time praying in a temple over it?"

"An excellent suggestion, Master Annelise," Vilmalia cheered. "Prayer is a direct way of communing with the gods."

"Yep!" Anne nodded with a smile, but her tone serious. "Sometimes they even play poker with you."

The priestess gave Annie a very perplexed look before shifting her attention back to Nyhm. "The gods are always willing to listen, if you are willing to talk. But be mindful of who you pray to, though," she warned him. "Not all gods are benevolent."

"Like dad would say: 'Lights be praised, that's the truth'!" Still serious, she nodded. "Some even cheat."

Completely aghast, Vilmalia threw back, "I should say not!"

"Sure! The ... un...benevolent ones." She paused, debating if she should tell about her father. "My dad spent time with the gods a long time ago."

"A very blessed man he must be." Vilmalia's tone indicated a lack of belief.

"He had died," Anne nodded. "They brought him back."

The priestess made a circle, tracing it back over her heart. "Lord and Lady... he's a very blessed man indeed!"

"Yeah," she smiled, obviously very proud of her father.

"Do you need further proof of the power of the gods, Nyhm?"

"I do not... I should be at the temple..." He turned and wandered off in the direction of the nearest one.

"Lord and Lady bless you, Nyhm!" she called out before turning to Anne. "He's a very confused young man."

"Yep. I kicked him a few weeks ago. It didn't help."

She turned to Anne, stunned. "Whyever did you kick him?"

"He said he was nothing." She shrugged. "If that were true, he couldn't feel pain." A broad grin lit her face. "Monk lesson."

Vilmalia didn't quite agree on the method, but could understand perhaps it was the training Anne had undergone to learn her path. It wasn't something she could truly address, so she turned to the tiny outfit the monk was wearing. "If I may speak on it," she whispered, "your dress seems... immodest."

"Yeah," she smiled, tugging at the hem. "I think my mom thought I was my older sister Nyx. She's even smaller than me." Nyx didn't even clear the five foot range that Anne barely hit. But she was uncomfortable in the dress and no one had seemed to like it on her. She excused herself to change, noting Amil and Cileria's tense conversation, and hurried back. Anne was much more comfortable in the loose pants and the wrap top. With a smile, she pressed her palms together and bowed at the waist. "My uniform."

Seeing the other woman much more at ease, Anne went on with the other matter she wanted addressed. "So this wedding stuff... We're planning the big to-do with the dress and everything, but there's this queen... if Amil has a chance to stop her, we're going to have to do a quickie service before he goes."

"Oh my," she murmured with a nod. "Aye, of course."

Absently rolling her ankle, letting her red slipper slide on and off, Anne couldn't keep the worry from her voice. "He's lost so much to this woman already..." And she couldn't help but think some of it was her fault. "He just needs to know someone will be there when he comes back from this. Y'know?"

"I'll include him in my nightly prayers to the Lord and Lady," she smiled. "It's been a very long time since my homelands saw that manner of conflict; a very, very long time. As I think on it, it was shortly before we left those lands before. Not that I was alive during all of that." The first hint of a soft laugh escaped her. "That was generations ago, by elven standards."

"Hey Victory!" Anne called out to the scythe-weilding Val'Sadar as he came into view. "C'mere. I want you to meet someone!"

He wandered over, casually drinking from a flask while merrily waving at the girl with his free hand. "Did you just say victory?" Vic knew that Anne loved to give people close to her nicknames. He was honored she'd think to give him one.

"Huh. I kinda like it." And how fitting for someone as amazing as he was.

"Villy, this is Vic. He's Amil's right arm in battle."

"Amil must put his faith in your skill at arms, to be considered so."

"Oh," Vicarious cleared his throat as he noticed the fair form of the young woman, his voice going flirtatious. "Hellooo."

"This's Priestess Vilmalia. She's gonna marry Amil and me."

"...Priestess?" His playfulness died, his tone going flat. "Oh."

She smiled politely. "There's no cause for concern on my title, is there?"

"Er, no." He kept a coy smile directed at the pretty girl while damning his misfortune. There would be no banter with this one; those connected to temples tended to be rather... stuffy.

"He's made sure Amil comes back to me every time they've gone out."

"Well, I *am* pretty amazing." Rather proud of himself on that fact, he buffed the fingernails of his left hand against his white coat. "No one gets past Vicarious. Unless they ask nicely. But they usually don't."

He grinned as that gained a laugh from both girls. "Speaking of Amil... I ain't seen him in some time."

Annie glanced around. "I left him talking with Cileria. Ooh!" Her face lit up as a good idea hit her." Y'know, Victory, you should go out with Cileria. You're entirely cute and a good arm with a weapon."

"Yeah, see... I've talked with her. She's got this problem with vidu..." he grinned, acting his typical arrogant self. "But she still has a crush on me. She just doesn't want to admit it. Makes her pretend harder."

With that the young priestess excused herself to her evening prayers. "It has been a great pleasure to meet the both of you." She formed a circle over her heart, back tracing a crescent moon within. "And may the Lord and Lady keep you both safe."

"Goodbye, priestess lady!" Vic grinned and waved as Anne pressed her palms together, bowing at the waist with the farewell of "walk in peace."

They stood in silence as she walked off. "Thanks," Anne said quietly, not looking at Vic, "for saving me." It seemed so little for all that had been done to free her from the clutches of the crazy women that had taken her.

"Oh that? Don't worry about it!" He turned to her, striking a heroic pose with a flirtatious smile. "It's what the great Vicarious does!"

"Yeah, well," she laughed, "you guys got to me in time. I appreciate it. Darned weapons and my oath and all. Yeah," she went on when one corner of his mouth came up and his brows knit together, "I'm a Tzee Divine, I've sworn to the gods not to touch a bladed weapon in exchange for their Gifts."

"Well that's a weird thing to swear." He didn't like the kind of oaths that placed one higher than another. Despite – or especially because of – being a noble back home, he kept that part of his history to himself. He didn't want to be treated any different than anyone else. The gods should be the same way; not making you swear and promise on crazy ideas. "Do they have something against blades?"

"When you're a monk that heals people, yeah."

He returned her infectious smile as he tapped his chin. Being a healer was a little different. That he could understand foregoing weapons for. "I guess that's fine then."

She nodded agreement. "They're good with everyone else using blades, so no worries for you there! Anyways..." Anne threw her arms around him, hugging him tightly. "Thanks."

"Alright, alright," he pushed her away with a grin. Didn't need some girl getting all mushy with him now... even though it did feel good to be acknowledged for his part in things. Better to deflect a little of that love. He pat his scythe, still at hand. "My partner feels better now." It had the desired effect, making her back up with a laugh. "Say," he changed the topic, "about those things Amil should know... Er... Heh..." he gave a weak laugh that held nervousness. They had discovered a few things that needed to be passed along. "Well," he made an "ahem" noise, clearing his throat. "Does he know about his cat?"

Blinking in surprise, Anne looked up at him in shock. "What about Cane? Did you find him?"

"Er... This might be hard for you ta hear..." he took a fortifying drink from a flask as Nyhm and Amil joined them on the plateau. "...Right." He waved halfheartedly at them.

Anne wasn't about to dismiss it that quick. "He knows

something about where Cane is."

The lighthearted moment between Nyhm and Amil fell away, Amil sheathing his blade with a quick motion and a clink as the crossguard snapped against the scabbard. Nyhm guiltily looked away, having known and not shared that information as the two of them had just been visiting. "I'm going to get some sleep..." He sidled off as Amil turned back in question to see Vic looking like a cornered animal and Anne standing militantly with her arms crossed.

Vic's hand went to his pouch of its own accord, caressing a bottle that was just waiting for him to take a steadying drink from. "We got reason to believe he's gone. And not in the good way. I mean the... sad kind of gone."

Anne moved to lean supportively against Amil as he asked, "And what reason do you have to believe that?"

"We've been working while you were doing other things. We saw the queen... through a magic orb thing. She was um... wearing a panther skin." Vic nodded when Amil repeated the last.

"Oh Amil!" Anne's heart was breaking. It was too much for one person to have to lose.

"I see..." he tried to ignore the soft support he longed for at his side. "Did you find out where the queen was by any chance?"

"Yeah, we did. We took out that Remy guy.. or rather... he kind of died."

"So you killed her, right?" Anne's worried gaze bounced between them.

"There is still the Warlord and herself then," Amil muttered when Vic shook his head to the negative.

"Yeah," the vidu added. "And we got a means to portal to her sanctuary, too. We weren't gonna attempt anything more without you, though. We used it more for a rescue mission." He glanced at Anne, knowing she wouldn't want to hear the next part. "Basically, we can go there whenever we want to. Once we're ready."

Amil nodded agreement, even as he sensed Anne's tension. "When we gather again, she will taste good ol' Atilian steel." He pat the sword at his hip.

"I think... I'm going to go pray. I'm not sure I want to hear about this mission. I'm going to hope the gods are listening and will bring you all back safe." Pulling on either side of Amil's hood, Anne went up on tiptoe to give him a kiss.

He returned the kiss, then offered a promise in a threat. "Pray for them; they will need it more than we will."

A rare flash of fury crossed her features as she fiercely swore, "I'll pray she goes down before you get near her. Vic, you keep him safe, okay?"

With a start of surprise, Vic stood straighter. "Ah... right!"

"And we have a promise, right?" She pinned Amil with a look she wouldn't release until he nodded. Only then did she smile, blowing both men a kiss. "I'm going back to Amil's then!"

Neither said a word until she had stepped onto the docks. There was planning to be done, and time was growing short for them.

Chapter Thirty-Eight
Not Today

Amil went first to the bathing room, letting the others raid his pantry. A long soak was just what he needed, letting the stress melt away as much as he could. He let the heat ease the aches in his back and his knees. It helped to know Anne was just a door down from the room he was in now.

It further helped to be clean, in soft linen sleep pants. Barefoot, he crept into his own room, mindful of the young woman asleep in his bed. She had long ago been given her own room in his house where she had taken to sleeping with his wolf and panther, but ever since her capture and return to safety, she had taken to sleeping in his bed. Even with his companions gone or missing now, he was glad she seemed to find his room restful.

Adjusting the quilts across the over-stuffed leather chair, he slowly lowered himself down into it, careful not to make any noise. He had slept in much more uncomfortable places over the years. And knowing he was still protecting her made it easier for him to justify sleeping this way. Catching the footstool with a toe, he pulled that close enough to put his feet up before pulling another quilt over himself. He lay there for a long time, watching Anne sleep.

The volcano had blown again in the past weeks. The few survivors had been sent to Lareah, but he feared there was nothing for the island anymore. The lava had even taken the forests closest to his home. Another explosion and his orchards, already in trouble, and his home would be destroyed. It was time to move Anne back to the mainland.

Items were nothing. As much as he had used this place to hang on to his past, the people that had mattered weren't there. He had faced his daughters and put that to rest. He had to trust that Firnos would someday take him to the Hunting Grounds, letting him, as unlikely as it would be, again see Oceania.

All that was left right now was Anne. And he wasn't going to let her be destroyed. Not when he could save her. She was well enough now that it was time to take care of the queen.

After a fairly restful night, he woke to have Anne curled in the chair with him, sharing the single blanket. Her cold nose was tucked just under his ear and her hair tickled his nose, but he wasn't about to move her. Careful not to lose the blanket, he moved just enough to put an arm around her.

"Are you leaving today?" her sleepy voice asked, one arm wrapping around his waist. She so rarely got to spend any time with him out of his armor.

He nuzzled against her hair, taking in the soft scent of her. She never wore perfume like Oceania had, but instead had the soft smell of clean linen and fresh air. "No," he whispered to her. "Sleep."

In response, her cheek rubbed against his bare shoulder. "You're not." Her voice was still sleepy and warm.

A breath of laughter escaped him, and he felt her smile against him. "I was planning on hiding your shoes," he teased. "And why aren't you in the bed?"

"Because you weren't." She snuggled further into his arms.

It hadn't been easy, but they had agreed the timing for more between them hadn't been right. "Soon enough." He kissed the top of her head, not wanting to tell her it probably never would happen now. Not unless they were to marry in the short time remaining yet, which he knew she wanted. He did as well, but he couldn't justify what he felt would leave her a widow before she could truly be a wife. If it wasn't for the fact that he remembered how happy she had been to get the ring from him, he might have called it off for now.

Her nose wrinkled against him about the same time he became aware of an acrid burning smell. She bolted upright, elbows digging into his chest, eyes as wide as dinner plates. "Fire!" She scrambled out of his lap, shaking the now-twisted blanket from her leg and bouncing in large, hopping steps as she grabbed at her clothes, pulling her gi on over the shorts and Amil's shirt she had been sleeping in. "Slippers....slippers..." She searched through the blankets on the bed (the gods only knew why on the bed) and under, finally pulling her favored red shoes onto her feet.

Amil darted to the door, making sure the fire wasn't on top of them. Smoke was starting to roll in their direction, but he couldn't see the flames yet. Any minute the house could burn. He spared a glance for where she was bouncing around the room, gathering her few things and spare outfits, throwing them into a bag. "I'm going to get dressed!" he shouted as he raced back to the bathing room.

With the ease of long years of practice, his armor practically donned itself. Sword. Dagger. Bow... He looked around. Bow...

Anne appeared in the hall, her bag over one shoulder and both their bows held close to her body. "It's not steel," she grinned. "Let's get out of here."

He spared a smirk for her that she couldn't handle steel, but would willingly take up a bow just to mimic him. "I've got them." He took them from her, racing down the hall.

Anne plowed right into the back of him as he slid to a stop. Through the smoke he could see the four chairs in his entry-way as a center of conflagration. All that was left of his previous life... gone now.

It wasn't the chairs that Annie noticed. It was the lava creeping and burning through that side of the building. The whole floor was a steaming mess of red-hot fluid. "We can't go that way," she yelled over the roar of flames and groaning of wood cracking and breaking. She pulled at his arm, tugging him back the direction they had come from.

His steps were a little slower as he forced himself to look away. His reverie was broken however when the ceiling creaked, groaned, and collapsed, covering the area. With a new burst of speed, they went back towards the bathing room. Anne was coughing now as the smoke became thicker. Explosions rocked the building behind them.

The windows in this room weren't meant to be opened, but only to provide light. Taking his dagger, he turned his face away and smashed the pommel to the glass. Anne screamed as the roar of flames appeared, snaking along the ground and creeping across the walls.

Hoping his gauntlets would protect his hands, he pushed out the last ragged edges of glass, lifting Anne up. "Out."

She wriggled, wanting down. "You first."

He set her down, giving her a stern look. "Anne, you're younger. I want you safe."

"I want you safe," she shot back.

"By Firnos..." he swore, picking her up again and pushing her onto the small ledge. "Out!"

"Amil!" she screamed from the outside as the crackling and popping came now from the benches and plants inside, hissing as the lava hit the bathing pool. She heard something scrape along the floor inside, the bows were tossed out, then Amil appeared, hoisting himself up and over the ledge to roll onto the grass, breathing hard.

He was too old for this; dragging heavy furniture around, climbing around like a cat... and there was no relief. Anne was tugging at him to get to his feet. "We need to get to the docks. We need to go, now!"

With a groan, he gave in to her goading, coughing the smoke from his lungs as they ran to the dock. The main boat that had ferried him across the last several years rarely came now. All that awaited them was a small dingy that would comfortably hold the two of them.

They took turns rowing back to the mainland, watching the last of his isle, his home and his orchards go up in flames. They went straight to the Defenders first, letting them know what had happened. Then they had to find a room at the lodge. At least he would have a night or two to hold her in his arms.

Chapter Thirty-Nine
Preparing for War

Messengers and couriers rode hard between the towns as word spread over the next week. In less than six months, Atil had been destroyed by industry, and was now being slowly consumed by volcanic ash and lava.

"Atil in peril. Island attacked by a queen bent on destruction, enslavement, and building a factory to produce machines of war. Ranger Amil's fiancée in danger. With the latest volcanic eruption, it is feared the foreign queen will move on our other towns. Request aid as possible. ~Defender Siril Te'lie."

It wasn't just the volcano, though. Others had seen the tunnels starting to show up through out the lands. A group of organized mercenaries calling themselves Gray Gryphons took up the message, running their own.

"It's bad," Gray Gryphon Farra sent back to her group. *"The volcano is erupting. The boatman refused to let me go ashore due to the danger, but did tell me a queen had taken all that belonged to the ranger. His girl is safe now, but the queen remains at large. She has had tunnels dug all under the lands, which may even reach as far as our holdings. Someone of rank may want to be in touch with either this Amil or the defender."*

After a quick briefing, it was decided they needed to throw in with the others. Farra's mate, a mage with the Gryphons, sent on to Siril, *"Let us know how we can help. Standing by."*

The king of Phaethredun, on the nearby island of Arindia, posted, *"My loyal guard, It has come to Our attention that Atil is in trouble. Via Lareahan Defenders to Garrison's Gryphons, one has made their way here to inform Us that Atil has been destroyed. High Council Ranger Amilmamir Mor Nermakiir is in grave distress. While We cannot leave Our city, We ask those of you who might, to offer aid. Our thanks, King Sigers."*

And so it went from the druids in the wilds to the clerics in the city temples as they sank to their knees, asking the gods to protect their cities. Rogues carried the news under the cover of shadows, passing information as they exchanged illicit materials in secret meetings while those with swords pulled glistening steel, making sure their blades were at the ready.

The bards caught wind of the worries of the people, not sure how to help, but wanting to be part of protecting the lands. Amil alone was reason enough to help. All knew him, all knew Atil and the welcome her people had always provided. But above that was the worry that this rogue queen might move on any of them next.

The people of Atil had been killed outright for not accepting a new ruler, or pressed into slavery - either alive or undead. To prevent attacks on other towns, increased protection walked the gates and walls. Any that could be spared began to rally near the Defenders Hall in Lareah, pledging whatever they had to the coming battle.

Word finally reached the Grove, a sacred space for the druids and rangers, as Amil, exhausted, found Kjorrath, one of the druid elders. He told the Elder that he had watched the island be destroyed rather than let this Queen Lutheria have it. He spoke of the troubles, the worries he had for the lands yet. Animals perk up at his words, listening intently.

"Firnos came to me," he informed the man quietly. "I was told that there will be heavy tolls for at least one brave enough to face this queen." It was with a heavy spirit, knowing that he would break Anne's heart, that Amil told the Elder, "I'm taking that burden on my own shoulders."

Kjorrath grieved with him for the loss of his wild friends and for his lands. They grieved all that had been taken and all that would yet suffer for this woman's selfish ends. "The Lord of the Hunt has set your course," the old druid finally said. "Others need to know."

It was a death sentence; one he didn't want to inflict on anyone. "I can't ask anyone else to join me."

Yet a loyal group remained ever present for him, despite such dark tidings. They had started the discussions while he dealt with the end of Atil. It was they who had started rallying the organizations, and they who had planned the mobilization.

Chapter Forty
Vigil

Amil stood on the cliffs high above the sea surrounding Atil, only allowed to set foot on the isle because it was his land. The night air blew a warm breeze across his face, making his cloak flutter with the wind. He took in a breath of the salty air, exhaling slowly, savoring the scents of the water. He gazed up into the celestial bodies shining brightly above in the clear night sky. His mind rolled over and over with the events that had led him to this point. Looking back inland, all he could see was destruction.

Atil, his island home, had once been damaged some years back by the volcano that had lain dormant for centuries. It had only started to show recovery when this queen had shown up with her war-mongering. The good people had either been taken for her use or killed. The machinations of this empire had caused the volcano to again erupt, destroying the land once more. Long had it been since he had needed to defend his own home from the terrors of others.

Malania, his wolven companion for the greater part of his life, trusted, and always near at hand no matter what hells he ventured into... dead at the hands of this woman's wrath. Cane, his panther, was now dead, skinned and worn as a cloak in the queen's attire. And his new love, now in constant danger, hunted for the twisted desires of a psychotic regime.

He had failed in the past; failed to protect Oceania and his daughters. Now he had failed his companions, coming too late to save them from their fate. Not again. He was going to strike before any more could come to harm, before any more had to suffer. If he could prevent war, prevent anyone else from becoming enslaved by this queen, to save those who were under her threat... even if it meant his death, he would succeed in destroying her cause.

The queen was trying to break him; so they had found out from their questioning. She was trying to drive him away.

She had failed.

His eyes narrowed as he looked across the sea to the distant shores of Lareah. He lifted his hand, a red carnation grasped lightly in his fingers. Looking over its petals and slender green stem, he thought of Anne. It was stronger than it looked, like she was. The stem didn't break, but instead bent in the shifting breeze, the leaves gently fluttering.

He didn't want to lose what happiness he had gained back in his life this last while, but if the lands needed him to... Anne kept saying nothing was permanent, to enjoy what they had been given while they had it. They had talked about him being older than her; that he would likely die before her. She swore she could, and would, deal with it when it happened. He worried that time was coming. It was time once again to trust his life into the hands of Firnos. If his god couldn't see him through...

Slowly, so slowly, one finger at a time, he opened his hand, letting the flower go. He watched it fall, sometimes catching on the breeze, turning and twisting, sometimes bumping against the rocks and crags, until it touched down in the crashing waves below.

Going to one knee, he bowed his head. He had lived his life in honor of Firnos, but had never been one for true prayer. Now he whispered words just barely heard over the breeze. He pulled a glove off, drawing the symbol of Firnos on the ground, then pressing his palm over the image of a bow with two crossed arrows in it. "Not my will, but yours be done."

Word had already been spread to all groups that might be able to aid him in the coming battle. Whatever happened, the queen would be taken down.

Standing silently, he looked one last time across the sea, white caps crashing below as the waves rolled towards the cliffs. He looked to his right where his blade was sunk into the ground. Wrapping his hand around the now cold handle of the sword, he pulled it from the earth, raising it in front of his face, the blade pointed straight up with the face staring at his own. The Atilian symbol engraved elegantly into it with the island markings running along its length reminded him of the gift this blade had been, lovingly made by a blacksmith trained by generations of forefathers on the same forge. It was a beautiful piece of work that he had been, and would especially in this coming battle, be honored to carry.

He was the last of a people he had called friends, brothers, and family on the island he had made his home. He would be the last of them to raise a sword against all those enslaved and twisted to a queen's will. They had resisted her unto death, sometimes beyond. He slammed his blade into the sheath with a quick snap and clink as the blade locked in.

    With the wind wrapping his cloak about him, he walked back to stand vigil over the smoking remains of what had been his life. Tonight he would mourn the isle, his home, and all the dreams he had long thought gone. Tomorrow he would go to war.

Chapter Forty-One
Magic Orbs

The time had finally come; Nang knew it deep down. As she waited with Nyhm for the arrival of Amil and the others, they found themselves talking to a member of the Truth's Light. In her mind, the man was a typical narrow-minded holy warrior. That was reinforced by his intent stare upon both Nyhm and herself. "I like to know who I'm dealing with," he said in a stoney voice, "friend or foe. I learned the hard way that betrayers can come from anywhere."

"Great," Nang muttered, "this should be about as much fun as working with that Steven fellow. Remember," she asked Nyhm, "that guy that kept racing ahead? Almost got us killed?"

"I don't mind a fellow of the Light," the young elf told Nang, giving the Lighter a pointed look, "as long as he doesn't point his sword at my throat for speaking what's on my mind."

Amil joined Nyhm and Nang to find them in dispute with the gruff paladin. He soon found himself engaged in the same conversation, discussing the morals of being evil or good, and what the basis was for each.

Vicarious strolled up whistling and twirling his scythe almost like a baton. "There you are," Nang tried to sound disapproving as Vic gave a wave with a goofy grin.

"Aye indeed," Amil added. "Been wondering where you have been. Kids? And teaching?"

"Yeah, didn't I tell ya?" His chest puffed up proudly. "I'm a great teacher as well!"

"Imagine that." There was no helping the dry, sarcastic tone from Nang. She could hardly believe it. "Vicarious; teaching children."

"And it came from Vic's mouth." Amil knew how capable Vic could be. He had seen him outside of this one quest for justice. The man was a little too liberal with the alcohol, but he knew his business when it came to a fight. "Obviously," he teased, "there is something amiss just yet to hear what it is. What are you teaching them, Vic?"

"Well, right now I teach the non-physical aspects of fighting.

But soon, when they're older, I'll have them doing the real thing. Besides that I have a good staff teaching them all kinds of other stuff." He took the pose of a hero's statue, hands on hips, shoulders back and shook his hair away from his face. "They all love me of course. *And* they call me Master Vic!"

Nang shook her head. "I still shudder at the thought of him teaching." She gave Vic a penetrating gaze. "Maybe I'll sit in on one of your classes... just to see."

"But I'm a great teacher! Plus, it's not like anyone was going out of their way to teach them nothin' before. These kids are from the orphanage. Way I see it, I'm givin' them options in their lives. Anyway! Seeing that Amil is here, I'm guessin' you got all your stuff in order?"

"I'm always in order." Amil said.

"Right! So am I! Are we waiting for the others?" He fished a bottle out of his coat and took a few drinks.

"Siril and Felicia," Nang answered with a nod just as Felicia gracefully came up the ramp perusing a book.

Vic waved at her while the paladin stared intently at the vidu. He was all for attention and being stared at – he was amazing, after all – but this man was sending shivered down Vic's spine. "He always do that?" he asked of the others.

"I think he dislikes elves."

The Lighter had the gall to look offended at Nang. "I have nothing against any race unless they are inherently evil with no chance of redemption."

A humorless laugh escaped Felicia. There was no such thing as a cut and dry "good" or "bad" person. "Back in the day, people thought Angon was far from redemption," she offered, throwing yet another name out that meant little to those assembled, "and yet he turned into a new direction. So your view is quite narrow." It didn't matter if they didn't know the name. The point was the same. And to drive it home, she pointedly didn't look at the holier-than-thou fool, instead keeping her eyes on the book, turning another page.

"Should we try for politeness then?" Nang cut in before the man could respond. She introduced each of them before asking for the man's name.

"Not necessary," he dismissed, letting them know he had no intention of ever seeing them in the future. "I don't think any of you will meet me after this queen is dealt with."

Nang gave him a cold smile. The 'Lighters had a reputation for high-handed self-righteous behavior that she wasn't sure they wanted along with them. "So if we need you to do something in combat, I should shout "hey you"?"

"Or 'you in the yellow'?" Felicia added. "Ooooor... 'Hey goldie'!" she threw out in reference to the man's very yellow uniform.

"Paladin is what people usually use," he said with a disdainful look down his nose at them.

"That's what you do, not who you are." Nang looked to the others as Vic grinned behind his bottle. "Remind me not to trust Truth's Light to be what they seem to be, if this man is an example."

"Some," Amil chided gently. "Not all. Some of them are really good people; some are extremists. The things that happen in your life help mold you into what you are or will become."

Felicia simply tapped the page she was looking at in contemplation, not even looking up as she noted Siril joining them.

Having heard the last few comments on his way up to them, Siril added, "If balors raised you and you never saw another human or heard of them, you wouldn't think being evil is a bad way of life. Come as a surprise then if you get killed for something you just did as part of your everyday life."

"That is why I do not attack unless they come at me first," the man shot back, still on the defensive.

"But then of course," Amil added, unaware that Vicarious and Siril were suddenly absent, "we can get into ethics, which could be a very long conversation; one which I do not have much time for."

Nang looked around as she realized the vidues were missing. "Where are Siril and Vicarious? Weren't they here just a moment ago?"

Looking up from her book only momentarily, Felicia muttered, "Maybe they walked off."

"No," Nang answered, pointing at the platform. "Siril was standing right there."

There was no discussion of splitting up to search. Too many times they had seen that happen over their hunt for the queen. Nothing good ever came of it. Instead they pondered the best method to find their comrades.

"Magic might find them."

Felicia shook her head at Nang. "In a city with its own magic school, picking his signature out would be too hard. Check for tracks?"

"In this city?" Amil shook his head. "I don't believe there would be any possible way. The grass and dirt is so trampled, and cobble is extremely hard, if not impossible. Maybe Siril's magical energy, if there was a way to sense for it."

"Why not scry the Defender's Hall?" Nyhm offered.

Amil didn't plan to use magic when he could just walk across town to the Defender's headquarters. He started off, leaving them to follow as they wished. They fell into the pattern they always used, with the holes showing where their friends would have stood; Amil to the front with Nyhm ranging slightly ahead to keep the way safe, Nang behind and to the right of Amil, her left side empty where Vicarious normal stood. Felicia came just outwards of that empty spot, her right side empty where Siril normally walked. The paladin straggled behind, unsure what to make of the group.

They went into the southern district of the city, noting the voices of multitudes getting louder the closer they got to the stronghold. One last turn brought the spacious area before the hall into view.

It looked like most of Kordathya's forces swarmed amidst the standards of different organizations and cities. The dark city of Kron'tir's militia mingled with the order of Truth's Light from the holy city of Phaethredun. The Gryphon Mercenaries stood alongside Lareah's Defenders. A few of the vidu, a force unto themselves and usually dependent upon no other race, had also come. All Amil's rangers that had been within distance had arrived and now stood with druids and Wild Elves that rarely stepped within city walls. They all had heard the call for assistance and answered to defend Kordathya from a queen who wanted to enslave the people and take the world for herself. Amil looked upon the force with surprise. He hadn't expected many to show, especially some of the more volatile groups. Seeing them standing side by side was beyond belief.

Unaware that the others had been searching for them, Siril Te'lie and Vicarious Val'Sadar turned as one to face their friends from the center of the crowd. Vic cleared his throat, throwing his arms wide as he grinned at them. "Vicarious' great charisma saves the day!"

Nang was astounded that he would claim something so outrageous, but Amil simply smirked his quiet smile. "Right. Explain?"

"As you can see," Vic purveyed the assembly, acting rather proud of himself, "these guys all got drawn here cuz of the awesome stuff I did. So they're gonna help us with the queen."

Nang saw it as the boast it was, and fought the smile threatening to come to her lips. He could be a showman when he wanted, and he was obviously a natural leader. Not that she'd tell him, though. "I'm officially worried now," she said loudly enough for him to hear.

Amil was stunned that so many had come to his aid. He looked to his companions, wondering how so many knew of this day. Siril met the gaze, smiling and offering a small nod that he had been behind it. "They came," Siril corrected the other vidu, "because a call went out for aid. I sent word to the Gray Gryphons. They in turn sent runners out to other cities. And now, as you can see, we are not alone in this."

Nang and Amil both agreed that made more sense, but Vic wasn't done yet. "You know that my exploits only helped of course. But, uh, what do we do with all these guys?"

"What they have all gathered for," Siril's no-nonsense tone answered the other vidu. "To do what we do best."

A true smile, one almost of relief, touched Amil. No matter what would come of this adventure, he would always know he had developed the best (and oddest) team ever assembled. Together they would see an end to this queen's tyranny.

The Kron'tir guards, given to shady dealings and dark promises, uneasily eyed the holy Truth's Lighters, but stood ready. The rangers swung up into saddled horses. "Mount up men! We're ready to move!"

Kjorrath, the Archdruid came forward, several druids at his back. He simply nodded, leaning on his staff of office as the slight form of the Wild Elves' queen gracefully stepped forward, wearing the minimum in leather skins that would count as decent. "I am Tenanye. We have all come to aid the one who would face this danger."

One of the vidu men from Vic's mountain home stepped forward, a dozen of their strongest warriors, men and women, behind him. The man respectfully inclined his head to Vic, recognizing the man slated to become the next ruler of the Val'Sadaran clan. "We will follow at a distance. Should you need us..."

Vic couldn't have been more proud. Even for them thinking he was the part he'd played as a fool, they were willing to follow him into possible death. They deserved better than someone like he thought himself to be; a profligate, someone only wanting freedom, someone running from duty. He should have let Nang know he had seen her attention on him, that he might maybe feel a little something back for her. He should have owned up in that instant, taking the mantle as the Vhalar of clan Val'Sadar, yet something balked within him. Instead, he grinned, clapped his hands together, rubbing them in glee. "Right! So we storm the queen's palace and waste her!"

Nang watched the conflict flash across Vic's features. She had hoped to see him step up; prove he was more than a silly drunk. She sighed as he purposely turned from her. "Which is...where?"

"Well..." Vic offered, "The orb. Right?"

"Indeed," Amil agreed. "Where is this orb?"

Siril stepped aside from his place near the orb, now moved outside to accommodate the large gathering of people. Standing waist high, the crystal had changed from the time Siril had started studying it, becoming more powerful, transforming from an orb to a floating blue teardrop shape.

Nang looked at it dubiously. "How are we going to get all of *these* people into that little orb?" she waved an arm at the amassed crowd of warriors, pleased in spite of the conundrum at how the arrogant Sirenian queen would have to take pause.

Looking over the amassed army, Amil wasn't sure either. "We need to know where this queen is first. Then figure out from there."

"I should warn you," the Defender cut in, "that when we tried to move it outside of the city, a few of our men were lost trying to handle it. It's more powerful now." He lowered his voice when Nang asked how they had been lost. "They were sucked in."

So that was their way to the queen: to enter the orb. Amil nodded slightly, looking over the crowd, back to the orb. "Then there may be men on the other side, possibly near the queen."

"Provided," Siril corrected, "they are still alive."

Vic pulled his fingers through his hair, shaking it into perfect form, and brushed non-existent lint from the flawless white coat. "Let's get ready to kill some goons!"

"Looking good, Vicarious." Nang wasn't sure herself if she meant it facetiously or as a compliment.

He grinned. "I look good *all* the time."

"So," Amil brought their attention back to the situation, "this thing possibly takes us near, or right to, the queen?"

Felicia crossed her arms, her voice dry, "I rather hope it doesn't put us too close to her, since logically speaking that would be the most guarded place."

With a nod, Siril approached the crystal. "It seems to be keyed to her location, although through a little manipulation, we can… or used to be able to… be a little selective about where we show up at."

"We got a large force," Vic added, "and probably the advantage of surprise."

A disgusted laugh escaped Felicia. "Yes, but never underestimate the enemy."

"They know we can get through the orb," Nang added, getting a motion from Felicia that claimed "see?" as she looked at Vic. "If I was the queen, I would move the orb or trap the entire area that the orb is in."

Playing the fool yet, Vic tapped his chin, drawing his words out. "Oh yeah."

"How did you do it?"

Siril gave a slight nod to Amil's question. "Before it changed, I simply moved my finger around the surface and 'moved' it from one place to the next."

"Can you possibly try it again?"

Careful to avoid placing his entire hand on it, Siril did as he had before, putting a single finger to the orb, sliding it across the surface as the view within shifted. The scene was shadowed as it rolled slowly past, the Defender walking clockwise around the crystal, never removing his finger as he tried to find some kind of landmark. Into view came a duskily lit area of sand. An old wooden chest with metal fittings sat partially buried, with a magical door hanging in the air behind it. "There… the door. Do you see it?"

Joining him, Amil peered into the hazy image. Whatever the place was they were looking at, it had to be the way to the queen.

"As long as everyone remembers," Vic addressed their group while eying the elf queen standing near to his right side, "the queen is Amil's kill. Everything else is fair game."

"Exactly," Felicia laced her fingers, palms out, cracking her knuckles with a wicked grin on her face. "We're the cleaning crew to get Amil a clear shot."

Vic agreed by taking a drink, lifting the flask in a salute and offering a loud burp.

"That doorway," Siril explained, trying to ignore the rude manners of Vicarious, "leads to a pocket of sorts. It's a spell. A very powerful one that creates a safe haven for a short time."

"You think she's hiding there?" Nang asked at the same moment Amil asked, "That door leads to our destination?"

"I'm not sure." Siril shrugged one shoulder. "Possibly? She would be safe there."

Felicia carefully came in at their side, a shoulder turned to them but not touching. "I doubt we can fly. Could make reaching a floating door hard, hm?"

"Agreed," Amil mused, "so we wouldn't be able to get to her then…"

Leaning between Siril and Amil, Nang and Vic studied the situation. "Feh," Vic muttered, glancing at Nang, "bring a ladder or something."

She looked back at him with a smile. "It doesn't look that high. Fairly easy jump."

"Guess we really won't know much more until we actually get in there," Amil said as he looked over the assembly.

"You lead," Archdruid Kjorrath said in a voice old but strong, "we follow."

He looked to the others that had stood at his back all this time, noting their nods, as the chant is picked up, repeated through the ranks in time to staves pounding against the cobbles. "You lead, we follow!"

Chapter Forty-Two
No Tears

She tried not to hover. Amil didn't particularly care for women that had to cling. But this was different. All the people that were gathered, all the different organizations that were looking to him for leadership; he could do it, she knew he could, but darn it! She should be going with! She should be at his side. *She wasn't god-touched for nothing*, she silently grumped to herself. One more time she tried telling him she should be at his back.

"Anne," he put his hands on her arms, his eyes peering out from under his hood at her, his voice determined and steady. "We've been over this. You're all I have left. I need to know you'll be here waiting when this is over. I need something to come home to."

She fought the tears that wanted to come. He didn't deserve that today. She bit her lip, forced a smile and nodded as she blinked back the tears. They were supposed to have married first. They were supposed to have had one night as man and wife. But the blasted woman had other ideas. The queen needed to be dealt with.

One last butt wiggle, making Amil laugh as he opened his arms to her. He knew what was coming from that, and she didn't disappoint. She threw herself into his arms for a last bear hug before he would take final charge of this growing army. "Come back to me," she whispered.

"I'll do what I can," he offered as a promise. He let her go, watching her step back into the crowd, hugging herself tightly, her blue eyes red with unshed tears.

Siril lightly touched Amil's arm. "This is what you have been looking for. Your army stands behind you, awaiting your command. Perhaps it's time to rally the troops."

Amil looked around at the assembly. It was easy to see the delineation of the groups, sections of gray clad mercenaries standing as a group next to Defenders in blue who in turn were next to the yellow uniforms of Phaethredun's Lighters. Kron'tir's black would have blended with Val'reveran's if not for the dark skinned vidu in the latter. And yet, despite their differences, they had found a common cause.

He had lead units to war, his rangers in battles, but he had never thought to stand before legions of forces from all fields of militia, all of them looking to him for direction. It was humbling to know they were putting such trust in him. "Defenders of Kordathya," he called out to them. "You have assembled under times of need; each and every one of you has felt this queen's wrath in some way; through the loss of family, friends, and even lands." He pointed in the direction of the cloud plume still rising from Atil's volcano. "She has taken our loved ones, killed and enslaved our people, twisting their souls! All to wage war upon us! Such is the cruelty of this women and she will not stop till she is victorious!" Amil raised a fist to the sky. "But we have the upper hand, for we are free! Look to the heavens and know that the gods favor us this day and have given us a chance – a chance to stop her tyranny. To drive our arrows! Our swords!"

Blades of every kind rose to the sky, thrust up over and over as they chanted, "hoo hoo hoo!" in exultation.

The tension of the past months faded, the fear disappearing. This was Amil's purpose. He was ready. He set aside all he had lost as resolve settled over him like a mantle, his spirit soaring to lead these men and women into battle. "Sirenians are a savage people, strong in forces!" He shouted over their rallying chants. "They take orders only from the one demanding Kordathya be hers."

Swept up in the fervor of the moment, Nang joined voices with the multitude. "Death to the queen!" It was time to end this.

Vic muttered, "None of ya are gonna kill more of them goons than Vicarious, of course." He toasted the crowd with a raised flask before downing the entire bottle.

"No one touches Kordathya without feeling our wrath!" Amil yelled as the roars erupted again over the clanging of shield and sword, and pole arms against the cobble. "Let's give her a taste of her destruction, forge a path to her fortress. She'll pay for her crimes against us! We march now! To victory!"

Anne stood at the back, proud of Amil, but her heart breaking to see him off to war again. It had been hard to have him leave when they had only started falling in love, but it had confirmed for both of them that they were in love.

She watched the Truth's Light touch shoulders, holding bridles of the horses, set their palms flat to the orb and each disappear as they moved forward. She wanted to watch Amil go; she wanted to turn and run; she wanted to go with; she wanted to honor his wish.

An arm settled across her back, slender vidu fingers settling at her shoulder. "We'll watch." Duval had heard and come. Either she would have been at Amil's side, or this, standing and watching him go. "I'm here."

Grateful for her friend's presence, she leaned against the mage, relying on his strength. "Thank you," she whispered.

He only gave her a slight squeeze of a hug. He had almost lost his love once, too. Duval knew the pain she had to be feeling, watching her other half walk into the unknown. "You'll come stay with Lex and I."

Annie nodded, her eyes fixed on Amil as he stepped up to the orb, his own group linked to him by touch as he pressed his palm flat to its surface. The teardrop crystal pulsed, growing in power at the contact again, making his group seem to disappear as they were sucked into whatever they saw inside it. She turned her head into Duval's shoulder, giving in to the tears once he was gone.

The remaining fighting men and women of Kordathya transported after that, followed lastly by Felicia, who somehow collapsed the crystal behind herself. The few citizens left before it, watched the power in the teardrop flicker and die, the shard then shattering in soft tinkling glass as it tumbled to the ground. There would be no coming back that way.

Chapter Forty-Three
Population Modifier

The light flared out, engulfing them, pulling them along into a sandy area. It was near pitch darkness and only a floating door and chest sat in the area they arrived in. Eery, dim lights flickered at intervals, not really providing any light or giving an idea to the size of area they were in.

"Wee!" Vic exclaimed as he stepped through, then stopped short. "Hey! This isn't the palace!"

With a last bang of magic imploding the portal, Felicia stepped next to him, dusting non-existent fuzz off her sleeve. "At least there is no snow."

They all started sorting themselves back into groups and units, weapons to hand, while Amil inspected the door. What they had thought was a massive door on closer inspection seemed sized to them... only hanging about half Vic's height off the ground. "Doesn't look very high at all."

"For an ant," Kjorrath offered, noting Amil's much shorter height compared to Vic, "it is high."

"Seems someone magical didn't want people getting in. An interesting chest." Felicia nudged Siril, who had been looking at the door, to look at the wooden box at the foot of the door.

"Why do you say that?" Amil leaned in, giving the box his own once-over.

"Nine o'clock," Nang suddenly announced. "Red glowing weapons. Sic 'em, Vicarious!"

"It's a pretty box and all," Vic's droll tone interrupted them, "but seeing as we got people that might be dying without us around..."

From behind the lights, hordes of Sirenia's elite mages, priestesses and cutthroats attempted to swarm on the group. Unfortunately for the Sirenians, these were the elite of Kordathya. With Vicarious at the front, they easily swept through their enemies.

The battle raged around them while a contingent of Defenders tried to protect the four still looking at the chest.

"Runes," Nang pointed, careful not to touch them.

Felicia frowned. "Magi don't put runes on a chest for no

reason."

Using her finely honed senses, Nang spotted a switch at the lower right of the chest in the front, but couldn't decipher the meaning of the runes around it. Siril could make out the runes, but not what they meant.

"Last ruined chest I ran into," Felicia offered in a bland tone, "took three to four other magi to chant forth a ritual, unseal it, and then open it."

Vic spun to a stop nearby, flicking the gore from his scythe to the ground. "You mean it can explode or somethin'?"

They all took a step back at that thought.

Catching sight of something, Siril crept back a little closer. "It's inscribed with 'For Sirenia,' and unless I am mistaken, it's trapped as well."

Nang laced her fingers, turning them palm out, cracking them away from herself. "Let me see." Careful not to push anything, she checked over the small switch she had noted. "This has to be the key to unlocking this thing."

"Here." Felicia noted further markings. "…population… modifier? I'm curious what that means."

"Magical bomb?" Nang offered. "That would certainly modify the population."

"Whatever this is then, is for Sirenia?" Amil eyed it dubiously, then looked out into the dark where their army waited for the enemy. "What if we just captured and asked someone about it?"

The sounds of battle rose around them in the inky darkness. Even with elven sight amongst them, they could see little other than vague shadows of their armies or the spark of two blades crossing just right. Nang notched an arrow, trying to find a target. "They could lie," she answered Amil. "Or know nothing."

Siril took a deep breath. "Would everyone move back, please? I'm going to try something." He placed his hand on the sigil.

The battle came closer, shapes starting to emerge as the chest clearly projected the queen's voice. "Speak the words of Sirenia."

Priestesses of Suffering emerged into their small circle, whips cracking and magic sparking. "All mine!" Vic spun into his dance of death as Amil and Nang fired arrows into any they could site. Felicia's fire took care of matters on the other side of the chest, her fire elemental at her side, while Nyhm and Kjorrath held the section opposite the magical door. Their forces came in around to surround those attacking, pulling them down.

"Capture one!" Amil called in vain over the screams of death and dying. He gave them all dark looks when none remained to speak to about the riddle of the chest.

"Just raise one," Vic said, motioning towards the elf with her hair up in a pony-tail. "That's what Nang does."

"Nang," Amil gestured with his chin towards the bodies. "Would you please?" A hand went up to stop the Defender whose hand still rested on the chest. "Hold, Siril. No need to blow yourself up yet."

Once again, Nang utilized her necklace and training to raise one of the fallen to unlife, forcing the soul back for a brief questioning. Pulling a small ankh she wore on a chain from beneath her armor, she murmured to the corpse, "I command you to raise yourself up, under my complete domination by the pact I bound myself to years ago." Vic took a seat on a nearby rock, alternately drinking and cleaning his scythe off, as Nang pointed to the chest. "Priestess, tell me... what that is?"

"The way home." When pressed if it was to Sirenia and if the queen was there, she answered as briefly as possible with a simple 'yes.'

"How do we open the chest?"

"The hand of a priestess, or the words of Sirenia."

When Nang pushed for the words, Vic leaned forward. "You could just put her hand on it, right?"

"She might need to be alive for that to work," Nang said, looking over her shoulder. "Technically, she's not alive anymore."

"And what of the door?" Siril asked, hand still on the chest.

"The key to the door is in the chest," the dead woman continued at Nang's prompting. "If he touched it, it awaits his words."

It was the one frustrating thing Nang found about dealing with the dead. They were more exacting than anyone alive would be, always answering only what was asked. She sighed, trying not to be frustrated. "And those words are...?" Finally getting an answer, Nang pressed her ankh against the priestess' forehead, letting the woman collapse back into death. "I release you from the pact."

As much as the Truth's Lighters hated such an abomination as undead, it had served its purpose this time. But the one watching felt he needed to grump about something. "We should have asked how heavily guarded the other side of the door is."

"Bah," Vic blew it off. "We'd still go in there anyway."

Felicia gave the yellow-clad man a vicious, battle-ready smile. "That's what Vicarious is for."

Clearing his throat, Siril looked at Amil. "When we are all ready…" A terse nod was his answer as everyone prepared for what might come from the chest. "Sirenia," he repeated, "expands through construction and domination."

Wheels and cogs slid back and forth as the wards on the chest dropped, the lid finally springing open. "Guess you don't get blown up today, Siril."

"Nor does my earth shield." Felicia negligently waved a hand towards the elemental, magically dismissing it.

"That's a good thing," Siril chuckled at Amil's assertion.

"Heh," Vic laughed. "There's still time." The words were meant to be light, but came across with too much meaning to them all. The only thing that off-set it was his salute with a bottle before he took a drink.

Under a mishmash of objects, Amil found the key to unlock the door. "Vic, you will love the chest."

"Oh, look," Nang said in a dry, flat tone. "Ale."

"Quite a bit," Amil added.

"I'm on it!" Vic shoved past them, gaining laughter as he greedily took up what he could. "Well then," Vic said when he couldn't add a single extra flask to his magic pouch, "That's that."

Chapter Forty-Four
Boom

They had taken the night to regroup, get some rest. None of them slept. None truly went into their Reveries, either. Amil spent his night propped on the cool stone floor, wondering why he hadn't taken the extra time to exchange the vows with Anne. But he knew. Deep down, he wanted her to have no attachments. He wanted her to not have to say she was a widow before she had been made a proper wife.

Pulling his hood lower, he prayed to Firnos that she remained well and strong. She'd survive, no matter what happened here. It was why he had fallen in love with her. He knew she had fought before her capture. She'd fight her way through her grief.

Coming to terms with their own mortality, the rest of the group took turns on watch while the armies got what rest they could. Some used a whetstone on their steel, others sat quiet with their eyes closed. None talked about the path ahead of them.

"Let's find out what's on the other side of our door then..." Amil inserted the key and turned it as slowly as he could, trying not to make any noise, as the armies fell into their groups with the dawn. He was surprised when it moved smooth and quiet. The path sloped gently upwards again.

Felicia spared a moment to wonder what had happened to the men Siril said had disappeared after touching the orb. Were they alive? Hostages? Had they been turned into more of the undead puppets that would force her friends to attack faces they had known in life? Just in case, she summoned her fire elemental to stand guard at her back against whatever might be coming.

Amil stepped in. The rest of his small group followed, lastly by Siril who made sure to keep his staff through the opening to ensure their army's ability to follow.

On first sight, the contents of the stone room appeared to be quiet and undisturbed. Siege equipment and work benches took up the space, but left plenty of room to maneuver between. Moving with great care, they were sure of their steps, not touching anything.

Not saying the obvious, Vic wondered how many of the others had noted that there wasn't a feeling of a palace to the place.

If this were the queen's domain, why weren't their guards? Soldiers? Servants? As heir to his own ruler-ship, he knew how busy a working keep or fortress needed to be. He stretched the fingers that gripped his scythe, letting them one by one settle back on the snath. This was too quiet. But to speak it would be to give away the one secret he kept from all but other Val'Saders.

As they made their way to the hall, other members of the army started to enter, taking up Siril's place so he could join his companions at the fore. Rounding a corner, they were confronted by men, Defilers that came ahead of the women in the lands they wished to claim.

Battle was tight in the passages. Amil couldn't shoot without the chance of hitting his own people, and Vic couldn't swing such a large weapon. It fell to Nang and Nyhm to pull daggers and take the charge. Felicia's magic sparked along the walls, fire biting into the men at the rear of the fight, while Siril cast missiles of energy in cascading bursts that focused on one man at a time.

"It's one of those bird things!" Nang shouted. The last of the men fell to the bite of Nyhm's dagger just as they spotted one of the strange creatures duck into a room, shutting the door. "Question him!" She raced the distance to the door, throwing it open only to have the creature slash out with a taloned foot. Another charged at her. Changing tactics, she ran back towards the group.

"What are you doing?" Vic yelled, trying to sound indignant while he was truly readying himself for more battle.

"Call 'em off!" She slid the last few steps, coming to a stop behind Vic.

Poofs of feathers flew and the creatures exploded in charred cinders. Squawks and chirps marked the last sounds of each as Felicia negligently pointed a finger at one after another, letting them crisp quickly, consumed by her fires.

"Hey," Vic cheered, "fried chicken!"

Amil dodged another's attack, glancing to Siril. "Use your magic to hold one of them!"

Felicia's magic took down all but one as a slight twist of Siril's wrist contained one to a space only big enough for the birdman to turn around just inside the doorway to the room they had come from. "Done." He focused his Will on the creature. "Answer their questions." He glanced to Amil. "He has no choice. Ask."

"What forces do you have up ahead?" Nang demanded.

"More goons I bet," Vic smirked before taking a drink from a bottle the same amazing red color as his hair.

In response it stretched its wing arms out to their fullest, lifting one leg to pose like some sort of ugly crane. They all stared at it in surprise, Vic losing a little of his alcohol as the bottle remained tipped in his shock.

"Last one," Felicia finally reminded them, "we had to make smarter."

"You can speak to animals," Siril finally mentioned to Amil. "Maybe you can communicate with it?"

Doubtfully, Amil looked it over. "Maybe... although it's more like us than an animal." He asked it several questions in the odd squeaks and growls that made up the language of the forest creatures, receiving nods and chirps in response.

"Don't set anything off," Nang warned Vicarious, who had started wandering around, drinking and inspecting different weapons lying about.

"Like the cannon over there," Felicia inclined her head towards it.

"Hammers don't explode." He waved his hand in dismissal.

"Hmph," Nang snorted. "Things tend to explode around you."

Purposely goading her now, he stepped over to the cannon, patting it. "There's a nice boom thingy over here though."

"No!" She stepped forward, hand outstretched towards him. Nang stopped, the panic fading as she noted the stupid grin on his face. He had purposely pushed her on that one. She didn't know if she should be furious with him or take it as a joke. Several times she opened her mouth, but was unsure what to say. Something scathing was biting to be said, but... she was pretty sure he wasn't trying to be a pain in the ass this time. He was intentionally teasing her. She shut her mouth again, glaring at him.

It gained her only a smirk from him. To make it worse, he gave her a wink before taking a last drink from an almost empty bottle.

"We are under the castle." Amil kept his eyes on the creature standing at the height of his chest. "It says there are no soldiers here."

"So we need to go up."

"Seems so." Amil nodded to Nang before turning back to ask the birdman.

Vic poked at a heavy metal door that had a large siege ladder leaned against it. The small being looked at Amil as if he were stupid, then motioned around the room, specifically at Vicarious, chirping at the ranger.

"Up we go." Amil relayed. "Only a few more doors preventing us from what we're looking for. It shouldn't be too much trouble to get to her." He thanked the beast politely before telling Siril to release it from the compulsion.

The creature looked around in confusion as the spell released not only the control Siril had maintained, but that of all the queen's people had done to it. It absently wandered around the room, heading out into the hall.

Nang stepped up to the door, giving it a quick inspection with small pokes from her dagger, looking for signs it would be trapped. "Step back," she warned, finally seeing the fine wires that would trigger something the moment they turned the lock.

"Release it," Amil instructed. "I have an idea for the door. Vic! Come 'ere." Amil looked for a way to drag the machine forward.

Nang watched them eying the cannon. "Gods above and below," she swore with a sigh, "men! You... do know that I can probably just disarm the trap *and* open the door?"

"I was liking Amil's plan better," Vic pouted, turning to their leader. "We were gonna use the boom thingy, right?"

"That's plan B." Nang turned to start on the fine task of disarming the wires.

"Don't hurt yourself," Amil warned just as she nicked her finger on a switch, several daggers ejecting from the doorframe, falling without any momentum behind them.

"Luck is with the daring ones," Kjorrath interjected.

"That," Nang grumped, "was pathetic. And badly put together. Honestly." Her tone indicated disgust, but she wasted no time on the thought as she turned her attention to next picking the lock on the heavy door.

Amil had wanted to try the cannon again. The war machine intrigued him, having never been used in any of the wars he could remember. And now that he had seen it once in action during this war, "My way would have been more entertaining."

"I wanted to see it," Vic agreed.

The lock clicked open, and Nang was able to push the door open. She quickly pulled it back to almost shut when she saw several of the large beefy dwarves ambling about the far end of the room. "Not as easy as we expected..." She moved for Amil and Vic to take a look.

Amil caught Vic's arm before he could go do more than lift a foot to move upward on the sloped floor. "Traps. Look where they're stopping."

"They look like they're messed in the head," Vic said, bemused at the odd behavior of them. The muscular monstrosities were muttering unintelligible taunts at each other, shambling about in confusion, but weren't coming any closer than a few feet from the door. "We might wanna just back out."

"Indeed. Vic, with me. Plan B." With the vidu's help, Amilmamir moved the cannon up in front of the door and started gathering the powder and cannon shot.

The sounds of further battle raged across the area at their backs as their army took on pockets of the enemy. Amil ignored all that, intent on moving forward. There was nothing to use as wadding. "Vic," he motioned to give over, "I need one of the dresses." He purposely didn't look to see which memory he was about to blow up as he shoved it into the mouth of the cannon, focused on pouring in the powder next. "I need a staff."

Siril sighed, using the blunt end of his magic staff to help pack the cannon. Vic stepped up, sparking the flint and tinder to the fuse as Siril hurried out of the way.

"Might want to cover your ears," Nang ducked, throwing an arm up to help shield herself. "These things are... very, very loud." The rest of their group either covered their ears or ducked behind shields as Amil and Vic watched in anticipation.

A low fffffft marked the hiss of the fuse burning down until the cannon rocked back slightly with the deafening boom. Those closest to the machine stumbled against the explosion. The door splintered into a deadly rain as members of the queen's army smashed against walls inside the room, bones shattering and the sound of squish marking ruptured bodies.

"Wow!" Vic exclaimed as Amil waved the smoke from his face. "That made a mess!"

Amil stepped around to the doorway to look closer. "Clear!"

"That... worked rather well." Nang was surprised. The only ones she had ever seen in her past had just as often caused damage to those using them. This had done as it was expected; only blowing forward. "And no soldiers."

"Trap's still here, though." Amil looked to Nang. "Can you disable it?"

"On it. This is easy." Quick work disabled the main trap. "Clear. Want me to check this door?" She crossed in silent steps to the far side of the room, looking over the next door forward in their venture. "Hrm," she offered thoughtfully, studying the hidden catches and mechanisms. Touching the point of a dagger to one, fire limned the door, in arches and fastenings. She scooted back from it. "I'm not a fan of getting torched."

"It looks pretty suspicious, right?" Vic inspected it from directly behind Nang.

Amil frowned. If Nyhm and Nang couldn't release the catches... "Felicia, can your elemental lend a bit of aid?"

"Felicia could handle this easy." Nang nodded agreement, letting the wizardess work her magic.

Chapter Forty-Five
Riddle Me This

With a bored expression, Felicia sauntered through them to the door. Under everything she was at heart a fire elemental herself. Fire was her companion. She casually extended a hand covered by her blackened glove, willing the fire to her. Not only did it come, it brought all its heat with it, leaving her charged with its energy and her glove smoking.

Looking back to the lock, the others saw it had become coated in ice. The magic already held within the spelled lock had turned the flames to the opposite end of the spectrum. Kjorrath considered a moment before picking up a stone and imbuing it with a druids earth magic before aiming and throwing it at the lock. Between the ice and the magic force, the lock exploded.

Careful of the cold now, Amil touched the latch several times with the briefest of contact until it warmed slightly. Only then did he push down, releasing the catch and pushing the door open. "Vic…" he carefully stepped back, eyes on whatever he saw, his voice humored. "Ex-girlfriend of yours?"

Vic and Nang pushed to the front, looking in at the same time. "Vic has better taste." At least, Nang hoped he did!

The leonine creature lounging within that next area had large feathery wings folded back behind its very human, very female upper body and face. It stretched its massive paws, letting the claws peek through as the "woman" looked them over. "A riddle, a passage," she said, "a riddle an answer." A type of sphinx then, and typical of its kind, it loved riddles.

"I love games!" Vic said, eyes intent on the bare bosoms on the creature. His scythe dipped, unheeded, towards the druid who leaned away from it.

"Nyhm!" Nang called over her shoulder, her irritated gaze on Vic. "Riddles!"

"Nyhm is a good riddler?"

She nodded to Amil. "He loves them, from what I can tell." He'd certainly told enough on their former meetings. But looking around now, they couldn't see the young elf. He had likely blended with the shadows to scout back along the way they had come, tracking how the rest of their army was doing.

They turned back to the female sphinx before them for their riddle. "In marble halls as white as milk, as soft as silk, a golden apple appears. No doors there are to this stronghold, yet thieves break in and steal the gold. Answer this, and I'll tell you about the passage behind me." Its gaze fell on Siril. "Others like you are here."

"Like me?" He wasn't sure he dared hope it was the men who had been sucked into the orb much earlier, but the feeling soared regardless.

"If you answer a separate riddle, I can tell you where the men are." Kjorrath and Siril both indicated interest. "It wasn't my sister," it recited, "nor my brother, but still was the child of my father and mother. Who is it?

"I'm thinking," Nyhm stated, seeming to appear from nowhere.

Siril glanced at the black-clad elf. To him the answer was simple. He turned back to the creature. "It was you."

It inclined its head, a humored smile directed at Vic, who was still staring. "Your men," it turned to Siril, "are in the northwest corner of the building, staked down. The first riddle again now."

"Staked down?" Amil frowned.

Siril couldn't think about that at the moment. Defenders knew the risk of the job they undertook, they knew the job needed to be completed. They would understand, even though there was a pang of guilt for the slight vidu in needing to leave them for the time. "Prisoners, most likely," he nodded to Nang. He would have to hope they survived just a little longer yet. The queen needed to be found and dealt with first. "Would you repeat the riddle?"

"In marble halls as white as milk," it repeated, "lined with a skin as soft as silk, within a fountain crystal clear, a golden apple appears. No doors there are to this stronghold, yet thieves break in and steal the gold."

"Give me a second..." Nyhm looked up towards the ceiling, his black hair hanging to partially conceal his dark eyes as he considered answers.

There were three doors; two on the wall behind the creature, and one that might have been designed specifically for the creature on the wall to their left. One of the doors likely led to the queen. The other... could the men in blue have truly survived? "Siril, did you send Defenders to move the orb from your office?" Amil thought the Defender may have mentioned something about that when they had first gathered around the crystal, but if they had been sacrificed...

A slight nod. "We had taken it outside so I could better move around it. The light seemed to affect it, though." His white hair barely moved with the shake of his head. "Once it changed shape, we didn't want the citizens endangered. They tried to move it again... and were almost immediately sucked in."

"Guess we found your lost men. Let's try the other door, and let Nyhm think on the riddle some. I'd rather see if we can get them out than stand and ponder riddles."

The beast padded over to the side, giving them access to the door they had riddled for. There was little room for the army to follow them and the sphinx seemed barely inclined to let them enter a small room with doors it meant to protect. The different units each assigned two or three to follow the group as they stayed back, guarding the way they'd come.

"Nang," Amil inclined his head towards their next path, "door."

Another metal structure was flanked by two very old and beautiful urns. Looking it over carefully, Nang noted tiny wires in the water, running up and through the doorframe. "It... looks like those two urns contain water, and that it's somehow trapped to the door. I'm not sure what it does, though."

Amil's hood barely tipped as he considered the situation. "Can you disarm it?"

She sat back on her heels, her hands resting on her knees. "I don't think it's poison..." she spoke to herself, "but I didn't sample any."

"Electrical trap maybe?"

Nang shrugged to Amil, turning to the others. She was at a loss as to what exactly the trap was. "Could be. Does anyone else want to take a look at this door? There's a fine wire." She turned back, tracing a finger just above it, careful not to touch.

Siril noted that disarming traps was far from his training, but Archdruid Kjorrath stepped up to contemplate the matter. He wasn't a trap-maker, but he worked with water on a regular basis. He frowned, tilting his head and rubbing his chin silently. His eyes glanced over the wires Nang had pointed out, but he wasn't interested in those. With a few murmured words to the water, he smoothly reached into the urn. Touching the water, he called to the element itself, coaxing it into his own form. It came readily to his hand, disappearing on contact, leaving the urns empty.

"That's... an interesting trick," Nang noted as the catches released with the last of the water.

"Ahem!" Vic gave a very polite, if loud, cough. "I'm pretty sure I solved that riddle thing."

Siril seemed to be looking down his nose at Vic, although he was more waiting for the joke's punch line to happen. "...really?"

"Yeah! I was thinking how it made me really hungry and stuff... riddles always do that." He grinned at the other vidu's raised eyebrows. "And so I thought that I never had breakfast this morning, and then I was thinking, I like eggs for breakfast. I'm pretty sure that's the answer though... An egg." Vic grinned at his own ingeniousness. "See? I'm completely amazing!"

"...the answer is an egg?" Siril didn't quite believe the big idiot could be the one to solve the matter. They'd have to discuss it before presenting it to the creature.

The large vidu shrugged his shoulders beneath his white coat. Let them think what they wanted. He knew he wasn't stupid. "What's with this door?" He pushed past them to open the door they had just unlocked.

"Vic!" Nang's voice held a girlish panic she didn't care for as she saw one of the large dwarves inside lumbering towards Vicarious.

"Vic..." Amil warned, pointing, as Siril watched with a raised brow, "big dwarf!"

His attention distracted to look back at them for only the blink of an eye, he did a sliding step into the room to give himself space. Adjusting the grip of the scythe and settling the weight in his knees, Vic grinned at his group before spinning in a whirl of white from his coat, his red hair flaring around him, perfectly fanned.

The scythe's chine bit deep across the beast's chest on the first round. With a roar of pain, one meaty hand bore down, crashing into the ground where Vic had been just a second before.

Moving the weight from his right to his left foot, he spun in the opposite direction, coming up behind the abomination. A quick stop as his right foot found purchase on the ground, weight balanced to push him forward again.

"HA!" He shouted, gaining its attention. As it started to turn, he threw his weight to his left again, using the force from his right to spin him, gaining momentum for the large weapon to bite deep. Arcing low, he turned the toe of his favored girl up, meeting the beast face to face as the scythe struck true, lodging in and pushing up, bursting the internal organs.

A second detached itself from a pod it had been resting in, tubes and wires disconnecting as it came away from its creational womb. The barest flicker of sentient thought, confusion, passed behind its eyes before that dulled to the vacant stare of all the others they had seen.

"Well," Nang spoke for them all as Vic put that one down as well, "I was wondering where the queen hid those things."

"Those are drugged up dwarves," Vic found it necessary to explain to Kjorrath and the troops at their backs. "Something called alchemy."

While Nang checked their next door for traps, Felicia nodded. "Alchemy and machine combined to create those huge dwarves."

"Life," the druid sighed, "is nothing that should be played with, to begin with."

"Preaching to the choir," Amil muttered, going up to Nang. "No trap?" At her assent that it was both untrapped and unlocked, he nocked an arrow to his bow. "Stand back."

The others fell back, readying their own weapons as he put his back to the doorframe. With a quick step he side-kicked the door open, his aim trained into the room. The heads of several dark warriors spun to look at them, weapons sliding free of sheaths. From out of the darkness that enveloped the furthest reaches of the massive room, their warriors came down the sloped plane of the floor.

"Twelve o'clock!" Nang stepped in on Amil's right, ready to advance.

"Watch my three!" The arrow flew true into those ahead as Amil saw several coming up behind Nang.

"I see it!" She turned the dagger underhanded in her left palm, shoving back and deep into the body of one.

Vic took the moment of distraction to race into the fray. Nyhm's dark clothing and crouched walk put him below the notice of the others as he crept towards the back of the room, blending with shadows where he could.

Felicia went gracefully to her knees, noting distance between those fighting in the doorway and the trajectory she needed. "This should keep them busy." A carefully controlled ball of fire shot from her hand, singing those it passed as it flew into the crowd of men coming at them, exploding with a boom that rocked through the cavernous space.

"Watch the coat!" Vic snapped, whirling further into the throng. Between his height and the reach of his scythe, the men were having a hard time reaching him.

Taking a place just inside the door, Siril stayed back from the heavy combat, letting their own troops pour into the battle zone. Not having any idea how many were hiding out of their reach, he cast light on random soldiers, bringing the entirety of the space visible to them.

This then was a staging area for the queen's army. Not only were their units to rival their own, but weapons of war and torture mingled in; guillotines, iron maidens and the bones of a few poor souls that hadn't survived the past.

Amil got his toe under several bones, kicking them up at two of the dark knights rushing at him. In the time it took them to deflect, he had trained his bow back on them, letting fly. Striking true, arrows lodged in their throats, they flew back off their feet.

The druid tucked in on himself, shoulder leading and bull-rushed a man running towards Amil. Kjorrath didn't understand all the details as to why this was so important to keep Amilmamir at the spearhead, but he respected the man enough to put his life in with the others. He took the man down as the sword came towards him, cutting deep into his left arm.

Seeing the pockets of fighting and the druid about to go down, Siril cast a force push towards the group with Kjorrath. A blast of energy formed like a large shield, slamming into one of the men. Thrown from his feet, the dark knight flew back towards the far wall, hitting with a squish that would mean his death.

Siril didn't pause, but cast several more, the last barely catching the man he had aimed at. The warrior pinballed against several of the siege weapons before falling to the floor. Staggering back up, dazed, the man found himself in front of Vicarious, lashing out blindly. Vic looked down to the small cut now visible in his amazing coat. "Damn me!" He glared at the man. "You ruined the coat!" As the dead piled around them, the fates favoring the side of the ranger, Vic pulled his fist back and let fly with enough force to knock the man back off his feet again, his face smashed in.

Dusting non-existent lint from the white sleeve, Vic shrugged to settle his armor and coat back into place. Leaning down towards the dying man, he put a finger out, shaking it in quick jerks. "That… is what happens when you mess with amazing."

Chapter Forty-Six
To Safety

Taking time to regroup, the troops took care of themselves, setting up a triage of who would live and who was gone. Amil's group moved towards an area with men hanging from shackles or staked out on the floor. Without a word, Siril pulled a dagger from his hip, one the others had never noticed on him, and knelt to start cutting the bonds of those still breathing.

Nang quietly joined his work on the floor, stripping rope away from the raw wrists of the men in blue. Kjorrath took in the injuries and the filthy conditions they had been left in. "Might as well put the water to use…" He slowly called back the water he had taken from the trap to help cleanse the wounds of a few still in fairly good shape.

The sounds of agony created a backdrop, not only from the prisoners, but from those injured or dying across the floor. Watching in a mix of horror and anger, Amil needed to do something. These men had risked their lives for him. "Vic," he put his hand out again, not looking towards the vidu. "Dress me."

"More room for ale!" Vic cheered as he pulled several of the dresses from his bag. He followed the ranger's lead then in ripping the fine satins to strips that could be used for bandages. The two handed the strips down to Siril, who parceled them out to Nang and to Nyhm as he joined them on the floor.

A few of the dark clad men appeared, pushing a last surprise attack, rushing into Amil from behind, knocking him to his knees. A sharp pain shot through one of the knees, having nothing to do with hitting the floor. It didn't stop Amil from rolling and coming back to his feet, his hood falling back from his face and his blade in hand.

Vic brought the heel of his scythe up into the groin of one before thrusting it forward, the chine biting deep into another. With a roar, Amil and Kjorrath both lowered their shoulders, rushing one standing before an open iron maiden. The man stumbled back into it, knocking it to the floor and the door slamming shut on it. The screams from within turned to gurgles before stopping.

"Are your men good?" Amil asked Siril, pulling his hood

carefully back up to cover his scarred face.

"Sir," an officer in a yellow tabard approached, addressing Amil and Siril both. "I'd like to take a few units of our Truth's Light and return our injured for aid."

Not to be outdone, the captain of the Gray Gryphons stepped up, rolling his shoulders, scratching the scruff on his cheeks. "We'll go as guard."

With the number that had fallen in the attacks, they needed to get them to safety. Amil knew if they were left, they would still need a contingent to protect them. And there were more they had already left along the path this far. He nodded curtly, sorting out five from each group, including scouts to keep their way clear. They'd need help in figuring out how to get the hells out of this maze of a building. "Go."

They helped the units ready themselves, then stood in silence as they moved out. There was no knowing if they would make it out. Amil had to trust to the captains that were leading the groups that at least some of them would survive. Ready to move on, he watched as Kjorrath gave Vic an apple. "You might want to stop drinking if you haven't eaten."

Vic merely grinned at the druid, took another swig from a bottle and palmed the apple. "Thanks pal." He led the way back to the large room with the sphinx in it. "We got that figured out," he announced after finishing both drink and apple, handing the core back to Kjorrath. "It's an egg."

"Very well," the female creature said after ensuring they were in agreement, "I can answer a question about what lies behind me."

"If it were me," Vic offered in an aside to Nang, "I'd ask why this thing is just camped out in the place."

"They make excellent guardians," Siril offered quietly. "I can't think of anything better."

"And," Felicia added, arms crossed, eyes narrowed in contemplation towards the sphinx, "they're very lawful creatures. If it took an oath to protect this passage, it will. Even if it isn't something it wants to do."

Everyone looked to Amilmamir, who considered several options. His guess was that the Sirenians had leverage on the sphinx, either a hostage or a threat to kill something – or someone – important to it. His duty though had to be first to stopping the queen.

That meant coming up with the right thing to ask at the moment.

Creatures like this could be tricky in exactly what they gave depending on the wording of the question. "Tell me everything we can expect to run into from the point you are to the queen."

"Be ready to face your past," it said, lying down again. "Ask your questions about the queen."

Amil had a moment of panic that he pushed back down. There was nothing left of his past. The only thing that had not been touched was his homelands, and those couldn't be here. His breath caught at the idea it might be the Oracle herself or his nephew. He had enjoyed what time he had been granted with the boy. Just on the edge of manhood, Elith had a fine career at the temple. Amil had hoped to go back to share stories and lessons he had learned over the years, considering that he would likely never have a son anymore. By Firnos, Sirenia wouldn't dare take that from him! Besides Anne, it was all he had left!

Glancing sidelong at Amil, Nyhm noted the worry and the fact that Amil wasn't mentally with them at the moment. He touched a hand to the ranger's elbow. "How about we get to know if the queen knows already that we're coming and if she's prepared for us?"

"What about weaknesses?" Felicia asked laconically.

"She does not," the sphinx answered. "And she is protected by her dwarves and the dark knights." Rising, the majestic creature pushed through the large third door.

They could momentarily hear the cries of what sounded like a child. Exchanged looks between them became a hard expression on Amil. They had enslaved a sentient creature, using the beast's young as a threat if there was no cooperation. It was just one more crime for this empire to pay for.

"I think question time is done." Nang gave Vic a look, letting him know his earlier question had likely been answered.

Going through the room now open to them, two men in the trappings of some holy order approached them, intent on their destruction. Shouts went back and forth as they called on each other to cast fire and force, arrows flew between them with only a breath of space from Amil's bow. One went down as Vicarious finished a bottle, taking the clay container and slamming it down over the man's head.

Nang paused, impressed despite herself. "I guess that wasn't so useless after all. Way to go, Vicarious." She cringed inwardly, rolling her eyes when he responded with a rakish grin and a wink.

The other was much stronger, continuing to fight. They called for their own holy order of Truth's Light to join as they could. Several came running from their position at the rear, taking up the attack. The man screamed, falling to the blessed weapons, disappearing in a heavy, rotten-smelling smoke, the light going with him.

Chapter Forty-Seven
Tears

Lareah was quiet, peaceful. A week had gone by since Amil had disappeared inside a crystal. There was nothing to indicate that the love of Anne's life was likely fighting for his life. She sat outside Duval's home, enjoying the sun when he came to sit beside her. The vidu made a great show of sitting with a groan, as if he were a much older man. Anne wasn't buying it. She knew he was only a little older than she was. "What's up, Cupcake?"

"Wondering the same thing, Squirt." He reached over and ruffled her hair into a brown rat's nest.

It earned him a scowl while she ran her fingers through it. "I was just considering the next set of forms for the trainees." The movements were slow, calculated, with the placement of each hand and foot timed to perfection. When her students could control each move without shaking, then – and only then – would she start showing them how to use those forms in combat. "They might be ready to start using some of them in practices."

Duval leaned his head back against the wall and stretched his feet out in front of himself. She was holding up remarkably well, considering. "You sure that's what you're thinking about?" He made sure to keep his tone light, neutral.

A long pause. "Damn you," she tempered the words with a smile and a playful shove. "Do you have to know me that well?"

He laughed, turning enough to tickle her, the red of his leathers blending against the red wrap she wore over the top of her gi as his dark hands flew against her white robes. She squealed and laughed, pretending to get away, only to allow him to capture her again. Du made a noise of humored outrage when she pulled a red slipper from her foot, beating against his arm with it.

They collapsed against each other laughing. But her hug became tighter, holding him as if he were a lifeline, as she gave in to the tears he had known she was hiding. He pet her hair, letting her cry. He knew better than most how hard this was. He had almost lost his Lexi years ago. It had nearly killed him then. There was no way he would say it now, but he knew in his heart that he wouldn't be able to go through that again. His heart was heavy for someone he saw as a younger sister to have to face that same unknowing.

"Shhh," he whispered, petting her hair. "Shh. I'm here." He knew better than to say it would be alright. Life wasn't fair; his mother had taught him that. Things happened, bad things that no one had any control over. He could promise Annie the moon and the sun, but what good would it do? All he had was his comfort, and that of his family. "I'm here. You aren't alone in this."

With a deep breath, she let her heart relax with that. She wasn't alone. And she trusted Amil. He said he'd come back.

Duval pulled back a little, smiling down at her ruddy, tearstained cheeks. "You have any idea how ugly you are?"

Laughter cut through her pain as she ran the heel of her hand over her face to wipe away the tears. "Takes one to know one," she teased back.

"No, no! Don't put this back on me. You've seen my kids. Cute little buggers."

She slapped playfully at him again. "Idiot. We both know that's because of Lex."

"Yeah, probably." He grinned, getting to his feet. "She is gorgeous." He stepped through the door before peeking back out. "Something you'll never be." It gained him the outraged squeal he'd expected as she got to her feet, tearing after him.

"No running in the house!" Lex called in vain as the two got the children all riled up with their antics.

Chapter Forty-Eight
She's Yours

Amil looked over his group, noting that his personal contingent had no humans. They would have no trouble seeing in the dim light. Down the line, he saw torches slowly flaring to life among the units needing it. "We're moving out!" he called back, turning quickly – but with no flash as Vic commanded – and approached yet another door.

Siril and Nang each checked for traps before they'd allow Amil to open it. "Exploding runes," Nang looked to Siril. "Ideas?"

"Depends on the kind of explosion," Felicia said, coming up with Siril to examine it.

"Localized," Siril determined. "Don't want the entire corridor brought down."

"Could be worse, it could be a death trap."

Giving Felicia a dark look, Amil warned her to hold those thoughts. "Don't give them any ideas for the next one!"

"Vic's right," Siril nodded when the other vidu made a suggestion. "If we can explode them without touching them, it should clear the path for us."

"Watch out, Siril." Amil nocked an arrow, pulling back as the others moved to find cover. They covered ears or eyes as they ducked behind shields and stones. In quick succession, several arrows flew, landing dead center on each rune, exploding in a shower of pebbles.

From that opening poured more of the beefy dwarves. Moving with more speed than should be possible for such an awkward body, their short legs and long ape-like muscled arms closed on them. Siril called for the Gryphons and the vidu Vhalar unit to come in. Rushing from their posts in the ranks, the two forces moved as a current around and past Amil's group to confront the massive creatures.

Fourteen of the mindless beasts focused on the battle, their fists smashing down as the Gryphons met them in melee and the Vhalar harried them at the edges of the fight. Easily twice the height of any of them, the groups tired, many falling below the massive blows. The Guardians and Rangers took up the fight, allowing Amil's group to slip past.

"This opens up to another room," Nang said as she peered through the now-broken doorway. "And it stinks of dwarf."

"More of the altered ones, likely." Amil readied another arrow, sliding forward with care.

Nyhm put a hand to the ranger's arm. "Let me look first." The young elf dropped to a crouch, creeping along the wall as he blended with the shadows for long moments. Amil admired the boy's skill; it almost rivaled his own.

"There's a cavern," Nyhm reported, seeming to appear out of nowhere, "and a bridge. I think all those dwarves are out here now, though."

As they carefully made their way into the damp stone room, the stench of unwashed bodies assaulted them. The overhang stretched for some distance with only a marginal ridge for a guard rail. Looking down into the darkness they could hear water running, a light mist rising up towards them. Nyhm pointed out the stone walkway that lead across to…

"Her," Amil spit. He began to have a sense of calm come over him as he set his sights on her. Finally he had found her; finally she had nowhere to run. Sitting on a chaise lounge of purest white with beautiful piled rugs, sat a woman of exquisite beauty. Dark flowing locks were held back by the crown atop her milk white skin. A shiny black corset was laced tight over a full bosom, flowing into a short, flared skirt over thigh high boots. This was no queen he could ever bow to, especially noting the black panther skin she had draped as a cloak. There was the past the sphinx had mentioned. She had taken everything. And she would pay.

Vic's scythe shot out, the wood stopping Nyhm from going first.

"I could…"

His red hair shook, falling perfectly back into shape. "That bitch is Amil's."

With a sharp marching step, a unit of her dark-clad knights came across the bridge. The old druid eyed them and their weapons, bringing his staff into a defensive position. "We will have enough business with this fight."

Guardian Siril Te'lie stopped in that moment from being "just a mage" with Amil and assumed leadership of the units sent from his own offices at home. Snapping orders and issuing direction, the reinforcements came at his call, dealing with the dark commanders of the queen. "All but her," he informed them as they fell into battle. "Leave the queen for Amil!"

True to their word, the men and women of Kordathya cleared the way for Amil. He didn't hesitate in his steps across the slick stone of the bridge as Vicarious came behind at his back, watching the way he'd come. Five of the dark guardians separated from the queen's protection to advance on the two. "Alright, Amil! She's yours! I'll take care of those knights!" Vic adjusted his grip. "They'll be easy to knock off the ledge anyway!"

Amil couldn't spare a thought as he was thrust into battle. His knees complained at the balance needed on the wet surface, but he wasn't about to have it end after having come this far. His blade came to his hand as an old friend, meeting in battle, holding, protecting, and slicing. He didn't hear Vicarious leave his back, returning to the far end of the bridge. He didn't see the queen's infantry enter behind his own troups. He didn't see the twisted dwarves lumber into battle.

"Two beefies!" Nyhm shouted at Vic while Siril cast a flurry of offensive spells to cover Amil's advance.

"Let's review after I win!" Vic shouted back, storming forward to lay in to the monstrous dwarves.

The armies clashed, men and women on both sides falling. Shouts and screams echoed strangely in the hollow sound of the cavern, mixing with the rush of water from below. Felicia's fire elemental chased after one of the large dwarves, fire blasting from her hands, while Kjorrath turned on the dark knights, his staff swept their legs out from under them, tossing them into others of their unit. A very few times he was lucky, their balance sending them pitching over the ledge.

Emerging from within the ranks of the enemy came the battle master, the queen's commander of her legions. A human no more, the warlord was an iron monstrosity, all vicious edges and burning hate. Armor as thick as a stone golem, his sword was gnarled and warped, much as the glare coming from within the dark helm. His blade rose to point, the rolling shout of thunder booming outward from the armor, demanding their queen be protected. More infantry charged in from the corridor.

Kordathya's finest stood their ground, despite the press of the other army. They met them bravely on the slick surface with the clashing of swords that brought splatters of blood. Screams of pain echoed on both sides as bones crushed and life was extinguished. Still they protected the bridge, preventing any from approaching Amil.

"You and I have some talking to do!" Amil shouted as he tossed his bow, letting it fall over the side of the bridge into whatever abyss waited below, and shrugged off his quiver. He strode forward, infinitely lighter, both in weight and in heart. The time had come. He pushed back his hood to better see his prey, blue eyes intent on her as his hand settled more comfortably on his sword.

Nang fell in behind Vic, back to back. This had become familiar and comfortable to her, fighting with the tall vidu at her back. Her own rapier and dagger easily guarded his back as he watched hers, her shorter weapons and stature a compliment to his height and scythe that easily swung overhead.

Rising, the queen seemed to strike a pose, hand on the hip of her tightly bound black corset. Only Amil saw it... and he had no appreciation for it. She wasn't his Oceania. And she wasn't his Anne. "You killed Atilians!" He spit at her. "You enslaved souls that aren't yours!"

Hate in her eyes, the queen drew her own sword, unwinding her whip, and stormed forward onto the bridge with a tight crack of the leather. "It's time to end this game, boy. Queen Lutheria Lianlenesh rules."

"Aye," Amil answered grimly, "this game will end, and so will your life!" With his offhand, he pulled his dagger and advanced closer to the center of the bridge while she did the same.

"Only if yours goes first, ranger," she spit back at him. "Atil will still be mine!"

"Keep an eye on the warlord!" Nang shouted to the rest of their small group.

"Kinda busy." Vic swept his scythe around, knocking knights to their death, before slicing high as now some of the bird creatures fluttered in, trying to land in the confusion.

Nyhm heard her though and crept in low from behind the battle master. He wasn't designed for heavy battle, but the group needed help and he had access. Striking hard, it gained the man's attention, turning it from the others to focus on the slight elf. Nyhm harried him, ran, harried again, ducking and dodging as he tried to stay ahead of the man's blade.

More fire erupted from Felicia's gloves as Siril took a place at her back, sending his own magic into the birdmen that continued to come from above. The sizzling scent of chicken surrounded them as feathers fell to the blood slicked stone below them.

"Atil will never be yours! False queen! And those you have enslaved will be free!" He pulled a dagger from the sheath at his belt, extending his left hand outwards, elbow raised slightly.

The queen sent her whip lashing at Amil's off hand. The sharp pain caused his fingers open, dropping his dagger. But as the tight rope of leather came up again, he managed to catch it, pulling tight and cutting the very tip with his sword. Off balance, she pulled the whip back, slashing towards his right shoulder as they closed on each other, their blades clashed, parrying swings left and right.

"There, Vic!" Nang indicated Nyhm's dance of death with the warlord. "There's your target! Keep going, the others will handle her minions!"

Felicia turned at Nang's shout, following her line of site. The bastard wasn't about to take down one of their own. She left Siril to fend off the last few of the birdmen that were now on the ground, sidling through the remnants of the war, hips unconsciously swaying to the pleasure she gained in the heat of battle. "Play with me, why don't you?" She purred in a sultry tone, a smirk touching her lips. Hand back as if to pitch a ball, a wisp of smoke appeared in her palm, quickly turning to a conflagration she tossed at the armored man fighting Nyhm.

"Oi, you!" Vic shoved the druid, pointing at a huge cauldron to one side. "Grab that forge while we hold him here! Pin him!" He launched into the fight, expecting the man to find a way to do it, as he had learned to just expect the rest of their party to always do as asked.

With a strength not apparent in his moderate frame, Kjorrath stepped over the dead bodies near him to rip the studs, stays and metal form from the ground. With a roar not meant to come from mortal men, he threw it towards the fire-reddened armor of the warlord. It landed just behind the man, exploding into pieces and causing scatter-damage to all nearby.

As the remainder of the queen's army fell to the Kordathyan forces, Siril beat them to the bridge, his back to the fight between Amil and his rival. It was his job to allow their commander this victory. The ranger was recorded in several documents in the city for his aid and bravery over the years. It would be an insult for them to now step in and finish for him when it was only one on one.

"No escape for you!" Nang shouted, joining the others against the warlord that still harried them.

Steel sang in the air as magic crackled and filled the room. Nyhm kept the attention of the battle master, ducking and twisting to stay just out of reach while the others struck at it from behind. "Why won't you just fall?"

And then it did. In a shower of sparks and flames, the pieces of the armor flew apart, scattering across the area. What might have once been a man, now only the size of a fire log, dropped at Nyhm's feet, burning as brightly as a fire. "What the…" Nyhm ducked low, throwing his hands over his head.

When the dust had cleared and everyone still standing could catch a breath, they had indeed been victorious. "We got it!" Vic high-fived Nang as she jumped around, whooping and cheering in exultation. They shared a glance and as one shouted across, "Your last man is dead, queen!" They turned, congratulating each other, sure Amilmamir would be joining them any second.

Chapter Forty-Nine
Enough?

Elith had been given a task by the Oracle to find Amil one last time. She had been almost frantic that Elith needed to find Amilmamir and return him to Tuarenlin. He hadn't expected it to be so difficult to track the man. Everyone seemed to mistake him for his uncle, with their armor so similar, but none seemed willing to share much with him.

He had found Cileria. The pretty elven maiden had shown him to the forest sanctuary of the rangers, but had also been unwilling to speak much on the matter. The sanctuary was quiet, few coming or going, let alone staying there. Over the intervening days, he found that a war was underway and that his uncle was leading it. None knew the location of the warzone, though, and the best they could do was mention he find Anne for other details.

It was a little disturbing to think that Amil's own rangers knew less than the girl, but he decided to try to locate her.

Anne made a point of going out every day, doing what she did best. As Master of the Tzee Dojo, it was her duty to see to the monks studying under her. She longed for word of Amil. She longed to have him back in her arms. Her world was incomplete without him… and she refused to bow under the weight of emptiness. Better to be busy.

The rangers that remained looked to her with a smile when she ventured into the forests. She wasn't trained to their ways, and didn't pretend to be. She was there as a reminder that he would return, something tangible they could hold onto. They were there as a promise to herself. They needed him; he'd come back.

Duval, her old friend, watched her head out the door again right after breakfast. His dark hands went around the waist of his elven wife. He couldn't imagine the strength needed for Squirt to get through this time. All he could do was offer his home and his family as a harbor in the storm of her heart.

"She'll be okay," his wife whispered. "She's stronger than you give her credit for."

"But should she have to be?" He brushed his smooth cheek against hers. "She's never had to deal with anything this hard before."

"Du," the light-skinned woman turned in his arms, giving him a serious look. "She needs a friend that's strong for her, not a father to worry."

He looked out the window to where she went through forms with her few students. He had almost lost his girl years ago, and knew the pain of not knowing. He wanted to prevent that for Annie, even though he couldn't.

For her part, Annie had to believe. She couldn't lie, not out loud; but she could try to convince herself that he was just away on patrol. He would be home soon. The few weeks he had been gone were nothing compared to those times. Any of those could have been deadly, but Amil was capable and experienced. He had always come home.

She smiled, going through the motions of teaching, knowing it wasn't true. He had scars and injuries that had never healed well. He had lost everything this time. What would be left for him to return to, other than her? Even she knew it might not be enough.

Chapter Fifty
Home?

"Atil will be mine," the woman had sneered at Amil. She had thrown the insult of "boy" at him, as if he were some green recruit. She had disarmed him of his dagger, but he had easily scored back in his strike at the whip. It didn't make the weapon any less dangerous though. Off-balance, she pulled the whip back, slashing with her blade towards his right shoulder.

Amil had already moved for his next attack, swinging for her head, as her blade flicked in under his guard. It didn't hit his shoulder as she'd intended, but did draw blood at his side. He couldn't help the grunt of pain as his own sword dropped at the shock, striking across her chest instead, just above the corset.

He staggered back a few steps, hand over the wound at his side. "Just a woman," he mocked, noting her own blood.

With a snarl, she stepped in to their deadly dance again, blades clashing, parrying left and right. Her blade grazed his hair, but the force of his own blade striking her side sent her spinning away, more blood now seeping through her fine black satin.

"Ha!" he crowed, "What do you have now, queen? You bleed like anyone…" his breath left him with a grunt as she recovered to spin back and hit him in his injured side with a high kick from her spiked heel. He stumbled back on the stone bridge, gasping as the wind was knocked out of him. "You… bitch…"

Recovering slower than he would have liked, he ran towards her, aiming for a strike to her midsection. The crack of the whip sounded, echoing loudly through the cavernous chamber. Amil slid to a stop, seeing the leather sailing towards him, but was still too far within her range. His hands came up to his neck as the whip wrapped around, pulling tightly, pulling him closer towards her.

Stumbling, he refused to let this be the end. Still fighting for breath, one hand trying to get between the weapon and his throat, his consciousness threatened to go black. A loud gasp barely whistled into his throat, not quite reaching his burning lungs. His knees went weak; not from pain this time, but with the lack of air.

Vertigo wrapped him as tightly as the whip did, the room

fading and spinning. He couldn't feel the sword in his hand, but knew it to still be there. *Never drop it,* he had learned young. *You let go and you're giving up the fight. Never let go.* And not once in all his battles had he. His fingers were locked around the grip, holding steady when everything else was leaving him.

He was letting his people down now. He couldn't hold out any longer. He swore he heard his eldest daughter's voice. *"You were never there for me! Never!"* And guilt washed over him. He hadn't been there as he should have been. But she had forgiven him. Juniper had forgiven him! Little Marie had never blamed him for his fault with her either.

Oceania's gentle smile, her beautiful music called to him from the past. Anne's joyful laughter in his mind reminded him that these were only memories. He could – and would – save the lands from this queen's further tyranny. It gave him the strength to blink back the darkness just as he felt her pull on the whip, jerking him towards her. He braced against it, seeing the glint of a blade in her off-hand.

She hadn't expected it. Her own balance temporarily offset, she swore at him in a language he didn't understand. Stepping forward as she once again jerked on the twisted leather, this time she did manage to pull him a little closer.

Half-rising, Amil stumbled at the pull, moving too far inside her range. She glared hatefully into his eyes, a snarl on her beautiful lips. It made her the ugliest thing he had ever seen. He watched in almost slow motion, unable to respond quick enough, unable to be the warrior he knew he was, as her sword came down towards him, piercing the leather armor over his chest.

With her minions taken care of, Siril and his companions had just enough time to see the queen strike Amil in the chest with her cursed blade. Siril had had enough. There was honor and then there was stupidity. He was not about to let that ranger die on his watch. Despite Nang and Vicarious moving to stop him, he unleashed every offensive spell at his disposal, throwing them as rapidly as he could towards the battle on the bridge. A few hit wildly, but most struck the area around them. It didn't stop him from trying.

Those with bows trained them on the fight, trying to find an opening, but there was no way to let fly without risking Amil's life. Felicia held a small orb of fire in her hand, but she knew. There was nothing they could do at this point. The battle was Amil's. For good or ill, it was Amil's now.

Trying to dodge, Amil was lethargic, the lack of air finally getting to be too much as he felt the kiss of steel against his skin. It was done. There was no turning back from this point. The magic exploded around him, burnt stone smoldering, small wounds showing on the queen's bare arms.

He attempted to give voice to the cry of pain as the blade pierced through, pushing deep into his chest, but nothing was coming. Blood and air bubbled around the sword, the agony bittersweet. He wouldn't see Anne again. But he refused to let this woman be the last thing he ever laid eyes on.

Knowing she had won, she loosened the whip, ready to step back. Haughty and full of her own pride, she looked past the man at her feet towards those he had dragged with him. They could attempt it next; she'd still win. She always won.

"You'll have to come back in a few days to find out," he had told her about her surprise.

"If I wait a few days, your laundry's gonna pile up," she had teased.

"I think I can manage doing my own laundry." He'd been doing it for just fine for longer than her lifetime.

"Don't forget to feed everyone," she had reminded with true worry. "Even the spiders."

"Of course I won't." Yet another thing he loved about her; she not only accepted that he had wild animals in his home, like mice and spiders, but she had learned how to care for them. And, to his humor, she had named them all. "Fred and his family will get plenty of food, and yes the spiders as well."

"And give Cane and Malania an extra hug for me."

"Of course I will." He had smiled at her, thinking how special she was to worry about creatures most would find beneath themselves, how she had turned his old wolf and panther into lap pets when she was around.

"And make sure they get scraps when you make supper."

"Yes, yes; they will get the scraps." He knew he was grinning, but couldn't help himself at the sweetness she showed everything that mattered to him.

He wasn't going home. It was time to make sure that wherever he WAS going, the bitch was going with him. This queen would never again touch the one good thing he had left. He would see all those little friends of his soon. He would keep at least that one promise to her.

Still on his knees, the queen sneered down at him in triumph.

Narrowing his eyes, he let his hand fall from the leather twisted around his neck, let her think for that one moment she had won. Summoning the very last of his strength, he grabbed the wrist of her sword hand, pulling her towards him as he thrust upwards, pushing as hard as he could with his own blade while letting momentum bring her down to him. Her blade slid deeper into his body with the movement, striking his heart, but his own bright sword found purchase as the Atilian steel bit into her stomach, moving up into her chest cavity.

The queen staggered, crying out in shock as she looked down in surprise. "Amil!" Nyhm cried as Vic spun around in time to see the woman collapse forward over the top of the ranger. His sword wedged tightly into the vile woman's chest, he had accomplished his goal.

Amil stayed on his knees, unable to get up. His strength all but used up, the queen laid heavy and dying on his shoulder. He could feel each pump of his heart against the slicing pain of the steel still lodged there. His vision faded in and out, letting him fields of wheat that traveled far off into the distance. *He let the fresh air envelope him before looking back. His family, his wife and daughters, were running towards him from a forest rich with autumn leaves.*

He smiled to himself at the sight as his knees could no longer take the blood loss or the weight. He fell onto his back, the sounds of far off footsteps running towards him along with yells and screams, blood trickling from his lips and from the heart wound staining the white stone.

As the two lay there, Vicarious and the rest of his comrades rushed toward Amil.

"Hurry!" Nang cried desperately, trying to drag the queen's body off their leader. "Help me!"

Vicarious touched her shoulder, letting her know he was there. He was always there when she needed him. She stepped back as Vic threw the dead queen off of Amil, her body limp as it landed near him.

"Could someone...?" Nyhm looked around as he stopped short at the dire sight of the ranger lying on the floor, blood pooling around the body, so starkly white now against the dark leathers, wanting someone to help him. "...Anyone?"

Racing with the others, Siril made a valiant effort to staunch the flow of blood from Amil's grievous wound. He tried in vain to stop the never-ending flow of the elf's life blood, as others tried various ways to bring him back.

"He's got to be..." Nyhm looked to the others, begging them to say Amilmamir would be alright. He looked back to the man at his feet, the look of peace on his face, haloed by the red tinge against his white locks.

With nervous care, a few remaining birdmen came down from far above, warily watching the group as they tried their magic and their healing on the man. Edging towards the dead queen, they pushed at her a few times, chirping to each other.

It wasn't a regular moment. The two mages now worked together with the druid, trying to find a way to save Amil. Vic noticed Nang looking small and fragile, although he'd never tell her he saw that. He moved over to stand next to her, then carefully put a supportive arm around her. She resisted, as he expected, then leaned against him, angrily wiping away tears he pretended not to see.

He eyed the birdmen as they cheered in their odd chirps. They pushed the queen off the ledge and flew off making all kinds of happy noise.

Siril didn't care about the woman. He was completely focused on the man he had come to count as both leader and friend, trying to heal the fatal wound. As the queen's body fell from sight, a final breath escaped the ranger.

"We have to make it work." Nyhm saw Siril sit back on his heels, stopping the attempt at healing, but wasn't ready to accept it. He took out a magic rod of healing, waving it several times over Amil. "Why isn't it working? Amil?"

The vidu defender got to his feet, laying a hand on the young elf's arm. "He's gone..." He knew the kid had had a rough start in life, had probably even seen death before, but the whole group had seen the way Nyhm had started looking up to Amil. And now that had been taken away.

"His soul won't come," Kjorrath murmured gently, not sure how to best help the young one. "He returns home."

"This... shouldn't have ended like this," Nang said quietly, watching the tears start for Nyhm, watched him drop to his knees, lowering his head.

"No," Vic agreed with Nang, giving her a slight sideways hug, not sure if it was more for her comfort or his. "But I think Amil knew it would. Or at least suspected."

Looking up, Nang's eyes widened as Firnos appeared before them. The realization hit Nang as she thought back to the words spoken by the gods in the past meetings. It was Amil's time – his was the life sacrificed.

Felicia scowled as the man in dark green leathers appeared, a quiver and bow at his back. "Who?"

"Lord of the Hunt," Siril explained quietly as he looked up.

"I did what I could, but Death insisted on one." The Green Lord offered with a heavy heart.

Knowing how much Amil had held to the premise of this god's ideals, Nyhm wanted to offer more than his own broken heart. Blowing out a long breath, he wiped his tears away and gained his feet, lowering his own hood to show a new maturity and seriousness. True youth had left the elfling.

Firnos inclined his head in acknowledgement, gaining a respectful nod back from Nyhm, then looked to the others. "He has one that waits for him back home. Take him to her. Grieve for him together." Partially turning away from them, the god disappeared between one blink and the next.

We... can't leave his body here." Felicia frowned. "Not like this."

They took up the body themselves as a single birdman appeared, clucking and cooing as it motioned them all to follow. Through the entire twist of upward-moving paths they had taken, it was still several levels up and up. The weeks through the forward push weighed heavy on them, but none wanted to relinquish their responsibility in this.

Only when they stumbled, only when they could barely keep their own heads up, would they allow others from the army to take their place. It took them time to realize that others were grieving just as much and wanting to carry their share of the burden.

Overland, the mages wore themselves out, jumping the units forward in small increments towards home. They didn't know where they were to start with, and could only orient on the direction of home. Not knowing how far they had to go, they wanted to speed things along because of the body.

As the days stretched, the heavy pain started to release on most of the army, and they were able to focus on the victory that had been gained. Amil's unit alone kept the burden. They still had a woman waiting for them to return Amil to her.

Chapter Fifty-One
Homecoming

Weary troops shuffled back into Lareah. Anne watched them laughing and talking as they congratulated each other or parted company. Amil, and those closest to him, were not with them. When she asked, one of the Gray Gryphons, not knowing who she was, simply pointed back towards the Eastern gate before turning back to his companions.

Anne raced through the residential area, going against the crowds still entering. Just inside the far gate, she could make out the backs of Amil's companions. "One of the Gryphons told me..."

Nang looked over, but quickly glanced away. Anne's movements slowed to a stumbled walk, her chipper words fell off in a gasp as the others turned, letting her see Amil's body at their feet. "No..."

Vic looked at Anne but had nothing to say.

"He can't be dead." Dropping to her knees, Anne laid one hand on his head and the other over his heart. She was a Tzee Divine, dedicated to healing others. Praying with all she had in her, she willed him to heal, to rise and give her his smirk that he'd been playing her for a joke.

"Firnos took him." Nang's voice was quiet with her own shock and her sympathy for the heartbreak of the woman on the ground.

Vic shared a look with Nang. He didn't like to see women suffer like this. He wasn't the nurturer any more than Nang was, but someone had to make the monk look at the facts. When Nang gave him a look that she wasn't about to be "the girl" and comfort another, Vic cleared his throat. "Firnos took his soul away already, Anne..."

She had never asked anything from the gods before. She never asked anyone for anything. Only two things had been requested from her to the man she loved. She had wanted to marry before this, and "He said he'd come back." Her gaze fell on those surrounding them. "He promised me. He said he'd come back." It couldn't be true. A pleading entered her eyes as she turned to Vic. "You said you'd bring him back."

Anne's tears were heavy and unrelenting, and Vic felt each one of them keenly. A warrior's honor was one thing, but he felt he had a hand in causing Anne to suffer. He, like the others, had stayed their hand in aiding Amil in that final battle... even though it had been the ranger's wish.

It was worse that he had promised Anne he would protect Amil. It was a promise that made Vicarious cringe inside, because honor had demanded that Amil face the queen alone. So in the end, at the most crucial point, Vicarious had needed to break his promise to Anne in order to keep the one to Amil. The ranger had needed to deal with his nemesis by himself.

Heart-sore with his own loss in the matter, Vic looked to the others for aid.

Siril gently laid a hand on Anne's shoulder, speaking carefully. "It's of no use; he's gone."

She sat back on her heels, looking to all of them to do something. Anything. "This is Amil." The truth was plain before her, but she wasn't ready to believe it. "He's been through worse, right? Right?"

"This was war," Nang apologized when no one else seemed able to say anything. "Good men died, but the queen is gone too. It wasn't in vain."

Silence stretched as Annelise simply brushed Amil's hair back from his face. "And Firnos took him? Personally?"

Nang nodded as Kjorrath opened his mouth and closed it again as he silently eyed Annelise. "He is home," his powerful voice came soft and gentle. "You will meet him again."

Annie laid her cheek to his chest, sobbing quietly into the leathers that still smelled of him; him, and the sharp tang of blood. Something about that pulled her back, making her sit up quickly enough to surprise the others while she angrily wiped the tears away. "He wouldn't like this. Not at all."

Vic's jaw dropped at the sudden change before them.

Clearing his throat in a manner just meant to get attention, Siril motioned the others to step away. "Maybe we should give her a moment to say private goodbyes."

"No." Determination entered Anne's voice. "He loved the sea," she offered before they could leave. "Let's finish this. The lake. I want ...he'd want... a pyre made. The body," she hiccupped back a sob, "will nourish other things. We need to burn him by the lake."

"Sure, Anne." Vic's voice was low, weighted with emotion as he looked to the others for confirmation. "We can do that." He looked to the others, as his fingers slid inside his pouch, caressing a bottle he couldn't justify pulling out. With nods of agreement from the others, he took up the hold on Amil he had earlier carried.

Nang followed Vic's lead, leveraging under Amil's other arm. Kjorrath and Nyhm lifted his legs and Siril lent his magic to keep Amil's head erect with some semblance of honor. Once he was again situated on the tower shield that had been serving as a makeshift stretcher, Nang asked Felicia to use her fire magic to light the way in the falling darkness.

"I thought I was strong," Nyhm said sadly, watching Anne too shaky to do more than hold Amil's hand, "but this truly wounds me…"

Anne felt alone, frozen in the warm night. She held tightly to Amil's cold hand, memorizing the calluses that had cradled his bow, her other hand wrapped tightly around her own waist. If it wasn't that her mind was in such shock, she might have thrown up. It certainly felt like a knife in her gut just thinking about this loss.

Felicia very lightly touched her shoulder before conjuring a small light to lead their way. The few still straggling into the city were careful at this point to lower their voices and avert their eyes from the small procession. There was nothing they could say that would help. Anne didn't want to hear anything. Nothing would bring him back to her.

Passing into the residential and then the poorest section of town, they went through a set of gates that marched them through the cemetery. Anne couldn't look. She didn't want to see the signs of death surrounding them. But she couldn't look at Amil either. She kept her eyes on the dusty path beneath her feet.

Finally the scent of water reached them. The lake was quiet and peaceful, just as Amil had loved it. The moon danced stars across the water, interrupted only by the small island at the center of the lake. Anne looked up to the overhang where she and Amil had sat so many times, just enjoying the quiet, just holding hands, looking out over the water. "That was his favorite spot. It overlooks this." She pointed to the center of the lake where there was a small isle with a single cherry blossom tree in bloom and a scattering of flowers blowing in the light breeze, the grasses undulating in their own mimic of the waves that surrounded them. "I want to take him there." He needed to be close to his Oceania.

Siril conjured a flat raft just big enough for all of them to step onto. No one spoke as they travelled the short distance. Anne let go of Amil's hand as she set foot on the little plot of land, going around the perimeter to pick up the gathered driftwood. As the others set Amil down in the center, Nyhm walked to the opposite side of the small isle, silently helping Anne gather enough for a fire.

Anne brushed off the aide of those who wanted to take the twigs for her, heedless of the splinters she garnered in her few trips back and forth. Even with Nyhm's assistance, the stack was pitifully small. She knelt beside it, taking flint and tinder, trying to be strong, wanting to be the one to start the fire. Striking it gained her a few sparks, but it kept falling from her shaky fingers.

"Allow me..." Siril touched his magic to it, letting the simple spell catch the wood on fire as Felicia used her Gift to pile more wood nearby.

"He has a nephew-ish guy that came looking for him. I don't know if he found him." She kneeled at Amil's side, her cheek against his still chest. "He needs to know."

"What's his name?" Nang asked.

"Elith." Anne brushed back Amil's hair again. "Can someone cut a lock for me? I can't use a blade."

Nang flipped out her trusty dagger and cut a bit off. Anne carefully tucked it away in her shoulder bag before pulling out a skirt and blouse embroidered on the back with the words "ranger mascot." She held it to her chest a moment, then carefully laid it over Amil. "You guys were there." It was more question than statement.

"Yeah," Vic answered, followed by Siril nodding with "we were."

"He fought to the end." Nang fidgeted with the dagger at her thigh, a tight smile on her lips.

Tears rolled down her cheeks unchecked. There were so many things she wished she could say yet, so many memories she could tell the others about Amil. But none of them would come. And he needed some sort of eulogy. "You say something about him," she implored the others.

The old druid Kjorrath rested a hand on Nyhm's shoulder as he looked to the merry flames licking at the twigs. "He lived the way he wanted and he couldn't have asked for a better return home. I'll remember his strength in the woods and his devotion to aiding the city in its protection from those who would do harm."

Vic looked over the small group, the firelight making everyone look a little haunted. They had grown, both personally and as they picked up more comrades along the way. The soothing sound of the water and merry crackle of the fire was at odds with the deep loss he could see in those he now counted as friends; Siril of the Defenders, Felicia the fire mage, and the young shadow user Nyhm. Vicarious had been their blade (or scythe as it were), and sometimes their shield while they utilized their own considerable talents to carry them the rest of the way. He had grown rather fond of each of them. Nang and Amil especially, followed closely by Siril and Nyhm... and Felicia, but she probably wouldn't like to hear that.

As if knowing she had been thought about, she spoke next. "I may not have known him as long as most, but he always treated people whom deserved it with kindness."

Nyhm didn't know what to say. Amil should have been alive. He had so much more to live for than Nyhm did; he had known what he wanted out of life. Watching the flames dance orange in the sunset, he felt that something good and right with the world was lost with Amil's passing. Trying to blink back the tears, he kept his lips pressed together as he looked to the others to speak for him.

"Cool," Nang said, pleased that her voice remained steady, "confident and collected. Amil was one of the best." She looked across at Vicarious, hoping he knew she thought of him in that same circle.

He caught her eye and looked away, clearing his throat. "Well, from the time I met him 'til now, he was the best guy I knew." He was proud that Nang would see that in him, and he swore to himself – and to Amil – that he would do better by his own obligations.

"I didn't know him well," Siril added quietly, wrapped in his own thoughts, "but what I did know of him was honorable and good. The world is truly a darker place without him here." He mumbled something under his breath and gently laid a hand on Amil's head. "... goodbye, my friend."

Anne wiped at her tears, smiling at their comments. It was nothing less than what she had already known.

Carefully taking his most prized possessions, she set them aside; the blue-rimmed shoulder plate from Tuarenlin, his bow, his blade, not caring that she would need to spend days in prayer to gain her Gifts of healing back. "For Elith," she whispered loud enough for the others to hear, deep emotion making her voice ragged. She swallowed hard, forcing herself to say what deserved to be said of him. "He taught me what it meant to really love someone, and how important that was. He showed me what duty meant, to others and to the forests. I... I never loved until Amil."

She let Felicia magically lift Amil's body, laying it atop the fire. Taking a small gold ring, she tenderly pushed it on to his ring finger. "That would have been your wedding ring." Careful of the flames already licking at his armor, she kissed his cheek. "I love you."

"It was a pleasure to serve with him." Nang held her head high, not shying away from the flames as Anne stepped back, nodding to Siril to raise the flames. Amil was being taken out of this world in the fashion of heroes of old. It would only dishonor the memory and the moment if she looked away.

The old druid took a slow breath, looking out at the shoreline and the trees that seemed to press towards them almost expectantly. "The land," he whispered quietly, a bittersweet smile touching him, "welcomes him home."

Vic pushed his perfect hair back away from his face, covering the need to brush away a few tears. Nyhm made no attempt to hide his emotion, while Felicia, unable to cry, looked to the ground with a sigh that carried the weight of her pain and Siril stepped back enough to concentrate, bringing the flames up to consume their leader.

Forlorn and quiet, Anne managed to only offer what any monk would give to another with great respect. "The Great Wheel goes around. What comes from the All, returns to the All. Too soon, but it returns." With a haunted look in her eyes, she finally looks away from the flames.

The red and orange flames flickered, taking a greenish tint to them before Firnos stepped in amongst them. His eyes found Anne, offering a slight bow. "I will take his soul myself," his voice held an undertone that said he understood their pain, but that this wasn't entirely a bad situation. "I'll take him to a place he will be able to

Hunt all the long years to come." He reached a hand out through the flames towards Amil. "Come, my son, we'll see you with your wife and children."

Vic stood a little taller, his scythe beside him, as he watched Amil's soul appear, standing above the body. Looking to Firnos, Amil took the Lord's hand, giving each of them a quick nod as he stepped away from his mortal anchor. As he walked away from them, towards the water, his already luminescent form started to fade. The last they saw was the ranger standing with the grace and strength of a young man, pulling his hood up, and readying his bow.

The vidu fighter waved one last time, sighing heavily in both regret and relief. Siril pulled his helm off, putting a supportive hand to Nyhm's back. The young elf smiled up at him with watery eyes before looking back where Amil had gone. "Forever in my memory Amil, you will never be forgotten."

"Never forget what was sacrificed to save your lands," Firnos intoned seriously, "or what greatness now leaves you." He turned to follow Amil's soul, seeming to disappear as a breeze blew leaves across his path.

Vicarious Val'Sadar stepped further back from the flames as they raised higher, consuming Amil's body. He pulled Anne with and into his arms, letting her sob her pain out against his amazing coat. A sense of closure surrounded him. Rarely did Vicarious let himself get involved in serious business. But he had been fated to come across Amilmamir and Nang in a time of need. He'd been tempted to just mind his own business like he usually did, but something had made him act differently that day. Maybe it was that he had seen they were in need of all the help they could get, or that sooner or later they would be outmatched by themselves... Or maybe it was just Fate and not any of that, but Vicarious offered his assistance, and just like that he had plunged into an epic story the likes of which one could only see to its conclusion or die trying.

The flames danced higher, reaching for the stars themselves. Those that kept their eyes on the fire watched the body slowly disappear as the flames closed in around it, slowly dying away. A breath of wind, the kiss of the gods, blew gently across the island, guttering the last few fingers of flame and catching the ash to dance off into the wind over the water and forest. A bare patch of land lay before them, man shaped, but with no body and no scorch marks.

Slowly, green tendrils pushed through. They all watched in amazement as first one then another formed into flowers, opening proudly to the night sky. Red tulips, the color of his elder daughter's hair, yellow buttercups to match little Marie, blue forget-me-nots reminding Anne of the blue plate on his armor, and a green creeping vine undulated and twisted in and around the flowers like waves. His family was together in the strange symbol of flowers that had sprung up.

That then, was the passing of the oldest and most esteemed ranger in Kordathya. Firnos had claimed his soul and the goddess Maleiin had reclaimed his isle home, leaving this gift to all as a reminder.

Chapter Fifty-Two
Final Thoughts

With the support of the others, Anne made her way back to town, glancing back to the flowers as long as she could. "Elith." In a fog, she finally stopped in town to lean against a stone wall, hiccupped sobs still breaking from her. "I need to find him."

Vicarious couldn't bring himself to talk to Anne; he didn't know what to say. He watched Anne twisting the ruby ring on her finger... the engagement ring that only reminded Vic of his failure to her. He had said he'd bring Amil back to her... he hadn't meant it the way it turned out. And for that, the guilt sat heavy in the pit of his stomach.

"Umm... Excuse me..." A man that could have been Amil's twin approached, lowering his hood. Even his armor was similar to the ranger's, right down to the blue on one shoulder.

Anne hastily wiped the tears away and turned. "Elith!" Unable to stop them from falling, more tears dripped from her cheeks. "He... um..." She looked to the others for help. But there was no help. This was her duty, to let his family know. "He...died."

Stunned, Elith could only repeat her words as a question. Felicia glanced at her compatriots as Vic looked between her and Amil's nephew before the fire wizardess nodded to him. "He gave his life to end an empire of slavery."

"That message for him," Anne asked again. "Could you please tell me?"

Elith saw the pain, but his was a sacred mission. And they had had this same conversation before. "I cannot just take your word for it... I will need proof of this if I'm to give you the message."

Her fingers went to the ruby ring on her left hand, twisting it. "I was... he was supposed to..." She swallowed hard, showing him the ring. "This was my engagement ring. And I have some of his things for you."

"If it helps any," Nyhm offered. "I was there. As was Vicarious, Felicia, Nang and that blue garbed elf. Kjorrath."

That man nodded agreement. "And if it's any proof, we can bring you to the place chosen to be his last resting place... even if his body was given to a pyre."

"Sorry, kid." Vic nodded in confirmation.

"He wasn't supposed to come back this way." Anne fought not to start crying again. This wasn't like her. "Firnos came himself to claim Amil's soul."

"So... he is dead then." Everything about Elith sagged, weighted down. "Then I failed my mission." A heavy sigh. "Mother forgive me." He pulled a carefully folded envelope with a red seal on it, handing it to Anne. "Though I don't believe this message will be any good now."

With shaky hands, she broke the seal, pulling the single sheet of rice paper out. *My Dear child, a great cloud awaits you. I have seen events unfold upon you that will bring terrible pain to those around you. If you venture after this woman, you will not return. Do not go, my nephew, for it is your doom. Leave your worries in those lands and return with Elith to me and your people. We miss you greatly. ~Seer Sithia Nermakiir*

"He should have gotten this sooner." Anne sniffled, giving Elith a sad smile. "I wish I'd known. I let him go." She knew he had needed to go. He couldn't have done any less. It was why she had loved him; that sense of right and honor. He had considered it a duty he needed to perform... and he had done it.

She took a sword carefully wrapped to keep her from touching it, as well as a few other personal items that had been Amil's. "These need to go to a family member." Her voice dropped as she averted her eyes, offering the items. "I wasn't quite family yet."

He reverently took the items that had always been on his uncle's person. "Thank you. I'll do them honor."

"Can... would you be willing to spend time with me? As a friend?"

"Of course. Amil knew you well. If there is anything I can do for you, ask and I shall try my best to assist you." He bowed to those assembled as Anne introduced him. "Pleasant to meet you."

"The people here," Anne motioned around the plateau, "are mostly those that went with him."

Vic nodded. "From start to finish."

"An honor to be in such presence," Elith offered, inclining his head in respect.

"Hey... kid," Vic indicated Elith, "Would you mind taking her home?" he motioned towards Anne who had a far-off, glassy-eyed look.

"Not at all." He smiled to Anne, giving a slight bow. "If you wish, I will be happy to escort you."

"I'll... just... go to Duval's," she said with a weak smile. "Amil's home was destroyed. I have nowhere else to go."

He wished he had been here earlier to spend more time with this uncle. Anne had obviously loved him very much, and was now in shock. "Very well then."

Nang shifted her weight, death heavy on her mind. In the end, she could only think of what mission would keep her going, keep her focused. "I... should get going as well... need to restock for the..." she paused, frowning. "... the... next mission."

Glancing at Nang, Vic understood. The next mission, the next adventure, the next day... only now there would be no more next. They had won, but at a cost higher than any of them had counted on. Firnos had told them that Death had demanded one of them. Amil chose it. They had lost a good man. And Vicarious was about to lose the one woman he had somehow let past his guard.

Unaware of the vidu's thoughts, Nang blinked the moment off, shaking her head. "Of course, the next mission." Offering her excuses, Nang made way back to... where? Amil had offered a room to her in Atil, but that was gone now. Lareah? It only made sense to remain behind in one of the many places she had recently defended. Perhaps success here would lead to another mission, one hopefully as meaningful as this had been. She hoped that Vicarious wouldn't forget her, and she hoped that Anne wouldn't spiral into darkness.

Nyhm had lost a man he had come to think of as a mentor, perhaps a father in some ways. He had never had one, growing up as a self-reliant orphan. He had respected the ranger, even knowing his pain now was nothing like what Anne had to be feeling. "I'm going to the Hall of Heroes." He took a few arrows, intending to leave them at the base of Amil's statue in homage.

They slowly drifted away from each other with a heavy and somber feeling in the air. Vicarious was left to himself to think his own thoughts. Most prominent was that he would miss Amil, who had become a good friend during their adventure. He had been an example of quiet dignity and true leadership.

A bottle found its way to his lips, pausing before he tipped the booze in. Maybe it was time. Vic wondered if he should honor Amil's memory and take up the mantle of leadership for his own people.

Nah, he thought. *I'm too amazing to not share with the world.* And instead he raised the bottle to the sky in a salute to the ranger and his eternal rest. He drained it in a single toss back. Shaking his perfect red hair to settle it over his awesome white coat, he headed further into the city with a whistle. Maybe Nang might still be around somewhere.

* * *

Siril sat quietly in a dark room, his thoughts on what had happened a few hours earlier. The scene played over and over again in his mind, refusing to leave him in peace. Amil and the queen locked in mortal combat, each trying to gain the upper hand. Siril had aided the others in keeping the queen's forces at bay, and in the end they had been successful; not even her Warlord had survived the battle. As they had worked on their fallen friend, Firnos had appeared as before. The Lord of the Hunt claimed the ranger's soul, taking him to a well-deserved rest, and reunion with those who had passed before him.

Now Siril sat alone in a dark room. Haunted by the fact that in the end, he had been able to do nothing to save one who he had considered a friend, if even for only a short time, he couldn't allay the guilt he felt in this one failure. Other images haunted the Defender now as well; the final vision of the fallen Ranger, laid out on his funeral pyre, the anguish in Anne's eyes. The flames that danced from his very own hand to ignite the dry timbers. The raw emotion that threatened to unhinge all who attended the funeral held by a lake. The words that each one spoke to eulogize a fallen hero… words that would most likely follow Siril for the rest of his days.

He sat there, and thought about all that had occurred since that day when he happened upon a small group at the docks, sorely in need of a mage to figure out a set of obscure runes. Many roads had been traveled and bonds had been formed in the process. Should any of them have need, Siril would do what he could to help.

The hour had grown quite late when the mage decided it was time to try and get some sleep. To help his cause, Siril uncorked a silver flask, much like one he had given to Vicarious during their journeys, and took a long draw from its contents. The wine would help him sleep; it always did. As he began to drift off, into what he hoped would be a dreamless sleep, a thought occurred to him. When his time came, would his friends be there, no matter what the end? When his time came, would he meet it with the same courage and valor that he had witnessed in Amilmamir Nermakiir?

Epilogue

Elith took great care with his uncle's treasure. She had been the one thing that had driven him, pushed the old ranger to save her and her way of life. With a hand around her waist and the other at her elbow, he stopped at the small home she said belonged to a family friend. "He's with the Mother now," he said when made herself say he was gone. "Let him smile on us. He would not wish to see you cry, I am sure of that."

"He'll never steal my shoe again, I'll never pounce him..."

"He may not be here physically, but he is still here." He placed a hand over his heart. "He is inside all who knew him."

She hiccupped a sob, putting a hand over her own heart. "Yeah. And... and we're better people for knowing him."

An understanding smile touched his eyes and lips as he nodded. "That we are."

"Would... you mind if I did something to you I did to Amil?" She couldn't help a small smile at his worried look. "Nothing that would break your vow. I promise." At his nod, she wiggled half-heartedly, bouncing towards him to give a hug. Shock stiffened him a moment, but he returned the hug. "Thank you," she whispered when he relaxed, "for understanding."

He smiled down at her as she stepped back. "I'm happy to be here for you."

Tucking her hair behind an ear, she gave him her bravest smile. "It's gonna be rough for a while. I'll take you up on that offer." Glancing inside to see the worried looks of Duval and his wife, she turned back to Elith. "I think I'm gonna get some rest." The only consolation this day had given her was in knowing Amil had been taken to his previous family, that Firnos would give him peace and the chance to rest with no more war. "This has been... shocking... to me today."

"Indeed. Some rest will help clear your thoughts some." He gave her a light hug. "You seem strong-willed. I am sure you will be fine after time."

She would be. She wasn't the kind to collapse over horrible circumstances. Life hadn't turned out the way she wanted, but she would find a way. And she knew Amilmamir would be watching from the other side. "I was raised to be," she told him, knowing it was true. "I'll be okay."

APPENDIX

Characters:

Amilmamir Mor Nermakiir – Elf that has lost wife Oceania (OSH en EE a) and daughters Juniper and Marie. The rangers blond hair has turned white over his centuries of life and hardship. Using a bow gifted from his god, as well as a longsword given from the people he protected. (AYmil mah MEER Mor NAIR mah keer)

Annelise Erickson – Human with heritage of vidu and celestial. Tzee Monk trained to reason and logic. Tzee Divine who has sworn to the gods not to use steel in exchange for healing gifts. Prefers martial arts first and a bow second.

Nang Teglen – Blonde haired elf of average height, lithe build usually seen in green leathers. Has a variety of weapons present on her person, including a rapier, dagger and bow.

Siril Te'lie – Vidu with natural white hair braided back behind ears. Mage that works as a Defender for the city of Lareah. (SIHR-ihl Teh-LEE)

Vicarious Val'Sadar – Tall vidu with amazing red hair, fine clothing, and a penchant for alcohol. Uses a scythe. Heir to his family's lands in the mountains. (Vy CARE ee us VAL se-DAHR)

Nyhm – Slight-framed elf with black hair and black, worn leathers. Pale skin. Prefers daggers and short swords, as well as creeping through shadows. (Nim)

Felicia Windsong – Elf with long brunette hair. Practical in pants. An official in the city of Kron'tir. Blackened gloves give the first indication to her skill in fire magic.

Vidu – The vidu were nothing more than a sub race of elves with pitch black skin and usually white hair. Some said they had always been dark. Some said it was to match their black hearts – a reference that they tended to be stronger and more violent than other elves, liking to fight. And for elves, they really were the best of the warriors; with blood just as red as any other elf.

Tzee Divine – A sacred group of monks that swear not to touch steel in exchange for god-given gifts of healing. Very rare to have the gift.

Oracle – A holy woman devoted to receiving messages from the gods and sharing them with the people of Tuarenlin (Amilmamir's homeland).

WEAPONS

RAPIER   SCYTHE

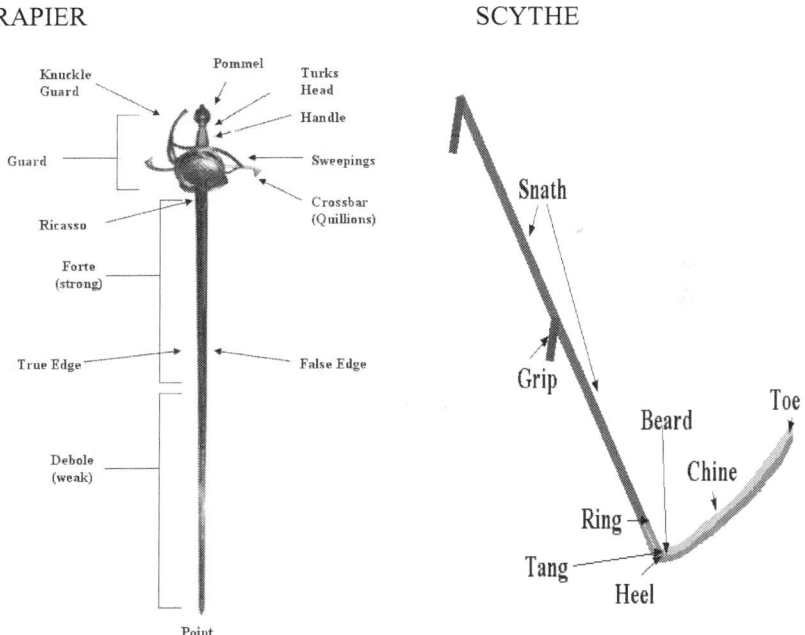

ABOUT THE AUTHOR

When not living her dream job of working in a library, Karlene is busy with organizations such as the SCA where she enjoys historical recreation as a thirteenth century Viking persona. If not travelling to new places, she lets her hips travel in beladi practice. She can be found at home northeast of the lone tree in North Dakota doing her myriad craft interests, gaming online or tabletop, playing with her parrot, or annoying her ever-so-tolerant and supportive husband.

Made in the USA
Charleston, SC
09 September 2011